Stephanie Julian started reading early, but it wasn't until ...
grade that she found her mother's stash of romance novels h...
under her bed – and realized they were much more interesting
than the books in the school library.

She went on to read English in college, became a reporter and
published a couple of sweet romances before she decided to write
the type of books she wanted – books where people actually get to
have sex.

Now she writes stories that combine heat with heart, and
is a happily married mother of two. You can find her on Twitter
@StephanieJulian, and on Facebook and Goodreads.

Praise for Stephanie Julian:

'Lush fantasies and dark obsessions provide a scrumptious buffet
on which we feed our senses in this deeply seductive erotic
romance. Beautifully written, this rich and detailed storyline,
coupled with beguiling and complex characters, takes us on an
emotionally charged journey filled with lust, betrayal and secrets'
Romantic Times (4½ Stars Top Pick)

'An incredibly sensual, deeply seductive read' *Sinfully Sexy Book
Reviews*

'An erotic romance that shines' *Romance Novel News* (Recommended
Read)

'A hot, sensual story, full of great heart and a pleasure to read'
That's What I'm Talking About Favorite Book

'This story hooked me from the start and didn't let go . . . A
steamy read I'd definitely recommend' *Happily Ever After-Reads*

'Ms. Julian too_ ... ...ew
author on my H...

By Stephanie Julian

Salon Games series
By Private Invitation
No Reservations
Over Exposed

Over Exposed
Stephanie Julian

headline
ETERNAL

Published by arrangement with Berkley,
a member of Penguin Group (USA) LLC.
A Penguin Random House Company.

First published in Great Britain in 2014
by HEADLINE ETERNAL
An imprint of HEADLINE PUBLISHING GROUP

1

Cataloguing in Publication Data is available from the British Library

ISBN 978 1 4722 1783 7

Offset in Garamond by Avon DataSet Ltd, Bidford-on-Avon, Warwickshire

Printed and bound by CPI Group (UK) Ltd, Croydon, CR0 4YY

Headline's policy is to use papers that are natural, renewable and
recyclable products and made from wood grown in sustainable forests.
The logging and manufacturing processes are expected to conform to the
environmental regulations of the country of origin.

HEADLINE PUBLISHING GROUP
An Hachette UK Company
338 Euston Road
London NW1 3BH

www.headlineeternal.com
www.headline.co.uk
www.hachette.co.uk

For you, my love, for never letting me falter

Acknowledgments

Thank you, Judi, for reminding me that this is a journey best shared.

One

"You sonuvabitch. What the hell were you thinking?"

"Hello to you, too."

Greg Hicks shoved a hand through his hair, ready to tear the shaggy curls out by the roots. He hadn't gotten the damn mess cut in weeks and it was bugging the shit out of him.

But not as much as the woman downstairs.

"Tyler, I swear, if you don't get her the hell out of here and right fucking now, I'm gonna do exactly what you want me to do. And Kate's gonna fucking hate me when I break that kid's heart."

"I take it Sabrina got to the spa. She said it wasn't snowing there as badly as it is down here. And wow, that ego of yours is still amazingly huge, isn't it?"

"Jesus Christ, Ty. I'm more than halfway into my second bottle of whiskey. I can barely see straight. And . . ."

Shit. He wasn't drunk enough.

Because he was still sober enough to look at Sabrina Rodriquez and want her so bad, his balls hurt and his dick was hard enough to hammer nails.

"And that's why you need a goddamn keeper. I know you, Greg. If you don't have someone up there to cook for you, you'll starve."

"I'm thirty-six fucking years old, Tyler. I think I can take care of myself for another few days."

"No way. Our deal was I let you stay at the retreat for two weeks so you can finish your damn screenplay, but you agreed to have a keeper. When Mrs. Banks asked me to replace her, Sabrina was available on short notice and close enough that the storm wouldn't delay her arrival. And she actually volunteered, so you will damn well *not* treat her like shit."

Fucking hell. "Shit."

Tyler Golden paused. Then Greg heard him sigh. Loudly.

"Greg, what the hell's going on with you?"

Greg heard the concern in Ty's voice but he didn't have the words. "Nothing."

"Bullshit." Ty's voice smacked at him through the phone. "You're insulting my intelligence. You don't want to talk about it, that's fine. But don't lie to me. And you'd better get your shit together, because if you do anything to hurt Sabrina, Kate *will* be all over your ass, and not in a good way."

Fuck.

Greg took a deep breath and released it, staring out into the hall.

Five minutes ago, Sabrina had walked through the front door of the not-yet-open Haven Retreat outside of Adamstown, Pennsylvania. Far enough away from civilization to make it the perfect place to hide.

Which was exactly what he was doing.

She'd called out to announce her presence, and he'd thought for a minute he'd finally passed out and was dreaming. He hadn't been sleeping well, which explained the liquid medication. If he drank enough, he knew he'd finally be able to get some rest.

Which was a slippery slope. He'd seen more than his fair share of friends and acquaintances fall off that slope. He'd always managed to stay just on the edge.

"Hello? Mr. Hicks? Are you here? It's Sabrina Rodriquez. I work for the Goldens. I'm here to take ca—ah, I'm here to help."

Fuck.

"Greg."

When he didn't answer, he heard Tyler swear under his breath. "I'll call her and tell her you don't need her. I'll find—"

"No." Shit, that wasn't what he should be saying, but he couldn't stop now. "No, it's fine. It's snowing pretty hard up here now so she's not going anywhere 'til morning. Why the hell is it snowing the first week in November anyway?"

"Well, damn, let me just get Mother Nature on the line for you and you can bitch at her. Seriously, Greg, what the fuck is going on with you? Are you okay?"

No, he wasn't. He was pretty sure he was losing it. "It" being everything from his sanity to his production company and, if he wasn't careful, the few true friends he had.

But that's what this time away was about. Getting his shit together and finishing the screenplay for the film that would make him love the business again.

"Hello?"

Sabrina's voice again, closer this time. She must be on her way up the stairs to the second floor, where he'd holed up in one of the rooms.

"I'm fine," he said to Tyler.

"Right." Tyler's tone suggested Greg wasn't fooling anybody and if he thought he was, he was more delusional than he realized. "Look, you're not gonna go all Jack Torrance, are you?"

Greg laughed, the noise startled out of him by Tyler's deadpan reference to *The Shining*.

"Not that far gone, buddy." Not yet, anyway. Fuck, he was going to have one massive hangover in the morning. And a serious case of blue balls. "I'll call tomorrow."

"Are you sure you and Sabrina will be okay tonight?"

That pricked at his pride. "So *now* you're worried about her? Jesus, Tyler, I'm not going to attack the girl. She's a kid."

A pause. "No. She's not. But you're right. This was a mistake and it was mine. You're not in any kind of mood to deal with another human being on any rational level tonight. I'm sorry—"

"Now you're just pissing me off. We'll be fine, Tyler. I need coffee. Or maybe another shot."

"Have Sabrina make you coffee. Then go the hell to bed and sleep it off. I'll talk to you tomorrow."

"Yeah. Coffee. Tomorrow. Bye."

Greg shut down the call before Tyler could say anything else. The guy was one of his best friends, someone outside the business whom he trusted implicitly, not only for his brains but also for his steadfast loyalty.

Tyler didn't like Greg because he was an Oscar-winning producer and director whose net worth was close to the budget of a small European country. Tyler actually liked him in spite of those facts.

Probably because Greg wasn't the same man around Tyler that he was in L.A. And Greg was starting not to like that guy from the West Coast anymore. That guy had started to lose his perspective.

He needed to get it back.

The knock at the door was almost too quiet to hear, but every hair on his body stood on end.

Only a few feet separated him from the girl he'd been obsessing over for months. Which was ridiculous. He was almost thirty-seven. He thought he'd gotten over the juvenile crush stage.

He'd had his heart broken more than a few times in his twenties and he'd figured, after all this time in Hollywood dealing with people who only wanted to fuck him because of what he could do for them, he'd be smarter than to let his heart get tripped up by a twenty-three-year-old with absolutely no agenda.

Hell, if she'd had one, he could've written her off, no problem. Taken her to bed, fucked her brains out, and forgotten her the next day.

The fact that she didn't made him want to throw her on his bed and sink into that luscious body all night long. And keep her there for a week. Or longer.

Fuck.

He took two steps to the door and pulled it open. She'd been heading back down the hallway and she turned sharply, looking over her shoulder with wide brown eyes. Dark golden hair fell down her back in waves he wanted to sink his fingers into and rub against his skin. The top of her head barely reached his chin and she had curves to rival his classic '65 Corvette. In all the right places.

She wasn't an anorexic stick with no breasts and hip bones sharp enough to take out an eye. The girl had tits and ass and hips and—

"I'm so sorry. I didn't mean to wake you. I just wanted you to know I was . . . here."

Shit, he'd been staring. And if the arch in her eyebrows was any indication, she'd caught him at it.

Another girl might've gone in for the kill. Fluttered her lashes, let her eyes narrow to slits as she smiled up at him. Sidle up to him, rub up against him, and offer him . . . whatever he wanted.

Sabrina just continued to stare up at him.

"Wasn't sleeping. On the phone."

Now her eyes narrowed and she checked him out from head to toe. And not in a good way.

He probably looked like shit.

He hadn't shaved in a couple of days. He wore a pair of holey jeans that were almost twenty years old. And his Avenged Sevenfold T-shirt had been new when the band first started playing gigs in the late '90s.

The girl standing in front of him probably hadn't been born at the time. And that was only a slight exaggeration.

Shit.

"Are you okay, Mr. Hicks?"

He straightened, realizing he'd been slouched against the doorjamb. "Yeah. Fine."

Her head tilted and her hair spilled over one shoulder, the ends brushing against the curve of a breast. He'd seen that breast covered in nothing more than satin and lace several months ago. And because he was a total dick, he kept one of those photos locked away on his phone.

Today, she wore a thick, deep-purple sweater that covered her from neck to waist but still couldn't hide those luscious curves. They were standing close enough that he could have reached out and touched her. Cupped his hand under her breast and felt the weight of it.

"Okay." She pasted on a smile he recognized as Pleasant Employee No. 1. "I'm Sabrina Rodriquez. I don't know if you remember me—"

"I remember you, Sabrina."

Those beautiful eyes widened and her lips parted but no sound emerged.

He wanted to kiss the shock off that mouth, had to hold himself steady before he curved a hand around her neck and brought her flat up against him.

"Oh." The shock started to wear off as she processed what he'd said. And tried to figure out any hidden meaning behind his words.

A flush crept into her cheeks, making her even more beautiful than she'd been a second ago, and he watched her remember exactly what she'd been wearing at the time.

"Oh. Okay. That's . . . great. That's . . ." She took another breath and mustered another smile. "Tyler told me you're working so I'll make sure I'm not in your way. If you need anything, just let me know."

Yeah, sure, honey. I want you in my bed. How about that?

"Anything, huh?"

Sonuvabitch.

He wanted to take the words back the second they escaped his mouth. Yes, he'd built his reputation on being a ruthless bastard in Hollywood. A ruthless bastard who got movies made on budget and on time no matter what and raked in millions doing it.

You're also the asshole who drove the woman you claimed to love to drink herself into rehab and pushed her into the bed of another man.

Her eyes widened again before they narrowed. Then one hand landed on one generous hip and she looked straight into his eyes.

"So, how about some food to go with the liquid diet you seem to be on? Have you eaten at all in the past couple of days? I can make you something. And maybe you could take a shower since it seems you haven't had one of those today, either."

* *

Well, damn. That was pretty stupid.

Sabrina snapped her mouth closed, knowing she'd probably just earned herself a pink slip.

Jesus H. Christ. When was she going to learn to keep her mouth shut? According to her mama, that time would probably be never.

"Oh, I'm so—"

Greg started to laugh, his voice deep and husky, and Sabrina had a hell of a time not falling at his feet in a puddle of pure goo.

The guy had that effect on her. And, oh, how she hoped he didn't know. How embarrassing would that be?

Several months ago, as a favor to her friend Kate, she'd agreed to model lingerie for a photo shoot. Greg had been the photographer.

She'd taken one look and fallen in insta-lust.

Of course, she hadn't recognized him then. He'd just been a towering hunk of man with unruly hair—a mix of light brown, bleached blond, and every shade in between—that hung around his masculine face in curls and waves. The kind of hair a girl sold her soul to get. Or at least paid a hair stylist a lot of money to create. She'd bet her ass his was natural. And she had more than enough ass to bet.

Combined with his broad shoulders, wide chest, and muscular thighs, she'd totally embarrassed herself by practically drooling on him the first time they met. When he'd made it perfectly clear he considered her nothing more than a kid.

Then she'd discovered who he was and, even though she had barely flirted with him, she'd been mortified to find out that the man who'd taken half-naked pictures of her was a world-famous,

Oscar-winning filmmaker who often dated women known to the world by only one name.

No wonder he'd seen her as nothing more than a prop in a photograph.

And thank *God* she hadn't thrown herself at him. That would've made this situation way too unbearable.

At least he was laughing, though she had no idea why.

If it'd been anyone else, she would've smacked him on the chest and demanded an explanation. But this man wasn't her friend. No, he was the special guest of the man who employed her.

She was here to work. Not ogle the guests. Or guest, as the case may be.

She stood silently while he laughed, trying not to notice how hot he was. Or how drunk.

It took him at least a minute to calm down, and when his laughter finally died, he still wore that smile that made her want to beg him to kiss her.

She bet he was one hell of a good kisser.

And that's probably not all he's good at.

Too bad she'd never find out. Although she could probably read about it in *In Touch* or *In Vogue* or whatever the hell those magazines were that her mother devoured when she put her feet up at night after working eight-hour days cleaning hotel rooms.

"I'm so sorry, Mr. Hicks. I didn't mean to offend you. I shouldn't have—"

"Sabrina. Stop."

She snapped her mouth closed, though she couldn't shut off her brain. She wondered if he was about to send her home, ending her four-month career with the Golden brothers and their boutique Haven Hotel and new Haven Retreat.

It was a dream job, especially for a girl with an associate's degree in hotel-restaurant management from a community college and a dream of putting that career to use somewhere other than a Motel 6.

He kept staring at her with those hazel eyes and her heart began to pound so loudly she heard it in her ears.

"You didn't offend me," he said. "I've got a pretty thick skin. And you're not wrong. So yeah, I could use some food. If you don't mind."

No, she didn't mind. Hell, she *wanted* to cook for him. Which was stupid and foolish and, if he knew what she was thinking, he'd pat her on the head and give her a pitying little smirk.

"Sure." She gave him what she hoped was a pleasant smile. Not an *OMG, you're so fucking hot, I want to climb you* smile. "I'll just see what they have in the kitchen. Anything you don't like?"

He snorted, not loud but audible, then shook his head. "Not really."

She kept her smile plastered on, even as her heart continued to pick up speed. Why was he looking at her like he couldn't decide whether to send her packing or . . .

Or what?

He's definitely not *looking at you like he wants to take you to bed.*

Obviously, she was reading way too much into the man's expression. Considering the fact that he was mostly drunk, it'd probably be a good idea for her to leave. Now.

"Okay." She perked up her smile a little as she started to retreat from the room. "I'll see if there's any steak."

There's a nice slab of beefcake right in front of you.

She felt a blush rise in her cheeks again and desperately tried to control it. It was a damn good thing he couldn't read her mind.

"Why don't you take a shower? By the time you're done, I'll have something for you to eat."

He never took his eyes off her, and she had to control her impulse not to run all the way to the kitchen. Away from him.

Because if she stayed . . .

"Sabrina."

His voice stopped her in her tracks just as she was about to make her getaway through the door and into the hall.

"Yes?"

"Will you eat with me?"

Her breath caught in her throat and her heart flipped into double time.

Whoa. Slow your roll. He's bored and you probably look ready to agree to anything.

"Uh, sure. If you want the company."

"I do."

Ooh-kay then.

She smiled. She couldn't help it. He looked at her with those eyes and that mouth twisted in a little smile and her thighs clenched.

Oh, this was *so* not good.

"Great." She took another step backward, hoping she didn't make a complete fool out of herself by slamming into the wall or doing something equally embarrassing. "I'll see you downstairs then."

She turned, breathing a sigh of relief when she saw she was right at the door. And it was open.

She took that as a good sign and made her escape downstairs to the kitchen, where she took a moment for a deep breath before opening the freezer. She considered sticking her head in there for a minute but realized she needed to cool down more than her head, and she didn't think her entire body would fit.

When Tyler had called her an hour ago and asked her to do him a favor, she'd never considered refusing. Until she'd heard what he wanted. Then she'd actually thought about saying no, thinking up some excuse as to why she couldn't come up here to take care of world-famous producer Greg Hicks.

Her youngest brother had the flu. Her middle sister needed a ride to her SAT test tomorrow. Her younger sister had wanted her to go shopping for a dress for the school winter dance.

All true and all of which her mama said she could handle. And Sherrilyn Michaels Rodriquez could handle pretty much anything, including two deadbeat ex-husbands and eight children.

So Sabrina could handle one cranky, hunky, way-out-of-her-league, world-famous Hollywood player.

First . . . food.

She was a decent cook. She'd been cooking for her brothers and sisters since she'd been old enough to figure out how to work the stove. Okay, she was more than a decent cook. She was pretty damn good.

But Greg was probably used to eating in four-star restaurants with gourmet chefs.

"Well, that's too freaking bad," she said out loud. "He's stuck with me."

And, oh sweet Jesus, she was stuck with him. For the night, at least.

Twenty minutes later, she had steaks on the indoor wood grill, thick-cut, rosemary-spiced fries in the oven, and a green salad in progress when he walked into the kitchen.

"Smells great."

She'd heard him coming down the stairs so she wasn't surprised. But she shouldn't have turned around to look at him because, holy crap, the guy made all her girly parts riot.

He hadn't shaved completely but he'd trimmed his stubble down to a shadow. A very sexy shadow. His hair was wet but now it curled even more. And his eyes seemed brighter, clearer.

He still wore a tight black T-shirt, but this one said Bad Religion across the front. She assumed it was a band, but not one she'd ever heard of. Her musical tastes tended to be more girly. Adele. Pink. Old Christina.

"Steaks and fries. Protein and carbs. Hope you're hungry."

"Starving, as a matter of fact. Thanks."

God, that voice. It made her—

Okay, time to pull yourself together. You can't melt into a pile of goo every time the guy speaks.

Pasting on "the smile" again, she flashed it at him over her shoulder. "No problem. That's what I'm here for. Why don't you go into the dining ro—"

"How about we eat in that lounge with the fireplace? Okay with you?"

And there went all those girly parts rioting again. "Sure. No problem."

She turned back to the steaks, expecting him to leave. Instead, she heard him lean against the worktable behind her.

"So how long have you been working for Tyler?"

Keeping her back to him, she put the steaks on a plate. She'd made two for him and one for her but she wasn't sure she could eat it sitting across from him.

Every time he looked at her, her stomach flipped. Sweet Jesus, she was acting worse than a kid.

Which was so freaking ridiculous. He was just a guy.

Enough is enough, Sabrina Jeannine. The guy's almost old enough to be your father.

The voice in her head was her mama's, and she totally agreed. She needed to snap out of this and do her job. Treat him like she would any other guest.

But he wasn't *that* old.

"I finished my degree in May and started with Haven in June. I couldn't start full time until mid-September because I'd already committed to the catering company for the summer. Tyler has been really wonderful about my schedule."

Retrieving the fries from the oven, she tipped them into a bowl before putting everything they'd need on a serving tray.

"Yeah, Tyler's a great guy."

She heard something in his tone that sounded like wry amusement. Frowning up at him, she opened her mouth to ask another question but he shook his head and took the tray out of her hands.

"Come on, kid. Let's eat. The food smells great and now I'm starving."

So she was back to "kid" again. Alright, maybe that would help.

She followed after him before she realized they didn't have drinks.

"Do you want something to drink?"

"Yeah, sure. Just bring whatever you're having."

Well, she was having a glass of milk. And it wouldn't hurt him to have one, too. But she'd also bring a couple of water bottles. Greg didn't need any more alcohol, that was for sure.

So now you're his mother?

No, damn it. She wasn't. Her last boyfriend had accused her of trying to mother him. Then he'd accused her of trying to smother him. Which she probably had. It was a habit she couldn't quit. As the oldest of eight with a mother who worked long hours just to keep them fed and clothed, she'd either had to step up or . . . well, there really hadn't been a second option. Not for her.

With a sigh, she put the water and the glasses of milk on another tray and made her way to the lounge off the larger common area. The common area was built to function like a gathering place and held an array of gorgeous furniture, much of it antique. Annabelle Elder, the local antiques dealer, had exquisite taste when it came to choosing diverse pieces that worked together, and she'd outdone herself with this room.

Sabrina preferred the lounge, though. It was meant to be used by only a few people at a time and had a large flat-screen TV, the only common room that did. Not even the intimate bar off the dining room had one.

Greg hadn't turned on the TV. Instead, big band music flowed from hidden speakers connected to satellite radio.

She noticed he'd put the food tray on the small table against the opposite wall from the door but she didn't see him right away.

It took her a few seconds to realize he sat sprawled out in one of the leather club chairs in front of the large picture window that looked out over a small courtyard. Right now, there was a cobblestone patio surrounded by a boxwood hedge and beyond that, a wall of trees. The property was almost completely enclosed by a small forest of pines and oak.

And they were all covered with an increasingly heavy blanket of snow.

He looked deep in thought so she didn't say anything, just took her tray to the table and began to set out the plates and glasses.

A minute later, she continued to fuss with the silverware, which was infinitely safer than taking the seat opposite Greg and asking him what he was thinking about.

Whatever it was, it was deep. Or maybe he really was just that drunk.

She sighed, the sound louder than she'd intended, and turned to tell him dinner was ready.

Only to gasp when she realized he stood only inches behind her.

"Holy crap!" She took a step back and bumped into the table, then reached for the chair to steady herself. He reached for her at the same time, grabbing her shoulders. "Jeez, Greg. You scared the hell out of me."

"Sorry, hon. You okay?"

Was she okay? Oh, hell no. Not when he still had his hands on her shoulders. Oh, my God, the guy had big hands. And he towered over her by at least a foot, which meant she had to tilt her head back to look up at him.

He ticked off every box on her perfect-man checklist.

And he was totally off limits.

Blinking, she looked away then sidestepped him, having to control a grimace when he released her. Then she gave him another totally plastic smile, which was beginning to make her face hurt. "I'm fine. Thanks. Why don't you sit down?"

He pulled out a chair and she paused a beat before taking it. "Thank you."

"I *was* raised with a few manners."

She couldn't help herself. She gave him a look he correctly interpreted as "Oh, really?" as he began to laugh.

"You have a whole flock of little brothers and sisters, don't you? I bet you've perfected that look over the years."

Had he actually asked Tyler or Kate about her? Or had he just taken a wild guess? She made sure to swallow the bite of steak she'd taken before answering. "I'm the oldest of eight. Had to develop skills to keep the minions in line."

His smile made her blood fizz and pop.

"Minions, huh? How old?"

"Seventeen, fifteen, two thirteens, ten, nine, and five. And yes, my mama did have me very young. She was sixteen. My sperm donor didn't stick around long and she basically raised me herself. My grandparents are great but my mom . . . she's something special."

He nodded, that smile still curving his lips. "Sounds like it. Did she teach you how to cook? The steaks are great, by the way."

That really shouldn't make her so damn proud. "Thanks but no, not my mom. My nana is a great cook and, since my mom worked a lot, I picked up a lot of tips."

"You took care of the younger ones. Must have been tough being a teenager with all those kids around."

Since he looked genuinely interested, she considered as she chewed. "Not really. I mean, I had friends and boyfriends."

Well, she'd had a huge group of friends, including guy friends she'd sometimes dated. She hadn't really had a steady boyfriend until college. And even then, none of them had made her feel a tenth as hot as this man did.

"What are you thinking?"

Her cheeks flushed as she considered telling him exactly what was going through her head. A year ago, she might have. Today, she had a job she loved that she wanted to keep.

And he was a guest of the boss. And his best friend.

Greg sighed and her head popped up in time to see him shake his head, his eyes steady on hers.

"We're gonna be stuck here together for a couple days. If you haven't noticed, it's snowing like a bitch outside and I'm pretty sure the road leading up here isn't high on the township's priorities. It's just you and me. Nothing you say will leave this place. And you can't say anything that's going to insult me. Trust me, I've been insulted by some of the best."

Ah yes, but what about when she told him how much she wanted to jump his bones and he laughed in her face? Or worse, gave her one of those pitying smiles she'd seen on the faces of her mom's boyfriends or husbands when they inevitably left?

"How did you get into the film business?"

He stared at her for a few seconds and she wasn't sure he was going to let her off the hook that easily. Then he shrugged. "I left for Hollywood a week after high school graduation. I slogged through a year of shit jobs before I talked my way into an intern position at Roger Corman's production company. Made no money but it was a foot in the door and when you work for Corman, you either swim or drown. I learned to swim, worked my way into a paid position, and the rest is history."

"I saw *The Virgin and the Terror*." Her smile widened as she continued. "Mama said it reminded her of *The Evil Dead*, so we watched that too but that freaked me out."

"And . . . ?" He looked at her expectantly. "What'd you think of *Virgin*?"

She debated what to say for a few seconds then took him at his word. He'd said she could say anything. "Well, the virgin had a thing for the dragon, which was kind of weird. And the gorgeous guy you thought was the hero turned out to be a dick. At one point, I swore I saw one of the extras talking on a cell phone even though it was set in the dark ages. Or maybe it wasn't even set on earth at all? And what was with all the little stone people? I totally didn't get that."

Greg was laughing so hard by the time she stopped to take a breath, she worried he was going to hurt himself. At least he wasn't pissed. Another man might've tried to defend himself. After all, she'd just torn his baby to pieces.

"I did think the story was really interesting," she added, which just seemed to make him laugh harder.

When he finally calmed down enough to take a drink of milk, she was positive he was going to go into some lengthy description about why his movie was much better than she'd just made it out to sound.

"You know I built my career on that film, right?" He waited until she nodded to continue. "I'd been working on that script for years. I started it when I was sixteen. I had no idea what I was doing but I knew what I liked. I grew up watching B-movies, like *The Evil Dead* and *Re-Animator* and *The Toxic Avenger*, and I thought, well, hell, if they can make money on those movies, I can do better."

Mesmerized, she watched him talk about his start in the film business. She heard most of what he said but mainly she got lost in his enthusiasm and his ability to tell a story.

She'd seen pictures of him on the set of *The Virgin and the Terror*. Okay, she'd searched long and hard to find pictures of him on the set. His hair had been shorter back then. He'd looked clean-cut, young, almost innocent—if you ignored the shit-eating, arrogant grin. He still had the grin but it was no longer arrogant. It was sexy. Really freaking sexy.

While he'd been almost too prettily perfect back then, now he had the age and maturity to back up his confidence. The guys she met now, the guys her age . . . most were jerks. They were cocky, which wasn't anywhere close to being confident. They acted like they had brass balls, but if you looked close enough, you could see the cracks beneath the surface. All bravado. No maturity.

This man . . . well, he *was* a man.

And you have major daddy issues, don't you?

Her face screwed up into a frown and he stopped mid-sentence, his eyebrows raised.

"What? Not a fan of Leo?"

She blinked, shaking her head. "No, sorry. I was thinking of something else and . . . "

She broke off when she realized she'd probably just offended him by admitting she hadn't been listening.

But he laughed again and she had to school her expression not to let her mouth hang open. God, could the man be any hotter?

She didn't think so and that was *really* going to be a problem.

"You're gonna be hell on my ego, aren't you, kid?"

A blush heated her cheeks. "I'm sorry. That's not— I didn't mean—"

She stopped with a sigh as he continued to laugh.

"Right. So I think I'll just clean up these dishes," she said. "I'm sure you want to get back to work. Or maybe you should get some sleep. You look like you could use it." She rolled her eyes when she realized what she'd said and stopped in the process of picking up the dishes. "And wow, did I just sound like my mother or what?"

He released another short, rough sound of amusement but when she flashed him a look, he wasn't smiling. He stared at her with an intensity that made her feel like she was naked. Which didn't help her rising blood pressure.

"I'm not ready for bed yet." He gathered his own dishes when she would have reached for them, and he motioned for her to lead the way into the kitchen. "I'll give you a hand with these then we can check for dessert. I'm in the mood for something sweet."

Had he looked at her for any particular reason when he said that? It certainly seemed that way.

But then he headed for the door and she got drawn along behind him. Achingly aware that he was only inches away from her, she tried not to keep looking at his very fine ass. Which was really, *really* hard to do because, oh, my God, the man had a great ass.

And broad shoulders. And that hair.

So not fair.

But she was used to disappointment so . . .

"You see anything in the fridge for dessert?" Greg headed directly for the dishwasher and would've taken the dishes out of her hands and loaded them himself if she hadn't put them out of his reach on the counter so she could open the door on the machine.

She was the one being paid to look after him, after all.

Giving him her best "employee" smile again, she reached for his dishes. "I did see a few different pieces of cakes and pies in there. Tyler obviously knows you have a sweet tooth and stocked the kitchen for you."

She almost breathed a sigh of relief when he turned toward the fridge and she didn't have to force that smile anymore.

"Huh. He's clearly trying to make me fat. Jesus, how the hell many Termini Brothers cannoli does he think I can eat? There must be twenty in here. How many do you want?"

Truthfully, she wanted about five right now. She ate when she was nervous and right now, her nerves were jonesing for sugar.

"Oh, none for me, thanks."

"Don't like cannoli, huh? Then you don't know what you're missing. There's chocolate cake in here and strawberry pie and . . . I think that's carrot cake."

Setting the dishwasher to run, she headed for the opposite side of the room. "I think I'm just going to head up to my room for the night. I don't want to get in your way—"

"You're not getting in my way." With a sigh, he shut the refrigerator door, the tray of cannoli in hand. Then he gave her that smile again, the one that made her thighs clench. "And truthfully, I could use the company."

* *

Greg watched Sabrina struggle for a way to decline his not-really-all-that-polite invitation.

If he were a decent guy, he'd give her an out. Tell her, sure, no problem. See you tomorrow.

But he wasn't going to. He wanted to spend more time with her. Screw it. It wasn't like she was underage. Hell, he knew older men than him who dated eighteen-year-olds. Of course, they were pricks but . . .

Goddamn it, he *liked* this girl. If she could get over the whole guest/employee thing, and get comfortable with him, they could have an intelligent conversation. For the past week and a half, he'd talked to no one except Camilla Banks, the first caretaker Tyler had sent. She'd had the grandmother-type down perfectly. Probably because she was, five times over.

But he hadn't had the faintest desire to talk about his screenplay with her.

He wanted to talk to Sabrina.

Yeah, he wanted to do other things with her, too. But that wasn't going to happen.

And maybe if he continued to tell himself that, he'd actually make it happen.

Leaning back against the counter, he watched her struggle for an answer. He couldn't tell if she really didn't want to spend time with him or if she did but didn't think she should.

He did know he'd seen her awareness of him in her eyes, seen the attraction.

With a barely audible sigh, he watched her worry her bottom lip with her teeth. Christ, if she wanted to stand in the kitchen for hours and discuss the merits of pie over cake, he'd dress up like the Pillsbury Doughboy and let her poke him in the stomach.

Was that the alcohol talking?

Probably not. He hadn't been able to get her out of his mind since the night they'd met. It had become a real problem. And now that he had the opportunity to spend some time with her, maybe he'd be able to work her out of his system.

Without an actual workout in bed.

"Sure," she finally answered, and that shy smile she gave him forced him to swallow a groan. "I can do that."

With the cannoli in hand, he led her back to the lounge and waved her toward the couch. He set the pastries on the coffee table then fell onto the other end of the couch.

"Did Tyler tell you what I've been working on?"

She shook her head. "No. Just that you're here to work. I did see something online about you writing a screenplay, though."

Had she been checking him out?

And there goes that ego again.

"But there really wasn't a lot of information. Will you tell me about it?"

Grabbing a cannoli, she settled back into the couch, watching him. Waiting. Like she was truly interested.

"It's an idea I had a few years ago. A parlor piece that takes place in the same house over the course of a weekend. A group of friends gathered for a wedding. Sort of *The Big Chill* with a little *Match Point* thrown in."

"You mean the Woody Allen movie?"

He laughed. "Yeah, have you seen it?"

"Oh, I loved that one. I don't go to the movies much but my

mom has a thing for Woody Allen so she and I went to see it. I couldn't believe how much I wanted that guy to get away with murder. I mean, it was just so—"

"Amazing how Allen made you root for the villain?"

Her bright smile made it hard for him to breathe. "Exactly. I thought about that for days."

"Yeah, it's a great piece of film. That's what I want to create."

Her lips remained curved in a sweet smile and he wanted to lean forward and kiss it off her face.

"Don't you think your other movies are great pieces of film?"

He shrugged. "I'm not in the business of making art. I make popular entertainment and I make damn good popular entertainment. I've produced two movies I think can be called art but I've never made one myself. This is my shot."

As soon as the words left his mouth, he wanted to take them back, even if they were the truest words he'd ever said. He hadn't said them to anyone else. Why he'd told Sabrina . . .

As she tilted her head, her hair fell over her shoulders again. He couldn't tear his gaze away as she brushed it back. His hands curled into fists from wanting to wind the strands through his fingers.

"So you're writing the screenplay, too? I thought you didn't write anymore. That you mainly produce now."

He caught back a grin because, again, she must have done some research on him. Juvenile? Yes. Did he care? Fuck no.

"Yeah, I'm doing the screenplay and directing. We film in December for four weeks. We're doing it here in Pennsylvania."

She nodded. "I did read about that in the newspaper. Why here? And in December? It could be miserably cold and snowy. Although"—she smiled as she motioned toward the window—"I guess you're not safe anytime."

Good question. It was the one everyone was asking, from his business partner to the media to every actor who thought they had half a snowball's chance in hell of getting a role.

People were lined up on either side of the divide between *It's a desperate attempt to regain credibility with a low-budget art-house production* or *His production company's in trouble and this project is a desperate, last-ditch Oscar-bait to give the company leverage when it comes time to sell.*

"Because I'm tired of the fucking rat race in Hollywood and I wanted to make a movie as far from the system as I could get."

He waited to see the doubt in her eyes, the cynical "Yeah, he's totally lost it" look he would've gotten from anyone in the business.

Sabrina just shrugged. "Sounds good. I can't wait to see it."

As she took a bite of her cannoli, Greg shook his head. *Amazing.* He felt like a ten-ton weight had been removed from his shoulders. While his jeans got tighter.

Fuck. He really needed to keep that under control.

When he didn't answer right away, she looked at him through narrowed eyes. "What? Don't believe me? I do actually enjoy movies that have a decent plot and not just half-naked guys running around saving the planet."

She stared at him, eyes wide, but a smile lurked around the corners of her full mouth. Christ, he felt like a fucking kid, wanting to lean forward and kiss the hell out of her.

He'd wrap that hair around his hand, pull her close, and keep her there. Plaster that lush body up against his and seal his mouth over hers.

And then . . .

"Greg?"

The amusement left her eyes and he wanted to kick his own ass.

"Yeah?

"Are you laughing at me?"

"Hell, no. I'm laughing at myself."

"Why?"

Because I want you so badly, I fucking ache and there's no way I can seduce you into my bed and still be able to look my closest friends in the eyes again.

"Because I can't decide if I'm finally having a midlife crisis or if it really is time for me to get the hell out of Hollywood for good."

Her eyes narrowed and he swore he saw worry in those dark depths. Worry for him as a person, not as a commodity.

"Don't you want to make movies anymore?"

"Making movies isn't the problem."

"Then what is?"

Good question.

A grin ghosted at the corners of his mouth for a second. "When I figure that out, I'll let you know."

She didn't seem to know what to say to that, so she nodded and nibbled at her cannoli.

Hell, she practically played with the damn thing, her tongue licking at the cream filling, her teeth taking tiny bites.

He had to tear his gaze away before he leaned forward and kissed away the tiny speck of filling at the corner of her mouth.

They sat in silence as they finished the cannoli, with the music barely audible over the sound of the wind blowing snow against the windows.

After a particularly harsh gust, she turned to stare out the window. Greg continued to stare at her.

Beautiful.

Her profile was softly rounded, like the rest of her. No sharp angles. A pug nose, curved chin, high cheekbones, and those gorgeous eyes.

He wanted his Nikon, the one he'd used to take photos of her in Kate's lingerie. He didn't want to film her and that shocked him. He wasn't framing her for a shot. Usually when he saw a beautiful woman, his brain automatically envisioned her on a big screen.

What did it say about this one that he didn't?

"I can't believe it's snowing this badly in November." Her voice had softened and he found himself almost mesmerized, waiting for her to continue. "I guess you don't see a lot of snow in L.A. Do you miss it?"

"Miss what?"

Drawing her legs up beneath her, she turned back to face him with a smile that made him feel like he'd been kicked in the stomach.

Jesus, what the hell was he going to do with her?

Not one damn thing.

"The change of seasons. I've never been to L.A. but I imagine it's warm most of the time."

Not as fucking hot as he was right now, that's for sure. "Not a lot of snow in L.A., no. If I want to see snow, I go skiing in Colorado."

Her nose wrinkled in a way that made his jeans even tighter. He needed to go to bed because if he stayed here with her much longer, he couldn't be sure he wouldn't seduce her.

His buzz had faded and rationality was seeping back. And rationally, he knew she was old enough to decide what she wanted.

That night, months ago, she'd wanted him. And he'd shut her down pretty damn fast, taking the moral high ground. He was quickly losing his footing up there now.

And what happens when she finds out you had sex with Kate?

"You will *never* get me on skis. Speeding down a mountain on two long pieces of wood? I seriously don't get the appeal."

He shoved away thoughts of Kate. "Not one for pushing limits, huh?"

"Not ones that potentially end with me in a body cast, no."

He laughed at her dry, sarcastic tone, soaked in the warmth of her smile, and felt his muscles unkink. He hadn't realized how tense his shoulders had been, how tight his arm muscles had been bunched.

Relaxing farther into the couch, he let himself sink into the conversation. He didn't pick it apart for underlying meanings or hidden agendas. He just enjoyed talking to her.

The girl had no guile. If he'd met her in Hollywood, he would've predicted she'd be on the first bus home after two weeks. She didn't have an ounce of hardness about her—until he asked about her father.

All she said was, "He left when I was young," and since he didn't want the conversation to get too heavy, he let that one go, even though he wanted to know everything he could about her.

The writer in him always wanted to know more, know everything. He'd asked a lot of inappropriate questions his first few months in California before he'd finally learned to rein in his mouth.

As the conversation continued, it ranged from family and politics to music and movies. Sabrina didn't seem to mind his questions and he couldn't seem to stop asking.

The night grew dark around them, the glow from the fire the only illumination in the room. They'd finished off the cannoli— she'd had two and, for some reason, he liked that—and neither of them let the conversation lag.

She wasn't a pushover. If she had an opinion, she spoke it. If she didn't, she listened to him and seemed genuinely interested in what he had to say. And not in the "Ooh, you're so interesting, Mr. Producer, please put me in your movie" way.

And every time she laughed, he wanted to reach for her, pull her across the empty cushion separating them and kiss the ever-loving hell out of her.

He wanted to put his hands on her skin, cup those breasts and bring them to his mouth so he could suck on her. She'd be so damn sweet. Then he'd pull her on top of him so he could smooth his hands down her back and over her ass.

He wanted her naked, wanted to be naked and pressed against her. Wanted to slip his cock between her thighs and—

"Greg, I think I'm going to head upstairs."

"What?"

He blinked out of the fantasy he had going on in his head and narrowed his eyes at that little smile he knew wasn't real.

"You seem to be zoning out on me, so I figured it was time for bed. It's getting late."

His gaze automatically went to the small brass clock on the mantel above the fireplace. The hands pointed almost straight up.

Damn. For her, it probably was late. She had an actual job so she probably kept regular daytime hours and liked to sleep.

He didn't like downtime. If he wasn't in a meeting, he was dealing with the day-to-day business of running his successful production company. That meant he often took calls at two or three in the morning from raging directors and weepy actors.

His ex had learned to put up with it, but then Daisy had been in the business. And Daisy hadn't been some self-obsessed twenty-year-old with mental health issues.

At the time, his ex had been a twenty-seven-year-old with a damn fine head on her shoulders who had a penchant for drinking too much, which had become more pronounced the more obsessed he'd become with building his company.

Well, he'd built the company but he'd lost the girl. And now, he might lose the company as well.

"Sorry. I didn't mean to keep you up. I'll probably do some more work."

He usually did his best writing in the dark, and he should be glad to send her off for the night so he could work.

But he didn't want her to leave, even though he was wide awake now. And sober. He could probably get a couple of pages done now that his head was clear.

She bit her lip, as if she didn't want to say anything else, but apparently curiosity got the better of her. "Aren't you finished yet?"

They hadn't discussed the film again while they'd been talking, which he realized was probably because he'd directed the entire conversation and he'd wanted to listen to her talk. Her voice mesmerized him.

"It's written. It just needs polishing. I'm trying to refine what I've got but it's harder than I remember. Then again, it's been a few years since I've written a screenplay."

And he hadn't been in the right frame of mind lately.

Now, he actually felt like he could get some decent work done. But he wasn't ready to let her go.

He wanted to pump his fist in the air when she didn't move.

"I can't even imagine doing what you do." Her nose wrinkled. "I had to take a creative writing class in college because I needed the credits. It was either that or a psych class and I figured making stuff up had to be easier than reading a whole lot of books about crazy people."

He laughed and her adorable expression became one that made

his heart pound and his cock throb until he'd be wearing the impression of his zipper on it for days.

Goddamn, he'd been fooling himself this whole time, thinking he could contain his attraction to her.

Now it really was time to retreat, because the way she was looking at him shook his control to the core.

It was late. It was dark. He wanted her and he wasn't used to denying himself.

But he had to deny himself her. Because if he took her to bed, they'd spend a couple of great hours together, maybe a couple of days. Then he'd say "Thanks, it was great" and never look back. She'd think he was an ass and cry to Kate, who would complain to Tyler, and then everyone would be pissed off at him.

And he had more than enough people pissed at him as it was.

"Greg? Are you okay?"

Because he couldn't tell her what he really wanted to say, he got something else off his chest.

"Not sure really. My partner in the production company tried to talk me out of taking the time off to do this film. He actually suggested I was having a really expensive nervous breakdown. Maybe I am."

Maybe that's why he hadn't wanted to take another woman to bed for the past six months. Not since he'd met her.

"You seem pretty sane to me." Sabrina's smile was back, this one sweet, comforting. She was trying to cheer him up.

"Up until three days ago, I felt pretty damn good."

"What happened three days ago?"

"I hit a wall. One of the characters just isn't working and I'm not sure how to fix it."

"I'm sure you will. Maybe it's not as bad as you think it is."

He wanted her like he wanted his next breath.

"Yeah. Maybe not." He kept staring into those dark eyes. "I better get to work or I'll never get it right."

Her gaze dipped as she nodded a little too fast and slid off the couch to her feet. "Of course. I'll just take this stuff back to the kitchen. Can I get you anything else?"

Jesus, yes, please just put yourself on the platter for me.

"No. Thank you, Sabrina. I enjoyed the company."

Her real smile enthralled him for two seconds before it morphed into Pleasant Employee. "I'll see you tomorrow morning . . . well"—she looked at the clock—"I guess I'll see you later today. Just let me know when you're awake and I'll get something together for you to eat."

Christ Almighty, he should be writing porn films. Apparently his sex-starved brain could come up with a scenario for anything she said. And right now, he had her spread out on the dining room table where he spread her legs and licked her until she came.

"Sure. I'll let you know."

After another brief smile, she picked up the tray and headed out the door.

His gaze followed the sway of her ass until she was out of sight.

With a mostly silent groan, he closed his eyes and let his head drop back against the cushion.

He hoped like hell the snow stopped right this fucking minute.

Two

Sabrina hoped the snow never stopped.

She stared out the kitchen window, dirty dishes in her hands, dishwasher open at her side.

That snow was the only thing keeping her here. If she'd been able to leave, if the streets were clear enough, she would head home because staying here . . .

Staying here meant she was only inches away from throwing herself at Greg Hicks.

She wanted him. Like she'd never wanted another man in her life. He made her palms sweaty and her heart race and her pussy wet.

And that had never happened all at the same time before, not in the five years she'd been sexually active. Which was a hell of a lot shorter time than he'd probably been having sex. With gorgeous women. Gorgeous, famous women who all looked like they had personal trainers and nutritionists on daily standby.

Greg had just watched her scarf down two cannoli. Stress eating sucked. And, sweet baby Jesus, was she stressed. She'd never been in this situation before.

If she wanted a guy, she went after him. She flirted. She got to know him. She went on a date. If she still liked him after a couple of dates, she might have sex with him, but there weren't too many guys out there who'd made it into her bed a third or fourth time.

She had yet to find a guy who made her want to lay in bed and talk all night.

Greg . . .

Shaking her head, she concentrated on loading the dishwasher with their dessert plates then setting it to run.

Greg was out of her league. Better to set her sights on one of the bellmen at Haven. Some of them were around her age—

She turned with a gasp when she heard a noise behind her.

"You know, I tried." Greg walked with a slow, steady pace across the kitchen, his gaze never leaving hers. "I really did. I was halfway up the stairs and then I heard you. I was standing here before I realized I'd turned around."

Her breath caught in her throat at the way he stared at her, his hazel eyes intent. She straightened to her full height but it still only brought the top of her head to his chin. When he stopped, he was close enough that she only had to lean forward and she could tuck her head under his chin. Which would bring her body right up against his.

Her hands clenched. Luckily, she wasn't holding a plate or it probably would've slipped from her grasp and shattered on the floor.

"Tell me no and I'm out the door." She felt his breath against her forehead and her lips parted to draw in air. Drawing his gaze to her mouth. "But I figure if we at least get this out of the way, we won't be climbing any more metaphorical walls. And that's all this is. A kiss. Nothing else."

He wanted to kiss her? And *only* kiss her?

Well, shit. Then it'd better be one hell of a good kiss.

She was in the process of lifting her arms to wrap her hands around his neck when he beat her to it.

He curled one big hand around the nape of her neck and closed the few inches between them. She had a split second to feel the heat and hardness of his body press against her breasts and thighs, a split second to think how much better this would be if they were naked, then his mouth closed over hers and she couldn't think.

Her brain blanked as his lips settled on hers. He didn't demand entrance right away—he seemed content just to feel her lips against his. He stood still, only the pressure of his lips against hers and the tightening of his hand around her nape. Not controlling or punishing. Demanding, but in a good way. A way that made her want to give him anything he asked for.

So when he parted his lips, she did too, giving his tongue a chance to slide into her mouth.

Heat spilled through her body as their tongues touched and their breath mingled. A moan worked its way free as he stroked his tongue along hers, tasting her, playing with her.

She kissed him back, not content to simply stand there. Her hands grabbed onto his waist, wanting him closer.

He had to bend so he could reach her mouth, and she wished she were taller so she could be plastered against him, feel every part of him, including the erection she'd seen him sporting when he'd walked in.

Tilting her hips forward, she sought to align them even more intimately as he kissed her deeper. As if he couldn't get enough of her.

Her own frantic need coursed through her, making her thighs clench and her heart pound.

Now he cupped her face with both hands and tilted her head to the side, allowing him more access. He seemed to want to devour her and she was perfectly willing to allow him.

Her hands tightened on his waist and she felt him take a breath, felt him slow the kiss without losing any momentum. It was almost as if, now that he'd tasted her, he was content to draw it out.

She didn't want slow. She wanted him to press against her, wanted to feel his erection against her belly. Wanted him to lift her so their necks weren't strained and she didn't feel so far away, even though she felt the heat of his body through her clothes.

Her breasts ached, her pussy ached—hell, her hands ached from clenching his hips. Without thought, her hands slipped down his hips then back to his tight ass.

Damn, he had a great ass.

He groaned and her lips curved in a smile as his fingers tightened on her cheeks.

Suddenly, he spun them around, grabbed her hips and lifted her onto the nearest worktable.

She had a quick second to suck in a deep breath and blink up at him before he insinuated his hips between her legs, wrapped one arm around her shoulders, and put his other hand under her chin.

Then he held her immobile and kissed the hell out of her.

If she'd thought that first kiss was good . . . sweet Jesus. Every muscle in her body went limp, every bone turned to jelly. If he hadn't been holding her up, she would've sank back onto the table in total surrender.

Whoever said you couldn't come just from a kiss had never been kissed by this man.

After a few seconds where she let herself float, she finally marshaled her strength and lifted her arms around his shoulders. She could reach them now, the table giving her enough height. She wanted him closer, tightening her arms, and he came, pulling her closer to the edge as he stepped forward.

Now she did feel his erection against her pussy and she wanted to moan and squirm and tear his jeans away. She wanted him to strip her down and do her right here, on the table—

He pulled away, jolting her out of her haze and leaving her scrambling to regain her equilibrium.

Eyes wide, she stared at him as she tried to draw some much needed air into her lungs.

Greg stared down at her, his expression unreadable.

When she opened her mouth to speak, he shook his head. "Okay, I totally miscalculated that one. Go to bed, Sabrina. We'll talk tomorrow."

Without waiting for a reply, he lifted her off the table. She had a brief moment to salivate over the fact that he made lifting her seem easy before she was on her feet and he was steering her toward the door.

He didn't say he was sorry, didn't say anything at all. And she was still too stunned to respond.

At the base of the stairs to the second floor, she turned to look up at him. He returned her gaze steadily but she knew he didn't want to talk. Not now.

Good thing for him she was tired.

"Aren't you going up?"

He needed to sleep. The dark half circles under his eyes looked like bruises and she wished she could reach up and brush them away.

But that would assume a deeper intimacy and, even though he'd just kissed her like he wanted to roll her into a bed naked and beneath him, they didn't have that.

"Not yet. I still have work to do."

Of course he did. Just because he'd kissed her didn't mean he was going to drop everything. Hell, he'd probably just been reacting to all the pheromones in the air and now that they'd gotten that out of the way . . . well, now they could just . . .

Oh, hell. She needed to go away so she didn't talk herself into thinking she should just kiss him again.

She nodded, not trusting herself to speak and therefore say something really stupid. Like "I bet we could find something a lot more interesting to do than work."

Which would be totally out of line and unprofessional.

And she'd already done enough damage.

"Okay. I'll see you tomorrow morning." She headed up the stairs but paused halfway up, turning to look at him. "Don't work too hard."

His expression never changed, that intensity never faltering.

He nodded and she turned away, forcing herself to go. Knowing he continued to watch her.

How the hell was she going to sleep tonight?

* *

Greg woke, fumbled for his phone on the bedside table, and looked at the time.

Well, damn, he'd slept more than five hours. A bloody fucking miracle.

And he'd had a breakthrough on that character last night.

He now had two new scenes that were some of the best he'd ever written.

That was great.

The reason he was able to get that much done . . . yeah, that was going to be this morning's problem.

No, actually, it was afternoon, 12:17 to be exact.

And Sabrina was probably already awake and downstairs, waiting to do his bidding.

Christ, what the fuck had he done?

Sitting up, he realized he'd slept in his clothes, so he stripped and headed straight to the bathroom. Twenty minutes later, showered and shaved, he figured he couldn't put it off any longer if he wanted to claim he had any balls at all.

He tried the kitchen first. No go.

The office suite behind the registration area. Not there, either.

In fact, he didn't find her downstairs at all.

Was she still in bed? Just the thought made him hard.

Running his fingers through his hair, he knew he shouldn't consider going upstairs to check on her. But, Jesus, he wanted to.

He had his hand on the banister and his foot on the first step when a noise caught his attention. He had no idea what it was, only that he hadn't heard it before.

Following the sound to the back of the building, he realized what he was hearing was music but not the rock and metal he liked. It was that shit they played in New Age shops and acupuncture studios. Daisy had dragged him to a few acupuncturists for his chronic neck ache. He still had the neck ache and he'd grown to hate the music.

Apparently this was something else he and Sabrina did *not* have in common. Too bad chemistry wasn't one of those things. Hell, their chemistry was off the charts, as they'd proven last night.

He should probably wait for her to find him. He should head back to the room he'd commandeered as an office and wait for her to finish whatever the hell she was doing.

Just like he shouldn't have kissed her last night.

But did he resist? Of course not. He didn't have enough self-control when it came to Sabrina.

And that was a major problem.

He made his way down a hall that led, if he remembered correctly, to the workout room. Actually, it was more like a dance studio with wooden floors and mirrored walls.

Or a yoga studio, because that's what he assumed she was doing.

Dressed in loose black pants and a gray shirt, she crouched on the floor, face down, arms stretched out in front of her. She'd pulled her hair back in a ponytail that spilled over one shoulder and onto the floor.

She must have had a routine memorized because there was no TV in the room, no instructor. The music plinked and plunked and annoyed the ever-loving shit out of him. But he would put up with it as long as Sabrina stretched and moved to it.

She hadn't noticed him yet, and he made sure he stayed far enough in the hall that she didn't catch him in the mirrors.

Yeah, maybe now he felt a little like a stalker. But that didn't mean he was leaving, because if he wasn't going to take the girl to bed, he could sure as shit just enjoy watching her move that gorgeous body.

Unfortunately, he must've caught her at the end of her routine because after only a few more minutes, she got to her feet, turned off the music, and picked up the mat she'd been using.

Since he knew he couldn't get away without her seeing him, he figured what the hell, he'd own up to his bad behavior.

After last night, she probably wouldn't be surprised by anything he did. Then again, he didn't want to frighten her.

He stepped into the room just as she was turning from replacing the mat on a shelf.

"Good morning."

She gasped and her hand rose to spread over her heart. "Holy crap! Jeez, Greg. What are you doing up already?"

He smiled at the cranky tone of her voice, wanting to go over and kiss that little frown off her face.

Yeah, last night he'd made a huge tactical error. Why the hell he'd thought he could just kiss her and not be tempted to push for more was a mystery.

He needed to back the fuck off.

And yet, here he stood, waiting for her to come closer.

"It's after noon, and I slept more this morning than I usually do. So, how long have you been doing yoga?"

She gave him a strange look, a little wary, a little confused. Like she didn't know what to expect from him.

Hell, he didn't know what to expect, either, so they were even.

She sidestepped him as she walked past and continued on toward the front of the building. He fell into step beside her.

"I started because I needed a phys ed credit and yoga seemed easier than basketball or Pilates. I continued because I like it. It's a great stress reliever."

He could think of a few more activities that were also great stress relievers, but he figured she wouldn't appreciate that now.

"So have you tried it?" she asked.

"What? Yoga?" They reached the kitchen and he pushed open the door for her to enter, his gaze catching on that swinging ponytail. He wanted to wrap it around his hand and pull her head back so he could kiss her again. "No. My ex did it for a while and she kept trying to get me to go with her but . . ."

He could never be bothered.

From the fridge, where she was removing stuff left and right, Sabrina looked over her shoulder at him, eyes wide. "You were married?"

"No." Engaged for five years, yes. And he'd been a total dick. "No, we never made it down the aisle." Totally his fault. "She's married to another guy now. They've actually agreed to be in the film."

Closing the fridge, she started opening cabinets, withdrawing canisters and bowls. "Sounds like you still have a good relationship with her."

"We do. Strange—well, maybe not so strange—but we get along better now that we're not together. She's still a good friend."

"And her husband?"

She'd gathered all her ingredients and she stood with the table between them, measuring dry ingredients into one bowl, wet into another. All that work gave her a convenient excuse not to look at him.

He should be happy she hadn't brought up that kiss. But damn it, he wanted her to. Wanted her to be as rattled as he was by it. Because that kiss had rocked him off his feet.

It'd also given him the fuel to get those pages written last night.

And he needed to keep that under tight control.

"Her husband is Neal Donahue."

She nodded, as if none of this surprised her, and again, he wondered exactly how much she'd researched him. Not that she'd had to do a lot of digging to know any of this. It was common fodder for the gossip rags. Still . . . he wanted to beat his chest in triumph.

"He's had some trouble, hasn't he?"

She said it without any sarcasm, when to say Neal had had trouble was like saying an alcoholic simply liked to unwind with a drink every night.

Neal had had a drug problem. A very public, very messy problem that had spilled over to his professional life for years. He'd made a triumphant debut on Broadway in a gritty musical about juvenile convicts at twenty, then made the jump to Hollywood and landed a pivotal role in an out-of-left-field summer blockbuster.

For a few years, Neal could do no wrong. But, like so many other brilliant artists, drugs finally got the better of him.

"That's a pretty big understatement," Greg said. "He racked up an almost-million-dollar debt by the time a few friends intervened and got him into rehab."

"You were one of them, weren't you?"

She'd stopped mixing to look at him and Greg had the uncontrollable urge to spill his guts. He never talked about this, not to anyone except Tyler, who'd dragged it out of him one very late night after several bottles of liquor.

"Yeah. Even though we were both sleeping with my fiancée at the time . . . yeah, I liked him."

Her eyebrows lifted but she didn't look shocked. "Did you know? About Daisy and Neal?"

She went back to mixing and he found it easier to talk about this when she wasn't looking directly at him.

"I knew."

"And it didn't bother you?"

How did he put this so he didn't sound like a total ass? Apparently he was fighting a losing battle. "Honestly, no. It was a relief."

She shot him a frown. "Why?"

Because she'd had someone else to worry about, someone else to talk to. Daisy had needed a hell of a lot more attention than he'd had to give and she'd desperately needed to take care of someone. Greg hadn't wanted someone to take care of him. He'd wanted someone to be there when he was home to sleep with, someone who didn't give him shit for working the hours he worked. He'd never cheated on her. The only other mistress he'd ever had was his company, and he'd married that one first.

Daisy had never really stood a chance.

"Because I couldn't give her what she needed and he could."

"Sounds like she might've gotten more than she bargained for."

She had. He'd spent a couple of nights with her in the ER waiting for her to get her stomach pumped while Neal puked his guts out in the next room.

Jesus, that'd been a fucked-up couple of years.

"Sorry." The hushed quality of Sabrina's voice drew him out of those dark memories and back to the kitchen. Where he'd much rather be. "I didn't mean to pry."

"You're not. Hell, most of my life has been plastered all over the Internet. Anyone with a blog and a camera can call themselves a journalist in California. They ask much more disturbing questions than you. And if they don't get the answer they want, they'll make it up."

"Must suck, having your every move scrutinized. I don't know that I could take it."

"You learn to deal with it." He shrugged. "Or you don't and you break."

"So you got used to it."

"For the most part, yeah."

Her gaze narrowed and she stopped stirring the batter. "You enjoy it."

He nodded. "Sometimes, yeah. I enjoy the challenge. I like talking to people about movies. I like talking about my projects."

She smiled and the bottom dropped out of his stomach. "Yes, I can tell."

Okay, so kissing her seemed like a really good idea at the moment. Tasting that smile was more important than breathing.

And he knew if he kissed her again, this time he wouldn't stop there. He'd have his hands on that ass, pulling her against his erection until he could get off just by rubbing himself on her.

Maybe he did need to send her home. Get her the hell out of here.

Then again, she was an adult and the vibe she was sending out was getting harder to ignore.

The conversation ground to a halt as she dumped out her dough and began to knead it on the marble countertop. Not for long and not hard, just enough for him to imagine her using those hands on his cock.

She must not have noticed all the heat he was putting out because she calmly finished patting out the dough and cutting it into triangles, then laying them on a cookie sheet.

She must have started the coffeemaker sometime earlier, because now she turned and grabbed a mug from the open shelving then waved it at him.

When he nodded, she poured him a cup then slid it across the table.

As he drank the coffee, he watched her watch him, wondering if she was trying to work up the nerve to talk about that kiss.

Finally, she sighed, shook her hair back, and crossed her arms over her chest.

"So, Greg. Are we going to have sex or are we going to pretend we don't want to?"

* *

Sabrina tried not to let the blush give her away, but the longer Greg stared at her, the harder it became.

She'd had a lot of time to think this morning. That kiss last night had made her see stars. Seriously, she swore she'd seen fireworks in her brain. Which had made sleeping almost impossible. After tossing and turning for an hour, she'd finally fallen asleep. And then she'd had *the* hottest dream *ever*. Yes, about him. Her panties had been soaked through this morning, and her thighs actually quivered.

Damn it, she wanted him. And he wanted her.

So after she'd tried to talk herself out of this ridiculous plan and started stocking towels in the linen closet, then moved on to an inventory of the toiletries, she decided to do her yoga routine and figure out a way to break the ice and get him into her bed.

Yeah, it was probably total stupidity on her part. Okay, more like definite total stupidity. But . . . being here with him felt like stolen time, out of sync with the rest of the world.

She had no doubt that what they did here would stay here.

She also knew that when they left, that would be the end of their brief affair.

And her heart would break and she'd eventually get over him.

At least, that was her plan and she was sticking to it. It had worked for her mom for years—why not her?

"I guess the question is," Greg finally said, halting her train of thought, "are you really sure you want to pull that trigger? Because when you do, we can't take it back."

She blinked, surprise making her lips part on a silent gasp. She'd almost expected him to laugh, pat her on the head—or the ass—and say, "Thanks but no thanks, kid."

Yes, he wanted her. She'd felt the physical proof his body couldn't hide, but guys got a hard-on when the wind blew. She really hadn't expected him to consider her question seriously. And now that he had . . .

Her heart began to beat so fast, she wondered if it might hurt itself banging against her ribs.

Her mind began to supply vivid images of them tangled together in a bed but, because she hadn't seen him naked, she didn't have a complete picture. And she *really* wanted the complete picture.

Right now, though, he looked dead serious.

And she wasn't about to take back her words.

"Yes, I am. I've wanted you since the first night we met."

Her voice had gone husky as she thought about how he'd looked at her that night. Those few hours had fueled her dreams for months. And if he said no now, they'd continue to do so for months to come. She hated to admit, even if only privately, that she'd allowed herself to weave fantasies around this man.

Fantasies that involved more than one night and a relationship built on more than just sex.

And that was oh so very bad. Real life never lived up to the fantasy, and the only way to keep telling herself that was to let reality keep knocking her down. Like it seemed to be doing right now. His expression hadn't changed since she'd asked her original question and doubt was beginning to creep in.

Damn it, she'd let her mouth get her in trouble again. She'd taken him at his word that whatever happened here, stayed here. But now . . .

Stupid. Jesus, she was so—

"You know," he said, his tone totally calm, "I took one look at you and wanted to get you in a bed and keep you under me for days. Shocked the hell out of me because that hadn't happened in a really long time."

It shocked the hell out of her, too. She took a deep breath, realizing she'd been holding hers, hanging on his every word.

"There's a lot of reasons why we shouldn't even be talking about this, much less thinking about it." He didn't wait for her to speak, just continued to watch her. "You know that, right? You work for my best friend. You're friends with Kate and that . . ."

He sighed, a grimace twisting that beautiful mouth, and she didn't have a clue what the rest of that sentence might have been. Yes, she and Kate were friends but that didn't mean they shared every little detail about their lives. Or maybe . . . he had a thing for Kate?

Oh, wow. Why hadn't she considered that?

She thought back to that night, to the way Greg, Kate, and Tyler had interacted. Tyler and Greg had a tight friendship that anyone looking at them could see. But Greg had treated Kate differently. There'd been an undercurrent of something Sabrina hadn't been able to put her finger on because she'd been too worried about not melting into a puddle of lust at his feet.

"Sabrina."

She'd heard vague rumors about the fourth floor at Haven, rumors about the decadent parties. She'd overheard a pair of housekeeping staff talking about the New Year's Eve party and what went on after, when a small group of Jared's friends retreated to the fourth floor and proceeded to have an orgy. And that was the exact word they'd used. Orgy.

"Sabrina."

What if Greg actually attended those parties? Was he laughing at her immature attempt to get him into his bed?

Oh, my God, she was totally out of her league.

Her gaze snapped back to his and now he stared at her with a frown.

"I am so sorry." Now a blush broke free, burning across her cheeks. "I never should've said anything. I'll call Tyler and have him send someone else today." Her gaze automatically went to the window over the sink, framing the snow still falling outside. "As soon as possible. Please forget I ever said anything but I'll understand completely if you need to tell Ty—"

"Jesus Christ." He took three steps around the table and grabbed her hands, which had been twisting a dish towel. "I'm not gonna tell Tyler a goddamn thing. And I have no idea where the hell your head just went but whatever you're thinking, you're not wrong about me wanting you."

His voice had dropped to a low rumble that made her sex clench and her nipples peak. How totally unfair was that? Her body had completely overruled her head, which was telling her to leave, to get away from him because she didn't have the skills to handle a man like this. But his gaze had an intensity she couldn't look away from.

"I have since the moment I saw you in that damn lingerie. Every time I even fucking think about you, I get a hard-on."

Her blush burned even hotter, but it wasn't in embarrassment. The more he talked, the more she burned for him. She wanted the fingers he had wrapped around her wrists on her breasts, between her thighs, inside her body.

He leaned closer, until she felt his breath on her lips and his eyes were only inches from hers.

"There are a lot of damn good reasons why we shouldn't take this any further. Hell, the age difference alone should be giving you second thoughts."

That made her chin tilt back. "I'm not some idiot teenager without a brain. I'm a grown woman—"

"Believe me, I know that." His jaw flexed and his gaze dropped to trace her body, making her breasts feel even more sensitive.

Oh, my God, she couldn't get enough air.

Her hands clenched into fists and she leaned closer. She couldn't help herself. "And you are not that old."

"Then let's just say I've had a hell of a lot more experience."

Did that mean he thought she wouldn't be any good in bed?

As soon as she'd thought that, his eyes closed and his mouth flattened into a straight light. "Damn it, don't take that— *Shit*."

He released her and stepped away, shoving a hand through his hair. She had to hold herself back from grabbing for him so he didn't leave.

"I'm sorry." She forced the words out of her mouth. "I never should've said anything. I'll call Tyler and have him send someone else. I'm so sorry that I made you uncomfortable—"

He started to laugh. "Oh, honey. You have no idea how uncomfortable you make me."

His laughter finally died but the smile remained. And again, she couldn't help noticing how utterly gorgeous the man was. Yes, he was older. He had a few tiny lines around his eyes, but they only made him more handsome.

He sighed and shook his head. "Look, Sabrina. This is my fault. I shouldn't have kissed you last night. Total miscalculation on my part."

"So why did you?"

Crossing her arms over her chest, she waited for him to answer. She could have pulled away. He wasn't holding on to her any longer. And it wasn't like he was going to grab her and kiss her again. He'd just told her he'd made a mistake. Okay, not a mistake. A miscalculation, whatever the hell that meant. But still, she had to know. If she was going to be humiliated, she might as well get it all over with at once.

He mirrored her stance. "Because I couldn't help myself. You make me want to throw you on the nearest flat surface, rip off your clothes, and spread your legs. I want to sink my cock between your thighs. I want to watch you come and feel you squeeze around me and make me come while you do. Then I want to take pictures."

The more he talked, the more the air in the room felt like it had simply evaporated. Oh, God, she was going to come just listening to him talk. Her thighs clenched as if he'd put his hands on her, and she felt moisture seep from her body to wet her panties.

And he knew it, damn him. His expression spoke volumes. He meant every word. But he still looked like he wasn't going to do a thing about it.

And that really pissed her off. "You know what, if you're not going to put your money where your mouth is, then just stop."

"See, that's the problem." He shrugged. "I don't want to stop."

"Ugh!" She couldn't stop the rush of frustration that made her reach out and shove at his chest. He was taking up all the air in the room and she needed some space. But she didn't even manage to make him rock back a step. "Then make up your mind. Either you put your hands on me and we do this or you step away and we don't. Just do *something*."

His grin reappeared, the one she knew made women fall into his bed because that's exactly what she wanted.

"Tell you what." He looked totally in control, and that just made her even more furious. "I've got to do some more writing today. Tonight, you let me know if you're still interested. If you are, I'll spend all night making sure you don't regret your decision. If you aren't, no harm, no foul. Either way, no one will ever know what did or didn't happen."

Then he turned and walked out of the kitchen, leaving her with her mouth hanging open.

The bastard. He'd worked her up then left her hanging.

She didn't want to wait. But even through the heat pounding in her blood, she realized he had a point. They shouldn't make this decision in the heat of the moment.

Then again, wasn't that what this was all about? Heated moments stolen out of time. Not something over-planned and over-thought.

By tonight, she might talk herself out of it. He might have second thoughts. Hell, by tonight, the snow could clear and he could make a break for it.

And how stupid was that thought?

The timer on the stove dinged behind her and she turned with a start. She'd forgotten all about the scones. Which meant she had the perfect excuse to track him down and . . . and what?

Throw herself at him again?

Yeah, because that had gone so well the first time.

Maybe he had the right idea. They needed to calm down and look at this from all sides before they made that irreversible leap.

Damn.

She grabbed a scone, blew on it for a few seconds, and took a huge bite.

* *

Christ, what the hell was he thinking?

Sabrina had practically thrown herself at him and he'd told her to *think* about it?

He must be fucking nuts. Absolutely fucking insane.

His dick was so hard, he swore he could bat with it. Every muscle in his body had tightened to the point of pain. He could still taste her from last night and he could barely breathe through the lust.

And he thought he was going to be able to write? No doubt about it. He *was* crazy.

He stopped halfway up the stairs on the way back to his room, fighting the urge to turn around, throw her over his shoulder like a caveman, and carry her back to his bed. Then he'd spend the rest of the day over her, under her, beside her . . . any which way he could have her.

Still . . . he continued to hesitate, that niggling sensation that he was doing the right thing deep in his gut.

Waiting wasn't something he had a lot of personal experience with, at least not in his sex life. If he wanted a woman, he asked her out, took her to dinner, took her to bed, and either called her the next day to set up another dinner or had his secretary send her flowers with a note that said, "Thanks for a great night. Best wishes." Which meant the sex had been great but he wouldn't be calling.

Damn, he really was a prick, wasn't he?

What the hell did Sabrina see in him? She had to have guys her own age hitting on her all the time. What did she see in him? Money? Power? Connections?

And why would any of that matter to her? She wasn't an aspiring actress and didn't even appear to want anything to do with the film industry. Of course, he was friends with Tyler and—

No, that didn't track. She was already good friends with Kate and, if Sabrina wanted someone to back her with Tyler then—

No, that wasn't Sabrina. It just wasn't. He'd made his fortune in Hollywood being able to read people and he could spot a user at five hundred yards.

Sabrina did not fall in that category.

"Fuck."

Frustration ate at his guts, but the part of his brain that was constantly churning out ideas screamed at him to get to his laptop and put this angst to good use. Channel it into the screenplay.

He started back up the stairs, this time with no hesitation.

That look on Sabrina's face had given him a damn good idea about the final scene.

He was sitting on a chair in front of the French doors to the balcony and had only just gotten into the scene when he heard the clink of pottery.

His head shot up and he turned just in time to catch a glimpse of Sabrina's backside as she left the room. Then the scent of fresh, hot pastry hit his nose. He spied the tray she'd set on the dresser just inside the door.

That smells great. She'd even put a carafe of coffee and a mug on the tray.

If this were a rom-com, she would've put the tray on his desk, knocked coffee on his lap, and tried to mop it while getting her hands all over his crotch. Then she would've tripped on her way out and landed in his lap.

He'd never been a fan of rom-coms. The conventions were bullshit and outdated. He didn't have one thing against a good love story if you told it right, and that meant having something new and interesting to say about love or you had characters so special you rooted for them to find their happily-ever-after.

But happily-ever-after wasn't something he expected in real life. There was always going to be too much bullshit in life to be happy all the time.

Since the tray was out of reach, he had to get up and get it but seconds later he was back in his chair, laptop humming, keys clicking.

The next time he looked up, he had a crick in his neck that made him swear like a sailor, and when he checked the time, he realized he'd spent more than three hours in the same position.

He'd also gotten through that final scene and finished the entire plate of scones and carafe of coffee.

Break time. He wanted to see Sabrina. Wanted to talk to her, tell her about the progress he'd made. Trying not to feel like a teenager with a crush, he stretched until he felt his spine and neck crackle and pop, then he picked up the tray to take it back down to the kitchen.

Good cover story.

Downstairs, he didn't hear her, and when he checked the kitchen and set the tray near the sink, she wasn't there. So he proceeded to check every other room on the first floor.

No, he wasn't obsessing much, was he?

He was on his way back to his room, determined to ignore the need to see her, when he heard his phone ring. He had gotten out of the habit of carrying it around with him everywhere because it continually buzzed and beeped and rang.

For so many years, he'd been tethered to the thing like he needed it to keep his heart beating. He'd answer it at any time of the day or night, whatever he was doing. Hell, he'd even answered it during sex every now and then.

He'd always considered it one of the costs of being in charge.

But over the last few weeks, he'd let his business partner, Fred Jamieson, handle most of the day-to-day stuff he usually took care of.

And that might prove to be your downfall.

Lately, he and Fred had started to butt heads over the company's direction. Fred wanted to go even bigger. Global.

Greg wanted . . .

Fuck, what the hell did he want?

Shit, he thought when he picked up his cell—he had to answer this one.

"Truly, babe, what's up?"

Trudeau Morrison sighed as she always did when he called her by his pet name. "I see you're feeling better than you were the last time we talked. Not that that's a bad thing . . ."

Greg laughed, picturing the look on his personal assistant's pretty face. Trudeau had been a kid just like he'd been when she'd fast-talked her way into a job in his production company six years ago.

She had a quick mind and the ability to sweet talk anyone she met, probably because she looked like everyone's kid sister.

Big blue eyes, pug nose, brown hair, and freckles. The definition of adorable on Wikipedia had her picture next to it. At least it had for her birthday last year, when he'd paid someone at the website to put it there for the day.

"But you just can't stand when I'm in a decent mood, can you?"

"It's not that I can't stand you. It's just that I've learned to be wary. Sometimes when you smile, you still cut people off at the knees. Sir."

Smiling like he hadn't in days, he settled into the chair overlooking the forest. "So why are you disturbing my peace today, Tru?"

A slight pause and he had the fleeting thought that he should hang up before she opened her mouth again. "Nothing's wrong. I just wanted to make sure you were aware that the contracts still haven't been signed. The deadline passed this morning and I tried to contact Vince but—"

"Vince is avoiding your calls, and Daisy and Neal have fallen off the grid again." He sighed and rubbed at his eyes with his thumb and forefinger. He knew the fact that his phone hadn't rung in several hours was a bad thing. "Shit."

Those contracts needed to be signed within the next couple of days if filming was going to start on time. Casting Daisy and Neal had been a no-brainer, at least for him. They were perfect for the roles, but Neal had burned a few too many people in the industry who'd thought a handshake over dinner constituted an ironclad deal.

Greg knew once Neal signed a legal contract, though, the guy would live up to it. Which was why he'd given them a deadline to sign. He honestly hadn't expected this to be a problem.

And maybe he should've listened to Fred and probably every other legitimate production company in the industry that'd black-balled Neal for good reasons, not the least of which was his cocaine addiction.

"What do you want me to do?" Tru asked. "I can drive over to the house and knock on the door if you want."

And what if they weren't there?

"No." Maybe he was sticking his head in the sand, but he didn't want to have to worry about whether or not Daisy and Neal had fallen off the rails. Again. At least not yet. "Give them until tomorrow. If you don't hear from either of them, then go to the house."

"Okay. So . . . how goes it?"

He paused and he was pretty sure he heard Trudeau suck in a sharp breath and hold it. His assistant wasn't normally easy to rattle. Then again, the way he'd been acting lately, he shouldn't be surprised she was worried.

"Actually, it's going pretty well. I think I'm finished."

She released her breath on an audible sigh of relief. "Great. That's great." She didn't even try to hide her relieved enthusiasm.

Damn, he must have been worse than he'd thought these past

few months. He made a mental note to get her set up with his masseuse for regular sessions. She deserved it for putting up with him. He'd add an unlimited account at M.A.C., too. Trudeau liked her cosmetics.

"Is that it?"

"Well . . ."

Aw hell, he hated when she said that. "Just spit it out. What else?"

"Mark's been awfully quiet the past few days and I've learned to be wary of that."

Mark Schumacher was his company's chief financial officer. Greg trusted him implicitly, but everyone knew when he went quiet, he was doing numbers in his head. And that meant numbers weren't adding up somewhere else.

"He only went silent two days ago but, well, you know what that means."

"Yeah, I do." It meant they had a film threatening to go over budget and that meant Greg would need to get involved.

"Shit." The curse came out a little harder than he'd intended. "Steven or Amanda?"

He couldn't imagine it was Amanda. Amanda Maitland was only twenty-two and out in the middle of nowhere Iowa filming a quirky, character-driven script she'd also written. Her last film had earned her Drama Desk and Directors Guild nominations and enough Oscar buzz to make Greg throw some money into a promotional push for the independent film he'd picked up at Sundance.

Steven Lawler's adaptation of a popular young-adult bestseller had blockbuster written all over it. If the famously temperamental director could keep a lid on himself. Greg typically managed to keep the guy on track, but he'd been out of touch lately, hadn't he?

So when Trudeau said, "Amanda," his brain hit a roadblock.

The girl had one hell of a brilliant brain, but she *was* young and this was her first studio film.

"Do I need to catch a flight?" Meaning, had Trudeau already booked him a flight? Sometimes his assistant was ten steps ahead of him, which was exactly why he'd tried to put a "'til death do us part" clause in her contract.

"Not yet. I'll corner Mark. See what's going on."

They rang off a few seconds later, after she'd promised to be in touch soon.

With the phone still in his hand, Greg considered calling Mark himself, but he knew if he made that call, his time here was over. And that's exactly why he'd tried not to have his phone close at hand all the time.

Okay, now he needed to get out of this room and leave his phone behind. He wasn't going to get any work done.

And he wanted to talk to someone—

No, not true.

He wanted to talk to Sabrina.

Usually, he had no problem controlling his cravings. Not so much today.

He checked downstairs first but didn't see her anywhere. Back upstairs, he checked her room. She didn't answer when he knocked and he debated just walking in. Good sense prevented him, knowing it'd be a huge breach of privacy. The other half of him wanted to kick in the door, maybe rifle through her underwear for a souvenir.

Yeah, maybe he should just go back to his room and lock himself in.

A faint thumping from somewhere above caught his attention and he followed it like a beacon.

The door to the suite at the top of the building hung open and he forced himself to stop and seriously consider his next move.

He'd been upstairs. He knew what the suite looked like. Jared Golden's fiancée, Annabelle, had taken a special interest in that room and created a sensualist's dream.

Where Jared had chosen a Victorian theme for the Salon at Haven, this room looked like something out of a sultan's wet dream. And he totally meant that in a good way.

He was halfway up the circular staircase before his brain said, "Ya know, this is probably a really bad idea."

Luckily for him, his feet didn't listen.

At the top of the stairs, he took a moment to appreciate the sheer visual beauty of the room.

He had no idea what it'd looked like before Annabelle had gotten her hands on it. He knew the round bed had come with the building, probably because the huge, custom-made piece would've had to be dismantled to get it out of there. It fit the dimensions of the circular room perfectly.

And Annabelle had gone from there.

Deep, rich purple and red silk covered the walls and windows. A canopy of white gauze draped over the bed along with white silk bedding. Every light in the room, all of which looked like lanterns, had a bulb that flickered and bathed the room in simulated candle-light. A chaise lounge made for two sat under the huge windows that took up nearly half of the wall space. A floor-to-ceiling armoire was the only other piece of furniture in the room. It really didn't need anything else.

Except for the artwork hanging along the walls from ribbons draped over a suspended rod.

Greg couldn't tell a Picasso from a Pollack but he knew what he liked. And he liked these.

They were black and white and looked like pen-and-ink drawings showing couples and threesomes in all manner of erotic poses. Nothing explicit, but just looking at them made his cock hard.

He wondered what Sabrina thought about them. Did she look at them and get hot?

Shit, he really should head back downstairs.

But did he? Of course not.

"Sabrina? Are you up here?"

A muffled thump followed by a curse came from the attached bath, and he headed for the door to find her on her knees on the floor, rubbing the back of her head.

"Hey, you okay?"

He crouched down beside her, cupping her nape as she gave him a dirty look. Which made him smile. Hell, everything about her made him smile.

"No. You startled me and I hit my head on the cabinet. Which is kind of hard, so, ouch."

"Yeah, sorry about that."

She shrugged and made a motion to get up, not meeting his gaze. "Not your fault."

Standing, he reached down to help her up and, when she tried to release his hand, he didn't let go.

Now she did look up, lifting her eyebrows at him.

"Yes, it was my fault. I didn't mean to startle you. What are you doing up here?"

She tugged on her hand and this time he let her go. "Stocking cabinets. I figured I could get some housekeeping stuff done. I get bored easily and it helps me think."

"I know the feeling. So are you finished in here?"

"Why?" Her question held a wary tone and his grin widened.

"Because I think we could both use a break."

Her arms crossed over her chest and he had to fight the temptation to look down awfully hard.

"And what do you have in mind?"

He wanted to go back on his earlier statement and throw her on the bed in the next room.

"How about you help me stage a few photos? I told Tyler I'd do some promo shots while I was up here."

He really didn't need her help and Tyler didn't really expect him to do those photos, but now that he was with her, he didn't want to be alone in his room again.

And he should have known she'd call him on it.

"I thought you didn't want to see me until tonight?" Her eyes narrowed and he found her suspicion hot as hell. "What changed? Is something wrong?"

"Why do you ask that?"

She paused. "No reason. I guess. So . . . what kind of photos?"

He had to laugh at the wariness in her expression even as he held back from kissing the look off her face.

"Not those kind." At least not now. But later . . . "Promo photos for the website and for print ads, but not your standard magazine shots. More artistic than promotional."

Her eyes narrowed even more as she thought about that. "Okay. But how can I help? I am the least artistic person you will ever meet."

"I bet that's not true."

She gave him a raised eyebrow. "You don't know me that well."

No, he didn't. And he wanted to change that. Didn't matter if it wasn't smart. "Don't worry. I will."

He underlaid the words with enough sexual heat to make her blush. Which then made her scowl.

He hadn't had this much fun flirting with a woman in . . . hell, he didn't know how long.

And even though in the back of his brain he knew he had a problem brewing in L.A., he managed to set that aside and focus on her.

"So, pictures." She didn't step away, and he liked having her this close. "Where's your camera?"

"In my room." And since he wasn't sure he could keep to his resolution not to touch her until tonight if she was that close to his bed, he didn't ask her to come with him. "I'll meet you in the lounge."

"Do you want me to get anything? Props or something?"

He hadn't thought that far ahead.

"Maybe a tray and some dishes?" she said. "Or a robe. Ooh, or maybe some of Kate's lingerie. She's got a few pieces stashed in the boutique."

His brain began to see images and he nodded. "Yes, to all of it. Meet me there in five minutes."

Three

Watching Greg work made Sabrina hot.

The camera looked small in his hands, and the way his fingers curved around it made her wonder how they'd feel cupping her breasts.

The last time she'd seen him with a camera in his hands, he'd been taking pictures of her and she'd been desperately trying not to show how turned on he'd made her.

Now, she honestly didn't care. She'd already made up her mind. She was going to have him tonight.

"Move that pillow to the left. Yeah, right there. Good."

He lifted the camera and she faded out of his sight line and out of his notice.

It gave her the chance to watch him unobserved.

He handled the camera with the ease of long use, almost as if it were an extension of his hands.

They'd started in the lounge, moved to the community room, then headed upstairs to the bedrooms. Since each one was different, they'd started at one end of the hall and worked their way down, skipping the rooms they were using.

While the tower room was Annabelle's masterpiece, all of the rooms were unique. And sensual. And filled with items designed to arouse and soothe. Strangely enough, it all worked. She'd chosen to stay in the night-sky room. At least that's what she called it. The walls and ceiling were painted a deep, midnight blue, and they gleamed at night because they'd been dusted with glow-in-the-dark glitter.

The artwork shared a common theme but, where the other rooms were all linked by one artist, this room had several. The only common theme was the outdoor setting.

Greg had chosen the room directly at the top of the stairs, probably because it was the first one he'd seen. Or maybe he liked the intensely masculine theme. Black silk sheets on the bed, black-leather upholstered furniture, wine-red walls. Beautiful, framed mirror over the bed. Yes, over the bed.

Only one painting hung in his room but its sexual nature was hard to mistake. It showed a woman artfully bound by ropes. Tastefully, of course. But still hot enough to peel paint.

"Alright, babe. Let's take a break. I have enough to get started. And you look like you could do with some food."

Blinking out of her thoughts, she looked up at Greg, standing not quite within touching distance.

"Um, yeah, sure. What do you want to eat?"

"How about I make you something? You cooked last night."

"But I'm here to take care of you."

The second the words were out of her mouth, she wanted to take them back.

Oh, hell.

And when he started to grin, well . . . had it suddenly become hotter than a furnace in here?

"Yeah." He let out a snort of amusement. "I know exactly why Tyler sent you. But it wasn't to be my slave. You helped me this morning, so I'll cook for you. Deal?"

When she continued to hesitate, he finally said, "I can cook, you know."

"I'm sure you can, it's just that . . . it's kind of my job."

Waving her out into the hall in front of him, he walked behind her as they went back to the kitchen.

"I don't want to be treated like a customer. For the time we're here, were not Guest and Employee. Just Greg and Sabrina. Okay?"

Yes. Please. She wanted that. She hadn't known how much she wanted it until he'd suggested it.

It wasn't right. The Goldens were paying her to take care of Greg while he was here. But she *so* wanted this time with him, knowing it would never happen again.

"Okay."

His smile made the bottom drop out of her stomach.

She took a deep breath to steady herself. "So what are you going to make me?"

They started down the stairs. "The best damn grilled cheese sandwich you ever had."

* *

"So now what? Are we doing more pictures?"

Sabrina leaned back in her chair at the small table in the kitchen, looking considerably more relaxed.

Greg had noticed the strain in her eyes before they'd stopped for lunch. He'd felt the same strain himself and it left him with an ache in his groin. The anticipation was making them both crazy but in a good way.

His brain kept coming up with a whole host of different ways he was going to take her, but they were butting up against the ideas flowing for the screenplay. He wanted to get back to his room and write, but he also wanted to lay her out on the table and sink between her thighs.

"No, I think I'm going to get some writing done."

She didn't look surprised or disappointed. "Okay. I have things I need to do."

The least she could have done was be a little pissed off that he wanted to abandon her for a while. "Oh, yeah? Like what?"

"Tyler asked me to work on the descriptions of the rooms for the website and the brochure." She shrugged. "I guess he figured I'd have time on my hands."

Greedy bastard that he was, he didn't want her to spend time on anything but him. Then again, the girl was just starting her career and wanted to make a good impression. He couldn't fault her for that. And he didn't want to stand in her way.

"Want any help?"

She smiled at him, a true smile this time. "No, but thanks. It'll keep me busy and I think I'll like it. I enjoyed the one business writing course I had in college so maybe I'll be good at it. Then again, I might suck, but at least I'll be busy."

He knew of several ways to keep her busy, but he bit his tongue and rose to help her clear the dishes.

He could tell she wanted to tell him not to help her with the dishes by the look she gave him, but she didn't open her mouth. Instead, she made sure they only had to make one trip to the dishwasher.

She shooed him out seconds later, and he headed back to his room with a smile and a brain full of ideas. He took the stairs two at a time, anxious to get back to his desk. And didn't get up for two hours straight.

When his neck finally protested that it'd been in the same position for too long, he wrote a few more notes before he forgot them, saved the file twice, then stood.

Stretching out the kinks, he spied the camera he'd used this morning next to his laptop. He picked it up, thinking maybe he'd take some more shots.

Or maybe he'd just find Sabrina and take some shots of her.

He checked her room first. Not there. Then he looked down the hall and found the door to the tower room open.

That's where he found her sitting cross-legged in the middle of the bed, laptop open in front of her, eyes closed, fingers typing away.

He leaned against the doorjamb and looked at her.

The girl was not what contemporary Hollywood would call beautiful but, damn, she was sexy as all hell. She had curves. Gorgeous curves he wanted to run his hands over. And those dark eyes. And that mass of golden brown hair he wanted to see spread all over a pillow.

The hunger he'd been diverting into writing for the past two hours renewed its focus on its primary target. He didn't want to wait until tonight to get his hands on her.

Standing away from the door, he lifted the camera and snapped off a few shots.

Fingers freezing on the keyboard, her eyes flew open and widened further with each step he took toward her.

When he stood by the bed, she closed the laptop.

"Are you finished?"

She shook her head. "I can put it aside for a while if you—"

Her teeth lodged in her bottom lip, halting whatever else she was going to say. Like, maybe, *if you want me.*

Which is exactly what he wanted.

Setting his camera on the bedside table, he held out his hand for the laptop, which she handed over silently.

Setting it next to his camera, he kneeled on the bed and reached for her. He wrapped one hand around the back of her head, tilting her face up to his.

Then he kissed her.

Holy hell. His blood turned to lava and his cock throbbed.

There was no hesitation in her kiss this time, no surprise. If anything, she seemed eager. And willing.

He didn't have the patience to coax her to open her mouth for him. He just demanded entrance with his tongue. She gave it to him willingly as her arms wrapped around his waist and her hands spread across his back.

She kissed with a sweetness he'd been expecting and a heat he was dying for. He'd burn in it for the rest of the day and ask for more.

With their tongues entangled, his free hand smoothed over the curve of her ass, pressing her closer. The warmth of her burned through her jeans into his skin, and he wanted to feel her naked and pressed against him. Wanted to lay her out on the bed and explore every naked inch of her body.

His hunger grew and he pressed his mouth harder against hers, wanting more of her. When he couldn't satisfy his craving with only her mouth, his lips slid away to press kisses along her jaw to her ear.

He bit the lobe, hard enough to make her flinch but not enough to cause pain. Well, maybe just a little. But he loved the feel of her body as she shivered against him. Nuzzling his nose into her hair for a second, he continued his exploration of her body with his mouth on her neck.

But he didn't get far. Her damn sweater got in the way. He pulled back, just enough to glance down at the mounds of her breasts pressed against his chest. Her fingers clenched on his back, as if she thought he was pulling away, making him grin.

"It's time to get rid of this." He released her and grabbed the hem of her sweater with both hands. Then he paused, checking to make sure she was still with him.

She stared up at him with wide, slightly dazed eyes, and he wondered if he was going too fast for her. Then he felt her hands move from his back to his sides and slide under the edges of his T-shirt.

"Only if yours comes off, too."

Desire made his balls tighten. "Anything you want, sweetheart."

She blinked and sucked in a barely audible breath before she started to tug up his shirt.

He released her sweater long enough for her to pull his shirt over his head. Her gaze immediately dropped to his chest.

"Very nice."

Her appreciative words made him laugh. Yeah, he worked out whenever he could because he had way too much energy otherwise. Side benefit being he didn't have an ounce of flab.

He reached for her shirt again but her hands landed on his chest and began to stroke through the fine hair that covered his pecs. He paused, his body responding to her touch like a lightbulb to electricity. His nerve endings lit up as she ran her fingertips along his collarbone then traced down the center of his chest to his belly button.

His stomach muscles tightened as she skimmed his belly button then continued on to the waistband of his jeans. Her fingers slipped just below the edge for a brief second before she spread her fingers wide and curved them around his hips.

Sinking his hands into her hair, he tugged her mouth up to his for another breath-stealing kiss before he released her and grabbed that sweater.

"Lift up." His voice held a definite rasp now—he wanted her naked.

She obeyed without hesitation, her gaze holding on to his as he dragged the sweater up her body and over her head. Then he let himself look.

Her bra had to be at least a C cup, black lace straining to encase gorgeous, golden breasts. They jiggled slightly as she breathed, and he wanted to bury his face between them before he pulled the lace aside and sucked on her nipples.

Lifting one hand, he traced the edge of a cup. He barely touched her skin but she caught her breath, forcing her breasts even tighter against the lace.

"One of Kate's?"

He'd bet money it was. It had the lingerie designer's sense of refinement all over it.

"Yes."

Her voice held a husky edge and she finally began to breathe again, which made her breasts move in ways that had his mouth watering.

"Beautiful."

"Kate makes them especially for me."

"I wasn't talking about the bra."

Her breath caught again but released on an audible moan when he cupped her with both hands and lowered his head so he could press a kiss to each plump mound. Her back arched, pushing herself more tightly into his hands.

Naked. He wanted her naked. Right now.

Snaking one arm around her back, he unclipped the bra then leaned away to look down. The straps fell down her arms but the cups stayed in place. Releasing her, he hooked one finger in the middle of the bra and tugged. It didn't come easily—it clung to her skin, but he was determined. Finally, he drew it down her arms and tossed it on the pile with her sweater.

She stayed still beneath his gaze as she let him take in her glorious nudity. So beautiful. So feminine. Full breasts, erect nipples, rounded belly, curved hips.

So fucking gorgeous. He wanted to take pictures. He'd never show them to another soul. He'd hoard them like a miser.

She was his. And he wanted her all to himself.

He wanted to brand himself onto her skin. Keep her under him and make her moan for the next several hours until she fell asleep, exhausted. Then he'd feed her and continue through the night.

Hell, he hoped they were snowed in for a friggin' week.

Cupping her breasts again, he drew on her already erect nipples with his thumb and forefinger. He rolled the tips between his fingers until she moaned, the sound barely audible. Then he pulled a little bit harder.

As he glanced up, her head dropped forward, her hair falling over her shoulders to brush against her breasts. He wanted to feel that hair on his thighs as she sucked on his cock.

Fuck. He needed to get a better handle on himself, or he wouldn't last more than a few seconds when he got inside her.

Of course then he'd just start all over.

"Bree, look here."

She didn't obey right away this time and he was ready to ask again when her head slowly lifted and those dark eyes connected with his.

He felt the jolt of that connection straight through his chest, down his spine, and into his balls.

With a groan, he released her breasts to wrap his arms around her and twist her body until he had her lowered onto the mattress beneath him. He covered her mouth and kissed her harder. Cupped her jaw in his hands and held her head at the perfect angle to go deeper. No hesitation, no adjustments.

She fit him perfectly and kissed him like she knew exactly what he wanted.

His cock, still trapped in his jeans, throbbed against her hip. He pressed even closer, the pain a heated pleasure. She tried to turn onto her side, toward him, but he held her steady with a hand on her shoulder.

When she acquiesced, he wanted to pump his fist in the air. Instead, he stroked his hand to her breasts, kneading each one in turn. They felt heavy, her skin soft against his. He allowed himself to play with her nipples while he kissed her, a steady torment that had them both struggling to breathe.

Finally, he had to release her mouth to draw in much needed air. It was that or pass out. And he had too much more he wanted to do to her to allow that to happen.

Like get his mouth on her breasts. She moaned when his lips covered one rigid tip and sucked it between his teeth, nipping at it and making her squirm. Her every move made his internal temperature rise, especially when her hip brushed against his erection.

The urge to rip off his jeans was a gnawing ache, but he didn't want to rush. Not her or himself. Sabrina was younger than the women he usually slept with, and maybe not as experienced.

That thought made him pause, made him lift his head to stare down at her.

What he saw was a beautiful young woman, eyes closed, hair spread out around her on the silk comforter. Her lips were swollen from his kiss and, when he glanced lower, her nipples were slightly red from where he'd been playing with them.

"Greg."

His gaze snapped back to hers, half-lidded and sexy.

"Why did you stop?"

Good question. Right now, she looked like a woman who knew exactly what she wanted.

Him. He let that thought burn deeper into his gut, let it roil and build.

When he didn't answer her right away, she lifted one hand to his hair and sank her fingers into it. Then she tugged.

His lips curved. "I'm not stopping. I'm admiring."

She blushed, this time from her cheeks to her breasts. Then she tugged on his hair again and he obliged her silent command to come closer. When he didn't completely close the gap between them, she lifted her head and sealed their lips together for a lung-searing kiss that made him groan into her mouth.

When she finally released him, he felt like she'd given him permission. For what, he wasn't exactly sure. Then again, he didn't typically ask for permission.

He'd wanted *hers*, he realized.

Bending, he put his mouth around one pebbled tip, sucking it into his mouth. With a little moan that sent heat arrowing straight to his groin, she grabbed his shoulders and pulled him even closer.

Jesus, she was sweet. He wanted to inhale her. Wanted to get as deep into her as he could.

He sucked harder, impatience riding him until all he could think about was making her come. Feeling her tighten around him while she did, driving deep and hard and having her beg him for more.

With his mouth tormenting her breasts, he smoothed his hand over her soft stomach to the waistband of her jeans. Yanking open the button, he ripped down the zipper and shoved his hand down her pants.

Only to freeze when he heard her suck in a sharp breath and still beneath him.

Shit. Shit. Too fast. Slow down.

He lifted his head from her breasts, but not before pressing an open-mouth kiss directly between them. He thought about taking his hand out of her pants but his fingertips just grazed the top of her mound and the silky hair there was too much of an enticement to leave. But he didn't press any further.

The lust glazing her eyes was unmistakable. It made his cock throb against his zipper.

"You need to tell me if I'm going too fast, Bree. Okay? I've been thinking about you here, like this, for months. If I listened to my body, you'd already be naked and I'd be fucking you until we both collapsed."

Her pretty, pink, kiss-swollen lips fell apart as he spoke, but he couldn't mistake the hitch in her breath for anything but desire.

Unable to resist temptation, he moved to seal her mouth with his. This time, her tongue pushed its way past his lips, her hands grabbing onto his shoulders before slipping to his back.

As the kiss deepened, she curled her hands and let her nails dig into his flesh, scoring light lines down his back.

He wanted those nails running along his shaft and making his balls tighten.

Later.

Hell, much later, because if she touched his cock right now, he'd come in her hand. He couldn't remember being so lost in a woman that he couldn't control himself. At least not anytime recently.

And holy hell, had he missed it.

With her nails digging into his back, he felt her thrust up into the hand on her mound, giving him tacit permission to continue.

He hadn't realized he'd been waiting for it. But now he wasn't stopping or holding back unless she pushed him away.

Releasing her mouth and pulling his hand out of her pants, he rose to his knees then stood beside the bed, grabbing her legs and pulling her closer to the edge of the mattress. As he stripped the jeans off her legs, she propped herself up on her elbows. Heavy-lidded eyes watched his every move as she wriggled and arched to help him.

Her jeans had been loose enough that he hadn't snagged her underwear, and he smiled at the sight of black lace panties that teased at the golden brown hair on her mound and covered more interesting secrets.

He reached for them but she grabbed his hands. "What about your jeans?"

"Those are staying on for a while. I'm not done using my mouth."

The flush on her cheeks deepened, but she said nothing as she released him so he could reach for the strings holding the back and front of the panties together. He wanted to rip them off her but he had too much appreciation for Kate's work to do it.

Instead, he pulled them down achingly slow. He could see they were wet, and the scent of her arousal made his mouth water and his heart pound even harder. By the time he pulled them away from her ankles, he could barely stop himself from dropping to his knees and spreading her legs.

Too fast. Need more time to play.

She'd closed her legs as soon as he'd released her so now he reached for her knees. But instead of holding her open, he ran his hands up her thighs, soaking in the feel of her skin. Damn, the girl was soft. Her thighs were smooth, her skin dotted with pale freckles he planned to lick later.

Watching his every move, she caught her bottom lip between her teeth, her stomach rising and falling with each breath.

She'd trimmed the hair on her mound to a small triangle and

when he ran his fingers over it, the softness tempted him to sink farther between her legs.

A small, husky moan slipped from her lips, making him smile. "A little impatient, babe?"

Her eyes narrowed, glittering at him in the hazy light coming from the windows. "Maybe you're just too slow."

"Don't you know good things come to those who wait?"

"Says the man who makes movies I need Dramamine to watch."

He laughed, a little surprised by her willingness to play with him. Most of the women he'd bedded would've pulled out the "ooh, baby, I want you, please do me" sex kitten act. And that's all it was with them—an act.

This woman wasn't playing a role. He *really* fucking liked that.

"Well, I can guarantee you won't need Dramamine now. But I will promise to feed you afterward. You'll need to replenish your energy."

He'd deliberately baited her, waiting—

Her eyebrows lifted. "You do know I'm more than ten years younger than you, right? Maybe you'll need a nap."

Now his smile became a full-blown grin and her eyes widened. Goddamn, he liked her.

"Oh, baby, if I need a nap, you can be damn sure you'll be passed out cold beside me."

Rising onto her elbows again, her head dropped back and she started to laugh, making her breasts jiggle and drawing his attention to them again. He wanted to rub his cock between her tits. They'd feel like the finest silk against his shaft and—

Her foot brushed against his erection, rubbing him through his jeans, making his grin widen.

"You don't have any confidence problems, do you?"

None that he'd ever admit to. And honestly, right now, with

the woman he'd been lusting after for months laid out in a bed right in front of him, with her foot teasing his cock, he said, "Not at the moment, no."

Something passed over her expression, a vulnerability that gave him pause. But she still hadn't said no.

He held out his hands and watched her frown for a second before she reached for them and let him pull her up into a sitting position, and then to her knees. The top of her head still barely reached his chin, and he bent to kiss her at the same time he put her hands on his jeans.

Her fingers began to move immediately, working the button loose and then grabbing the zipper tab and pulling it down.

A groan rumbled in his chest as she released his aching cock by tugging the jeans over his hips and down his thighs. The boxers he'd been wearing went with them, exposing his cock to the slightly cooler air in the room. It jerked in anticipation, as if it had a mind of its own and wanted her to take notice.

It didn't have long to wait.

She abandoned his jeans around his knees, cupped his balls in one hand, and wrapped her fingers around his erection with the other. He nearly came in her hand.

"Holy fuck, yes. Harder."

Wrapping his hands in her hair, he tugged her head back and let himself kiss her like he hadn't yet. With the full force of his desire.

Her hands clenched tight around him and her head bent farther back as he devoured her. His lips demanded more and more and, after a few seconds, she gave it to him. She met him kiss for kiss and her hands tightened on his cock and balls with purpose.

Then she started to play with him, stroking his cock from root to tip. Way too gently. Almost as if she was teasing him. He wanted harder and faster, but just the fact that it was Sabrina was enough to make it better than any other hand job he'd ever had.

Her other hand massaged his balls, rolling and squeezing his sac. Gently. Making his cock throb and a drop of liquid form at the tip. On her next stroke upward, she caught that drip on her fingers and spread it down his shaft.

The lubrication made her hand pick up speed, and his pulse began to pound in his ears. Releasing one hand from her hair, he reached for her breast, cupping its weight. He wanted to pet her all over, wanted to get his hand between her legs and feel if she was as wet as he wanted her to be.

He held back his inclination to toss her on her back and plow between her legs. Even though it was exactly what he wanted to do, there was another part of his brain that wanted to make sure she was just as satisfied.

Yes, she had her hands all over him but this wasn't some jaded thirty-something who'd been around the block more than a few times.

This was a twenty-three-year-old small-town girl who worked for his best friend.

Who seems to want you as much as you want her.

She kissed him with a passion nearly equal to his own, her hands caressing him with increasing surety. Her body responded to his every touch like they were connected on another level.

Right now, she was totally his.

And it was time to prove it.

Grabbing her hips, he lifted her off her knees, breaking their kiss and her hold on his cock, then laid her on her back. Okay, maybe he tossed her just a little. He had the supreme pleasure of watching her sprawl there for a second, hair fanned out on the silk, dark eyes blinking up at him.

He grinned as he kneed her legs apart then sat back on his heels. Now he had her spread out in front of him like a willing sacrifice and there was no more time for doubts.

"So fucking pretty."

Letting his gaze drift down her body, he noted her bottom lip caught between her teeth again, the puckered nipples, the rapid rise and fall of her chest, and the quiver of her belly.

Finally, he got to that tiny vee of hair on her mound. She obviously trimmed that darker brown hair and waxed between her legs. Smooth, pink flesh beckoned.

Putting one hand on her left thigh, he pushed her open even more. She didn't resist, let him move her leg where he wanted it, her fingers curling into the comforter beneath.

Then he reached for her with his free hand, laying it flat on her stomach before drawing it down her body. He ran his fingers through that soft hair then twisted his hand to cup her, the heel of his palm pressing against her clit while his fingers slid along her pussy lips.

She moaned and he glanced up for a second to see her eyes close and her lips part before he returned to watching his fingers play with her most sensitive flesh.

Her pussy lips were flushed and plump. And hot. And wet. He rubbed his fingers in the moisture, coating them with it as he worked her clit. He heard her breathing increase and felt her thighs clench, trying to close, but his knees didn't budge.

"I want to watch you come, just like this, sweetheart. Spread out in front of me with my fingers inside you. Then I'll make you come with my mouth. After that, I'll work my cock inside your pussy and fuck you hard and fast."

Her mouth parted, her slightly shocked expression only making him more determined.

Breaching her with his fingers, he watched her hips arch off the bed as he stroked, gently at first, only giving her the tip of one finger, crooking it inside then dragging it back out.

So soft. He wanted to feel that softness against his tongue.

Soon.

On each inward stroke, he went a little deeper. Then he added another finger.

Releasing her thigh, he used his thumb and forefinger to tease her clit, exposing it to the air and watching her suck in a sharp breath, then tweaking it until her hips thrust in time with his fingers.

His breath came harder now, watching her work toward her climax. His cock stood stiff and ready—he was going to have to rethink this plan. He wouldn't be getting his mouth on her this time. He wouldn't have the patience.

Increasing the pressure on her clit, he gave it a rough tweak and felt her pussy clench around his fingers in a short, sharp orgasm.

"Greg."

His name fell from her lips and sealed the deal. He ripped the condom out of his back pocket. The one he'd stashed in there this morning after that kiss. He didn't want to use the damn thing but that was going to require a conversation.

And that sure as hell wasn't happening right now.

Reluctantly, he pulled his fingers from her body, groaning when she grabbed his wrist and tried to hold his fingers inside her.

"Hang tight, sweetheart. Just let me—"

He got the condom unwrapped and rolled on in mere seconds. Not bothering to lose his jeans, he planted one hand on the mattress and used his free hand to guide his shaft straight to her sex.

In the next second, he was working his way inside.

Tight, so fucking tight.

Still working through her orgasm, her pussy grasped onto him, trying to take him deeper.

He tried not to go too fast, to lose control, but the feel of her closing around him, the heat of her pussy, and the strength of her arms as she wrapped them around him and held on when he started to thrust . . . it was too damn much.

He went hard and deep from the first second and he couldn't stop himself.

Their height difference was more noticeable in this position and he had to lift his upper body away to kiss her. Which made his hips press closer and his cock sink even deeper. He groaned as he fucked her mouth with his tongue in the same rhythm as his hips.

She moved with him, her body a sinuous dance beneath his. Her breasts pressed against his chest made him want to flip their positions and let her ride him while he sucked on her nipples.

Next time.

Now, he moved one hand to her right leg and tugged. She took the hint and wrapped her legs around his waist, letting him slide even deeper.

Her arms and legs tightened around him as she gasped, turning her head to the side. He froze, afraid he might've hurt her.

Then he heard her gasp out, "Don't stop," as her fingernails raked his back.

He bucked like she'd smacked his ass with a crop, then fucked her hard and fast. He lost himself in the tightness of her body and the warmth of her skin pressed against his. In the scent of her arousal and the sound she made every time he thrust back inside her.

He didn't know how long he could hold out, his attention focused on the sensation of his cock being clenched by her pussy. It made him lose all rational thought.

When she cried out, not more than a breath of sound, he felt her sheath grip his cock like a vise. He had the vague notion that he could ride this out, hold back his own orgasm so he could wind her up again.

But it wasn't going to happen. He'd reached his breaking point.

With her legs locked around his waist and her arms around his shoulders, he thrust and held deep as he came.

* *

Greg collapsed over her with a sigh, his cock still pulsing deep inside her.

Sabrina had to turn her head to the side so she could breathe, but refused to release her arms and legs.

Oh, my God, oh, my God, oh, my God.

The words would not stop going through her head.

Exhaustion and exhilaration made it hard for her to catch her breath while every muscle in her body tingled . . . and her sex throbbed.

And when he pulled out, she thought she might come again. Every inch of her was sensitized to him. Every breath he took, she felt as if his lungs kept hers going as well. Every breath she took was filled with his scent, so deeply male she wanted to lick his skin to see if he tasted the same.

His heart pounded against her chest, calling to hers to join his rhythm.

Oh, my God, she'd had sex with Greg Hicks.

And holy crap, it'd been amazing.

For several long minutes, she lay there, holding on to him. Not ready to let go, though she'd have to soon enough. He had at least sixty pounds on her and needed to breathe to remain conscious. But—

Damn, he must have read her mind because he rolled. But he

took her with him, rearranging them so he was on his back and she lay curved against his side.

I could get used to this, every night.

Draping her arm over his chest, she put her head on his shoulder and tried to catch her breath.

Which was pretty damn difficult to do when he wound one hand into her hair and put the other on her bare ass. She shivered, not at the room temperature but at the possessive way he held her. His hand on her ass began to smooth over her skin, from her lower back to her thighs.

Oh, my God, if he kept doing that, she'd be ready to go again in minutes.

"You cold?" Greg's voice, husky and deep, made her shiver again.

"Hmm. A little."

He shifted beneath her. She shouldn't have said anything. She didn't want him to move. Not yet.

But instead of leaving the bed and handing her clothes to her, he reached across her to grab the comforter they were laying on and drag it over her.

The silky material slid against her already sensitized skin and raised more goose bumps. As she huddled closer to Greg, her mound bumped against his hip and she bit back a moan, wanting to grind herself on him to satiate the already building lust.

Maybe she'd made a serious miscalculation here—

"So, I've been thinking about this scene," he said. "It's pretty late in the film and I'm not sure yet if I'm going to keep it."

—because she'd thought maybe the ache would lessen after they'd had sex. Maybe it'd even go away. Like scratching an itch.

"But it's pretty pivotal to an earlier scene I've been thinking about adding, and that could push the run time into two hours."

And now he wanted to talk about his movie?

Yeah, so what do you want to talk about?

Good point.

"What do you think?"

She thought she was in deep shit because all she wanted to do was lie here naked and warm against him and talk about his movie.

When she pulled away enough so that she could look up at him, he looked like he was actually waiting for an answer. A coherent answer.

Luckily, she'd been listening, mostly because all she wanted to do when he spoke was listen.

"I think if you need the scene, you should add it. I watch movies all the time where I feel like they rushed things just to get the film to fit a certain time frame. That's cheating."

He smiled at her, and her stomach did that thing where it felt like it turned end over end.

And when he leaned down and kissed her, she had to control her first reaction to crawl onto his body and rub against him until he was hard, she was wet, and there was no question about what would happen next.

When he pulled away this time, after scrambling her brain once again, she could tell from the look on his face that his brain was already back to thinking about his screenplay. She couldn't decide whether to be pissed off that he'd already dismissed her or relieved this wasn't going to be awkward.

Turning toward the other side of the bed, she began to gather her clothes.

"Sabrina?"

Snapping out of her thoughts, she turned, holding the sheet to her breasts like a shield. Which was ridiculous considering what they'd been doing only minutes ago.

"Yes?"

His eyes narrowed. "Stay. Just like that."

Her eyes widened and she had half a mind to remind him she wasn't a dog he could order around.

Then he reached for his camera.

She froze. "Greg, what—"

"No, no. Don't freeze up on me, babe." *Click, click.* "Just look at me."

Her cheeks burned and she clutched the sheet higher as he walked around the bed, camera still trained on her. "What are you doing?"

"You look amazing and sexy."

The blush that had started in her cheeks became a full-body flush. No one had ever said that to her and she didn't know how to respond. He made her want to give him anything he wanted.

"But . . . I don't . . . I'm not a model."

"Don't want you to be." *Click, click, click.* "Models sell a product. I'm capturing a mood."

She frowned as he continued to snap away.

"And what are you going to do with these?"

He lowered the camera, his gaze intent on hers. "No one else will ever see them. I promise you that. If you want me to, I'll give you the SD card as soon as I'm done here. Just let me take them and show you what I see when I look at you. How sexy you are."

She remembered how she'd felt when he'd taken the pictures of her before. Sexy. Confident. Completely feminine.

But that had been different. She'd been showing off Kate's lingerie. Now his emphasis was totally on her.

And it made her wonder what her hair looked like and had the little bit of mascara she'd put on this morning smudged.

He lowered the camera just enough that he could see her over it. "Now your head's not in the right place. What are you thinking about?"

She pulled a face at him and the camera went back up. And she started to smile as she shook her head. "I'm thinking I probably look like a hot mess."

"Sweetheart, you are in no way a mess."

"Yeah, but this just seems so weird. If you're going to take pictures of me, you have to talk to me while you do it."

"Okay. Sure. What do you want to know?"

Hmm. "Have you always been into photography?"

"Yep. Got the bug from my dad pretty young and I never really lost it, even when I realized film was what I wanted to do."

"I guess the two aren't that different."

He shrugged, the camera still at his eye. "They're just two different mediums. Photography is the capture of a moment in time. A photo can be a perfect distillation of a thought or emotion. Film—good film, anyway—draws you into its world and makes you part of it. It engages you."

As Greg continued to talk, she almost forgot that he was taking pictures of her. She became so enthralled with the peek he was giving her into his head.

The man was brilliant but then she'd known that, at least subconsciously. He'd created a successful business and managed to hold it together when so many had gone down in flames. But the way he talked about film, about the art of it, it made her hot for him all over again.

The camera began to click faster. Obviously Greg had noticed. Blinking, she looked away.

And the camera stopped.

"Hey, you okay? What happened?"

Looking back, she saw Greg had dropped the camera to his side and stared at her through narrowed eyes.

He hadn't put his shirt back on yet and she had a hard time keeping her gaze from dropping to his chest. He had a couple of tattoos that she hadn't noticed before, probably because her attention had been focused on . . . other things.

"I'm fine. Just, uh . . . I really should get back to work."

She tried to make her voice sound normal, like she always stopped to have sex with hot guys in the middle of her workday.

She smiled and turned toward the opposite side of the bed to pull her clothes back on. He continued to stand there, watching her dress, but she didn't turn around until she was completely covered.

Which was ridiculous because he'd spent the better part of an hour with her body pressed up against his and had just spent the last fifteen minutes taking pictures of her mostly naked.

Reaching for her laptop, she forced herself to walk to him as if the last hour hadn't happened.

"I'm just going to head downstairs and work in the lounge. I'll see what I can put together for lunch. Do you want me to bring you a tray?"

His eyes had narrowed down to slits as she spoke and she knew he was picking apart her every word, trying to figure out any hidden meanings.

While she was being very careful not to have any. No hidden meanings. No thoughts at all.

Mentally, she was writing a list of all the things she needed to do today, including washing the sheets on this bed.

Guess you can cross "Greg" off that list.

Forcing another smile before her face turned a very betraying shade of red, she headed for the circular stairwell and the sanctuary of the empty building.

Greg followed on her heels but she didn't stop to look behind her until she'd passed the door to his room.

Doubts about everything had started to crowd her mind, and she really didn't want to have him see her freak out completely.

"I'll be downstairs. Just let me know when you want to eat lunch."

His narrowed eyes had become a full-blown scowl, his arms crossed over his chest. "Sabrina, are you sure—"

"Greg, I'm fine. Really." And since she couldn't help herself, she added, "Yes, the sex was great. Yes, I'm sure I'll want more. But I really do have to get some work done or Tyler will wonder what I've been up to, and I don't think he'll be thrilled with the fact that his employee had sex with a guest, so I'd rather not give him any more reason to fire me."

Greg started toward her but she held up her hand and he stopped, shaking his head. "No one is going to fire you."

"Good to hear because I really love my job. And I'm going to go do it now. It was fun. I hope we can have more. But later. Let me know about lunch."

This time, she turned, not waiting for him to say anything more, and walked down the stairs.

Proud of herself for not running, she hit the first floor and headed for the kitchen instead of the lounge.

She didn't think she could settle down enough to make her brain work, but she knew she could work on instinct in the kitchen.

And try to figure out how she was going to compartmentalize all the pieces of her life that had just been blown into so many different fragments.

* *

Greg got about two hours' worth of decent work in before his conscience got the better of him and he figured he better go find Sabrina.

He'd been an absolute ass to let her go downstairs by herself right after he'd fucked her. Hell, he couldn't even pretty it up and say they'd made love because that's not even close to what'd happened.

He'd wanted her. He'd taken her.

And then he'd gone back to work.

Christ, you're an asshole.

No wonder she'd practically run down the stairs to get away from him.

And did you follow?

No, of course not. He'd already been in his room, furiously typing because the great sex and the amazing photos he'd taken of her had not only stimulated his body but his mind, as well.

And if he was honest, he could admit to there being a little avoidance going on, too.

He hadn't gotten to the stairs when his phone rang.

Pulling it out of his back pocket, he checked the number before answering. And nearly shut it off without picking up.

"Fuck." Taking a deep breath, he answered. "Tyler. What's up?"

"Just checking in. How's it going?"

"She's fine. We're fine."

Tyler paused. "Ooh-kay. Did I get you at a bad time?"

Greg sighed as he leaned against the wall. "No. Sorry. Just finished writing and am going in search of food."

"And how's the writing going?"

"Pretty good, actually." At least he didn't have to lie about that.

"And Sabrina?"

"She's fine. She's working on whatever project you gave her to keep her busy."

Tyler paused again. "That's not busy work. She's gonna make a damn fine marketing manager in a few years. She's got the ability to grasp big concepts and cut them into manageable pieces."

"I didn't say she was stupid, Ty—"

"True. But you just reduced the project I gave her to busy work. When have you known me to be stupid or too generous with my money? I'm paying her to do a job. I expect her to do the job."

And apparently that job was not supposed to include being a sex toy for his best friend. Christ, he was an idiot. Before he could say anything else, Tyler continued.

"So how are you two getting along?"

Greg was ready for the question, just not for the immediate instinct to lie to his friend. "Fine. She's actually given me some good feedback on the script."

"You let her read it?"

The shock in Tyler's voice grated.

"No." But he'd been thinking about it. He wanted her opinion on it. Hell, he wanted her to like it. "We talked about a few scenes, though, and she had some good insight."

He didn't add that they'd had that talk in bed. And unless Tyler was a long-distance mind reader, Greg figured he was safe from having to reveal that information.

"I told you she was smart."

"And so she is. Is there anything else you want to know or are you just bored with your hotel at the moment?"

Tyler laughed, knowing Greg was trying to get rid of him. "Actually, I got a call this morning from a very good friend of my father's asking for a favor."

"Oh, yeah. What'd he want?"

"For us to rent a suite to his son for a few months."

"So? You've done long-term rentals before. What's the big deal with this one?"

"His son has a few issues."

Greg snorted. "Don't we all?"

"Not like this. Have you heard of Sebastian Valenti? He's the—"

"Lead guitarist for Baseline Sins. Yeah, I know who he is. Had a pretty spectacular meltdown last year at a festival in England."

"That's the one. He's been through rehab and he's been clean since, but his dad wants to rent him a suite so he can work on new music away from temptation."

"And how does working in a hotel get him away from temptation?"

"I guess because his dad figures I won't put up with a bunch of rowdy musicians, but I could be talked into letting one kid with a gift for the piano and a sob story stay for a few weeks."

"Ah. You're becoming a soft touch, my friend. That icy exterior is starting to crumble. Kate's good for you."

"Yes, she is. She's also on the phone with Sabrina at the moment. Sure there's nothing you want to confess before I hang up?"

"Fuck you, Ty."

"Uh-huh. That's what I thought."

Greg knew Tyler was goading him and was smart enough not to let his guilt get the better of him. "Gotta go. Work to do."

"Hey, I called the township. They should be able to get a plow up there sometime tomorrow."

And Sabrina would be able to leave. "Okay, sounds good. I'll let Sabrina know."

"You do that. Filming still start in December?"

"Yeah. The crew arrives right after Thanksgiving. They'll stay at the farmhouse. I plan to stay at Haven most of the time and do the editing. Give me a little distance."

"Are Daisy and Neal staying at the farmhouse, too?"

"Yeah, but in a separate cottage. Let's just hope they show up."

Tyler paused. "Have they gone off the grid again?"

"Not yet. At least not that I know."

"That doesn't sound good."

"I'm trying not to read anything into it but Trudeau hasn't been able to reach them to sign the contracts."

"You don't think they're—"

"Like I said." He cut Tyler off before he could voice Greg's own doubts. "I'm not reading anything into it yet. They'll show."

"Hopefully sober."

"They will be." He couldn't let himself think anything else. He needed this filming to go off without too many hitches. They only had a thirty-day shooting window. Tight but doable. He'd actually padded the shoot with a couple extra days. Just in case.

They were shooting in the winter in Pennsylvania. The smarter move would've been to shoot in California but that wasn't the look he wanted.

"Hmm. Are you still planning to be back here Monday?"

"Yeah. My flight leaves Tuesday at three a.m. Then I'll be back the day before Thanksgiving."

"Okay. And Greg?"

"Yeah?"

"Don't break her heart."

Four

"So?"

"So what?"

Kate huffed and Sabrina covered a sigh, knowing she wasn't going to distract her friend by playing dumb. Kate knew her too well.

"Fine. I'll spell it out. How are you and Greg getting along?"

"Fine." *He kisses like a god.* "Everything's fine." *The sex was freaking amazing.* "We're getting along just fine."

"Oh, no. What happened?"

Shit. One too many fines. "Nothing happened." *Except great sex.* "He's been working a lot." *True.* "And I'm working on the copy for the brochure."

Kate paused then apparently decided to let her off the hook for the time being. Or she was simply regrouping for another attempt at information. "And how's that going?"

"Pretty well, I think. At least I hope it is. I have some ideas I want to float by Tyler, but I'm having fun with the descriptions."

"I'm sure Tyler will love them. And he told me to tell you the plows should make their way up there by tomorrow morning, at the latest."

Was that supposed to be good news?

"Okay. Great." She tried to force enthusiasm into her voice but probably failed miserably. "Thanks. So hey, I've been doing a little work on the boutique. I had a few ideas about displays and stuff."

They talked for a few more minutes, Sabrina explaining her ideas for displaying Kate's lingerie in the retreat's small boutique, and Kate gushing over them.

"You'll definitely have to be there when I bring the rest of the stock up," Kate said. "Opening day will be here soon."

"Are you getting nervous?"

"Of course I am. What if people hate my lingerie?"

"Oh please, no one could hate your lingerie," Sabrina said, totally believing every word. "You're gonna kill this."

Kate laughed. "You're so good for my ego. Smooches. Uh-oh. Tyler just walked back into the room and I got the raised eyebrow. You know what that means."

Yes, she did. All Tyler had to do was raise an eyebrow and everyone in the vicinity stopped what they were doing and attended to him. He just had that air about him.

Sabrina would've gladly admitted she'd had a slight crush on Tyler. Okay, maybe she still had a slight crush on him, but now it was only for his business skills. She *so* wanted to be half as good at what he did one day.

After saying good-bye to Kate, and promising to call if anything "interesting" happened, Sabrina shut off all the lights in the small boutique in the front of the building and made her way back to the kitchen. She didn't hear any movement upstairs so that probably meant Greg was still working.

She'd kept herself busy all afternoon so she didn't constantly think about him. About Greg naked. About him over her and inside her. Because every time she did, she wanted to do it again. And again.

And that, my friends, is the start of an addiction.

Her stomach growled and she realized it was almost six o'clock. They could both do with some food. Maybe he'd want to eat in his room and keep working. She certainly didn't want to get in his way.

"There you are. I was just coming to look for you."

Greg walked out of the kitchen just as she was ready to walk through the door, and she barely managed to catch back a sigh as her heart kicked up its beat and her lungs tightened. Her skin tingled in anticipation of his touch and her thighs clenched as her pussy went wet.

Maybe those snowplows could get here just a little faster, because she was *not* going to be able to say no to him. Not about anything.

Still, she was here to do a job. "Are you hungry? I was just about to start dinner. Is there anything in particular you'd like?"

She saw his eyes narrow and realized he was going to flirt with her. And that could spell disaster. She needed to define some boundaries here, before he wiped them all out of existence.

"I thought I'd make pasta, if that's okay with you," she continued, not wanting to give him an opening. "I think I saw meatballs in the freezer and I make a pretty decent marinara."

"Sure, sounds good."

As he leaned against the worktable, she pulled out a pot then headed for the pantry.

"Did you get a lot of work done?" she asked when she emerged with the ingredients.

"Yeah, actually, I did. I'm pretty sure I have you to thank for that. The sex was amazing."

She nearly tripped over her feet. Luckily, she was close enough to the table that she could put the cans of tomato sauce and jars of spices down before she dropped them. When she looked up at him, she knew her face had turned beet-red.

"Jesus, Greg. Do you go out of your way to make me blush or is it a gift?"

The gleam in his eyes should have warned her that he wasn't finished. "I'm not in the habit of saying things I don't mean."

Crossing his arms over his chest, he walked around the table to stand right next to her. Not close enough to be in her personal space, but that didn't matter. No matter where he stood, if he was in the same room, he was too close. Or too far away.

"Well, do you have to say everything that comes into your mind? It's disconcerting."

"Not arousing?"

She blushed again but forced herself to continue opening the cans. "What do you want me to say to that?"

"How about the truth?"

She shot him a quick glance. "Fine. The truth is I get hot just looking at you." She looked up again, so wanting to stick out her tongue at him but afraid he'd think she was being childish. Or see it as an invitation to kiss her.

Which she really wanted.

Because the snowplows would be here tomorrow. He was scheduled to go back to Haven on Monday, which was the day after tomorrow.

And then he was probably flying back to Hollywood.

She'd known there was a time limit on this affair. She'd actually been counting on that to help her get through the inevitable heartbreak when he told her, "It's been fun, kid. See you around."

But she hadn't expected him to want to tease and flirt. She'd expected more typical guy behavior. She'd almost expected him not to pay her any attention now that they'd had sex.

Which probably just showed the quality of guys she'd dated.

And Greg was *so* not a typical guy.

He stared back at her, his mouth curved in a wry smile that made her want to throw things at him. And kiss the smirk off his face.

"Is that what you wanted to hear?"

He shrugged, that smile widening just a little. "Truthfully, babe, I want to hear anything you have to say."

She stared up at him, shaking her head. "Why?"

He continued to smile. "So what are you putting in this sauce? You are going to finish it, aren't you? I worked up a pretty decent appetite today."

Her eyes widened. "Seriously? Now you just want me to cook for you? Why don't you go ahead and make sure I'm barefoot, too."

His smirk turned into a full-blown grin. "See, this is why I like you. You're not afraid to give me shit."

She huffed, secretly pleased that she had something that set her apart from the beautiful women who surrounded him the rest of the time. "Well, at least make yourself useful and open these cans for me."

They worked side by side to put dinner together. He let her tell him what to do and he did anything she asked. Almost as if they were a couple. Two normal people sharing an ordinary life.

And she enjoyed it way too much.

Let go, Sabrina. Live a little and enjoy.

Oh, how she wanted to. But every time she tried, that little voice in the back of her brain continued the countdown.

Obviously, she wasn't one of those people who could live in the moment. She lived in this moment *and* the one happening two days from now when he patted her on the ass and kissed her good-bye, and the next time she saw him at the hotel, he'd nod at her as he walked by then forget her.

She managed to keep a smile on her face all through dinner, where Greg complimented her on the sauce and told her all about the changes he'd made to the script.

He drew her into the story, got her to tell him what she thought about the plot and the characters, and it was after eight when they finally got up from the table. When he offered to help her load the dishwasher, she didn't bother to argue because he wouldn't listen anyway.

Afterward, she stood staring out the window over the sink. It had finally stopped snowing and the bright moon illuminated the winter wonderland outside. A blanket of white covered everything as far as the eye could see. Only the tree trunks were dark stains against all that white.

"You look about a thousand miles away. You tired?" Greg stepped up next to her. "Looks beautiful, doesn't it? You can make snow, but it never looks right. At least I don't think it does."

"Not tired, not really." She didn't want to go to bed alone but she wasn't going to throw herself at him and beg him to take her, either. If he wanted her, he'd say so. She knew that much about him.

"Good. You want to watch Margo and Mason Holder's latest film? Won't be released until next March. I've got an early copy. They wanted notes so . . . ?"

Sabrina turned to him with a smile, tossing the dishtowel onto the counter. "Seriously? I loved their first movie. I thought *Inmates* was brilliant."

Greg caught himself before he leaned down to kiss the excitement off her beautiful face.

He'd planned on taking her straight back to his bed after dinner, but she'd gotten quieter as dinner had progressed. Something had been bothering her all day. He'd wanted to ask what was going on, but he wasn't sure she'd tell him.

Had she been waiting for him to do something, say something? Was she expecting him to whisk her off to bed and bang her brains out?

That's what *he* wanted. But he didn't want her to think the only reason he wanted her was because she was convenient.

Sure, he wanted to sink inside that gorgeous body and lose himself. He still planned to later. And he wanted to stay there for the rest of the night.

But right now, he wanted to have her next to him on the couch while he watched this film. Wanted to hear what she had to say about it, wanted to discuss it with her.

Then he'd tell her that when they returned to Philadelphia, he wanted to continue seeing her.

Yeah, it was going to be problematic. He had to go back to L.A. for several days. And she'd just started working for Tyler. To make matters worse, it was her first real job. Which made the fact of her age smack him in the face again.

Christ, what a fucking minefield. But he'd dealt with worse before.

"*Inmates* was a great first film," he said as they walked back to the lounge, "but I know they can do better. I've seen some of the dailies and they're funny as hell. I'm hoping the rest of the film lives up to the promise."

As he put in the DVD, she settled onto the couch. He'd wondered if she'd take the chair. Wanted to pump his fist in the air when she didn't. If she had, he would've scooped her up and settled her on the couch. Where he wanted her.

He sat next to her but contained the urge to draw her into his side. He wanted her snuggled up against him, her head on his chest, but didn't want to seem demanding.

Hell, maybe he should be worried about becoming obsessed. Too possessive.

Which had never been a problem for him before. Well, at least not the possessive part. Obsessive . . . yeah. He'd cop to that. It's what made him good at his job.

And if he wanted to continue this relationship beyond these few days, it was probably good to get it out in the open right away.

So he grabbed the remote, hit the play button, and reached for her.

Wrapping his arm around her shoulders, he pulled her against him. She slid across the leather cushion without protest or hesitation.

Now he had her settled against him exactly how he wanted her—her side against his, her head on his shoulder and her hand on his thigh. His cock started to harden as he rested his chin on top of her head and breathed her in.

He realized about halfway through the film that he'd have to watch it again, alone, because he'd paid more attention to Sabrina for forty-five minutes than he had to the movie.

Every time she'd laughed, he'd felt the sensation ripple through his body. Every time she shifted, getting more comfortable against him, his muscles tensed a little tighter.

And then, halfway in, they hit the love scene.

Because he'd been following the film only half-assed, it was like a blow to the solar plexus when the characters started ripping off their clothes and having sex against a wall in the pouring rain.

It was hot and raw and, by the time it was over, not more than two minutes later, he was ready to rip Sabrina's clothes off and fuck her on the couch.

He hadn't been able to take his eyes off the scene, it'd been that well done. But as it cut away, he realized he was breathing like he'd just run a six-minute mile.

Sabrina hadn't been unaffected. She'd gone rigid against him. The hand she'd had on his thigh clenched until he felt each individual fingertip through the fabric of his jeans. His aching cock pounded against the zipper, demanding she put that hand to better use.

He heard her breathing deepen. Felt her shudder when he shifted beneath her, trying to ease the pressure on his cock.

Then he muttered, "Fuck it," and reached for her. She was already reaching for him and let him rearrange her until she straddled his lap. Then he put his hand on her ass and pressed her down against his aching erection.

She moaned as their mouths met and melded. This time, they didn't ease into anything. The hunger had already infected his every cell and his body needed hers with a wildness he didn't want to rein in.

With one hand on her ass, he got her rocking over his cock, pressing her mound against him and rubbing then withdrawing for seconds before coming back in and winding him up more.

She didn't need his direction for long, taking over the rhythm as his hands moved on to other things. One sank into her hair, wrapping the long strands around one fist and tugging her head back so he could kiss her deeper. The other slid beneath her shirt and spread over her back, pressing her even closer.

With a moan, she cupped her hands around his jaw before sliding them to his shoulders, where she kneaded him, fingers digging into the muscles. Then they slipped lower, trailing over his pecs, stopping to pinch at his nipples poking through the cotton. He groaned into her mouth as the slight pain amplified the pounding desire in his veins.

Christ, he loved having her hands on him. Almost as much as he loved putting his hands on her.

When she grabbed the hem of his shirt, he bent forward so she could pull it over his head. As soon as it cleared his arms, he reached for her shirt and whipped it off before he reached for her bra and added it to the pile.

She reached for him again, hands grasping at his shoulders, but he held her away and just looked at her.

So fucking gorgeous. And he wanted to taste every single inch of her.

Putting one hand on her back, he urged her to arch, thrusting her breasts toward him. He bent, sucking an already pointed nipple into his mouth. He didn't start out slow, didn't ease into it. He pulled her in hard and deep then drew back to nip at the tip, making her writhe on his lap and moan. The sound made him want to growl.

When he switched to the other side, he already had one hand on the button of her jeans. But he knew he couldn't get her clothes off in this position.

Pulling back, he lifted her, shocking a gasp out of her as he stood, setting her on her feet.

"Strip. Everything off. Right now."

He didn't temper his demanding tone and he didn't relent when her eyes widened and her hands grabbed his forearms. He couldn't tell whether she wanted to draw him closer or push him away but she obeyed, her hands falling to her jeans.

Then she said, "You, too."

He grinned and watched her shiver as he cupped her breasts and rolled her nipples between his thumbs and forefingers.

"Greg."

"Yeah, babe?"

He bent before she could answer, licking at her nipples and making her moan. Her hands sank into his hair, holding him to her. He obliged, mainly because he couldn't get enough of her. Rubbing his cheeks against her breasts, he felt her quiver as his stubble abraded her skin.

"God, I love that." Her voice had a husky quality that made his balls tighten and his cock spill a drop of moisture. He needed to watch that or he'd be coming in his jeans.

Pulling away, he crossed his arms over his chest. "Take yours off then you can strip me."

She gave him the look, the one that meant "you're pushing it." And he was. But not only did he think that look was fucking adorable, he loved that she wasn't completely cowed by him. Another woman might've reached for him right away, ready to do whatever he wanted. Give him whatever he wanted.

Sabrina was going to give him what he wanted but she was going to make damn sure he knew he had to deserve it.

Smiling at her, he dug the condom out of his pocket and tossed it on the couch cushion, watching her return his smile.

Keeping her gaze on his, she opened the button on her jeans then unzipped them and pushed them down. Since he didn't want to miss the show, he let his gaze drop, saw her shove her pants to her thighs, taking her underwear with them. Bending at the waist, she got them to her ankles then stepped out.

Goddamn, she made him so fucking hot. He couldn't remember the last time he'd wanted another woman as much as he wanted Sabrina.

This girl had curves that made him want to put his hands everywhere at once. And *this* woman was his, said the primal heart of him. She looked at him like Kate looked at Tyler, and he realized only Daisy had ever done that before.

Yeah, and look how that turned out.

Shutting down that train of thought before it poisoned the moment, he watched Sabrina straighten and take another step toward him. Then she stopped, leaving only centimeters separating them. If she took a deep breath, her breasts would brush against his chest.

His fingers itched to reach for her hair but he waited, watching as she slowly reached out and let her fingertips brush the hair on his chest then follow the line over his stomach and down to his waistband.

His abs clenched but he held himself in place, keeping a rigid leash on his instinct to pounce. But if Sabrina didn't get rid of his pants right fucking now, he was going to show her why people usually jumped to do exactly what he wanted.

Then again, maybe patience really was a virtue, he thought as she brushed her fingers along the bare skin above his waistband. Flashes of lightning coursed through him, making him shiver.

His head dropped forward and he pressed a kiss to her forehead as she slowly worked her way to the button. He bit back a command for her to rip it open then groaned when she did. She didn't take her time now, almost as if she couldn't wait to strip him. She had his jeans around his thighs in no time and bent even farther to get them to his ankles.

"Fuck."

Her lips brushed against the head of his cock for a brief second as she straightened, but it was enough contact to make him shudder and want to force her to take him in her mouth.

He stopped before he did but couldn't stop himself from threading his fingers through her hair. He needed that semblance of control.

"Now what, Greg? Tell me what you want."

Her breath brushed his chest, lighting sparks low in his gut.

"I want your mouth on my cock, sweetheart. I want you to suck me but I don't want you to get me off. I want to come inside you. But only after I return the favor and lick you until you come on my tongue."

She shivered, goose bumps covering her skin, and looked up at him with eyes hazy with desire.

"I think that'll be okay."

Laughing because he couldn't help himself, he kissed the burgeoning smile off her lips then drew her back to the couch.

He was just about to push her onto it so he could kneel between her legs and suck her off when she put her hand on his chest and gave him a shove.

He went because, well, why the hell wouldn't he? But he didn't want her kneeling on the floor. Reaching for her hips, he pulled her forward until her knees hit the cushion next to him and she took the hint.

Sliding onto the couch, she leaned forward to meld their lips together, her hands cupping his jaw, caressing, stroking. Her kiss made him steam, made him grab for her nape to hold her to him, even though he knew she wasn't going anywhere.

Except down.

When she wrapped one hand around his cock, he groaned into

her mouth and couldn't help but tug on her hair to tilt her head back just a tiny bit more. She allowed it for a second, her hand steady on his shaft, but then she moved her lips to his jaw and twisted her hand.

Fuck yes.

His head fell back as fire spread every place her mouth pressed a kiss. She moved from his neck to his chest, where she stopped to lick at his nipples, while the hand on his cock began a slow but steady pump that made it thicken and throb.

If he let himself go, she could bring him off just like this, with her teeth sinking onto his nipple and her hair falling over her shoulders to brush against his stomach.

He wondered if she'd let him take photos of them like this one day. Just the thought made him grit his teeth with pleasure.

"Christ, Bree."

He felt her mouth curve in a grin. "Everything okay?"

"You know it is. Don't stop."

"I don't plan to."

After a slightly harder nip, she continued kissing her way down his body. Nothing about her seemed practiced but every movement was arousing. So fucking hot.

His body alternated between being on edge and melting into the sofa. Her hand on his cock made him want to pump into her hand, but her lips on his skin turned his bones to jelly. Clenching his fingers in her hair, he rubbed it against his stomach, making sure not to yank or take her off course.

Because he felt her breath on his cock. His own breath stuttered in his chest and he closed his eyes, waiting.

He shuddered as every muscle in his body slammed to attention as her lips closed around the head. He had to make a conscious effort to control his hips because all his body wanted was to thrust up to fuck her mouth. To sink his cock deep in her warmth and let her suck him dry.

As if she'd read his mind or, more likely, his body, she took him deeper. Her lips slid down his shaft, her tongue flat against the side of his cock. As she did, one hand slid down to cup his balls and the other curled around his waist. Then she sucked.

Yes.

The gentle suction of her mouth wreaked havoc with his mind and body. He could barely breathe and every muscle tingled and his brain buzzed with static. The sensation of her hair on his thighs made him ache to feel it on his balls. The hand caressing his balls tightened, drawing another groan from him.

"God, yes."

She picked up on his cues, learning what made him groan, what made his hand tighten in her hair and exactly what pushed him to his limits.

Pulling back to the tip of his cock, she flicked her tongue at the slit, making his eyes roll back in his head before she sank down to the root and held him there. The wet heat of her mouth nearly made him spill on her tongue but he forced back the urge by grabbing the base of his cock and squeezing until it passed.

She eased up a little to allow him to do it then released him, but not before placing one final kiss against the tip.

That sweetly erotic caress broke his control.

She'd barely lifted her head when he grabbed her under her arms and lifted her over his lap. She spread her legs, putting her hands on his shoulders to steady herself as her knees hit the cushions on either side of his thighs.

Watching her face, he reached for his cock and pulled it straight until they were perfectly aligned. With his other hand, he grabbed her hips and brought her down. The slick lips of her pussy met the head of his dick, but he didn't pull her any farther. Instead, he rubbed the tip against that plump, hot flesh, coating it in her moisture.

"Jesus, you're wet. I'm going to go down on you next time and suck you until you scream. Then I'm going to fuck you with my tongue until you beg me to stop and fuck you with my cock."

Her eyelids slammed closed, as if trying to shut him out, but the expression on her face and the clench of her hands on his shoulders made it clear she liked hearing him talk.

And her body obviously liked having his cock rub against her clit. Each time he made contact, she shivered. Her hips began to rock with him and she tried to lower herself onto him but he wasn't going to let her. Not yet.

He wanted her to ask for it, to beg him to fuck her. To lose all her inhibitions and give herself over to him completely.

She was close. He wanted total.

"Lean forward, Bree. I want to suck on those beautiful nipples again."

Her eyes opened as she moaned and the flush on her cheeks burned a little brighter. But she did move closer, arching her back and thrusting her breasts toward him.

He was almost too tall to make this work, but he was determined. Wedging his cock between her sex lips without penetrating her took monumental control but it allowed him to use that hand to cup her breast and lift it to his mouth.

He had no more patience for easy. He wanted hot and rough.

Sucking on her nipple, he drew her between his teeth, letting the edges graze her flesh. She moaned and the hands she'd had on his shoulders immediately reached up to grab his hair. Her hold was tight and made his scalp sting, but he liked it.

He liked that she responded to him, how she writhed against

him when he bit and licked and made her nipples so tight they had to hurt. He liked how she rocked on his dick but didn't sink down, because she knew he wanted her to wait. Instead, she teased herself . . . and him.

His chest ached and his cock throbbed but he played with her breasts until he literally couldn't hold himself back anymore.

Growling as he pulled away, he released her nipple at the very last second. With her soft gasp echoing in his ears, he grabbed the condom, covered himself, then grabbed her hips and brought her down.

His cock sank only about halfway, the angle of her body just slightly off for him to get deeper. That was okay. He didn't want to fuck her too hard right away.

But Bree apparently had plans of her own.

She leaned forward to kiss him—a hot, wet, tongue-melding kiss that took him by surprise—and shifted just enough so she sank onto him until her ass met his thighs. Her pussy tightened around him, squeezing him, holding him steady.

But not for long.

With a little moan, she rocked her hips and took him even deeper. Then she rose up on her knees and sank back down, her rhythm slow at first but picking up speed.

Her lips softened even more against his, her body arching toward him. Since he wanted as much skin contact as possible, he leaned farther back into the couch, bringing her with him, changing the angle of penetration.

She whimpered as his cock shifted inside her and hit other, more sensitive areas. Her fingers tightened in his hair then released to cup his head and hold him to her with one hand while the other curled over his shoulder. Giving her a more stable base.

Then she rode him harder.

He slid one arm around her back, stabilizing them both as they both started to lose control. Greg felt it in the tremor of his muscles and the sudden uneven rhythm of her body on his. He felt her reaching, trying to make him give her what he was instinctively withholding. Because he didn't want this to end.

He wanted to fuck her all night. Wanted to fall asleep buried inside her, wake up, and start all over again. Just the thought had his orgasm pounding at the base of his spine.

As if she'd realized how close he was, she pushed him harder. But he wasn't about to go over alone.

He slid a hand between their bodies and pressed his thumb against her clit.

She moaned into his mouth, her ass slamming down on his thighs as her pussy tightened around his cock like a fist.

Then she came.

And, holy hell, she felt like heaven. Like he'd found the perfect fit, the perfect woman, and no other would ever satisfy him again.

His orgasm blasted out of him, bowing his back until he couldn't get any farther inside her. And still he wanted more.

He thrust until she clung to him like a second skin, until he knew he was making a mess of the damn couch and he didn't give a fuck.

And when he finally gave into exhaustion and sank into the cushions, his arms so tight around her he wasn't sure he could've released her if he'd tried, he knew she'd dug a hole in his heart he wasn't sure he wanted to fill.

Five

"What about the car? Are you just going to leave it here?"

"For now, yeah." Greg tossed her overnighter in the back of her fifteen-year-old Jeep Cherokee on Monday morning, right beside his battered black backpack and his weathered leather duffle bag. "I don't want you driving back alone."

Sabrina bit her tongue before "You do know I'm an actual adult who's been driving for seven years," slipped out of her mouth.

Damn him. She was totally out of sorts and it was all his fault. She'd thought, come Monday morning, she'd go back to Philadelphia. Alone.

Hell, she'd been counting on it.

These last four days had been like a really great fantasy where she'd spent the nights in a bed with the man of her dreams.

But now she needed to get back to the real world. Back to work. Back to her life, the one that didn't include him.

She'd wanted to clear her head on the drive back to Haven, to cry him out of her system.

Greg did *not* have a place in her real life. He'd been a brief, hot fling before the rest of her life happened. Every girl deserved at least one, right?

Sure, she'd briefly considered that maybe he'd follow her back to Philadelphia, but figured when they got there, he'd say, "Thanks, kid. It was fun."

And she'd say, "It was nice," or something equally stupid. And then the next time she'd see him, it'd be a passing glance in the lobby of Haven as he left for filming or dinner or, God forbid, with some other woman. She imagined he'd smile the first few times, but eventually he wouldn't even notice her.

She'd be heartbroken. And over him.

He wasn't sticking to the plan. Of course, he didn't know about the plan . . . but still.

"Bree? What's wrong?"

He'd taken to calling her that. It wasn't a nickname anyone else had ever used and it made her heart trip over itself whenever he said it. It was so stupid but it meant the world to her, as if she actually meant something to him other than a good time in bed.

Which didn't mean she thought he was a douchebag who'd only slept with her because they'd been together and bored. No, she thought he actually did care about her.

Then again, she could just be fooling herself. He was a guy. A rich, gorgeous, famous guy who could have any woman he wanted. And she'd been the only woman available and she'd practically thrown herself at him.

She so didn't need this. Not now.

She shook her head, not bothering with a smile because he'd

know it was fake and he'd continue to ask what was wrong. "I'm just anxious to get back to work."

His gaze narrowed as he closed the hatch but she turned back toward the building so he couldn't see her face. "I'm just going to make sure the front door's locked."

She'd already done that twice but she needed a few seconds to catch her breath.

He didn't say anything, just felt him watching her the entire way. She took her time, sucked in a couple of deep breaths, and made sure she didn't look like she was ready to cry when she returned to the garage to find him leaning against the front of her Jeep, looking so hot she thought she might just swallow her tongue.

"Mind if I drive?" he asked. "I used to have one of these. Wish I'd kept the damn thing but some asshole totaled mine when he ran a red light in Vegas."

"Sure. No problem." Truthfully, she didn't want to be behind the wheel with him in the car. She wasn't sure she'd be able to keep her mind on the road.

Adjusting course for the passenger side, she buckled herself in and tried not to sigh over the fact that she liked having him in her car. He had to shove the driver's seat back as far as it would go, then he put one big hand on the wheel and the other on the gear shift.

She had the brief thought that maybe she should've asked if he could drive stick shift, but he answered that by shifting into reverse and pulling out of the garage as if the car was his.

Of course.

The plows had cleared the road yesterday, and the private plow Tyler employed to do the lane up to the retreat had followed shortly after. She'd almost wished they'd had another day, but she'd known their interlude had to end sometime and better it end now, before she really fell hard.

Right. Like that hasn't already happened?

Shifting in her chair, her legs ached and her clit throbbed from the shower sex they'd had this morning. Her breasts still felt tender and heavy and . . . God, she still felt him all over her.

As they hit the highway headed toward the turnpike, he broke the silence that had fallen while he navigated the still-dangerous back roads.

"So you want to tell me why you look like you're going to your own execution? Are you that anxious about going back to Haven?"

Her cheeks burned with a blush. How the hell could he read her so easily? Maybe she shouldn't be surprised. He'd spent most of the last three days watching her as he fucked her, so . . .

"Yeah. A little. Now that you brought it up," she said as she took a deep breath, "maybe we should talk about what happens now."

He slid a brief glance at her and she had no idea what he was thinking. "You mean with us?"

"I mean, I'm working for the Goldens. You're a friend of theirs and . . . I guess I just don't want there to be any . . . problems."

Namely, she didn't want the other workers at the hotel wondering if she'd gotten her job because she was screwing the boss's best friend. Everyone already knew she was friends with Kate, the boss's girlfriend. And with Annabelle, the other boss's girlfriend. They also knew she was the youngest and greenest management trainee Tyler had ever hired. She'd told the few people who'd outright asked how she'd gotten the job the truth—that she'd met Tyler through Kate and he'd offered her an internship for the summer that had turned into a full-time position when he'd started hiring staff for the retreat.

"You don't want anyone to think you're getting special treatment. I get it. It also means you probably work five times harder than anyone else."

She shrugged, silently acknowledging she probably did. She wanted to learn everything she could and she didn't want Tyler to regret hiring her so, yeah, she probably worked a little longer, tried a little harder.

She knew what a great opportunity had fallen into her lap, and didn't want to screw it up.

"I love what I'm doing so it's not a hardship. Everyone I work with is nice, and they've been really helpful. But most of them are older and we don't—"

He started to laugh and she realized she'd been about to stick her foot in her mouth.

Sliding him a scowl, she smacked him on the shoulder because that's what she did with her friends.

Before she could pull away though, he grabbed her hand and pulled it to his mouth, where he brushed a kiss against the inside of her wrist.

A shiver spread through her until it made the ache in her pussy even worse.

When he released her, she tried not to yank her hand away too fast.

"Hey, now, sweetheart. Don't get mean. You're already hell on my ego."

She snorted at that, which only made him laugh harder.

"I only meant that they have their own friends and family," she continued. "When they leave work, they go home to their boyfriends or their husbands or their kids. They've made me feel welcome but . . ."

But hanging out with the boss and his girlfriend on her nights off wasn't going to endear her to her coworkers or make them want to invite her out for drinks or dinner.

"It's tough being the new kid. I get it. And you're living at the hotel right now, aren't you? Do you like it?"

Her smile felt a little forced. "I do. Mostly. I was going to commute from home until Tyler transfers me to the retreat, but I realized when I was interning over the summer that that just wasn't going to work. The drive was murder. So Tyler leased me one of the smaller suites. He said they've done it before when employees have needed to find an apartment. I love it, it's just not—"

"It's not home."

Exactly. And she was homesick. And lonely. Yes, she worked long hours but Tyler wasn't a slave driver. She had downtime. Some of that was spent with Kate and Annabelle. Some was spent exploring the city. Mostly though, she worked, went back to her suite, ate, and watched TV until she fell asleep. Then she started all over again.

"You still feel out of place."

She nodded. "Yeah, I do." And wow, did she sound like a whiner. "But I'm not bored. And I love what I'm doing. I never thought I'd say this but I really miss my family."

"Tough to go from living with a houseful of people to living by yourself."

"The thing is, I thought I'd love it." Turning slightly in her seat so she could see him better, she held back a sigh. He really was a beautiful man. Not pretty, just . . . so damn handsome. "You know, a bathroom all to myself, no one eating my cookies. But—"

"You're lonely."

She grimaced. "Sounds stupid, I know. I'm living in a city full of people and things to do and I miss my younger sisters coming to talk to me about school, and playing games with my brothers."

"Sounds like you're close to your family."

"I am. But even when I move to the retreat, I plan to get an apartment. Just not that far away."

"I didn't have a lot of money when I moved to California and I was broke most of the first year, so I didn't do much but work whatever jobs I could get. And I was always close to my sister, so when I moved to Hollywood, there were nights I'd spend hours on the phone with her." He laughed and her chest got tight. "Of course, I always called collect so my parents' phone bill had to be astronomical. But they never complained." He smiled at her, their gazes connecting for a brief, heart-stopping moment. "It'll get better. You'll meet people."

A silence fell then, and if she hadn't been watching him, she would've missed the look that crossed his face. The one that made her wish for things she knew she couldn't have.

Then he reached for her hand resting on her knee and squeezed. Without thought, she flipped her hand and laced their fingers together.

* *

When Sabrina laced her fingers through his, Greg wanted to beat his chest like a caveman. Which made him feel ridiculous. But hopeful.

He'd already decided he wasn't ready to end whatever this thing was they were doing when they got back to Philly. Yes, he had to be on a plane for California early tomorrow morning. But he'd be back in less than a month.

He wanted to see her when he got back, and he would do everything in his power to make sure it happened.

But he'd figured he was going to have an uphill battle with her.

Then she'd started talking about work and he'd realized exactly what pursuing a relationship with him would mean.

First off, they'd either have to do it in complete secrecy or . . . well, there really wasn't an "or," was there? And they'd have to be superhero stealthy about it because once the paparazzi got wind that he was seeing someone, it'd be all over the rags. With Neal and Daisy scheduled to arrive for filming right after he got back, there'd be additional press and . . .

Jesus, what a bad fucking time to fall for a woman. A twenty-three-year-old with absolutely no idea what hell he'd bring to her life just by virtue of sharing his bed.

He should be smart about this, at least for her sake. He should've let her go back to Haven by herself and left her alone. It's what she'd expected. He'd seen her surprise when he'd told her he'd be driving back with her. Which had pissed him off because she'd *expected* him to dump her.

Damn it, he wasn't that much of an ass. At least, he hoped he wasn't.

And now that he'd made up his mind to continue seeing her, he wasn't about to give her up.

They fell silent as he drove, and he realized there was music playing. Pink, he thought. For the rest of the drive they talked, first about music, which became a discussion about how the singer used her personal life as fodder for some of her songs, which became a discussion about the way Hollywood stars were portrayed in the tabloids and how their lives became public domain.

By the time he pulled her Jeep into the garage at Haven, he'd pretty much convinced himself he wouldn't have to worry about seeing her again because she'd go out of her way to avoid him.

She'd shuddered when he'd talked about the paparazzi. About the lack of privacy and the lies and the general shit you had to deal with. He also knew he'd do whatever he needed to not let her get away.

She stared straight ahead silently as he pulled up to the guard's booth and exchanged hellos with the off-duty Philadelphia cop manning it.

The guy was good. He'd probably recognized the Jeep as Sabrina's but he'd shown no surprise when he'd found Greg behind the wheel. He said hello to Ms. Rodriquez, who gave him a weak but genuine smile, then told them to have a good day as he raised the gate.

She directed him to the employee parking area then fell silent again as he parked and turned off the engine.

Her smile was totally fake as she held out a hand for the keys.

"I should get upstairs and tell them I'm here. I'm not scheduled to work today but I should check in, let the manager know I'll be available to work tomorrow."

"Sabrina—"

"I'm sure you've still got lots of work to do so I'll just—"

"Sabrina, stop."

Her mouth snapped shut, her lips pursed as she stared up at him. She didn't actually check to see if anyone was around to overhear them but he knew she was probably worried about that.

And he understood. He did. It just . . .

Fuck.

Leaning closer, he spoke directly into her ear. "This, us . . . we're not through. I want to see you again."

When he pulled back, she looked directly into his eyes, a blush coloring her cheeks. He couldn't tell if she was turned on, furious, or embarrassed. He really hoped it was the first.

She didn't answer right away and, when he heard her take a deep breath, he wondered if maybe he didn't want to hear what she had to say.

"I thought you were leaving tonight."

"I am. But I'll be back for Thanksgiving. I want to see you then."

She paused. "I'm not sure that's a good idea."

"I think it's a great idea."

"Greg—"

He kissed her—hard, hot, and no holds barred. He figured if this was the last chance he was going to get, he'd better make it a damn good one.

She froze, totally unresponsive. Which just made him all the more determined to get a response.

Cupping her face in his hands, he kissed her deeper, sliding his tongue along the seam of her lips and taking advantage of her tiny gasp to lick his way into her mouth. He couldn't get enough of her. He wanted to take her back to his room right now and spend these last few hours before he had to get on a plane in a bed with her.

When he pulled back, she clung just the tiniest bit. And he loved it.

"Come to my room." He let her hear the demand in his voice. "Dump your stuff and come to my room. I'm staying on the fourth floor."

She blinked up at him. "I don't have access."

"Here." He reached into his back pocket and held out his key-card. "You just need to swipe it when you're in the elevator and it'll take you straight to the fourth floor."

She didn't reach for it. Instead, she looked at it like it was a poisonous snake.

"I can't. I need to check my schedule. I'm not sure when I work—"

"Text me and let me know your schedule. We'll work something out."

"Greg . . ."

She paused and he knew she wanted to tell him she wasn't going to show up. That he was too much trouble, way too demanding, and she had to think of her job first.

"I'm sorry. I can't. It was fun"—her cheeks burned with a faint but noticeable blush—"but this . . . affair isn't going anywhere. I thought we both understood that."

Goddamn it. He understood exactly what she was saying and he knew he shouldn't push. He also knew what he wanted, he usually got.

And he wanted *her.*

He'd never had much patience. Not for anything. And people who knew him knew he didn't give up when he wanted something. He slipped the keycard into her coat pocket.

"What I understand is that I enjoy spending time with you and I want to spend more time with you. I totally understand that you might have to work. I also understand that this thing between us . . . it doesn't happen often. And I want to see where it goes. Give me your phone."

"Why?" The dazed look he'd put on her face with his kiss hadn't lasted as long as he would've liked.

"Because I'm going to give you my phone number. Here." He pulled his phone out of his shirt pocket and held it out to her. "Put yours in mine."

She didn't take his phone, didn't move at all, just sat there staring at him. Contemplating. He swore he could see the gears moving in her brain and his chest started to tighten.

"Bree—"

With a sharply indrawn breath, she reached for her purse and took out her phone.

A minute later, he continued to hold back his grin as they exchanged phone numbers.

"I really need to get upstairs."

"I know. Hold on. I've got something else for you."

He held out the SD card from his camera. He really didn't want to give it up, but he'd promised her.

Confusion made her frown for a brief moment before she realized what he was offering her.

"I'd prefer to keep this," he said when she didn't reach for it right away. "I want to take these with me so I have a piece of you until I come back. But if you want them, they're yours."

It took her several seconds, but finally she lifted her gaze to his again. "I trust you."

Then she turned, opened the car door, and slid out.

But not before giving him a glance that was so blatantly sexual it made him groan.

After they'd gotten their bags out of her car, he watched her ass as she walked toward the service elevator and thought about all the things he was going to do when he got his hands on her tonight.

When the elevator doors closed, cutting her off from view, he let his lips curve with the smile he'd been suppressing and headed for the guest elevator.

* *

Minutes later in her room on the ninth floor, Sabrina dropped her bag by the door to the bathroom then dropped onto the bed, staring at the ceiling.

She should take a nap. Her body vibrated in that state between hyper-alert and exhausted. She'd gotten maybe three hours of sleep last night. Not that she minded, but if she didn't get some rest now, she'd be dead on her feet the rest of the day.

What she really wanted to do was curl up next to Greg.

The keycard he'd given her felt like a lead weight in her coat pocket. Digging it out, she held it in front of her and stared at it. This card was red instead of the standard Haven blue and had no identifying marks on it. No words, no numbers, nothing. So—

Someone knocked on the door, making her gasp and bolt upright.

She immediately wanted it to be him.

Scrambling off the bed, she stuffed the keycard in her back pocket and hurried to the door. If he was out there, she didn't want him standing in the hall where the security cameras could—

"I have been *dying* to talk to you!" Kate Song practically jumped into the room and grabbed her in a tight hug as soon as Sabrina opened the door. "Tell me everything."

Sabrina closed the door behind Kate with a rueful grin. "Hi to you, too."

Kate dropped into one of the two chairs in the small seating area in front of the window in the spacious room. Her dark hair fell over her shoulder in a sleek wave, her dark eyes sharp and inquisitive. "Oh, please. What's a few formalities between friends. How are you? Are you okay? How was the sex? I want to hear everything."

Sighing, Sabrina sank into the chair opposite Kate and propped her head on her hand. "And by everything you mean . . ."

"Whatever you want to tell me. Which should be everything. I thought maybe you'd need to talk."

Did she? "I'm not sure there's anything to talk about. It's just sex."

"Really? Just sex?"

"Sure. What else could it be?"

Kate's gaze narrowed. "You do know the man has had the hots for you since he met you? Have you *seen* the photos he took for my portfolio? And you can bet he kept some of those photos for himself."

Heat flushed Sabrina's cheeks as she thought about the other photos he'd taken more recently. "You don't know that."

"Yeah, actually, I do. Tyler told me."

"Oh, my God. That's . . ."

Amazing. Arousing. Encouraging.

"How about 'not surprising,'" Kate finished for her. "The guy has a serious jones for you. The question is, how do you feel about him?"

Giddy. Breathless. Horny. Terrified.

"Sabrina?"

"Yeah?"

Kate's nose crinkled. "I'm pushing, aren't I?"

"Just a little."

"Sorry. It's just . . . I love you and I want you to be happy. And Greg . . ." Kate paused and Sabrina saw unease cross Kate's expression. Like there was something she knew that she didn't want to tell her. "Greg expects people to want something from him. All the time. He doesn't tend to really *like* people, if you know what I mean. He respects some people, he enjoys working with others, but . . . he *likes* you."

The blush was back, but this time it wasn't embarrassment. It was heat.

"I like him, too. It's just . . . there's no future in a relationship with him. I guess I just need time to come to terms with that and make sure I don't fall head over heels for a guy who's always going to leave." *Like most of the men in my life.* "That this is just a fling."

"And how do you know that?"

She pulled a face. "Oh, please. The man runs his own film

studio. He lives in California and he's basically a workaholic. I swear his phone never stops vibrating and he barely gets four hours of sleep a night."

Yes, she wanted him, but she'd always be a couple of steps below the top of his priority list. And she didn't know if she could take that.

"So you had sex and that's it?"

"We had sex, yes." She paused, not sure she wanted to reveal anymore. But she couldn't help herself. "And yes, he wants to see me again but that was probably just so I wouldn't make a scene—"

"No. No way." Kate shook her head, hair waving over her shoulder. "That's not Greg's style. If he didn't want to see you again, he would have said, 'Thanks. Have a great day. See ya later.' Greg doesn't say what he doesn't mean."

"Well, maybe I don't want to see him again."

"Don't you?"

She hesitated too long and Kate began to grin.

"Alright, of course I do. Who wouldn't? He's—"

"Gorgeous? Hot? Amazing? All of above?"

Sabrina grimaced. "A force of nature. And he's used to getting his own way."

"Yeah, I see where you're coming from but . . . try to keep an open mind, okay? Don't just write him off as a fling right away. Give him a chance to prove himself."

And let him break her heart?

That might be too much to ask.

* *

"Sabrina, glad to see you made it back okay. I hope you didn't have any trouble on the road."

Dredging up a smile for her immediate supervisor, Sabrina

turned from the computer monitor where she'd been checking her schedule in the reception office.

"No, the main roads are pretty clear. We didn't have any trouble."

Shit. She wanted to bite her tongue and take back that one little word.

"Yes, I heard you had company on the way back." Marissa Vale's dry tone made Sabrina cringe. "Greg Hicks is definitely one handsome man. Too bad he's such a . . . difficult person. He didn't give you any trouble, did he?"

Choosing her words carefully this time, Sabrina turned to face the other woman. The front office manager had a reputation among the staff for being demanding and exacting and the absolute best at what she did, which was take care of the guests. Didn't matter if they were heads of state or a couple celebrating their sixtieth wedding anniversary with their first trip away from the family farm in Wisconsin, Marissa made sure they all enjoyed the same high level of service at Haven.

At fifty-eight, she was the highest-ranking hotel employee and had been with Haven since Tyler had hired her before the hotel opened. She had a management degree from Cornell University, wore four-inch heels every day, and nothing and no one escaped her sharp blue gaze.

"No trouble. He talked about his new movie a lot." Totally true and she decided she should stop there.

Apparently Marissa figured Greg couldn't have much interest in Sabrina because she didn't continue her questioning. "Well, I'm glad you're back. I know you're supposed to be off tonight but Laney was in an accident last night on her way to work and is going to be out of work for a few days."

"Oh, no." Sabrina liked the always-smiling Laney. "Is she okay?"

Marissa nodded, her gaze softening the tiniest bit. "She'll be fine. Just banged up and sore. Luckily she didn't have her son in the car with her. But she won't be in for a few days. I need you for the overnight tonight and possibly to cover another of her shifts later this week. Unless, you have other plans."

Sabrina forced a smile. "No, no other plans. Of course I can fill in."

There really was no other response.

Apparently, her affair with Greg was destined to die a fast death.

Six

Three weeks later

Pasting on a smile for the lone photographer hanging out in front of Haven, Greg stepped out of the limo and acknowledged the man with a wave.

Greg had no problem helping a decent guy make an honest living.

Tony DiGrigorio snapped a few photos to sell to whatever tabloid paid the highest, waved back, then hopped on his motorcycle and headed off, probably back home to his wife and two kids.

Considering it was nearly seven on the night before Thanksgiving, Tony probably had better things to do than wait in the cold for a few photographs.

With a nod for the grandfatherly doorman, who always had a smile, Greg entered the lobby and immediately looked toward the desk.

Sabrina wasn't there.

He hadn't figured it was going to be that easy. And frankly, he wasn't sure she was going to want to see him. It'd been three days since he'd texted her.

Yes, he had a legitimate excuse. He'd been busy as hell, barely a minute to spare with last-minute details and crises to handle before filming started in just a few days. And that didn't take into account the shitstorm brewing at his production company.

Still, for two weeks after he'd left her, he'd managed to communicate with her at least once a day. And then last week . . . Shit.

Heading for the elevator through the mostly deserted lobby, he nodded at the brunette behind the reception desk, who returned his acknowledgment with a brilliant smile.

Was she even in the hotel? If I text her when I get to my room, how long will I have to wait before I can get her naked and in my bed?

And how much would he have to grovel to get her there?

Greg hadn't even gotten his keycard in the slot in his door when the door to Tyler's apartment opened.

"Hey, how was your trip?"

"Long." Greg pushed open the door to his suite, walked through and dumped his bags on the couch before heading for the tiny kitchen. "Fucking exhausting, actually."

Tyler followed, stopping to lean his back against the door when it had closed.

"Bitch, bitch, bitch. Just like an old woman," Tyler ribbed before his expression turned serious. "Anyway, I'm sorry but it's about to get longer. Daisy's here. Arrived this morning, went to her room, hasn't been out since."

Grabbing a can of Coke, Greg turned to scowl at Tyler. "What the fuck? Trudeau said she hadn't talked to Daisy or— Wait. Just Daisy?"

Tyler nodded, his expression grave. "Yep."

"Fuck."

"Yeah, that's what I figured you'd say."

Greg slumped into a club chair next to the sofa. "Press figure out she's here yet?"

"Not that I know of. The desk hasn't fielded any calls for her yet."

"Shit." He let his head drop back, his eyes closed. "I need to go talk to her."

Son of a fucking bitch.

He'd been planning to spend the night in bed with Sabrina beneath him. Or on top of him or in front of him. He wasn't picky. He just wanted her here with him.

The thought of seeing her tonight had kept him going for the past three days of hell.

The last time he'd texted her, she'd told him she hadn't been scheduled to work tonight but that she was having Thanksgiving dinner with her family around noon tomorrow and then she had to work the three-to-eleven shift.

Now he had to deal with this.

"She looked pretty wiped. Maybe she's asleep and you can let it go until tomorrow morning."

Cracking open the soda, Greg took a sip before he opened his eyes and stared back at Tyler. "Yeah, you know it's never that easy with Daisy."

"True." Tyler's bland expression grated on Greg's last remaining nerve.

"What? Spit out whatever it is you want to say. It's been a hell of a long day. Actually, life's been a bitch pretty much for the past three weeks. And why are you dressed like you're going to a funeral?"

Tyler didn't bat an eye at Greg's bad-tempered diss at his dark suit and muted tie. "We're hosting the staff for dinner tonight. We close the dining room and hire outside waitstaff. We'd hire a chef, but you know Marco would never allow it. He and the kitchen staff fix dinner and then we all eat."

So Sabrina would be at dinner. And she'd be missed if she didn't go.

Greg laughed but it was more in frustration than amusement.

"Do you want to join us?"

Hell, yes. He wanted to see Sabrina any way he could. It'd be hell not being able to talk to her, touch her, hold her. Shit, he wasn't even sure she'd allow him to after all this time.

Maybe she'd decided he wasn't worth the trouble. He wouldn't blame her.

"Kate told me you've kept in contact with her."

"Oh, yeah? What else did Kate tell you?"

"That you better not fuck with that girl's head."

Greg had to set the soda can down before he crushed it, wanting to punch the wall.

"I don't want to fuck with her head."

"Did you sleep with her up at the retreat?"

"What? You don't know already? And how is that any of your business?"

"Because she's one of my girlfriend's best friends, you ass. And she's my employee."

"Which is exactly why this should be none of your business."

"You made it my business when you decided to pursue her."

His temples started to throb and he let his head fall back on the cushion again. "Jesus, Tyler. Why is that such a bad thing? You practically delivered her to me on a silver platter. What's changed?"

Greg opened his eyes again to see Tyler's smirk. "Not a damn thing. You know it's okay to actually like her, right? Or is there something else going on here that I'm not seeing?"

Greg gave Tyler the finger. "You're worse than my grandmother, you know that? I tell her not to read the tabloids or watch those shows but she still does. And then she calls me and wants to know why I don't bring any of those nice actresses I date home to meet her."

Tyler gave him a raised eyebrow. "What the fuck does that have to do with this situation?"

"Because you're acting like an old woman, butting into a situation that's already filled with enough landmines. Christ almighty, yes, we slept together. It was fucking amazing. She's sweet and smart and I like her. I want to see her again. Enough already."

Tyler's only response was a shrug. "Okay. So where do you think Neal is?"

Greg ran a hand through his hair, trying not to anticipate disaster or get whiplash at Tyler's change of subject. "Who the fuck knows. I guess I'd better go find out."

"Do I need to brace the hotel for an onslaught of paparazzi?"

"I'll let you know after I talk to Daisy."

"She seems pretty upset."

"I'm sure she is."

"Of course, you can never tell with Daisy," Tyler continued. "She's a damn good actress, after all."

Greg eyed Tyler without speaking. Daisy and Tyler had met several times when she and Greg had stayed at Haven as a couple. Tyler had never treated Daisy poorly but he'd never warmed up to her, either. And it was hard not to like Daisy.

Yes, she could be demanding but she was never a diva. She treated everyone as a potential best friend—which usually backfired on her. People thought because she was so sweet, she was also a pushover.

Not so much. In fact, you really didn't want to piss off Daisy.

She could cut your heart out with a few words and leave you bleeding to death, but when she loved you . . . well, you were the center of her world.

It's what had allowed her to put up with him for all those years. She'd loved him. And then she hadn't because she'd met Neal. And anyone who'd seen Neal and Daisy together could see how much they loved each other.

Yet Greg had only seen how potentially devastating that relationship could be to both of them. Like what was happening now. Except Greg hadn't expected them to take him along for the ride.

Finally, Greg responded. "Yeah, she is. Give me a few hours. I'll figure out if she was able to get here unseen."

Christ, if anyone figured out Daisy and Neal hadn't arrived together the tabloids would go crazy. Considering filming was supposed to start next week, Greg didn't need an onslaught at the set. He'd managed to keep the exact filming site under wraps by having Trudeau lay out several decoys. He'd hoped to get at least a couple days of shooting in without the press hounding them.

He'd planned to schedule interviews at the end of shooting but now he might have to rework that timetable. He needed to call Trudeau—

Tyler stood and headed toward the door. "Just let me know what's up."

"What? That's it? No more third degree?"

"Nope. I figure you've got enough on your plate right now. And you know how I feel. Hurt Sabrina and I maim you. And after that, I'll let Kate go to work on you. That will be even less pleasant. Let me know what's up with Neal." Tyler opened the door but turned before he closed it behind him. "Hope this doesn't fuck your shooting schedule. I know it's tight."

"Yeah, me too. Hey, Ty."

"Yeah?"

"You see me screwing with her head, you have my permission to kick the shit out of me."

Tyler gave him a look that said he thought Greg was being fucking hilarious. "Don't need permission. I'd do it anyway. See you at dinner?"

"Thanks, but I doubt it."

"She's working the overnight shift. Just FYI."

Tyler closed the door, leaving Greg to consider adding something a little harder to his Coke before he headed up to see Daisy.

Nah, might make things worse.

Taking a detour through the bathroom to splash water on his face, he checked his email and messages, just to make sure he hadn't missed anything. Trudeau hadn't contacted him at all. Neither had Daisy.

No, she'd simply shown up here. Four days early. By herself. Without the man who'd been glued to her side since she'd left Greg for him.

Fuck.

On the elevator, he texted Trudeau, who got back to him in seconds.

No, haven't heard from either of them. Let me know what you need.

He needed this fucking shoot to go well. He needed this film to be exactly what he wanted it to be.

He wanted to see Sabrina.

First things first.

The top floor of the hotel consisted of six suites, three each on either side of the elevator. He stopped at the door to Daisy's, took a deep breath, and knocked.

He almost hoped she didn't answer.

No such luck. The door opened just as he was getting ready to knock a second time.

The second Daisy saw who it was, she flung herself into his arms and started to cry.

And Greg watched all his careful planning go up in flames.

* *

". . . heard she checked in without her husband. Could mean nothing. Could mean there's trouble in paradise."

"And when isn't there trouble in a Hollywood marriage? Seriously? How can anyone have a normal relationship in that business?"

Sitting at a table with other members of the registration staff, Sabrina had been trying to have a good time. Really, she had. But Greg was returning sometime tonight.

Would he call her? Would she see him?

Beside her, Darryl Heister gave her shoulder a nudge and smiled at her. "You've been awfully quiet. Not interested in Hollywood gossip, huh?"

Sabrina returned the smile of the tall, slim man with skin the color of cocoa and eyes as gray as storm clouds.

"Just a little tired. Feel like I've been fighting a cold."

"You've been working way too many hours," piped up Teresa Dumbroski, her riot of brown curls contained in a ponytail that fell most of the way down her back. "Heard you drew the short stick for tonight. That sucks. But I'm going home to two toddlers hopped up on sugar because my mom is babysitting and doesn't know how to say no to her demon grandchildren."

Darryl laughed. "Your children are *not* that bad. Did I tell you what Shawn did to Derek last night?"

The two thirty-somethings continued to trade tales of their children as conversation at the table swirled around her. Sabrina made sure she smiled and added to the conversation, but mostly, she tried not to think about Greg.

And didn't correct Teresa's assumption that she'd been given the overnight shift.

In reality, she'd asked for it.

Coward.

Absolutely. She'd known Greg was coming back tonight and she'd wanted to be busy when he did.

"Did you hear about Daisy Devlin? She showed up early this morning." Teresa leaned closer to Sabrina so she could talk to Danica. "She seemed nice enough when she checked in but she looked like she was crying. And her husband's not with her."

"Ooh." Danica's eyes went round. "And Greg Hicks just rolled into the hotel an hour or so ago. I wonder if they're starting up again. They'd been engaged for years before she and Neal hooked up."

"Well, she and Neal have been inseparable since then, according to *ET.*"

Darryl shook his hands and screwed his face up in mock horror, making the women laugh. "And we *all* know how reliable a news source that is."

"Hey, I have kids, give me a break. I don't get out much."

Sabrina barely heard another word.

Greg had arrived.

And he hadn't contacted her.

She had to bite her tongue so she didn't interrogate Danica.

How had he looked? Had he asked about her?

Of course he hadn't. If he had, Danica would've been interrogating her.

Instead they were discussing the possibility that Greg was sleeping with his ex behind her husband's back.

Her stomach rolled and she put down her fork.

Why hadn't Kate told her?

Sliding a glance at the table behind her, Sabrina saw Kate and Tyler engaged with several other couples. Jared and Annabelle were at another table, talking and laughing.

Because they were busy with their lives, that's why.

Daisy. Greg's ex. Here alone.

Of course that was the reason she hadn't heard from Greg. He was with Daisy.

And maybe you aren't giving him enough credit. The guy is filming a movie in less than a week. Daisy is working for him.

Maybe Daisy had arrived early to do publicity or rehearse or . . .

Then why hasn't he been in touch with you?

She tried to ignore the growing ache in her chest as dinner went on. What she really wanted to do was go back to her room, curl on her bed, and fall into unconsciousness. Which wasn't going to happen because she had to work. Hours and hours of alone time to think.

Lovely.

She managed to make it through another half hour at dinner before she was able to plead work as an excuse, go to her room to change, then head back to the reception office.

Laney, fully recovered from her accident, was more than happy to give up her post early so she could enjoy dessert with the rest of the staff. She thanked Sabrina with a tight hug then promised to bring Sabrina a piece of whatever the chef was serving. Sabrina didn't have the heart to tell her not to.

By three a.m., she'd devoured the slice of decadent chocolate cake and was following it with some highly caffeinated, highly sweetened tea, trying not to let her brain become caught in a rut.

So was he up there with Daisy now?

She huffed. "No, I'm not going to think about it."

"Think about what?"

She bit back a surprised squeak as she shot up from the chair she'd been sitting on at the computer terminal.

A man stood in front of the reception desk, baseball cap low on his forehead, black leather coat collar shadowing the bottom half of his face. She couldn't believe she'd completely missed his entrance into the lobby. And now she wondered if that was on purpose.

Her gaze slid toward the door, where the bellman should be. And wasn't.

She swallowed down the flash of fear that sprang up. He couldn't have come in through the front door because it was locked this late at night. Which meant he had to have come through the garage, and the only way into the garage was through the bellman, who doubled as security this late at night. Which would explain why there was no one at the door.

"I'm so sorry. I didn't see you come in." She dredged up a smile. "Welcome to Haven. How can I help you?"

"Well, for starters, I'm sorry I scared the crap out of you, but you looked pretty intent on what you were doing."

Setting his bags on the floor, one of which was a guitar case, he folded down the collar then took off the hat.

Sabrina felt her eyes widen as his face emerged. At first glance, he wasn't conventionally handsome. Shaggy, dirty blond hair flopped over his broad forehead, almost obscuring light eyes that were either blue or green or maybe somewhere in between. His nose was slightly too large for his face, and his chin made up for the nose in being perfectly masculine and covered with reddish-gold whiskers. And that mouth was something else.

Running a hand through his hair made it fall in crazy ways that were just as attractive as before. "I was told to contact Tyler Golden when I got here but since it's three in the morning, I figured I'd just check in and touch base with him tomorrow."

"Oh, of course. Do you have a reservation?"

"Honestly, I'm not sure." He grimaced and looked like the next words out of his mouth didn't taste all that good. "I believe my dad was going to take care of that."

She brightened her smile, wanting to put him at ease. The closer she looked at him, the more she could see exhaustion in the pallor of his skin and the dullness of his eyes.

"Okay, let me check. Can I have your name?"

"Sebastian Valenti." Then he paused, as if waiting to see how she reacted. When she didn't, he continued. "Might be under my dad's name, Arthur Valenti. Like I said, I'm not even sure he made the reservation. He only told me Golden would be expecting me."

"Just give me a minute."

She had already double checked the registration roster when she'd started tonight, but maybe she'd missed something. Her concentration had been fractured.

Haven wasn't the kind of place where people walked in off the street to book a room. Yes, visitors came for the bar or the restaurant and, very occasionally, a few of those guests would book rooms for the night, if there was one available.

They did have rooms tonight so registering him wouldn't be a problem.

But if he really was supposed to contact Tyler when he arrived, she figured she'd better do just that.

"I'm sorry I don't have you on the list but let me contact Tyler. If he's expecting you—"

"He is." Sebastian sighed, grimacing. "Unfortunately. Look, I really don't want to wake him this late at night. I'll just check my bags. I think I saw an all-night diner just down the street—"

"No need for that." Tyler walked out of the elevator just as she'd been reaching for her phone to text him. "Sebastian, I'm Tyler. Nice to meet you."

Sebastian visibly tensed as Tyler came toward him, hand outstretched, smile firmly in place. Almost as if he didn't want to meet him.

When Tyler was almost on top of him, Sebastian finally took his hand.

"Thanks for taking me in." The words sounded almost bitten off. "I appreciate it."

"Not a problem. We're glad to have you."

Taking him in? Her natural curiosity kicked in but she didn't have time to indulge it because Tyler turned to her.

"Sabrina, we're going to register Sebastian under a false name. He's going to be staying with us for several weeks and he'd rather keep his whereabouts secret."

"Of course." She flashed Sebastian another smile, noticing the tight set of his jaw and the clenched fists at his sides.

Obviously this guy was someone famous. And she had absolutely no idea who he was. He did look like he could use a friend, though. Which totally wasn't in her job description.

And neither was sleeping with Greg Hicks.

Better stick to work. At least she knew what she was doing there. Mostly.

*   *

Greg stepped out of Daisy's room, pulled the door shut behind him, then leaned against it and closed his eyes.

The queasy feeling he'd been fighting off since he'd entered her room hadn't abated, but now he had a headache to go with it.

He needed some food. He hadn't eaten since a late lunch on the plane and that had been about, oh, nine hours ago.

But he'd forgo food if he could see Sabrina.

Goddamn it.

He'd wanted this shoot to fly under the radar. Now, he didn't know if that was going to be possible. Luckily, he'd already fought some of the battle. He'd managed to track down Neal after nearly five straight hours of phone calls. Then he'd sent Trudeau to get Neal's ass on the first plane to the East Coast. He'd also told her not to leave Neal's side and to make sure he wasn't high as a kite or falling down drunk by the time he got here.

And to please *God* do it as discreetly as possible.

Once he'd assured Daisy that Neal was in one piece and on his way, she'd finally fallen asleep.

And all Greg wanted to do was talk to Sabrina, which made him feel like he'd fallen into a John Hughes movie, if Hughes had written love stories about thirty-somethings instead of teenagers. Then again, he felt like a teenager, complete with raging hormones and a constant hard-on.

There was no way he was going to get any sleep right now, and he had a million little things he should take care of. He should head back to his room and crack open the laptop . . .

He'd punched the button for the lobby before he'd made a conscious decision. When the doors opened, he stepped out of the cage but didn't move out of the alcove. He heard voices. One was definitely Tyler's.

What the hell was he doing down here this late? Had something happened to Sabrina?

He was halfway across the lobby when he saw Tyler talking to another guy. Then he heard Sabrina speak and the new guy answer. Even though his back was to the lobby, Greg could tell the guy was smiling at Sabrina.

And she smiled back.

He wanted to grab the interloper and toss him across the lobby.

Cue the fight scene from *Pretty in Pink*.

Jesus, he needed to get a grip.

Instead of heading for the desk, he veered off, ending up in an alcove next to the doors to the atrium.

He forced himself to look out over Tyler's masterwork in horticulture design. Still dressed for Thanksgiving, the atrium would undergo its Christmas transformation next week.

Right now, it still looked fall-like. And a little drab. But that could just be his shitty mood talking, which wasn't getting any better listening to Sabrina try to charm the asshole at the desk.

Could he tell Tyler he didn't want her working any more night shifts until he left? Or would that make him too controlling?

Do you really care?

The real questions were, would Tyler do it and would Sabrina be pissed off if he did.

Maybe he wanted to get her riled. Then get her naked and riled in bed.

"If you need anything, please don't hesitate to ask," he heard Sabrina say.

"Thanks. Nice to meet you, Sabrina. Hope to see you again."

Flicking his gaze to the right, Greg could just make out the scene at the desk. He saw Sabrina smiling and saw the guy, who still had his back to Greg, reach over the desk to take the keycard she held out.

Her smile softened as the guy turned to Tyler, who waved a hand toward the elevators.

When the men turned, Greg realized why Sabrina had been smiling.

Sebastian Valenti. Tyler had said the guy was coming to stay for a few weeks. He hadn't said when.

Watching the reflection in the glass windows, Greg saw burnout etched in the guy's face.

Been there, done that.

His attention returned to Sabrina, caught by her compassionate expression.

The girl had a big heart.

And damn it, he wanted it. Wanted her. Wanted all of her attention focused on him.

So what the fucking *hell* was he going to do about it?

Checking the clock on the wall, he realized she still had another three hours to go before her shift was over.

Fuck.

He should go back upstairs. He didn't think she'd seen him yet, so he could slip back down the hall to the second bank of elevators on the other side of the atrium.

Then again, if he stayed here, he had the perfect vantage point to watch her unobserved.

When did you turn into a creeper?

Yeah, he liked to watch but . . .

With Tyler and Sebastian gone, she turned to look at the clock on the wall above the registration desk. Then she sighed. He swore he heard her from here.

Was she tired? Was she wondering why he hadn't contacted her yet? Did she think he wasn't going to?

His phone vibrated.

Yes!

He nearly pumped his fist in the air and did a touchdown dance.

Trudeau had Neal. They'd be at the hotel, barring bad weather or a plane crash, in eight hours. And he knew that even if that plane went down, Trudeau would deliver Neal in a full-body cast.

The click of heels made his head snap up, and he saw Sabrina in the glass, walking straight for his hiding spot.

He took a second to examine her features before he turned, trying to guess her mood from her expression so he could be prepared for whatever she threw at him.

She didn't look pissed. No, it was worse. She was wearing her Pleasant Employee face.

"Hello, Greg. Nice to see you again."

And wow, he really fucking hated that bland smile. It made him want to kiss it off her face. But he wasn't sure she wouldn't punch him in the face if he tried.

"Sabrina." He thought about what he should say and settled for the truth. "I really fucking missed you, babe."

Her eyes widened with shock, then her expression softened with pleasure and he knew he'd chosen the right tactic.

In L.A., honesty didn't get you far. But he wasn't in L.A. And Sabrina was no vapid starlet.

"I'm sure you've been busy."

"You could say that. Still, I'm sorry I didn't text you tonight when I got in. I've been dealing with a . . . situation."

Her teeth lodged in her lower lip. "I heard Daisy Devlin arrived earlier today."

Christ, he'd probably be trying to fend off press as soon as tomorrow if the staff was talking. "She did."

"And there's something wrong with that?"

"Unfortunately, yeah. She came without her husband."

"And that's a problem?"

He nodded. "Can you sit for a few minutes?"

Her gaze flashed back to the desk. "For a few minutes, sure."

She eased onto the chair across from him, barely sitting on the edge of the cushion, the hem of her plain blue skirt riding up just above her knees. He tried not to let his gaze linger, but it was so damn hard when he knew how soft the skin was on the inside of her thighs.

Fuck.

His fingers dug into the arms of the chair because he really wanted to pull her onto his lap. But then he wouldn't be able to help himself. He'd kiss her and wouldn't want to stop.

Consider this an exercise in self-control.

Something he typically didn't have to worry about.

"Considering she didn't know where Neal was, yeah, it was a problem. But my assistant found him and she's got him on a plane. They'll be here in eight hours."

"That's great." Her genuine smile made an appearance now, her eyes lighting up. He really liked this girl. "So you'll be able to start filming on time."

He nodded. "The crew arrives Saturday. The rest of the cast'll be here Sunday. Filming starts Tuesday."

"You'll be pretty busy then."

Did he hear a wistful note in her voice? "I will. But I'll still have time for you."

She didn't say anything right away, just stared at him with a look he couldn't decipher.

"Sabrina—"

"I'm glad to hear that."

Yes.

Smiling, he watched a blush color her cheeks, as if she knew what he was thinking, that he wanted to drag her back to his room now and bury himself between her legs.

Which was exactly what he planned to do the second he had her alone.

"I'm going to apologize now for the long days and the ten thousand phone calls at all hours and the hundred people asking me twenty million questions."

"You're busy. I understand."

No, she really didn't, but she would soon enough. Hopefully by that time, he'd have her tied to him as tight as he could. He'd fuck her until she couldn't see straight and wouldn't want to leave his bed. Of course, he wouldn't be spending all that much time in bed . . .

Really fucking bad timing.

"So, I'm assuming you didn't recognize the guy who just checked in."

She gave him a look that clearly showed she had no idea what he was getting at or why he'd suddenly changed the subject.

"Sebastian Valenti. Lead guitarist and singer for Baseline Sins. A rock band," he added when she raised an eyebrow at him. "A pretty good one, too."

"Are you a fan? Why didn't you come over and introduce yourself?"

"It's late. I'm sure I'll see him around."

"He looked . . . tired."

"Yeah, he did." He didn't add that the guy had had some major problems recently. She'd discover that on her own soon enough.

"So do you." Her voice softened. "You should get some sleep."

"Trying to get rid of me?"

"No. Would it work if I were?"

"Probably not. Do you still have the keycard I gave you?"

She blinked. "Yes."

"Come to my room when you're finished with your shift."

She bit her lip. "My mom's making dinner for noon so I can be there. I have to work again tonight at four."

"You get off at seven?"

"Yes."

"Then you've got a few hours before you have to leave. Give me two of them."

After a short pause, she nodded. "Okay."

She stood, her lips curving in a way that made him want to reach for her, have her straddle his lap and kiss her until he wanted to yank up her skirt and do her right here.

"Maybe you should go up and get a little rest. Wouldn't want you to be too tired when I get off work."

He laughed, the sound echoing through the empty lobby. "I'm not that old, babe."

"Maybe I'm just that horny."

Heat flashed from his balls, up his spine and through his cock, making it stiffen almost painfully.

"Jesus, Bree—"

She walked by his chair, brushing her fingers through his hair and making his cock throb.

He couldn't fucking wait to get her back in his bed.

* *

By the time seven a.m. finally arrived, Sabrina was ready to crawl out of her skin.

She'd been counting the minutes until her replacements arrived and, when the Fiorelli sisters, Casey and Danica, walked out of the registration office, she wanted to rush to the elevator.

But she didn't want to make her coworkers suspicious, and everyone knew Casey and Danica, who'd been hired a year before

Sabrina, were the biggest gossips in the hotel. And if she went all smiles and hightailed it out of here, the sisters would suspect a man because they always suspected a man behind anyone's good mood. Usually they were right. She couldn't risk them having even a hint of suspicion.

She already knew the daytime security guard might catch her heading for Greg's room on the security cam in the elevator but, unlike the Fiorelli sisters, he knew how to keep his mouth shut.

After filling in Casey and Danica on the new arrival and giving them his assumed name, she headed for her room to change before she went to Greg's suite—

Which was on the same floor as her boss's apartment.

Oh, my God, what if she got off the elevator and Tyler was standing there? Talk about awkward.

Maybe she should rethink this.

And maybe you should stop overthinking everything and have a good time.

Back in her room, she did the fastest change ever, throwing off her skirt and blouse to pull on comfy, worn jeans that didn't make her ass look huge and a purple T-shirt that made her breasts look great.

She knew she should be tired, figured the adrenaline crash was going to be pretty bad later, but she'd pulled all-nighters before. She'd catch a nap at her mom's before she came back for her shift at seven. She could catch up on her sleep on her next day off.

Which was in two days.

Thinking about how much sex she could have with Greg before then made her want to fan her burning cheeks, but the elevator dinged to announce her arrival on the fourth floor.

Taking a deep breath, she stepped out into the hall.

No one there.

She breathed a sigh of relief. She wasn't doing anything wrong. There was no company policy about fraternizing with the guests. Besides, Tyler knew what was going on between her and Greg. If Tyler didn't want her to see Greg, he would've told her.

Turning right, she headed for the door at the end of the hall.

Greg was staying in Suite C, which she knew from visiting Kate was at the opposite end of the hall from Tyler and Jared's apartments. And from the room the other employees called the Salon.

The registration staff had told her it was the Goldens' private room for entertaining. But the looks Casey and Danica had exchanged when they'd told her that said something else entirely. Like there was something really interesting about that room. Kate had mentioned it a few times in passing. So had Annabelle. And whenever Annabelle said anything about it, her fair skin turned bright red.

Her curiosity would get the better of her soon enough, and she'd ask exactly what kind of entertaining they did in that room. But not now.

Now she walked straight to Greg's door and barely hesitated when she slid the card in the lock. She didn't want to stand in the hall too long in case Tyler or Jared emerged from their apartments.

She'd texted Greg to let him know she was on her way and the moment she opened the door, he was there. She had a second to draw in a short breath before he had her pinned against the now-closed door, his mouth sealing hers as his tongue demanded entrance.

This was no tame "Hey, how've you been" kiss.

This was a "Get your clothes off now, I want to fuck you" kiss.

Her arms automatically rose to circle his shoulders and her head hit the door as she tilted it back to let him kiss her more deeply. He barely let her up for air, kissing her with such intense focus her toes curled.

It felt like she'd been waiting ages for him to kiss her again.

Arching her back, she tried to get closer, to press her breasts against his chest and her mound against his cock. Better yet, she wanted to be naked and riding him, hearing him say her name in that husky growl and telling her how much he wanted her.

This doesn't seem like you're working him out of your system.

She told the little voice in her head to go pound sand and she sank her fingers into his hair as her legs circled his waist.

He held her there for several seconds, letting his mouth explore hers in the most sensual way, drugging her, dragging her deeper into a state where passion ruled.

When he finally let her up for air, it was so he could turn and carry her into the room.

"You're late."

The lust-roughened tone of his voice made her shiver, and the intensity of his gaze made her feel like a mouse in the sights of a hawk. That look promised that he was going to devour her.

She had to swallow before she could answer. "I wanted to change."

"And I wanted you here."

A smile pulled at the corners of her mouth. "Kind of impatient, aren't you?"

"Hell yes. I've been waiting too long to get my hands on you again." His mouth curved into a wicked grin that made her chest constrict as he nudged open a door on the far side of the room. "When are you due at your mom's?"

"By noon, but I wanted to get there a little early to spend time with my sisters and brothers. It's been a while since I've seen them."

She saw his jaw clench, as if he had something he wanted to say but didn't think he should. "Fine." That one word sounded like he didn't like the taste of it. "Then don't blame me if this is a little faster than normal."

"Sometimes fast is good. It also means we might be able to do it twice."

"Damn, I like the way you think."

The next thing she knew, she was falling. He'd reached the bed and dropped her on it, watching her every move with narrowed eyes.

"I'm gonna strip you naked and put your legs over my shoulders and make you come with my mouth. Sound good?"

Her eyes widened and her jaw dropped but she had no idea what to say to that bald statement of intent. Her body, however, knew exactly what to do. She drew in a shaky breath and her thighs clenched.

His gaze fell from her eyes to her lips, which made her press them together so her moan didn't escape. She could barely breathe, and all her energy and awareness had shifted lower.

As his gaze continued its downward journey, her nipples peaked into hard nubs, pressing against her bra, straining for his mouth. Her abdomen tightened as if he'd put his hands on her and had started to caress her.

And her pussy . . . well, that was drenched and needy.

"Finally rendered you speechless, huh?" He sounded pleased with himself. "Let's see if I can change that. I want to hear you scream my name when you come."

Her breath hitched as Greg's smile evaporated. Coming up onto her elbows, she watched him reach for her legs, lifting them to remove her shoes and socks. He rubbed her feet for a few seconds each, making her bite back a moan at the pleasure.

Then he reached for her jeans. "I think I like you better in skirts. Much easier to remove."

That spurred her into speech. "Maybe you shouldn't always get what you want."

Popping the button on her jeans, he worked them down her legs, his gaze now latching onto the purple satin panties that matched the demi bra under her T-shirt.

"What would be the fun in that? I'm going to suggest Kate make your underwear crotchless from now on."

"Greg!"

He laughed at her breathless shock, throwing her jeans on the bench at the end of the bed. "Hell, we didn't even get started and you're already crying out my name."

She couldn't help but laugh. "You have no shame, do you?"

"Nothing to be ashamed about in here. Damn, I can't wait to get those legs spread. Sit up, babe, and let me take off that shirt."

She obeyed without hesitation, still shaking her head. The way he talked made her feel like she was a fizzy bottle of soda that had been shaken for days.

Grabbing the hem of her shirt, he had it over her head in a flash. In the next second, his hands cupped her breasts, molding them through the satin.

"Definitely crotchless panties. Damn, you are *so* fucking gorgeous."

No one had ever said that to her before. No one had ever looked at her the way Greg was looking at her now.

She wanted to agree to anything he asked.

Slippery slope. Oh, so very slippery . . .

"What about you?" she asked. "Don't I get to strip you?"

"I'm glad you asked."

Releasing her breasts, he reached behind his head to grab his shirt and pull it over his head. Now her gaze was level with the center of his chest and she leaned forward to press a kiss right there.

She heard him groan, low and deep, felt his hand cup her head, fingers threading through her hair. Those fingers clenched when she worked the button on his jeans through the hole then eased the zipper over the impressive erection pushing against it.

Reaching for his waistband, she stopped when he put his hand over hers. "I think we're gonna leave those where they are for now. Lay back, sweetheart."

She did what he wanted because it's exactly what she wanted, too. But that little voice in the back of her brain began to pipe up again.

Have a little backbone, girl. What the hell are you—

Greg went to his knees at the side of the bed, spreading her legs with his hands on her inner thighs. Staring at the ceiling, she tried to breathe normally but couldn't because he was opening her even more.

She swore she felt his gaze on her like a heat ray—

"You're wet, baby. Have you been thinking about me?"

"Greg . . ." Her fingers grasped at the silky comforter as his breath brushed along the inside of her thighs. Her pussy clenched and she felt even more moisture dampen her already wet panties.

"I sure as hell have been thinking about you." His breath drew closer to where she needed him to be, his fingers stroking closer to the edges of her panties as he wedged his shoulders between her thighs to hold her open. "I think you're becoming a serious addiction."

He put his mouth directly over her clit, nipping at her through her panties. The sensation was decadent and all the air rushed from her lungs as he made her panties even wetter than they had been.

When he moved to the bare skin of her thigh she wanted to complain, but then he bit her. Not hard. Just enough for the sensitive nerves at that spot to send heated pulses through her body, making her back bow. He made a growling sound of approval as he bit his way up her leg, deliberately avoiding her mound as he headed to her other thigh.

It wasn't enough, not nearly enough.

She reached for his head, but he withdrew. "Grab the other side of the mattress, babe. Stretch out for me. There you go. I'll apologize to Kate later."

His muttered last sentence didn't make sense until she heard the distinctive sound of satin ripping.

She couldn't find it in her to care. As long as—

He put his mouth directly over her core for an intimate kiss that made her writhe so much he had to put his hands on her hips to keep her from bucking away from him.

But, oh, my God, she didn't think she could stand the overwhelming sensations.

He used his tongue and lips in ways she'd never imagined, evoking so much pleasure. He used the flat of his tongue to lick at her clit, the rough surface just abrasive enough to make her shudder. His lips sucked at her tender folds until they were plump and so slick.

His single-minded focus brought her to the edge of orgasm twice. Each time, he eased off just as she was about to come and now she lay panting and shaking.

"Greg, please."

"That's what I love to hear. You asking me for what you want."

"Then give me what I want."

His low laugh made her internal muscles shimmy. "Soon enough. First I'm going to suck on those pretty nipples."

Her breasts tightened to a point just below pain and, when he sucked one between his lips, still wet from her juices, she felt a short, jolting orgasm that made her moan.

He looked up at her. "That's one."

Heat suffused her face. "You are *not* going to count my orgasms."

"If I don't, how are we going to keep score?"

She lifted onto her elbows to find him grinning at her, his hands braced on the bed on either side of her body.

He looked breathtakingly sexy, with his hair hanging around his face, and that smile and those eyes that promised so much more pleasure.

She had to smile back. All sense of embarrassment, all thought of propriety was blown away by the strength of his desire for her.

He made her want to be bad. Or maybe she'd always had it in her but he'd been the only one to bring it out.

She didn't care. She liked it.

"Then maybe I need to count yours."

Laughing, he bent to kiss her and she felt his laughter against her lips, her chest, deep inside.

"You do that, but I can assure you, you'll have more than me."

"Is that a challenge?"

His eyes widened, surprise and something wicked lighting in the depths. "Honey, I love a challenge. And I never lose."

She cocked her head to the side, feeling her hair waterfall over her shoulder, and watched him shift his attention. "But you've never played with me."

He leaned down to lick her other nipple before he took the tip between his teeth and bit. A breath hissed between her lips and she caught back a moan. The muscles in her abdomen, thighs, and arms all clenched. But this time, she staved off the immediate surrender, knowing he'd deliver later. And knowing the buildup was sometimes just as satisfying as the payoff.

"That's right, sweetheart. Make me work for it. I like that."

He played with her breasts for several wonderful, tortuous minutes. Then he pushed her flat on her back, shifting her farther onto the bed so he could crawl onto the mattress beside her. The king-size bed gave them more than enough room to spread out.

She found herself sprawled on her back while Greg discovered every erogenous point on her body.

Like the one behind her ear where all he had to do was breathe on her to make her shudder. Or the one on her wrist that he found when he lifted her hands above her head and held them there with one hand while his other stroked down her abdomen. That one led him to the one on the inside of her thighs, which he bit, pushing her closer to another meltdown.

When he slid back up her body after making her moan and writhe, she used the split-second it took him to move to reverse their positions.

He let her push him onto his back. If he hadn't wanted to go, she'd still be on hers.

She was breathing more heavily than he was, a situation she planned to change in the next several minutes. And when she looked down and found him grinning up at her, she knew exactly what he was thinking. He was going to make her work for his surrender.

Pausing for a beat, she smiled down at him then pushed herself onto her knees next to him.

Lacing his hands behind his head, he watched her contemplate his jeans.

"Go ahead. Take 'em off."

Since that's exactly what she'd planned to do, she paused, putting her hands on her hips and staring at him with raised eyebrows.

"I'm not sure you deserve to have my mouth on you yet."

"How about your hands? Tug my zipper down. I need a little relief here."

Her gaze slid down his body to his crotch. The bulge behind the placket did look a little painful. She'd already undone the button and she could just see the tip of his penis peeking out of the tiny gap.

Instead of reaching for the tab, she touched the tip of her tongue to her top lip as she reached out and ran the pad of one finger over that soft, soft skin.

She heard him suck in a short breath, his abs flexing in fascinating patterns. Her finger gravitated to those muscles, petting through the valleys and dancing over the ridges.

"Pretty."

He huffed out an amused sound. "Not sure what you're talking about so I'm just going to say thank you. And if you don't do more than touch me with that finger and stare at me, you're gonna find yourself flat on your back again and me fucking you through a couple more orgasms."

Her cheeks flared with heat, which spread throughout her whole body.

"That doesn't seem very fair. And shows a distinct lack of control on your part."

"I know. And that's typically something I don't have to worry about."

His tone held the slightest hint of introspection and that's not what she wanted. She didn't want him thinking about anything but her and pleasure.

She gave him her sexiest smile and watched his eyes narrow.

Several months ago, when he'd taken those pictures of her in Kate's lingerie, he'd told her to smolder. And she hadn't understood what he'd meant until he'd gotten close enough to make her.

She let the heat curled low in her body show through her eyes. And had the satisfaction of seeing how she affected him.

His expression hardened, his eyes burning and his chest expanding to take in more air.

"I think I like that you're going to have to worry about it with me," she said.

Gripping the tab on his zipper between her thumb and forefinger, she began to ease it down. It came reluctantly, probably because his erection pressed against it so tightly.

He hissed in a breath as she got near the end, but she knew she hadn't hurt him. At least, she hadn't caught him in the zipper. He may be in pain, but it was a good pain.

"Why don't you take them off for me? Wouldn't want to damage anything."

He hesitated only a second before he grabbed the waistband and shoved his jeans and boxer briefs below his ass. Then he crunched his stomach and pulled up until he sat on the bed, working his jeans the rest of the way off his legs. Tossing them on the floor, he lay back. Beautifully, gloriously naked.

She wondered what he would do if she asked to take pictures of him? Would he let her?

Before he could do anything else, she straddled his thighs and put her hands on his chest. Her nails bit into his nicely defined pecs, just hard enough to leave a slight impression. His gaze glued to hers, she dragged her fingers down his torso, loving how his eyes narrowed the farther she got down his body.

His cock bobbed, as if to entice her to stroke it, too. Instead, she let her nails graze the skin on either side.

"*Fuck.* Do that again."

She obeyed, in the opposite direction, leaning forward while she did. She wanted to rub her breasts against his chest, feel the heat of his body. And press his cock against her clit, where she ached.

Bracing her hands on either side of his shoulders, she leaned down to kiss him, her hair falling around his face, a curtain that shut out the rest of the room.

He let her kiss him but she felt the control he was exerting to hold himself back. When he lifted his hands to push back her hair and twist it around his fingers, she thought he might take over.

But he didn't, and she gave herself over to the sheer pleasure of molding their lips together and slipping her tongue into his mouth. His heat made her want to breathe him in.

Her nipples poked into his chest and, even though she hadn't yet pressed her mound against his cock, she felt the heat radiating from him.

Her moan felt like it came from deep inside and their kiss deepened. One hand cupped her jaw, the thumb stroking against her skin, while the other landed on her ass.

The sharp sting made her suck in a quick gasp, even as her pussy clenched.

Oh, God, she'd never thought she could be so turned on by even the slightest hint of pain. He smoothed a hand down the back of her thigh then back up again to knead her ass. She groaned as he traced the valley between her buttocks and reached the wet, hot channel between her legs.

She broke away from his mouth to breathe when she felt his fingers slip through the folds of her sex. "Yes. Fuck me with your fingers."

She almost didn't recognize her own voice, couldn't quite believe she was the one saying these things. When she was with Greg, she became a different person. A sexy, confident woman with no inhibitions.

A woman this man wanted.

Her eyes closed and her head tilted down until they were forehead to forehead as he dipped his fingers into her channel, sliding two in just to the first knuckle.

Then he withdrew. The next time, he went a little farther.

Bent over him like she was, she didn't have a full range of movement, but she could move just enough to rub his cock against her mound and manipulate his fingers in interesting ways.

"You like that, don't you?" His voice sounded so close to her ear, it was almost as if he spoke inside her head. "And I like that you're so damn tight. I can't wait to get my cock inside you again."

Suddenly, he impaled her with his fingers as far as he could go and pulled her head back to bite her neck.

"Oh, my God." She was so close to another orgasm and this time she didn't care if she lost their little competition. She only wanted to come.

Holding his fingers steady inside her, his mouth moved slowly up her neck. When he reached her chin, he nipped her.

And stroked his fingers high inside her.

She moaned into his mouth as he kissed, squirmed against his hand as he worked that spot until her body quivered from an over-load of sensation. His fingers filled her, stroked her, coaxed her into coming apart again.

He groaned as she rippled around his fingers. Releasing her hair, he gripped her hips. Then suddenly, he pulled out. Tears wet her eyes. She needed—

A millisecond later, he shoved his cock inside her, making her cry out as she stretched to accommodate him. Her pussy welcomed him, tightening around him like a fist, drawing him deeper.

"Up, baby. Sit up."

She did what he wanted, her brain barely functioning except to listen to him. Bracing her palms against his abs, she straightened, taking him even deeper, making them both gasp.

She stayed still for several seconds, absorbing the feel of him being bigger in this position. Filling her until she thought she'd burst.

His breathing sounded amplified and she opened her eyes to stare down at him. His eyes had narrowed to slits, his mouth flattened into a line she wanted to kiss. But she didn't want to move and lose this sensation.

Greg had other plans.

Hands on her hips, he urged her to lift up then sink back down.

God, yes. His cock hit all sorts of different erogenous zones inside her body and her burgeoning orgasm felt like a living thing, hungry and not about to stop.

She took over the rhythm after a few seconds, her body understanding what he wanted. Working her thighs, she rode him harder and harder until her ass slapped against his thighs.

When he no longer needed to guide her, he released her thighs and reached for her hands. Their fingers meshed as she rode him, their gazes locked.

His face showed the strain of holding back his orgasm. She didn't want him to hold back. She wanted that tic on her scorecard.

Tightening her pussy around him each time she slid down on him, she watched with growing satisfaction as he lost that grip on his control.

He was breathing like a freight train now and when his eyes closed that last tiny bit, she swiveled her hips, just enough to make his cock twist in the slightest way—and grinned in triumph when he groaned, his head kicking back into the mattress as his hips pressed forward.

His finger bit into her hips as he held himself deep and came inside her.

Without a condom.

* *

Greg realized what he'd done a millisecond after it happened.

And he still didn't pull out.

No, he lay there staring at the ecstasy on her face and thought, *Mine*.

Yeah, but for how long?

A few seconds later, she collapsed onto his chest and he wrapped his arms around her, holding her tight.

His cock continued to twitch inside her. The feel of her squeezing his bare flesh was something he wouldn't give up for all the money and power in the world. But, Jesus . . . There could be consequences.

"Bree. We didn't use a condom."

She didn't say anything right away, her breathing continuing to slow as the seconds passed.

Finally, she sighed. "I know. It's okay. I'm on the Pill." She paused. "And I'm fine. I mean, there's nothing you should be worried about. Healthwise, I mean. I'm sorry. I didn't realize until it was too late—"

"Whoa. Hey, that's not why I said anything. This is not your fault. It's mine." His arms tightened around her as she stiffened against him. "You've got nothing to worry about from me. I'll get you my health records later today if you want." He paused, thinking. "I can't honestly tell you the last time I had sex without a condom. I just don't want you to think I don't care about what happens to you."

After a few deep breaths, she tried to move but he refused to let her. He wanted her right where he had her for as long as he could keep her there. He liked the feel of her breasts pressed against his chest and her hands in his hair.

Finally, she fell still again, nestling her head under his chin. He relaxed, though he kept his arms around her.

"I've been on the Pill for years. And I've never had unprotected sex. My mom—"

"Your mom what?" He wanted her to talk to him, wanted to hear whatever she wanted to tell him.

"My mom got pregnant at sixteen but I think I told you that. My sperm donor was never in the picture. Mom used to say when he found out she was pregnant, he ran so fast he left skid marks. I've never met him. With my grandparents' help, she finished school and got a job. She met my first stepdad, Diego, when I was five. He adopted me after they had my first two sisters. He died twelve years ago. Brain cancer. My mom was pregnant with the twins."

"Jesus, that sucks, babe. I'm sorry."

She rubbed her cheek against his chest, the motion making him want to hold her even closer. "It does and thank you. I kept his last name because he was the only real dad I knew. A year later my mom met Dan and he seemed nice. At first. They got married and my mom had my younger brothers. And then he left one day and said he wouldn't be back. My brothers occasionally get cards for their birthdays but she doesn't cry over them like she used to. A few years later, my mom met Charlie."

He heard something hard in her tone and he knew this part of the story wasn't going to end well, either. "How old were you?"

"Thirteen."

Fuck. He really hoped he didn't know where this story was heading. "What happened?"

"Nothing. At first. He seemed okay. Then my mom had my youngest brother."

"And?"

"And I was seventeen."

Every muscle in his body went rigid. "You tell me he touched you and I will pay to make him bleed."

She shifted again and he felt her lips brush his chest. "He never got the chance. My mom picked up on it right away. He was out the door five seconds later. None of her friends could figure out why my mom had dumped him. Everyone thought he was such a great guy. And she had eight kids and a barely minimum-wage job. I know Mom told a few people. And a few of those people told her she was crazy for kicking him out. He hadn't touched me. Why the hell would she get rid of a decent man who provided for her?"

His arms tightened around her. "Because she loved her daughter."

"Yeah. I've never doubted that."

"Sounds like a great lady."

"She is. One of the best." A loud yawn seemed to surprise her. "Oh, wow. Sorry. I can't believe how tired I am. I had a nap yesterday. I shouldn't be so sleepy."

"Maybe I'm just that good at wearing you out."

Her low laughter made his gut clench and his cock finally slid from her sheath. He wanted to roll her over and start again.

"Hang tight. I'll get a towel."

"Do you mind if I use the bathroom?"

"No, of course not."

With a sigh, she shifted, then rolled off the bed and headed for the attached bath.

Turning onto his side, he watched her ass the entire way. Damn, he loved the way that girl was put together.

He wondered if she'd let him take more pictures. A little more risqué this time.

He hadn't been able to delete any of the photos he'd taken of her at the retreat. Just couldn't do it. And he'd spent a little too much time looking at them these past three weeks they'd been apart.

He wanted to take more. Pictures only he would ever see. Would she agree?

He thought he might be able to convince her.

His phone vibrated on the nightstand and he glared at it. He really should pick up the damn thing and start going through his email and texts. Both were probably exploding, even though most of his email went to the general account Trudeau handled. Only a select group had his private email. Still, that probably had a hundred things in it he had to take care of. A few probably needed immediate attention.

He was still running a company, one that needed a strong hand, especially now.

Christ, why the hell had he thought directing a film again would be fun?

"Greg," she called, "do you mind if I borrow your shirt?"

Yeah, he did. He wanted her to walk back out here naked, so he could watch her. Then he wanted to lay her out on the bed again. "No problem."

The door opened again and she emerged in the blue button-down he'd tossed on the hook last night.

It reached about mid-thigh and hung loose around her chest, though he could still see the jiggle of her breasts. He really had a thing for her breasts.

She glanced at the clock as she walked toward the bed. As he pulled himself up and sat on the edge of the bed, her eyes tracked his movements. "I really should get on the road to my mom's. Besides, I'm sure you have a lot— Hey!"

He grabbed her hand and yanked her toward him, twisting until he had her on the bed again, trapped under him this time.

She looked so sexy, her hair messy and falling all over the sheets, and her eyes half-lidded and smoky. He bent and kissed her, loving the way she seemed to melt beneath him.

"Stay for another hour."

Cocking an eyebrow at him, she shook her head. "If I stay another hour, I won't be able to help my mom finish dinner. I told her I'd be there. Besides, I thought you were going to your parents for dinner."

"We're not eating 'til later." She hadn't reached for him, her hands palm up on the mattress next to her head. "Put your hands on my shoulders."

Her nose crinkled in an adorably puzzled expression. "Why?"

"Because I want you to hold on to me while I do this."

He took her mouth, kissing her hard and deep until she finally put her hands on his shoulders. She clutched at him, opening her mouth to him and kissing him back.

When he finally let her up for air, she blinked up at him after taking a deep breath.

"You know," she said, "I'm beginning to realize why you have the reputation you do in Hollywood. You don't take no for an answer, do you?"

"Not usually."

"And do you always get what you want?"

"Usually, yeah." He sighed. "Look, I know I'm not going to have a lot of free time over the next month. And I know you're busy, too. But I want to see you as much as I can."

Her smile made his heart pound. He liked it. A lot. And he was glad he hadn't added "while I'm here" to the end of that sentence.

He'd realized years ago that if he didn't tell a woman up front there was a time limit to their affair, she tended to think he meant forever.

Which was how he'd gotten a reputation for being a cold bastard. Daisy had been the only woman who'd stuck around long enough to leave him first.

As if she'd read his mind, her smile disappeared. "My schedule is going to be totally screwed up the next few weeks. I switch between the seven-to-three and the three-to-eleven shifts."

"What about the overnights like last night? Any more of those?"

"A few, although that could change in a second. Since I'm the newest employee, I'm always the first one who gets asked to take the crappy shifts. And I don't mind, not really. This job is such a great opportunity for me and . . ."

He waited, having some idea what she was about to say.

She sighed. "What should I tell Tyler? I don't like feeling like I'm going behind his back."

"What we do here has nothing to do with him."

"He's my boss."

"He's not your keeper."

"What happens if I see him in the hall coming to your room? This level is usually off limits to the staff and—"

"You're not working now and you're my guest." He held up one hand as she opened her mouth to speak again. "I'll talk to Tyler. Tell him if he sees you in the hall to just ignore you, okay?"

She gave him another one of those looks that said she didn't think he was funny. And he wasn't trying to be. For the most part.

"That'll be kind of stupid. It's going to be awkward."

"Only if you let it."

He wanted her to say okay, to give in. And when she didn't, he realized he wasn't going to be civilized if she said she didn't want to see him again.

"Bree, do you want to see me again?"

She nodded immediately. "Yeah. I do."

He smiled and watched her lips part so she could draw in air. Yes, he liked knowing how he affected her. He liked it a hell of a lot. "Then we'll figure it out."

His phone vibrated again and he knew he couldn't ignore it any longer.

Glaring at the damn thing made it continue to shake. "Shit. I gotta get that. I'll talk to Tyler as soon as possible." Of course, he'd already talked to Tyler but he wasn't sure he wanted to confess that little conversation just yet. "You're already navigating the boss-friend thing, right? We'll figure this out, too."

He kissed her again before he rolled away and reached for the phone. Before he could get up, she brushed a hand across his back, holding him in place.

He looked over his shoulder at her. Her half smile made his cock twitch.

"You can text me later, if you have time. I'll be off at eleven. If you're too busy, just let me know. No problem."

He had a feeling he would never be too tired for her. "I like my shirt on you, hon. Looks good."

He watched her smile as she took it off then started to dress in her own clothes.

"Then I guess you can keep it for me until next time."

With one last kiss, she walked out the door.

And his phone buzzed until he wanted to throw it against a wall.

He opened it and started to swear.

Seven

"Sabrina, come have lunch with me and Annabelle. We're going over her dress. Again. Please, please, please. We need a new perspective because we're driving each other crazy."

Sabrina laughed at the childish air of pleading in Kate's voice as she checked the clock. It was around noon on Saturday and she'd been thinking about doing the wash. Which she hated. "You showed me the last sketch you did last week. I thought that was final."

"It is. I've already cut the pieces for the practice dress and I even caved on the amount of cleavage she's showing. Personally, I think she should go for more but she said she doesn't want to look like Kim Kardashian at the MTV Video Music Awards. As if I'd ever let her."

Even though she hadn't had much sleep, Sabrina was still able to laugh at Kate's sarcastic tone.

"She has to pick the fabric so I can order it. *Please* come back me up," Kate pleaded. "She has to make some hard and fast decisions or I won't have the dress finished for the wedding."

Annabelle and Jared, Tyler's younger brother, had chosen the first Saturday in April as the date of their wedding. All Kate and Annabelle seemed to talk about now was the dress.

Sabrina and Kate had already chosen their dresses as her bridesmaid and maid of honor. Kate hadn't been thrilled about taking dresses off the rack but she had her hands more than full with Annabelle's dress.

And the way the two women argued about every little nip and tuck, you'd think they hated each other.

"Sure. I'll come. You want to meet in the restaurant?"

"No, let's go out. I'm in the mood to be bad. Crepes at the Terminal Market?"

"Wow. You must be having a bad day."

"Not bad, just . . . nerves, I guess. I need to get some air." Kate sighed loud enough to be heard over the phone. "Dress warm. I want to walk. See you in ten."

Since she was already dressed in jeans and a sweater, Sabrina didn't have to do anything more than grab her coat and purse. She wasn't scheduled to work until seven tonight. She was taking a half shift until eleven for Darryl, whose son had a music recital at school.

She hadn't heard from Greg since late Thursday, when he'd texted her to let her know he was staying at his parents' house for the night and wouldn't be able to see her but he'd text her Friday.

She'd texted him back. No problem. I understand.

And she had. Honestly. She loved her family.

Friday morning, he'd told her he was going to be busy all day but he'd be back at the hotel late Friday.

No problem. I understand.

Only, he hadn't been back last night. And he hadn't texted.

Frankly, she wondered if she was ever going to see him again. Yes, she'd known he wasn't going to have much time the closer he got to the start of filming. But she'd hoped . . .

What exactly had she hoped for?

Maybe she didn't want to look at that question too closely.

Taking the elevator to the lobby, she waved at Danica behind the desk—and stopped cold when she realized who Casey was smiling at farther down.

Greg.

He had his back to her but she could clearly see Casey beaming at him. Almost as if he were flirting with her.

No, no, no. Don't even go there.

Still, she couldn't contain the pain jabbing at her gut like a knife.

Turning on her heel, she headed for the front door. She'd wait for Annabelle and Kate outside. The fresh air would do her good.

And maybe help her stomach stop churning.

She walked through the door, gave a smile and a wave to Charlie, the white-haired grandfather who manned the door most days, then headed for the front of the building, which had been built far enough from the street to allow for a tiny courtyard.

A row of boxwoods hid the area from the street but still allowed a view of the hotel's front door. Two ornate marble benches formed an "L" in one corner of the courtyard. A small bronze fountain sat in another. And a little garden bloomed all year long in the last corner. In the summer, it held bright flowers. Now it was filled with tiny evergreen trees waiting for their Christmas decorations.

She was just about to sit when she realized someone was behind her.

"Sabrina. Wait."

Greg.

She took a second to suck in a breath and put on a smile. Then she turned.

She couldn't hold the smile because the look he gave her practically burned through her skin.

Swallowing, she managed a quiet "Hi" before she lowered herself onto the marble. The cold from the stone seeped through her jeans but she didn't get up. She needed that shock to keep from throwing herself at him.

"Hey." He stopped in front of her, standing with his hands on his hips. "Are you going somewhere?"

"Lunch with Kate and Annabelle." She actually thought about offering to cancel if he wanted to spend time with her but swallowed the words before they escaped. She didn't want to sound pathetic and chances were he didn't have the time. Which he confirmed in seconds.

"Wish I could ask you to bag them and have lunch with me but I've got another meeting in half an hour."

"No problem. I understand."

He grimaced and she realized she'd said exactly that the couple of times he'd texted her about his schedule. "Yeah. I guess I deserve that."

"I'm sorry," she said. "I didn't mean . . . That wasn't a—"

Seconds later, she found herself sitting on his lap, his thighs warm and hard beneath hers, her mouth covered by his lips. Sinking fast toward combustion. Whenever they kissed, combustion wasn't far behind.

Greg launched a full-out erotic assault on her mouth, heat and hunger radiating off him. She wanted to shove her hands beneath his battered leather bomber jacket and rip his shirt out of his slacks so she could put her hands on his bare flesh.

Instead, she grabbed the front of his jacket and held on.

Too soon, he pulled back, breathing hard enough that she saw little white puffs in the air between them.

"Damn, I've fucking missed you."

She shook her head, her lips curving at his raw words and her heart skipping a beat at the force behind them. "Hi to you, too. And it's been less than two days since you saw me."

His husky laugh made her tingle between her legs, where she'd been aching since the last time she'd seen him, and his eyes peered into hers with that intensity she'd come to crave. No one had ever looked at her like he did, like he wanted to see *into* her.

"You are just hell on my ego. Here I've been, wanting to get you back in my bed since the moment you walked out my door Thursday morning. Sorry about Thursday night. I had an emergency to deal with and I was late getting to my parents' house so I stayed the night to spend a little time with them Friday morning. Then yesterday . . ." He shook his head. "Did you have a good time with your brothers and sisters?"

She nodded, her smile wistful. "Yeah, I did. But is it wrong to say I was kind of glad I had to work Thursday night? I forgot how *loud* all those kids can be in one house."

Laughing, he pressed a kiss to her neck. "I totally understand. I love my sister's kids but they're a hell of a lot of work."

"How old are they?"

He paused, a thoughtful expression crossing his face. "Eight, six, and four. I think. Damn, I'm a shitty uncle. I'm not honestly sure how old they are."

"I'm sure they love you."

"Yeah, they love me. Especially when I bring them videogames that won't be on the market for months. So, you work tonight?"

"Yes. Until eleven."

He pressed another kiss to her neck, this one longer. And then she felt his teeth graze her skin. The shiver that went through her body had nothing to do with the air temperature.

"Then be at my door by 11:02. I think I may have actually cleared a little time in my schedule to sleep. And other things that require a bed."

This time, he kissed her on the mouth, his arms tightening around her.

Unable to worry about anyone from the hotel seeing them because, at this minute, she didn't really care, she wriggled on his lap, earning a smack on the ass that energized all of her nerve endings.

"Keep that for tonight. Right now I've got to deal with a depressed canine and a pissed-off fire marshal. Then I've got a read-through with Neal and Daisy and a meeting with the crew."

"So what you really want to do tonight is sleep."

He leaned closer, rubbing his nose against hers in an affectionate way that made her melt inside. "After I get inside you. I thought I said that. *Shit.*" His coat vibrated beneath her hands and she realized his phone was ringing.

With a rough sigh, he kissed her again. "Gotta go, babe. See you tonight."

Seconds later, he was gone.

And she was sitting on the marble bench again, the cold seeping through her jeans. While her internal temperature continued to hover right below boiling.

She blinked and caught sight of him grabbing for the front door and holding it open for Kate and Annabelle to walk through. They stopped for a second, Greg giving Annabelle's shoulder a squeeze as he bent to kiss Kate on the cheek. Then he nodded in Sabrina's direction before continuing into the hotel as Kate and Annabelle made a beeline for her.

Kate's raised eyebrows and Annabelle's smile made her want to groan.

Standing, she walked to meet the other women, who flanked her as soon as she got close to them. Each took an arm and they started walking in the direction of the Reading Terminal Market.

"So." Kate gave her a wicked smile. "I guess we have something more than Annabelle's dress to discuss."

* *

Trudeau met him just inside the door, tablet in hand, stylus tapping away.

"I have several forms you need to sign, two phone calls you need to return, a budget to approve, and I sent the emails you need to handle personally to your private account. And you've got to decide on a composer because I need to get started on those contracts."

Falling into step beside him as he headed for the elevator, his assistant barely came up to his shoulder. This morning, she wore blue pants, a white blouse, and had her hair pulled back in a high ponytail that bounced in a perfect curl.

"I've managed to put off most of the local press for the moment," she continued as they crossed the lobby, "but they're not going to leave you alone for much longer. We've got requests for interviews from every TV station, cable access show, daily local, weekly tabloid, regional magazine, and merchandiser in a three-hundred-mile radius. By the way, what is a merchandiser?"

The elevator doors opened seconds after he punched the button and he stepped aside to let the older couple inside exit.

He'd been listening with half an ear to Trudeau, knowing she wouldn't let him forget anything. The rest of his brain was back with Sabrina.

Stepping into the elevator, he leaned against the back wall, willing away the stiffness in his cock and the clench in his jaw.

He shouldn't have followed her out of the hotel but, like a fucking teenager, he'd let his cock dictate his actions. Now he was going to pay for it the rest of the fucking day.

He was going to be beyond busy for the next thirty days. He'd barely have time to eat and catch a few hours of sleep.

He needed all of his concentration on his film, but thoughts of her managed to sneak into his head every few minutes. Through no fault of hers, she was fucking with his head.

That was going to be a major problem if he couldn't keep a lid on it. A problem he'd never encountered before. Which just pissed him off.

Maybe if he fucked her at least once a day, he could keep his focus where it had to be. On the film.

As the elevator began to rise, Trudeau went silent.

"Greg? Are you okay? Do you need something?"

Turning, Greg realized she looked worried. "Like what?"

Trudeau shrugged, the action so uncommon, his attention focused more fully on her. "I'm not sure. You seem distracted. It's a bit . . . alarming."

He laughed, a short bark she'd surprised out of him. "Alarming, huh? I thought nothing could rattle you."

Her lips pursed in a way his mother would be proud of. "I work hard at cultivating that image. Keeps the jackals at bay."

"And by jackals you mean . . ."

"Anyone who wants something. And they all want something, don't they?"

His eyebrows raised. "Well, damn. So jaded already. Something happen I didn't get a memo on?"

She shrugged, her gaze never wavering. "Nothing you need to concern yourself about."

And that's what he paid her for. To make sure the little shit didn't get to him. He'd never stopped to think how much of a toll it might be taking on Trudeau.

Hollywood assistants burned out faster than social workers. Trudeau had been with him for almost three years. She'd never asked for a raise, although he gave her one annually. And her workload had increased exponentially the second he'd decided to direct this film. He'd already told her she was getting an associate producer credit and she deserved it.

"Is it a guy?"

She didn't even blink. "When would I have time for a relationship?"

Good question. Hell, he didn't have time for one and it pissed him off that he couldn't spend the time with Sabrina he wanted.

"So it is a guy."

"Do you really want to know or are you looking for an opening to talk about the woman you're seeing?"

He shouldn't be surprised. Trudeau probably knew him better than anyone except Tyler and his sister.

As the elevator slid to a stop and the doors opened on Daisy's floor, he put a hand on the elevator to stop the doors from closing but stayed inside the cage. "What do you already know?"

Trudeau's expression didn't change. "Only that you followed a woman out of the hotel this morning. And you've been more stressed than normal and I've never really seen you like this so I made an educated guess. I'm not digging for dirt. I only need to know enough to be prepared for any fallout when the press gets wind of it."

"I don't want the press getting wind of it."

"So what do you need me to do? Are you going to need a decoy?"

Greg started to laugh. "I like you, Truly. If you ever decide to use your powers for evil, I'm going to make sure I'm not on your bad side.

A smile twitched at the corners of her mouth. "Who says I don't?"

It was always the quiet ones you had to watch out for, wasn't it?

"I'll talk to Sabrina and let you know what I'll need. Now," he said with a sigh, "let's go figure out how to deal with our Neal-Daisy dilemma."

* *

"So." Kate drew the word out to at least five syllables. "Greg talked to Tyler on Wednesday morning."

Kate had been remarkably not-pushy as the three of them walked to the market. Kate and Annabelle had discussed the dress while the cold air allowed Sabrina to regain most of her senses.

Then they'd gotten their crepes and managed to find a small table near the back of the overflowing seating area. But now Sabrina's reprieve had come to an end.

Trying not to blush five shades of red, she nodded, deliberately cutting her crepe into bite-size pieces.

Maybe if she ate it slowly, her body wouldn't immediately add five pounds to her hips. She'd managed to keep her weight steady since she'd started working at Haven, but that wouldn't last long if she kept taking Dominique the pastry chef's advice to try her dessert every night. Or made too many trips to the market for crepes.

Of course, the stress of dealing with this relationship might burn some calories.

"Hellooo, Sabrina. I said—"

"I heard you. You're not exactly subtle, you know."

"I wasn't going for subtle," Kate said. "I was attempting nonchalant."

"Well, you missed that by about a mile." She sighed as Kate continued to stare at her with raised brows. "He told me he was going to."

Kate and Annabelle exchanged a glance.

"And . . . ?" they said in unison.

Sabrina put down her fork. "And you already know what he told Tyler, so why are you giving me the third degree?"

Kate's eyes widened as if she'd attacked her, and Sabrina wanted to take the words back right away. "Sorry. I'm sorry. I didn't mean that to come out so . . . mean."

Annabelle smacked Kate on the shoulder. "You're not being mean. Kate's being Kate. What she *meant* to say is, we're here if you want to talk. About anything."

Kate huffed. "Or specifically about Greg." She stared at her, gaze boring into hers with laser-like intensity. "I've noticed the past few days you've seemed kind of on edge. Did he do something?"

Sabrina's fork paused on its way to her mouth. "What do you mean?"

"Did he say something to hurt you?"

She frowned. "No. Why would you think that?"

Kate rolled her eyes. "Please. He's a guy. So he gave you a key to the fourth floor and his room. Have you stayed with him?"

Sabrina deliberately took a bite of her crepe and chewed. Slowly.

Kate rolled her eyes and groaned. "Come on, Sabrina. I know you want to talk. No one can hear us over the noise. Are you *sure* you don't have anything you want to talk about?"

Sabrina had an entire army of nosy minions at home. She knew how to deal with one beloved friend. "You want to talk, let's talk.

You first. There's something going on that I don't know about, so spill it."

Kate couldn't quite conceal the flash of something in her eyes that looked a lot like guilt.

Again, Sabrina wondered exactly what sort of relationship she and Tyler had with Greg.

And then Kate and Annabelle exchanged the look. The one that meant they were telepathically communicating. Or at least reading each other's minds.

"Oh, now that's just not fair." Sabrina barely managed not to throw her fork at them. "Spill it. You two want to know what's going on in my life but you're allowed to keep secrets? So not fair."

Annabelle grimaced. "You're absolutely right. It's not fair and I'm sorry."

Kate and Annabelle exchanged another look, apparently coming to some conclusion. Then both stared straight at her.

"We're breaching about five different legal contracts here so you have to swear that what we talk about here stays here. And when I have you sign a contract later that says basically the same thing, you need to sign it."

Sabrina started to laugh at what sounded like the plot to a film but Kate looked totally sincere. Her laughter cut off and her smile turned into a frown.

"Seriously? That sounds ominous."

Annabelle smiled and reached for her hand to squeeze it. "Just agree."

Sabrina pulled a face. "Okay, fine, I promise I won't say a word and I promise to sign whatever you want. Now spit it out."

"Has he shown you the Salon yet?" Kate asked.

She shook her head. "No. And there would have been no time because I haven't seen him since Thursday morning."

"Really?" Kate looked shocked. "I thought— Oh, hell, never mind. I thought . . . Shit."

She and Annabelle glanced at each other again.

"You thought there was something more going on than there is."

Obviously she didn't hide the hurt in her voice well enough because Annabelle shook her head. "Oh, there's definitely something going on. You can't help but notice how much he wants you when he looks at you. I'm sure he's just busy right now."

"He is. I get it. The guy's a world-famous producer directing his first feature in years. What was I thinking? Of course he's not going to have time for me."

"Yeah, the timing really does suck, doesn't it?" Kate shook her head. "But that doesn't mean you should give up."

"Who said I'm giving up? But it's not like we're planning to spend the rest of our lives together. We're just having some fun."

Kate paused then her smile returned. "Well, I am glad to hear that. So, what's your plan?"

"Plan? Why do I need a plan?"

"Please." Kate rolled her eyes. "You don't do anything without a five-point plan."

That arrow hit the mark and Sabrina wrinkled her nose. "You make me sound like I'm an evil genius plotting world domination. Greg and I are just—"

"Just what?"

She wished she knew. "Having a good time while it lasts?"

Kate narrowed her gaze. "And that's it?"

"Well, it's not like we're going to fall in love and live happily ever after."

Even as she said the words, she felt a little pang in her chest. Which was stupid. Seriously stupid to even say the words out loud.

"So you're just in it for the sex." Annabelle looked like she totally understood. And approved. "Good choice."

Sabrina shoved another two bites of crepe in her mouth. Well, she didn't have to be *that* agreeable.

"Hmm, I guess Annabelle's right." Kate started to dig into her crepe. "Greg is pretty much married to his company. He doesn't really have time to care about anything else."

"He's much too intense and too focused on business. So, what do you think about ivory for my dress instead of white? Or maybe pink. I wasn't so sure about the ivory at first but, as much as I hate to admit it, I think Kate's right. The ivory looks better against my skin."

Sabrina's fork stopped midway to her mouth before she forced it to continue, shoving it in her mouth and starting to chew, barely tasting the Nutella, strawberry, and banana crepe she usually loved.

"I think ivory will look amazing."

Annabelle and Kate exchanged a glance then both turned their full attention back to her.

"Alright." Kate stabbed her fork into her crepe and let it stand there. "Who are you and what have you done with the real Sabrina? The one who would never let a guy treat her like nothing more than a fuck buddy."

Wincing at the volume of Kate's voice, even though no one would be able to hear their conversation above the noise from the rest of the market, Sabrina's heart started to pound. "I don't know what you're talking about. Greg and I both know the relationship isn't going anywhere. We're having fun. I like him. He seems to like me. When he's finished with his film, he'll go back to Hollywood and I'll be here. Doing the dream job I've been lucky enough to fall into."

Kate's gaze narrowed. "So this is about your job? You think

Tyler's going to have a problem with you seeing Greg? Seriously, the only problem he's going to have is with Greg if he hurts you. Tyler thinks of you as a friend, not just an employee."

"And that's a huge potential problem. Don't you see? Greg's his best friend. I don't want to be a wrench in their relationship. And I love my job. I don't want to lose it."

Kate looked shocked. "You think Tyler would fire you because of Greg?"

Sabrina immediately shook her head. "No, no. I know he wouldn't do that. But . . . what if I can't stand to see him. What if—"

"You fall in love and you're forced to see him whenever he comes to the hotel to see Tyler." Annabelle's tone was kind, sympathetic. "Yeah, that would suck."

"So then don't let it come to that." Kate's voice held a strong note of determination.

It was Sabrina's turn to give Kate the lifted eyebrows. "It will."

"Why are you so ready to talk yourself down?" Kate stabbed at her crepe again. "You're not giving yourself enough credit. The man's been half in love with you since that night he took the pictures for my portfolio."

Sabrina refused to blush. "No, he's in lust."

Kate rolled her eyes. "If it was just lust, he wouldn't be telling Tyler not to give you a hassle about him."

"Why would Tyler do that?"

Kate gave her a nod. "He wouldn't. So that demonstrates Greg's totally unusual response to you."

Little sparks of hope that she tried to crush continued to flare. "But it's still not going to develop into anything. In a few months, he'll be back in Hollywood and I'll be here and there'll be three thousand miles between us."

And she'd be left with a broken heart.

Isn't that what you wanted? For him to break your heart so you could move on with your life?

"Sometimes things work out." Kate's determination showed in the set of her chin and the gleam in her eyes.

"Sure, sometimes."

She dug up a smile that tried to be sincere but probably just looked pathetic. Things had worked out great for Kate and Tyler. Even though Kate had turned down her dream job in New York, she was going to open her own boutique at the retreat and she'd found a man who loved her with an intensity that was palpable when they were in the same room.

Even Annabelle's messy, tragic life had gotten a happy ending. She'd recently revealed she was the daughter of a famous painter and his wife, who, along with their lover, had been murdered by a psycho, and she had subsequently seen her private life splashed over the tabloid pages.

Jesus, the things those rags said about her, the lies they printed about her family were horrendous. Annabelle had done a couple of interviews with a very few select magazines, the ones that had allowed her to talk about her parents' artistic passions more than their bedroom habits. Jared had already set his legal team on several magazines that had dared to print some of the most objectionable stories.

Annabelle had handled most of it with grace, although there'd been quite a few bottles of wine downed while she cursed a few so-called journalists.

Sabrina cringed to think what the supermarket tabloids would make of her.

White trash. Money-grubbing—

"Hey." Kate drew Sabrina out of her head, which wasn't a very nice place at the moment. "I'm really sorry. I didn't mean to badger you. Honestly. We're just worried. I saw the way Greg looked at you this morning—like he wanted to devour you."

"And can you imagine what will happen if anyone else sees him look at me like that? He's got enough on his mind without me freaking out about paparazzi taking pictures of us."

"So you're worried what other people will think about you and him?" Kate asked.

"Shouldn't I be? I don't know that I want my life splashed all over a tabloid. Annabelle, you have to know how I feel."

Annabelle's expression looked pained. "I do."

"So that's your excuse to hide your affair?" Kate's tone was drenched in disbelief. "Because the paparazzi might take a few pictures?"

She wondered what her friends would think if they knew about the photos Greg had already taken of her. But those were private.

"It's not only that. I just don't want my life to be . . . lived in the media. I'm fine if we spend most of our time in his suite. Besides, now that the film's ready to start shooting, that time's going to be cut to nil. I just feel like it's the beginning of the end. And there wasn't that much of a middle to begin with so maybe it's better that things just kind of fade away, because there's no future."

There. She'd said it out loud, exactly what she'd been thinking. Sure, she could dream, but when she examined all the pieces rationally, she knew they'd never fit together into a whole.

Annabelle shook her head. "Sabrina, you're way too jaded for your age."

"You're just way too jaded, period." Kate huffed. "Is that seriously what you want? For this affair to fade into the woodwork like it never happened?"

No. Absolutely not.

She looked at Kate and watched the other woman start to smile.

"You're damn right you don't." Kate knocked on the table with her fist to punctuate her words, making the already wobbly table tremble in fear. "Now what the hell are you going to do about it?"

Sabrina had the childish impulse to stick her tongue out at Kate. So she did, which just made Kate laugh.

"Honestly, I don't know what the hell I can do about it."

Kate stopped laughing and her expression got serious as she leaned across the table. "Alright, listen up. I'm going to tell you a secret Tyler told me about Greg when we first met. Show him genuine affection. He doesn't expect it from anyone. Give him a little piece of yourself and he'll be your slave."

If only it were that easy. "What if I give him everything and he makes me *his* slave and then he leaves?"

Kate's gaze narrowed. "Then you've got to make him see that his life is better with you in it."

"And again I say, my life is here. My family. I don't want to give up everything and move across the country."

"A relationship should be fifty-fifty." Annabelle glanced at Kate before giving Sabrina a little smile. "Who says he won't do some of the bending?"

"Because he's Greg freaking Hicks. He doesn't have to bend. And why should he? It's not like the guy has declared his everlasting love. Hell, I'm not even sure I could live with him. He's bossy and demanding and . . ."

"Sexy?" Annabelle grinned.

"Freaking hot?" Kate added.

Sabrina threw up her hands. "Yes, yes. He's all that and great in bed. Okay, happy? I admit it. The man is a sex god."

"And he's yours," Annabelle said.

For now, at least. Sabrina didn't say that out loud, however, because she knew Annabelle and Kate wouldn't let it go. And she really didn't want to talk about it anymore. So she smiled. "Yeah. So Annabelle, pink for your dress? That could be really pretty."

Eight

"Hey, Sabrina, right? Can you point me in the direction of the music room? Golden said I could use it while I'm here."

Sabrina had filled in Laney and was about to make her escape to her room when George Duggan, aka Sebastian Valenti, caught her before she left the desk Saturday night.

Since Laney had just picked up the phone, Sabrina smiled and nodded. "Of course. Let me get a key."

Sebastian flipped his hand up with a keycard clutched in his fingers. "That I've got. I just forgot how to get there."

"Not a problem." She started toward the atrium. "Follow me."

"That will *not* be a problem."

Though he'd said the words under his breath, Sabrina heard them clearly.

Was Sebastian checking out her ass?

Glancing over her shoulder, she caught the guy grinning at her. And wow. When he smiled, she understood exactly why women threw their panties at him during concerts.

She'd had time tonight during her shift, so she'd looked him up. Beneath the long-sleeved T-shirt he wore, he had a full sleeve of tattoos on his left arm, an intricate design she could just see peeking out from beneath the wristband of his shirt. On his right arm, he had a beautifully detailed Celtic cross. Across his back, he had the word "Surrender" in gothic script. And on his chest and torso, he had several other artistic designs.

If she hadn't searched him on Google, she never would've guessed the tattoos. Sure, his hair was a little long but he looked . . . normal. Like the boy next door. Especially compared to his band-mates.

One had a blue Mohawk. Another's head was shaved completely and, combined with his bulging muscles and piercings, made him look like someone she'd cross the street to avoid on a dark night. The other had straight black hair that reached his shoulders and several facial piercings that made her wince just to think about.

Not sure whether she should be offended or pleased by his attention, she raised one eyebrow at him to let him know she'd caught his remark.

And heard him laugh as he fell into step beside her.

"Wow, you've got that look down solid. And if you're wondering, yeah, I like the view. But don't worry, if I make a move, you'll see me coming."

Nonplussed, she slid him another look. "Are you always this straightforward, Mr. Valenti?"

He winced. "Hey, please. Call me Sebastian. Or Baz. Mr. Valenti is my dad. And trust me, I'm nothing like my dad."

Pushing through the doors into the shadow-shrouded atrium, Sabrina felt the humidity brush against her skin as she waved Sebastian through.

"The music room is straight through here."

She started to walk then paused when she realized Sebastian wasn't behind her. He'd stopped just inside the door and she saw his head turning to look around.

"Holy shit, this is pretty cool."

She smiled at the complete surprise in his voice. Obviously, Sebastian hadn't been in here yet. As a matter of fact, she couldn't remember seeing him around the hotel at all the past few days. Then again, she'd only been interested in seeing one man. And she hadn't had much success there.

"It is, isn't it? They'll be installing the Christmas decorations overnight tomorrow. I can't wait to see that."

"So you haven't been working here that long?"

Hands in his pockets, Sebastian continued toward her but at a snail's pace, his interest seemingly consumed with the atrium.

"Only since the summer."

"Good gig?"

"I enjoy it, yes."

"Good. Work sucks when you hate it."

The bitter note in his voice made her take a closer look at him. "And do you hate your work?"

He sighed then continued walking, his expression closing. "No. I don't. So . . . the music room?"

She blinked at his sudden mood change then plastered on her most pleasant smile. "Of course. Right this way."

They walked the rest of the way in silence, Sebastian keeping his distance. When they reached the practically hidden door on the other side of the large space, she stepped aside and pointed to the slot for the keycard.

"Just let Laney at the desk know if you need anything. I'm sure—"

"So, yeah." He shoved his hands in his pockets and rocked back on his heels. "I could use a fresh pair of ears on this piece I'm working on. I know it's late and you're probably tired but . . . do you have a few minutes?"

Did she?

Sebastian stared at her, almost as if daring her to stay with him. But beneath that, he looked . . . lonely.

She didn't know this man at all. But what was she going to do? Go back to her room and wait for Greg to text? What if he didn't?

She wasn't at all tired. She didn't want to be alone and Sebastian looked like he could use the company, too.

"Sure. I have some time."

* *

"I'm so sorry, Greg. I know this could totally fuck up your filming schedule but I didn't know what else to do and I was afraid . . ."

Greg wrapped an arm around Daisy's shoulders and pulled her against him. "Not a problem. I'm glad you called. We'll figure something out."

That's what he did, wasn't it? He figured things out.

When Daisy had called three hours ago, he'd almost let it go to voicemail. He'd been in the middle of a meeting with the crew but Trudeau had warned him that, even though Neal and Daisy had appeared to make up, there was still trouble in paradise.

Since Neal had arrived, Greg had spent as much time as he could with the couple. What he'd seen had made his jaw tense until he wasn't sure it would unlock.

Neither one of them was admitting to a problem. And that in itself was a problem because when those two didn't talk, whatever was happening was beyond bad.

Daisy's call had confirmed that.

Neal had finally cracked.

In fucking public. At a fucking popular restaurant. On one of the busiest fucking days of the year.

Of fucking course.

With the help of Michael, Neal's assistant-nurse-bodyguard-fixer, Daisy had been able to get Neal out of the restaurant and into the limo before the other restaurant patrons had figured out what was going on and who was involved. However, she was pretty sure the few paparazzi hanging around outside the restaurant had gotten some pictures.

Daisy had called Greg in tears from the limo. He'd been able to hear Neal in the background alternately crying and raging as Daisy had the limo driver bring them back to the hotel.

With Tyler's help, Greg had gotten them into the service elevator and back to their apartment without anyone seeing them.

Neal had been almost incoherent by the time Greg and Michael had dumped him in a bed in the second bedroom.

Michael had stayed with Neal while he sat Daisy in a chair in the living area and started the hard part. "Do you know what he took?"

She shook her head, tears still dripping down her face. "Nothing that I know of. Honestly. We had a few drinks with dinner. He just seemed so depressed. He was talking about his mom and dad and then he started to talk about how he's not good enough for me and . . ."

Greg listened with a sinking feeling in his gut as Daisy told him everything else Neal had said. It sounded like the guy was dealing with severe depression, and the alcohol really hadn't helped.

And if he'd taken anything besides alcohol, he'd have to go back into rehab.

Fucking hell.

"Greg, I'm so sorry."

Daisy had stopped talking and he hadn't noticed, he'd been so damn stuck in his own head. Now he took a closer look at his ex and saw a woman who'd reached the end of her rope.

"How long has it been this bad?"

She didn't answer right away, and he knew she was trying to rein in her crying jag. "About three months. But I noticed the changes starting six months ago."

Right after they'd agreed to do the film. Fuck. Just . . . fuck.

Had he pushed Neal too hard too fast? Maybe—

"Greg, stop it." Daisy reached for him, cupping her hand around his jaw. "I know what you're thinking. I can't even read your expression but I know. This isn't your fault. It's Neal's. And mine. I should have told you . . ."

"What?" He forced a smile. "What should you have told me? That he was acting erratic? That's just Neal. We've seen him do this before. Hell, we've seen him pull himself out of worse spirals. Let's just wait 'til he sleeps it off then we'll see what's up."

Daisy continued to stare at him, her eyes going a liquid blue. He knew that look. Knew how it used to make him feel.

She used to look at him like that and he'd throw her on the nearest flat surface and fuck her brains out.

Right now, all it made him feel was how much he missed Sabrina. He couldn't comfort Daisy, not like that. Because the only woman he wanted right now was the one who was probably cursing his name because he'd broken their plans for tonight.

Goddamn, his gut burned.

With a wry twist of his lips, he removed Daisy's hand from his cheek, pressed a kiss to the back, then stood. "Try to get some sleep, babe. Call me when you get up in the morning or before, if there's anything Michael can't handle on his own."

Daisy actually managed a weak laugh as she looked up at him.

"Always the gentleman. You get some sleep, too. You don't look like you've been getting enough."

"I'll sleep when I'm done filming."

"No, you won't. They'll be another project after this film. There always is. Just don't burn yourself out, Greg. Are you at least getting laid?"

He grinned at her bald question, secretly relieved she still had somewhat of a sense of humor. He'd been worried that Neal's darkness would dim her normally vibrant personality.

"None of your damn business."

"I'll take that as a no. Greg—"

"Actually, you'd be wrong."

Her eyebrows lifted in unfeigned surprise. "Wow, you've been able to keep that under the radar."

"And I plan to continue, so you're not getting any more out of me."

"Obviously she's not in the business."

He rose, knowing if he didn't leave now, she'd have the entire story out of him. And that wouldn't be fair to Sabrina. "I'm going back to my room. Call me if you need anything."

He left before she could say anything else.

In the hall, he gave himself ten seconds to lean against the wall and take a few deep breaths to stave off the sensation of falling.

He'd bang his head against the wall as well, but he knew from experience it wouldn't help.

He also knew he could get through this. He just needed a decent night's sleep. Tomorrow morning, he'd have a plan.

Too bad what he really wanted to do involved a bed but not much sleep.

In the elevator, Greg swiped his card and sighed as the doors closed.

He had every intention of heading back to his suite, taking a shower, and getting some sleep. Only one problem. He wasn't tired. Okay, two problems. He wanted Sabrina so badly, his entire body ached with need.

What he should do is go back to his room, take a hot shower, get some food, have a drink, and go the fuck to bed. It'd been a long day and he needed to sleep.

But Sabrina had texted him earlier today that she'd be working until eleven and would he like to get together. That had been three hours ago. He hadn't been able to text her back since he'd been dealing with Neal and Daisy.

He wanted to text her now but he didn't want to wake her if she was already asleep.

Shit.

With a deep sigh, he caught a glimpse of himself in the elevator doors. They reflected back the image of a man who looked like he didn't belong here. The worn jeans, chamois shirt, and too-long hair clashed with the refined elegance of Tyler's hotel.

He needed a shave, which he'd do tomorrow morning. He also needed a haircut, but that wasn't going to happen anytime soon. Besides, he liked having Sabrina's fingers in it and she seemed to like it just the way it was.

Pulling his phone from his pocket, he checked the time. Nearly one a.m. Her shift had ended two hours ago.

Just text her. If she answers, great. If she doesn't, she's asleep and she'll get the text in the morning and know I'm thinking about her.

He hesitated so long the elevator opened on the fourth floor before he'd typed anything.

Shit.

With the door standing open, he typed in three words.

Hey, you up?

Then he punched the button for the lobby. If he didn't hear from her, he'd have some food and a drink at the bar. He needed time to unwind. Then he'd hit the sack. He could function perfectly well on four hours of sleep. He just hoped Sunday lived up to its reputation as a day of rest.

Yeah, right. He needed to have another sit down with Neal. Just the two of them, without Daisy to fuck up their focus. He needed to know if Neal was in any shape to film or if he had to rearrange the shooting schedule.

His phone vibrated and he grabbed it before it stopped, only to find a text from Trudeau.

Extra camera on the way. Will talk to fire marshal tomorrow. Have given all guards updated photos of your family. They won't get delayed at checkpoint again. Will have editing computer set up by tomorrow afternoon. Will make sure Dale gets what he needs. Another boom mic already ordered. Will be at set by 6. Get some sleep. Long day tomorrow.

Shaking his head as he smiled, he stopped by the door to the atrium to text her back.

What the hell are you still doing up? Go to bed. And don't bother to be on set before 10. I've got to deal with Neal so I won't be there until at least 11.

He hoped.

I've got things I need to do so I'll be there by 6.

The girl was getting to be as bad a workaholic as he was.

And why the hell hadn't Sabrina texted him back?

Goddamn it, he wanted her to be awake. Now he felt cranky as shit.

His gaze flicked toward the desk, knowing she wasn't going to be there.

And he was right. The brunette behind the desk was taller,

slimmer, and older. He seemed to remember her name was Laney. As she caught sight of him, she smiled but it faltered in seconds. Probably because he looked like he wanted to tear someone's head off.

Taking a deep breath, he forced back the frustration and nodded to acknowledge her. Then headed for the bar. He'd scheduled two days of rehearsals for Sunday and Monday before filming started Tuesday. His crew had arrived, most of the equipment was accounted for, and the set was dressed. He'd already scouted the outdoor locations and knew they were ready to go.

Jesus, he hoped Neal wasn't going to take down the entire production. The rest of his principal cast had arrived today and he'd managed to greet each one before the shit with Neal had gone down. He'd worked with nearly all of them before and he considered them friends as well as colleagues.

He'd almost reached the bar when he realized alcohol and his mood probably weren't a good mix. Maybe he should think about a workout instead—

His phone vibrated and he whipped it out of his pocket.

Yes. I'm in the music room behind the atrium. Come join us.

He grinned, feeling like he'd won a bidding war at Sundance. Then two thoughts crossed his mind.

Where the hell was the music room?

And who was "us"?

Turning, he headed for the desk.

Laney gave him another bright smile, as perky as if it was nine in the morning. "Hello, Mr. Hicks. What can I do for you tonight?"

"I'm looking for the music room."

"Of course. Just follow the path through the atrium. Past the fountain on the far side, the path will split. Take the right branch and that will take you straight to the music room. You'll need your key to open the door."

After a short thank you, he headed for the atrium, pushing through into Tyler's playground.

Where Jared had sunk so much of his creative energy into the Salon, Tyler had channeled his into the atrium.

But Greg barely gave the indoor garden a second look tonight as he followed the directions. It didn't take him long to find the door and, when he did, he realized Tyler had carefully concealed it.

He heard nothing coming from inside but, knowing Tyler, the room was probably completely soundproofed.

Slipping his card in the slot, he cracked the door then paused as piano music spilled out.

Whoever was at the keys had a gift. Was it Tyler? That would make sense.

Pushing the door open until he could see into the room, he found the baby grand right away.

But that wasn't Tyler.

The man hunched over the piano had his back to the door, completely oblivious to Greg's arrival. As was Sabrina, who stood at the side of the piano, her attention focused solely on the player.

Greg wanted to close the distance between them, grab her, and head back to his room. But he knew he'd be acting like a caveman and he didn't want to embarrass her.

There were so many other things he wanted to do to this girl, whose ass looked amazing in a prim blue skirt that fell just above her knees.

She had her hair in a braid tonight and it lay against the back of her white blouse like a gold rope twisted with pale bronze.

The door closed behind him without a sound as he stepped into the room, but Sabrina turned. And the smile that lit up her face made him feel like he could roar.

A second later, the music stopped as the player took his hands off the keys and turned.

Sebastian Valenti stared at him with the look of a guy who wasn't happy to have the competition.

Tough shit. Sabrina was Greg's. The sooner Sebastian realized that, the sooner he wouldn't wind up with a fist in his face.

"Greg." She looked like she wanted to say more but wasn't sure what. "Hi. I'd like you to meet Sebastian Valenti."

"Sabrina." He didn't bother to hide the heat in his eyes. He was staking a claim and, while she might not realize what he was doing, Sebastian would.

The younger man's eyes narrowed as Greg nodded at him then held out his hand as he came closer.

"Sebastian. Nice to meet you. I'm Greg Hicks."

Sebastian stood, taking Greg's hand and meeting his gaze. "The producer?"

"Yeah, though right now I'm wearing my director's hat."

Sebastian's eyes widened and his expression lightened. "Seriously? You're making another film? Is it a sequel to *The Virgin and the Terror*? Man, I wore out that DVD when I was a teenager. Loved that film."

Greg smiled, some of his immediate animosity leaking away. "Thanks but no, sorry. Not a sequel."

"Too bad." Sebastian sat back at the piano. "That film was epic."

"And I never get tired of hearing people say that, so I appreciate it. But not everyone thinks that way." Greg pointedly looked at Sabrina, who shook her head, her smile turning rueful.

"I never said I didn't like it. I think it's really, um, creative. It just isn't . . . my style."

Sebastian and Greg both laughed.

"And if that isn't damned by faint praise," Greg said, "I don't know what is."

As Sabrina smiled up at him, Greg felt his shoulders unkink, along with the muscles in his back and his arms.

He wanted to put his arm around her shoulders, draw her into his side, and kiss her. And he didn't want to have to worry about who saw them.

But he didn't know Sebastian other than by reputation. And that was of a hard-partying rock star. Greg also knew reputations weren't always true.

Still, he didn't want to make Sabrina uncomfortable, so he stood next to her at the piano, leaving a couple of inches between them.

"Gotta say, I'm a fan of your music, Sebastian. The last album was amazing."

Sebastian nodded but his smile fled. "Thanks. I think it was our best yet."

"How many albums has your group released?" Sabrina asked, her genuine interest showing through.

"Five. One independent and four through our label."

"Are you working on music for the next one?"

Sabrina's innocent-sounding question had a scowl forming on Sebastian's face.

"Yeah. Maybe. Not sure yet. The band's kind of on hiatus. Don't know for how long."

Now that was interesting. Greg didn't follow much of the music industry but he read enough music blogs to keep up with the bands he liked. And he liked Baseline Sins.

"Caught your show at Club Nokia last year," he said. "Great set."

"Thanks. That was a good night."

It'd also been the last show before his meltdown in Europe.

"So what are you working on now?"

Sebastian released a barely audible sigh and settled his fingers back on the keys. No discordant crash but a collection of notes that sounded melancholy.

"Nothing. I'm not sure." He shook his head. "Might not turn out to be anything."

"Do you do all your composing on the piano?"

Sebastian's fingers began to move over the keys and the classical melody piqued Greg's attention.

"Not usually. But I'm classically trained. Ten years of lessons before I got my first guitar. My parents expected me to go to Juilliard or Berklee." In a flash, the music became an assault and Greg was pretty sure he recognized the opening notes of one of Baseline Sins' biggest hits. "Instead I formed a garage band with a couple of guys who hung around the skate park and drank Wild Turkey until they puked. Needless to say, the parents weren't thrilled."

Yeah, Greg could see where that might've been a problem for middle-class parents who'd produced a musical prodigy.

"Do they go to your concerts?" Sabrina asked quietly.

"Yeah, they do now."

Sebastian flashed Sabrina a grin and Greg had to consciously loosen the fist he had formed.

Greg let Sabrina and Sebastian carry the conversation for the next few minutes, talking about nothing more serious than the strange Pennsylvania weather.

And all the while, Sebastian continued to play. The guy had a gift, no doubt about it. Piano, guitar . . . didn't matter. Greg knew Sebastian wrote most of the band's music. Singer-guitarist Max Brody handled the lyrics. Together they'd created some of the best heavy rock to come out of the scene in years.

Their almost-instant fame had come with the expected back-lash, but it hadn't been enough to keep them from headlining gigs all over the world. The weight of that could still be seen in the dark circles under Sebastian's eyes.

Maybe he and the kid had more in common than their mutual attraction to a certain smiling female leaning against the piano. Did she realize when she did that, her shirt gaped open and he could stare at the perfect mounds of her breasts?

Probably not.

Then again . . .

She flashed him a smile, as if she'd felt his attention. That smile made lust burn through his veins like acid.

Time's up, babe.

Reaching for her, he did what he'd wanted to do the second he saw her. He put his arm around her waist and drew her into his side.

Her startled glance quickly turned heated.

And it was definitely time to go. Because if they didn't leave now, he might end up showing Sebastian exactly how much he liked her. And while he didn't have a problem with a little public display of affection in the right situation, Sabrina probably wouldn't want him to bend her over the piano and fuck her while Sebastian played.

Hell, the guy could watch if he wanted, but he couldn't touch. Sabrina was his and he didn't want to share her.

The logic was totally fucked. He knew it. He'd had no problem sharing other women in his life. Daisy. Kate. There'd never been anyone else in his life who he'd had such a visceral repulsion to sharing.

Sabrina was his.

Yeah, but for how long?

He wasn't even going to think about the answer to that question, because he might find the answer had changed in the past day.

Pulling his hands from the keys, Sebastian's narrowed gaze took in the situation in a heartbeat.

Beside him, Greg felt Sabrina still, caught the blush that painted her cheeks. He also noticed she didn't pull away.

"Thank you for playing for me, Sebastian. It was beautiful." Sabrina's voice held a husky note that made his cock twitch. "But I think it's time for me to go up. It's been a long day."

Sebastian nodded slowly. "Thanks for listening."

"If you're going to be here for a while, maybe we can talk a little more about your music and what some other options might be," Greg added. "But for now I'm gonna say goodnight."

After Sebastian's intrigued, "Sure," he turned with his arm still around Sabrina's waist. They walked out together but, about halfway through the atrium, Sabrina stopped. "I think you should head out first. That way Laney won't suspect—"

He bent and kissed her with all the pent-up passion currently making him feel like he was hooked up to an electrical current.

Cupping her face in his palms, he angled her head to one side so he could get a better angle, licking at the seam of her mouth until she opened for him.

So fucking sweet.

Her taste flooded his system like a hit of his favorite drug, pure heroin or the best damn scotch. So very, *very* addictive.

As he devoured her mouth, her hands gripped his hips, fingers sliding beneath the waistband of his jeans and shirt to stroke his bare skin. Lightning arrowed to his groin and his cock hardened with a rush of blood that should've made him lightheaded, it was so fast.

He wanted to shove up her skirt, hold her against a wall, and pound into her.

Slow down.

Fuck that. He wanted to go faster.

Tearing his mouth away from hers, he looked around the atrium, searching—

She moved her hands to the front of his pants and let the tips of her fingers brush against the head of his cock.

"Fuck, Sabrina." Dropping his head, he laid his cheek against her hair, trying to suck in enough air to breathe.

"Yes. Please."

Jesus Christ, she was going to kill him. Or he was going to die of a passion-induced heart attack as she slid one hand into his jeans and wrapped it around his cock.

With a growl, he wrapped an arm around her waist and took her off her feet. She had to let go of him but he knew it wouldn't be long before he had something much better wrapped around his erection.

"Where are we going?" She whispered the words directly into his ear then bit his earlobe. "You can't take me into the lobby like this."

He shuddered but continued to walk because, holy fuck, that felt good.

"Not going to. Hold on."

His voice sounded strangled and he nearly faltered when she began to press open-mouth kisses along his jaw and down his throat.

Just a few more feet.

He stepped behind the piece of modern art that looked like nothing more than a long, wavy strip of highly polished steel. During the day, it reflected the colors of the garden. At night, it emitted a low-level glow. Just enough for him to see her but not enough for anyone who might wander into the atrium to see them. Not that he expected anyone to come in here this late. And Sebastian was still in the music room.

Anticipation honed his desire to a fine edge and, when he finally had her where he wanted her, he dropped all restraints and let lust take him.

Except, it didn't feel like lust. It felt like craving and need and some other deeper emotion that had him slowing their kisses, trying to ease the frantic race.

But Bree didn't want slow. And apparently, she wasn't going to balk at their surroundings.

As soon as he set her on her feet, her hands went to his waistband. She worked the button free then released the zipper, easing the pressure on his cock but making him groan when she wrapped her fingers around his shaft through his boxers.

As she explored him through the barrier of cotton, she tilted her face up to his, staring at him through her lashes.

Taking the hint, he caught her chin between his thumb and forefinger and held her steady for his descending mouth. He couldn't seem to get enough of her taste. It made him feel slightly wasted.

He liked it. A lot.

Her lips moved under his as she continued to stroke his cock. Sliding his tongue into her mouth, he licked at hers, wanting to devour her.

She let him but she didn't surrender. No, she came at him from another angle. She slowly stripped his defenses as she worked his jeans and boxers down his hips until she'd exposed his cock. Then she wrapped her warm fingers around him and squeezed.

It was a testament to his will that he didn't come right then but,

Christ, he wanted to. His balls tightened in warning but he clamped one hand around the base and squeezed until he'd staved it off.

Bree didn't let up on him. She continued to stroke him with short, hard tugs and longer, more languid pulls and twists.

As his knees started to go weak, he turned until he had his back braced against the wall. Then he started his own campaign.

He plucked open the buttons on her shirt until it gaped in a vee, baring her bra. The lace and satin matched the color of her skin, and the design lifted her breasts into mounds that quivered with every breath.

He cupped the underside of her breasts, lifting the mounds higher, then bent to rub his cheeks against them.

Bree sucked in an audible breath as his whiskers abraded her delicate skin. His thumbs moved to rub her nipples, which had tightened into hard points.

Her hands stilled as he pressed kisses to her flesh, stringing them from one breast to the other before he made his way to a nipple poking through the lace. He licked at it, wetting the fabric. Then he bit it, grinning when he heard her moan and felt her hands tighten around his cock again.

"Keep stroking me, baby. I like your hands on my cock."

She shuddered but didn't obey right away. So he moved to the other nipple and bit her again.

"Greg."

Sucking her nipple into his mouth, he laved the tip with his tongue before releasing her.

"Come on, Bree. Make me even harder."

Her fingers tightened convulsively around his erection and he bit back a groan at the slight hint of pain laced through the pleasure.

"That's right. Tighter."

Goddamn, she knew exactly what he wanted, and she gave it to him.

She slid one hand between his legs, cupping his balls and rolling them in her hand, while her other stroked his cock from root to tip.

His head fell back against the wall, hard enough to send a shaft of pain through his temples. It only managed to make him more aware of her.

His hands fell to her hips as she worked him, his fingers tugging up her skirt in tiny increments. Each inch of thigh he bared made his heart pound a little harder until he could hear his pulse beat in his ears.

"I'm going to fuck you right here unless you say no."

He felt he owed it to her to give her the choice but he really hoped she didn't balk. He didn't want to wait. And he wanted her to get a little wicked with him.

Her head cocked to the side and her mouth twitched into a smile.

"Well, you better do it soon because I'm so horny, I may take care of myself."

His hands clenched around her skirt as fierce victory arrowed through him. "No need, babe."

With her skirt hooked on her hips, he used his hands to shove down her underwear. With a twist of her hips, Bree made them fall to her ankles then stepped out of them.

"Hands on my shoulders. Now."

He didn't wait for her to comply. He sealed her mouth with his and reached for her hips. She gave him one last squeeze before she released him and put her hands on his shoulders.

When he leaned back, she looked up at him and smiled. "You need to hurry."

"Be careful what you wish for."

"Why should I? I'll never get anything good if I don't wish for—"

She sucked in a gasp as he lifted her against him, her legs automatically wrapping around his waist.

Her mound brushed against his cock and she tilted her hips into him.

Biting back a groan, he bent to whisper in her ear. "Condom? I've got one in—"

"Just do me, Greg. I'm on the Pill. I trust you."

And he trusted her. Grabbing the rope of her braid, he pulled her head back so he could kiss her and shifted just enough to—

Yes.

He slid inside her with one thrust, letting her slide down as far as she could, enclosing him in wet, hot heaven.

He groaned. "God, yes. I could stay inside you all night and not care if I ever got any sleep."

With a slow roll of his hips he sank even deeper, loving the way her pussy clenched around him and her legs clasped around his hips.

Her arms tightened around his shoulders, her hands splayed across his back, fingers digging into his skin through his shirt.

"Move, Greg. Please. I need—"

She didn't need to tell him twice. Settling her weight more fully in his hands, he began to move her up and down his cock, hitting sensitive spots on their bodies he'd never known existed.

At this rate, he wasn't going to last more than a few minutes. Every breath she released brushed against his neck, stroking him deep inside.

Increasing the pace, he braced his back more steadily against the wall and fucked her like he wanted.

Clinging to him, she let him. Have her. Control her.

Fuck, he liked that. Liked that she gave herself over to him.

His cock swelled, throbbed, his climax building in his balls. Listening to her breathing, he tried to tell if she was close.

The low moans she made brought his inner caveman a little closer to the surface. Making sure he had a good grip on her with one arm, he used his other hand to grab her braid and tug her head back.

"Look here, babe. Open your eyes."

It took a second but, on his next thrust, she did what he'd asked. She opened her eyes.

So dark. So sexy.

"Ah hell, honey, next time I'm setting up a camera by the bed."

"Only if you're going to be in the shots, too."

His cock pulsed a warning. He was close, too damn close.

Shifting her just a bit, he changed the angle of penetration . . . and watched her suck in a breath as her eyes fluttered closed.

Yes.

"Oh, my God. Greg, do that again."

"Gladly. I want to watch you come."

Her head fell back as she tilted her hips forward. Now she worked with him, moved with him as they chased the ultimate pleasure.

Her gasping breaths sounded insanely loud in the quiet atrium but he didn't give a shit if anyone heard them now. All he cared about was making her come.

He thrust harder, higher, shifted her closer.

"Come on, sweetheart. Damn, you're so fucking tight. I fucking love it."

She moaned, biting her lips as she clenched around him, her thighs tightening on his hips.

Then she came with a muffled cry, shoving her face into the crook of his neck and biting him. Hard.

Which made him come in an explosive rush that nearly buckled his knees.

They stood there for at least a minute as they caught their breath.

And Greg tried to find his center of gravity. For a few minutes there, he thought he'd lost it.

Finally she shifted, straightening her legs until he took the hint and let her stand.

Grabbing her underwear off the floor, she pulled them on as he tucked his cock back into his jeans and zipped up.

After she'd pulled her skirt down and fiddled with it, she finally looked up at him again.

"Nice to see you, too," she said.

The glint in her eye and the smile on her face made him laugh.

"How about we see a little more of each other? Come back to my room. Stay the night. Rehearsals start tomorrow so my free time is about to become nonexistent. But that doesn't mean I don't want to see you. It just means we have to be a little flexible."

Her eyes rounded in mock surprise. "And I wasn't flexible enough for you for the last fifteen minutes?"

He reached over to stroke a finger down her cheek. "Oh, honey, let me show you just how much more flexible you can be."

She continued to grin up at him and he bent to steal another kiss.

"Okay." She finally responded. "You go out first. I'll follow in a few minutes."

His gaze narrowed. "So we're gonna continue to be stealthy about this?"

Her teeth fastened onto her bottom lip for a second and her

expression got serious. "I'd prefer to, if you don't mind. I'm just not sure I'm ready to tell the world we're . . ."

"Screwing around?"

Her eyebrows raised, probably because of the edge in this tone. "Are you telling me there's more to this than just screwing around?"

Hell, yes. "Yeah, that's what I'm telling you. I want to spend as much time with you as I can. Right now, the only time I have is at night. If that means we spend most of our time together in bed, I'm okay with that. The question is, are you?"

She paused. "Yes. I am. But I'd still like to keep our . . . involvement quiet, at least for now."

"I can agree to that."

A slight smile curved her lips. "You're used to getting your way all the time, aren't you?"

It was his turn to give her wide eyes. "Why would anyone want to deny me anything?"

With a laugh, she put a hand on his back and gave him a little push toward the door. "I don't have any idea. I'll see you in a few minutes. I want to go to my room and change first."

He bent and put his mouth right at her ear. "If you're not at my door in ten minutes, I'm gonna come looking, babe. And I'm not gonna be subtle."

Shaking her head, she gave him a harder shove this time though he didn't move. "Don't push your luck, big guy. I said I'll be there."

"And I'm holding you to it. Ten minutes." He leaned over and bit her earlobe. "And then I'm gonna make you wonder why you just don't give in and move into my suite."

Nine

"No, I'm sorry, that's just not going to happen. If you call this number again, I will call the police."

Sabrina couldn't help but overhear the one-sided conversation Saturday night.

Even though Daisy Devlin had moved to an out-of-the-way alcove away from the lobby and was keeping her voice to a whisper, the alcove was just behind the registration desk, so Sabrina had a front-row seat to the drama.

And apparently it was gearing up to be a knock-down, drag-out fight.

Though she tried to keep a respectful distance, the hotel was close to capacity and, even though it was close to ten at night, clusters of people kept coming through the lobby. Most were on their way to and from the atrium, where the Goldens were hosting a holiday cocktail party for local small-business owners.

Sabrina and Teresa had been oohing and ahhing over the

dresses, ranking the men on a one-to-ten hotness scale, and having a decent night.

Which was more than Sabrina could say for Daisy.

"I don't care what you write, you son of a bitch. But if you so much as mention me or my husband by name, you can bet your *ass* it'll be slapped with a libel lawsuit the next day. Trust me. You'll be strung out to dry so fast, the only writing gig you'll ever get will be reporting on the opening of a grocery store in Bumfuck, Iowa."

Ouch. Sabrina almost felt sorry for the person on the other end of that call. Then again, he probably deserved whatever Daisy was dishing out. According to Greg, the press had heard about Neal's meltdown at a local restaurant a couple of weeks ago and had been hounding the couple ever since.

In the few minutes over the past few weeks that they'd managed to spend alone—when they weren't having sex, of course—Greg had given her a crash course in film industry politics and publicity. Most of it made her head spin. The deliberate leaks of careful information to the press by the publicity department. The "anonymous" calls to trusted photographers about "secret" appearances by the actors.

Everything he'd said made her more convinced than ever that she'd made the right choice to ask Greg to keep their relationship secret. No way did she want to be subjected to the hell Daisy Devlin was apparently going through.

Some people said she brought it on herself by choosing to be an actress and pursuing fame. Casey and Danica totally believed that once you made the choice to become a public figure, your life became fair game for every sleazeball looking to make a buck off someone else's misery.

Sabrina believed everyone deserved a private life. But if you didn't work hard to keep it private, then you were just asking for trouble.

Still, she couldn't help but feel sorry for Daisy. It wasn't her fault her husband had problems and was dragging her down with him. Sure, Daisy could always leave him. But Sabrina actually respected the woman more for sticking by her man.

"I have no comment except to say Greg, Neal, and I have known each other for years. We have a working relationship and a personal relationship." A pause. "I care about Greg a great deal. He's been a part of my life for a decade. My husband and I are thrilled to be working with him again."

Damn. Sabrina really didn't want to hear this. She should walk away before she heard something she really didn't want to know.

"I have no comment about any relationship with Amanda Patton. And that's the last thing I'm going to say. I have no comment on any other questions you might have."

Silence from the alcove, then an audible sigh.

Though she hadn't been eavesdropping on purpose, Sabrina felt guilty as Daisy emerged from the alcove. Hair shoved in a baseball cap and wearing no makeup, she had her head down as she dug through the huge purse hanging from one slim shoulder.

When Daisy sniffled, Sabrina reached for the box of tissues beneath the desk and set it on the top.

"Can I help you with anything?"

Daisy's head popped up and Sabrina saw her red-rimmed eyes and the fierce set of her mouth. And knew she should've kept her mouth shut.

"No, you can't," Daisy snapped. "And next time, I'd appreciate if you wouldn't blatantly eavesdrop on a private conversation. That'll get you fired."

Sabrina felt her entire body flash hot then cold as Daisy stormed away to the elevators, but not before sending Sabrina a death glare.

"Well, damn. That woman always seems so sweet. Guess I really shouldn't be surprised to find out she's a royal bitch." Teresa bumped shoulders with Sabrina, who felt rooted to the floor. "Hey, don't worry about her, hon. She's obviously upset, and not at you."

"I wasn't eavesdropping."

Teresa waved off her statement. "I know that. Hell, she could have gone in the bathroom if she wanted privacy. Or at least waited until she was in her room to deal with whatever she was dealing with. Seriously, you didn't do anything wrong."

But the incident wouldn't leave her alone.

Had she deliberately been listening to Daisy's conversation? The question bugged her for the rest of her shift.

She knew she wouldn't be seeing Greg tonight. He had a night shoot and she wouldn't see him until tomorrow. Maybe. If he had time.

She hadn't seen him since Wednesday and when she thought about that night, she couldn't breathe. Not because she was embarrassed but because she burned with arousal.

Anyone could have walked into the atrium that night, could have caught them. And that only made the thrill that much better.

What the hell was happening to her?

Well, she knew the answer to that question, didn't she?

Greg Hicks, that's what. He made her crave things she'd never considered doing and . . .

He was shooting scenes with Amanda all night.

She knew that not because he'd told her but because she'd seen it on *Entertainment Tonight*. The TV had been on in the employee lounge when she'd taken her dinner break. It would've all been background noise if she hadn't heard Greg's name. And the veiled innuendo in the announcer's voice when he mentioned Greg and Amanda in the same sentence made her stomach roll.

The scene with Daisy brought back that feeling that stayed with her until midnight when she finally left the desk. The reception in the atrium had broken up minutes ago, the last guests shaking hands with Jared, Annabelle, Tyler, and Kate.

Her friends looked gorgeous in their fancy dresses, both of them smiling, shaking hands, and looking the parts of wealthy socialites with nothing to worry about but their manicures—

Okay, wow. Just . . . wow.

That had been incredibly bitchy and unspeakably mean-spirited. And about her best friends.

Jesus, she needed to get a grip.

"So you look like you need a drink, and since I *really* need a drink and I don't want to drink alone, you're coming with me."

Sabrina's smile was already forming as she turned from the elevator to face Sebastian.

"Hi there. Haven't seen you for a while. Have you been working?"

He nodded. "Nonstop. Or at least it feels like it. Thought I'd take the night off, maybe hit the bar for a drink."

"The hotel bar?"

A frown crossed his expression before it cleared. "Nah. Let's take this show on the road. Do you have someplace in mind?"

She smiled. "Actually, yeah, I do. Let me go up and change and I'll meet you back here in ten minutes."

The bell dinged for the elevator as Sebastian tapped his watch-free wrist.

"I'll give you fifteen. There's no way you can be back in ten minutes. It'll take you that long to figure out what to wear."

Laughing, she stepped into the elevator. "If I'm back in ten, you're buying the first round."

"If you're back in ten, I'll play you my new music. I'm buying tonight anyway."

Eight minutes later, she found Sebastian standing by the front door, talking to Jimmy, one of the overnight security guards. A year older than her, Jimmy and his older brother, Rob, switched off nights on the door.

Nice guys. Handsome guys, too, with their dark Italian hair and eyes. But they weren't Greg.

"Dude, Metallica's still got it but Korn has lost their credibility. All that electronic crap. Makes me wanna slit my wrists. Now, Volbeat . . . love 'em." Jimmy's head turned and he smiled. "Hey, Sabrina, you heading out with his guy? Make sure he takes you somewhere decent."

"I thought we'd go to South Street and hit JC Dobbs."

Sebastian smiled. "Wow, I haven't been there in years. Baseline Sins played one of our first gigs there. When do you get off, Jimmy? Wanna join us?"

"Seriously? I'd love to." Jimmy looked between her and Sebastian. "Unless . . . I'd be a third wheel."

Sebastian shook his head before she could disabuse Jimmy of the notion. "Nah, man. It's not like that. We're just going out for a drink."

Jimmy grinned at both of them. "Then, hell yeah. I'll be there in half an hour."

An hour later, Sabrina was halfway into her second Long Island Iced Tea and Jimmy and Sebastian had finished off their first pitcher of lager and had circled back to discussing music. She and Jimmy's boyfriend, Brian, had been having a hell of a time watching the women eye Sebastian like a side of beef and the guys fall over themselves to shake his hand.

The manager had told them drinks were on the house and he'd given them a table along the wall that was as secluded as possible. The stream of fanboys and girls with barely covered breasts had finally slowed and Sabrina had started to unwind.

"You look like you're finally having a good time."

Sebastian leaned in but actually had to lower his voice so it wouldn't carry. This close to closing, the music had been turned down to a more manageable level. She'd never been a fan of hard rock for the simple fact that people apparently thought it only sounded really good if it was turned up to eleven.

"I am. Thanks for asking me to come with you. I didn't want to spend another night in my room."

"Waiting for him to call, huh?"

She met Sebastian's gaze head on. "He's busy. We picked a really bad time to . . . do whatever it is we're doing."

"But you're still waiting for him."

She forced a smile. "Well, not tonight, obviously. I haven't looked at my phone since we left the hotel. And here I am, listening to really awful music with you."

Sebastian laughed. "Hey, Jimmy. I don't think Sabrina appreciates the sheer awesomeness of Anthrax. Maybe we should request a little Pantera."

As the guys laughed and talked about bands she'd never heard of, she felt that knot in her shoulders loosen even more.

By the time they left an hour later, Sabrina had a buzz and a smile as she and Sebastian waved good-bye to Jimmy and Brian, then folded themselves into a taxi for the ride back to the hotel.

"Now you're smiling." Sebastian touched a finger to her cheek. "Glad to finally see it."

She let her smile widen, grabbing his hand and lacing their fingers together. She had the fleeting thought that she was crossing a line but, other than the first night they'd met, Sebastian had treated her like a friend.

"Guess I needed a night out."

"You've been working a lot of hours and not doing much of anything else. That'll fry you faster than a microwave. Hicks giving you problems?"

Sighing, Sabrina shook her head. "We haven't seen each other enough to have problems. I've spent more time with you in the past two weeks than I have with him."

Which was totally true. It had started with that first night in the music room. Since then, Sebastian had asked her to join him there a couple nights a week. He'd said it was because he wanted someone who didn't know his music to give him an honest opinion but, in the past several nights, it'd become more about two friends talking. With Annabelle and Kate so wrapped up in their men's lives and careers of their own, Sabrina had started to feel like a fifth wheel.

She knew it wasn't a conscious decision on their parts. It was just the way things worked. It still sucked but it forced her to widen her circle of friends.

She'd never expected her new best friend to be male. Or a rock god. Of course, with her, Sebastian didn't play the part of the hard-partying, trash-talking womanizer he appeared to be on the Internet.

He was just Sebastian, who made her laugh with his stupid-ass jokes and made her feel comfortable enough to tell him anything. Yes, the guy was totally hot but she didn't want to climb all over him like she wanted to do to Greg whenever she saw him. Which hadn't been a lot lately.

"I hate to go to bat for the guy but I heard he's having some trouble with a couple of his actors. It's tough to have all that money and expectation riding on your shoulders."

She squeezed his hand before releasing it. And, if he didn't release her immediately, well, she chose to ignore that.

"I know." She shrugged. "And I know it's stupid to be jealous when I knew going in that this . . . whatever it is we're doing was going to burn out soon enough. Sure, it's been fun but maybe it's time to tell him so long and move on?"

She realized as soon as she'd stopped talking that she wanted Sebastian to tell her what to do. Wanted him to tell her she was right, that she should cut and run.

Sebastian just looked at her with raised eyebrows.

So she stuck out her tongue. "You suck, you know that, right?"

He huffed out a wry laugh. "Hey, babe, I'm not gonna tell you what you should do. If it was me, I woulda been long gone. But then I've been told I'm a real prick by most of the women I've dated. Usually as I'm walking out the door. Guess it comes down to how you feel about him."

Good question. How *did* she feel about Greg?

She thought about that in silence the rest of the way to the hotel. She still hadn't come up with an answer when the taxi came to a stop.

Sebastian reached for her hand to help her out and, when her ankle turned just enough to throw her off balance as she stepped out of the car, he put his arm around her shoulder to steady her.

She let him hold her against his side for a few seconds and rested her head on his shoulder.

"You know someone could get ideas here."

His low growl held a hint of humor, and she turned her head to smile up at him. That's when she noticed the look in his eyes didn't match his tone.

Stepping to the side, she shook her head. "Then I'm sorry—"

Sebastian sighed and rolled his eyes dramatically. "Yeah, yeah. I know. Tell me again how you really don't know how you feel about Hicks."

Scowling at him, she smacked him on the shoulder. "Not fair, Valenti."

"Life's not fair. Blah, blah, blah. Sing me another ballad. Oh, wait. Please don't. I've heard you sing."

She was still laughing when they walked into the lobby—until she saw Greg and stopped cold.

He stood in the shadows near the now-darkened atrium with his back to the door. She had no idea how she'd known it was him, considering she couldn't see his face. Then she realized she'd be able to pick him out of a dark room blindfolded.

Her entire body seemed to know he was there, like he sent out a frequency she picked up subconsciously.

He, however, didn't seem to have the same problem.

He and a woman Sabrina didn't immediately recognize were having an intense conversation. Her gaze shifted to the glass walls of the atrium, where she could see his reflection. See the intensity she'd only ever seen him display with her in bed. That he was showing it now with another woman made all the air leave her lungs in a rush.

The tiny blonde looked like a fairy princess—all big tits, wide eyes, shiny white teeth, and bright smile. Amanda Patton, she realized. That's who stared up at Greg like he was a god and she was his willing sacrifice. Or she was an actress and he was her director.

She stumbled and Sebastian reached for her shoulder. "Whoa. Didn't think you had that much to drink. You're a lightweight."

Forcing a smile, she tore her gaze away from Greg to look at Sebastian. "I think it's time for me to go up. Thanks for taking me out tonight . . ."

Sebastian had started to frown as she'd spoken and his head shot up. She knew exactly when he saw Greg and Amanda. His eyes narrowed and his mouth flattened into a tight line.

And all she wanted to do was retreat to her room. When the hell had her life become such a damn drama?

"Baz, I really just want to go to bed."

"Right. You do that. I'm gonna hit the music room for a little while."

He looked pissed and she knew that was because she felt threatened. Which was stupid. She knew the woman was an actress. She was too adorable not to be. And Greg was making a movie. She was being stupid.

"Thank you." She leaned in and brushed a kiss on his cheek. "I had a good time tonight. I needed to get out."

"Yeah, me too." He refocused his attention on her with a smile she recognized from a couple of his videos. Total smart-ass.

She took a step back before he could do something crazy to piss off Greg. Who didn't even seem to notice she was there.

She was well aware that Laney was watching from behind the desk. The other receptionist had asked her earlier tonight if there was anything going on between her and Sebastian, and Sabrina had honestly answered no, they were just friends.

She enjoyed his company but the man she wanted more than she wanted to breathe was currently engrossed in what looked to be an intimate conversation with another woman.

Get a grip. Go upstairs and if he calls, you don't have to answer. Better yet, turn off your phone.

Because she knew she'd never be able to say no to him.

* *

Out of the corner of his eye, Greg saw Sebastian stalk by, probably on his way to the music room.

Still listening to Amanda babble on about her inspiration for her character, he caught the musician's eye and nodded at him. Sebastian glared back and kept moving.

What the fuck?

"Greg? Are you sure you wouldn't like to come up to my room and talk in private?"

No, he didn't want to go to Amanda's room. He'd texted Sabrina about a half hour ago to see if she was up but he hadn't heard back from her. She was the only woman whose room he wanted to be in tonight.

He hadn't seen her since Wednesday, and tonight he'd realized why he'd been biting off everyone's head if they so much as looked at him.

He missed Sabrina. Plain and simple. He wanted to see her tonight and then maybe tomorrow he wouldn't want to kill anyone.

"No, but you go up. I've got to track someone down."

Amanda pouted . . . gorgeously, of course. There wasn't anything Amanda did that wasn't gorgeous. Act, sing, dance. Broadway loved her and he'd courted the hell out of her to get her to take this role. It was her first film and she was killing it. But she'd taken a distinct liking to him, and apparently what Amanda wanted, Amanda was used to getting.

He was having a hard time getting her to understand that he wasn't going to take her to bed. He was obviously out of practice handling actors.

"Okay, fine. I'll see you tomorrow." Sighing, she leaned in then dragged a finger across his chest and smiled up at him. "Sweet dreams."

He gave her a nod in return but managed not to pat her on the back like a child and steer her in the direction of the elevators.

Having his actors at the same hotel was proving to be a pain in the ass. But Daisy and Neal needed the space from everyone else and New York City–native Amanda had taken one look at the woods surrounding the farmhouse where she was supposed to be staying and freaked.

The rest of the cast and crew had bonded over their separation, and Greg almost wished he'd planned to stay at the farmhouse himself.

But then he wouldn't get to track down a certain hotel employee.

He fucking *missed* seeing her, especially at night. He'd give up sleeping until this film was completed if he could spend a few hours with Sabrina.

But he hadn't even had a few minutes to spend with her. And yes, it was way too late to text her again.

So maybe he'd just go to her room and knock on her door. Quite frankly, he didn't give a shit if anyone saw him. Let them talk.

But . . . that wasn't what Sabrina wanted.

So he'd go find out what the hell was up Sebastian's ass.

He'd been able to spend a little time alone with the musician, listening to some of the guy's new music and what he'd heard convinced him Sebastian was the perfect choice to score this film.

Trudeau had been hounding his ass to choose a composer. He couldn't wait to see her face when he told her who he'd picked. Trudeau and Sabrina had pretty much the same taste musically and, even though he'd tried to expand her musical horizons, Trudeau rolled her eyes at him and changed the subject.

Without waiting to see if Amanda went upstairs, he headed through the atrium to the music room.

He didn't bother to knock. Sebastian would know it was him.

A wall of sound assaulted him as he opened the door.

Okay, wow. The guy was definitely pissed off.

Shutting the door behind him, Greg leaned against it as Sebastian pounded the keys.

When Sebastian finally took his hands off the keys several minutes later, Greg heard him suck in a deep breath then release it on a sigh.

"Bad night?"

Sebastian didn't answer Greg's question immediately. He seemed to need to catch his breath. Or maybe control his temper.

When he finally swung his legs over the bench to face Greg, it didn't take a rocket scientist to realize Sebastian was pissed at him. And yeah, Greg knew what had set Sebastian off. He'd seen the way Sebastian looked at Sabrina. But there was no fucking way Sebastian was going to have her.

That didn't mean he didn't like Sebastian. He did. A lot.

"Wanna talk about it?"

Sebastian crossed his arms over his chest as he leaned back against the piano. "I'm not sure you want to talk to me right now. You're not gonna like what I have to say."

"Jesus, Baz, did I forget your birthday? What the hell's going on?"

"Who's the hot blonde piece you were talking to in the lobby?"

Greg's gaze narrowed. "Amanda. She's one of my actors. Why—"

"Are you fucking her?"

Greg felt like Sebastian had taken a swing at him. "Why the fuck would that be any business of yours and hell no. And—shit!"

Sebastian jumped off the bench and took a swing at him. A wild roundhouse that glanced off his jaw. An inch higher and he would've done some damage. Reacting out of instinct, Greg jabbed out with his right and popped Sebastian in the nose. He managed to rein in the strength of his punch just before he hit the guy. He smelled the alcohol coming off Sebastian and knew it had to be messing with his judgment.

As Sebastian stumbled back, cursing and holding his nose, Greg shook out his right hand and rubbed at his jaw with the left.

"Alright, *now* do you want to tell me what the fuck that was all about?"

"Damn, what's your jaw made of?" Sebastian cradled his hand against his chest and scowled at him. "Granite? And yeah, I'll tell you as soon as my nose stops bleeding."

Looking around, Greg saw a box of tissues on a table in the corner. He snagged the box then threw it at Sebastian. "Now spill it."

"You don't deserve her."

Greg stilled, watching Sebastian stuff tissues up his nose like a champ. Obviously he'd done it a few times before. "Are you gonna tell me what that means exactly or are you just going to—"

"You're treating her like some piece of ass you're gonna toss aside when you're done, and that makes you a prick."

Greg felt anger burn like lava in his gut but he wasn't going to give in to it. "You don't have any idea what you're talking about so you better—"

"She saw you in the lobby. With the blonde who was all over you."

Shit. Just . . . shit. He hadn't seen her. And obviously, she'd been out with Sebastian. "Amanda wasn't all over me and I certainly wasn't coming on to her. And I don't know why the *fuck* I have to explain anything to you."

"Because I *like* her, you prick. And for some dumbass reason, she's hung up on *you*."

Jealousy rose up like bile, and Greg had the urge to take another shot at Sebastian's nose.

"So you two were out tonight." He didn't make it a question.

Sebastian smirked at him, though the effect was muted by the tissues hanging from his nose. "Yeah, we were. But don't go getting all pissy, especially not at her. She was sick of waiting for you to call and she's been working extra shifts because the hotel's fucking busy. She needed a little down time. So yeah, we went to a bar, had a few drinks and, when we got back here, she saw you huddled up with the flavor of the month."

Crossing his arms over his chest, Greg took a deep breath. It was late. He was tired. And this conversation was only going to get worse.

And so was his guilt level. The words "I've been busy" were on the tip of his tongue, but he knew them for the excuse they were.

Not that it wasn't true. But that didn't mean he shouldn't have made more of an effort. Should've texted or called or—

"Shit. I need a drink. And I don't want to drink alone. Come on, Baz."

The younger man looked at him with wary surprise. "Where are we going?"

"My room. I've got the liquor. You're gonna be the sounding board."

* *

Sabrina woke Sunday morning with a throbbing headache.

Correction. It was a hangover and it was Sunday afternoon, close to one, according to the clock on the bedside table.

With a sigh, she reached for her water bottle next to the clock and drank half of it before she took another breath. Then she waited for it to hit her stomach. And for her stomach to accept it.

When it did, she drank the rest and reached for her phone. She had five texts.

One from her mom, telling her to call when she had a few moments. One from Kate, inviting her to lunch Monday. Two from Sebastian, asking her how she was feeling and did she want to get dinner tonight.

The last was from Greg.

Call me when you're awake.

That last one made her heart kick into a higher gear.

And she wanted to kick herself for it.

Damn him. He didn't contact her for several days and, when he did, her first instinct was to jump to do his bidding.

"Bastard."

No, that wasn't fair. She'd known what she was getting into when she'd agreed to see him. She'd known he wasn't going to have much time for her.

So if you don't want to continue with whatever it is you're doing, tell him.

The problem was, she didn't know what she wanted.

And that was bullshit.

She wanted Greg.

Then you've got to be willing to put up with the rest of the shit, don't you?

How much was she willing to bend?

She grabbed her phone then debated what to text for at least a minute. *Such a dweeb.*

Hi. I'm awake.

Then she put it aside and headed for the shower, figuring he was probably sleeping.

Emerging from the bathroom after a twenty-minute shower, the pounding in her head had eased and all the muscles in her body had relaxed.

She'd just reached for underwear when her phone signaled a text.

I've got a few hours free. Let me take you out for brunch.

Did he mean *out* out? In public?

Was he going to break up with her and wanted to do it somewhere publically so she wouldn't make a scene?

Which was totally stupid because why would he bother to expose their . . . whatever this was . . . when he could continue on the way they were going and never see her again?

Did he actually want to take her out? Like on a date?

Longing made her suck in a deep breath. And right on its heels was trepidation.

Was he asking her for more than a date?

And if he is?

If she asked to make him breakfast in his suite, he'd agree. But if he'd wanted to stay in, he'd have said that. He'd specifically asked to take her out.

OK. Just got out of the shower. How about half an hour?

His answer was almost immediate.

Oh, yeah? Pix?

She laughed and shook her head, charmed in spite of the fact that she knew he wanted her to take a picture of herself naked and send it to him.

The thought didn't shock her as it might have before.

Still grinning, she took her phone into the bathroom and snapped a picture . . . of the wet shower walls.

Another almost-instantaneous response.

Tease. You'll pay for that.

She broke out in goose bumps at the thought of what he might do to make her "pay." She knew a few things she wanted to do to him.

Not what you wanted?

You know it's not but I'm patient. Come down when you're ready.

Half an hour later, she knocked on his door, trying not to grin like a fool. It seemed like it'd been weeks since she'd seen him. She wanted him to kiss her the second he saw her. She didn't care if they went out to eat. In fact, she'd prefer if they didn't. Of course, there was no way she was going to tell him that.

The door opened seconds later, and she knew she was about to get half of her wish.

"Hey."

He looked stressed, his mouth pursed like he was gritting his teeth, his hair a mess.

"What's wrong?"

"Nothing I can explain right now. Daisy's inside, crying her eyes out on my bed. Sebastian's sleeping off the liquor from last night in the other room. Trudeau will be here in a few minutes to take care of Daisy, but I have to go talk to Neal before I can leave."

"We can resched—"

"No." As if he knew she was about to take a step back and away from him, he grabbed her hand. "I don't want to reschedule." He tugged her closer. "Come in and as soon as Trudeau gets here and I make sure Neal isn't going to do something stupid, we can go. I fucking *miss* you."

He'd stolen her breath with those last four words, with the force of the emotion behind them. She froze and his eyes narrowed as he started to pull away. Which is *so* not what she wanted. Tightening her hand around his, she got him to stop.

"I want to go out with you. I just don't want to get in your way. I understand this is a busy time for you and—"

"And I know that's no excuse for treating you like a toy, which someone accused me of last night." He stared intently into her eyes. "That's not how I think of you."

Smiling, she nodded and watched his expression lighten just a little. "I'm glad to hear it. But the next time I see Sebastian, I'm going to smack him."

She didn't need someone else fighting her battles. Especially not one as personal as this. Besides, she still didn't know exactly where the battle lines were being drawn. Or even if there was a battle to be fought.

"He's got a hard head." Greg smiled now and tugged on her hand. "Come in. Sit down. I'll be back in five minutes and we'll leave. Sebastian's still asleep and Daisy's probably passed out by now. They won't know you're here."

Taking a deep breath, she nodded and followed him inside.

The second he had the door closed, he had her back pressed against the door and his mouth sealed over hers.

Her arms automatically went around his shoulders as she arched into him. She blocked out the fact that they weren't alone, that Sebastian or Daisy could walk out and find them on the brink of tearing off their clothes. Which she totally wanted to do.

Greg kissed her like he wanted to devour her. It made her want to wrap her legs around his waist and let him do her right against the door.

She had no idea where her inhibitions had gone. And honestly, she didn't care.

As long as he wanted her, she'd be willing.

Finally, he pulled away, breathing hard as he pressed his hips against hers, letting her feel his erection. Groaning when she pressed back, he moved his hand from her hips to her ass to hold her against him. "Don't leave until I get back. Promise."

"I'll be here."

Another kiss and he pulled away. "Be back in a five."

Then he was gone and she took a deep breath, trying to regain her equilibrium.

Walking to the couch, she eased down onto the cushion. She couldn't have been sitting there more than thirty seconds when the door to Greg's bedroom opened and Daisy emerged.

The other woman shuffled toward the kitchen, dressed in a man's T-shirt and apparently nothing else. She looked like she'd been fucked hard and well.

Her body reacted like she'd been kicked in the stomach even as she tried to get her thoughts under control.

Had he slept with his ex?

No, she couldn't believe he'd do that.

Sure he could.

No. She was being totally unfair to Greg.

"Who the hell are you?"

Sabrina's gaze snapped to Daisy, who was holding an empty

mug and glaring at her. Sabrina recognized that glare. She'd gotten the same one last night.

"Hi. I'm Sabrina."

"What are you doing in Greg's room?"

"Waiting for him to get back."

"That doesn't tell me who the hell you are."

Daisy spoke to her like she didn't belong, as if Sabrina were encroaching. The words "screw" and "you" popped into her head but she managed to hold them back, knowing Daisy's life was in a pretty shitty ditch at the moment.

Still, Sabrina refused to be a pushover. Or a whipping post.

"No, it doesn't."

Daisy's eyes narrowed. "Wait. I recognize you. You were the clerk listening in on my conversation the other night."

Sabrina took a deep breath and reached for calm. "I wasn't listening. You happened to be talking loud enough that I could hear from the desk. I'm sorry you thought I was eavesdropping."

Daisy's sneer made Sabrina's blood pressure spike. "You know what? I don't really care. Just leave."

Sabrina silently counted to five. "I'm waiting for Greg to get back." Then she took a page out of her mother's book. Sugar, not salt, her mom used to say all the time. You attract more bees with sugar than you do with salt. Although why you wanted to attract bees was beyond her. They stung. "Why don't you let me make some coffee? You look like you could use some."

Daisy's mouth dropped open and Sabrina swore she could hear the other woman's gears grinding. As Sabrina headed for the kitchen and pulled the coffee out of the refrigerator and the filters out of the cabinet, Daisy's expression slowly loosened from pinched anger to understanding. Leaning back against the counter, Daisy watched Sabrina handle the coffeemaker.

"So you're sleeping with him. I wasn't aware he'd lowered his minimum age to teenagers."

"You'll have to talk to Greg about that."

"Can't speak for yourself?"

She'd have to try for a little more patience, as she nearly cracked the coffeepot when she set it in the sink to fill.

"Actually yes, I can, but I don't respond well to bitchy innuendo."

Damn it. Shit, shit, and shit. She'd sworn she wasn't going to get involved in a pissing match then she'd gone and let Daisy get under her skin anyway.

"Well, good for you." Daisy sighed. "And hell, I'm sorry for being a bitch. It's been a crappy couple of weeks. If you don't mind, could you finish filling that? I could really use the coffee."

Blinking in shock at Daisy's complete one-eighty, Sabrina finished getting the coffee ready to brew then turned to face the other woman, who'd pulled herself onto one of the stools at the breakfast bar. Daisy had her chin propped on one hand and stared at Sabrina with a curious expression that made her even more nervous than Daisy's previous attitude.

"So, you're the woman Greg's been keeping under wraps. I knew he was seeing someone. He's never been good at hiding things from the people who know him really well."

Was that another dig? Sabrina was still trying to wrap her head around Daisy's personality adjustment and wasn't sure what to make of anything that came out of the woman's mouth. Was she needling her for information?

And what the hell was taking Greg so long?

"So how did you guys meet?"

Now the woman looked positively friendly, although sadness lingered in her eyes and Sabrina remembered why Daisy was here in his apartment. And why Greg wasn't.

"Last spring when I modeled a friend's lingerie for her portfolio. Greg took the photos."

"Ah, yes." Daisy's smile appeared for a second. "Greg and his camera. I used to think it was an extension of his hand sometimes. The man certainly has a gift."

"Yes, he does."

Daisy laughed, though the sound was muted. "And you're probably wondering when I'm going to turn my head in circles and become the bitch again. Sorry about that. It's been a seriously bad few months. I've been lucky enough to have Greg at my back and he actually seems to be more stable than I've seen him in a while. And now I'm wondering if that has something to do with you. So how old are you? I'm guessing not much more than twenty-five."

The coffee gave a last gurgle and Sabrina turned for the pot. By the time she'd turned back with another mug in her hand, she'd come to a decision.

"Twenty-three. Greg and I started our . . . relationship in November, when we were snowed in together at the retreat for a few days."

Taking a swallow of the coffee Sabrina poured into her mug, Daisy cocked her head to the side. "Huh. I wondered . . ."

"Wondered what?"

She paused, took a sip of coffee. "He'd been having trouble with the script. Did he tell you that?"

Sabrina blinked, her brain stuttering at the abrupt change in direction. "Um, not really. I mean, I knew he was having trouble but I didn't know with what."

"Hmm. Did he tell you most of the actors signed on without having a finished script? Most of the cast and crew have known and worked with Greg for years, so when he decided he was going to direct his first film in a decade, we all signed on. I'm not sure he realizes this, but in his very tight circle of friends, he's beloved. We would do anything for him. So when he asked, we said of course."

Sabrina understood that completely. If he asked, she'd give him whatever he wanted. Hopefully he hadn't realized that.

"The guy can be such a pain in the ass, and when he wants something, he doesn't stop until he gets it," Daisy continued. "He's really choosy about who he loves but when he decides you're one of his, he's pretty damn loyal. Almost to a fault."

Was Daisy warning her away? That's what it sounded—

"He shouldn't have signed Neal."

Sabrina shook her head, not quite sure what Daisy had said. She'd spoken in barely more than a whisper but Sabrina heard the pain in her voice.

"I should've warned him. Should've told him about the problems. But I thought if Neal had something to do . . . if he had something to work for . . ."

Sabrina didn't know what to say. Didn't figure anything she did say would help.

But she couldn't sit there and not respond at all to the pain in Daisy's voice. "Don't you think Greg already knows this? I mean, the man is somewhat of a genius with people. Yeah, he's pushy and can be a bulldozer and he's too much of a smartass for his own good and sometimes I just wanna smack him but he genuinely cares about his friends."

Daisy snorted then covered her mouth with her hand and continued to laugh. "Wow, I think I understand what Greg sees in you. You really fell hard for him, didn't you?"

She almost didn't say anything before she realized that Daisy had just poured her heart out. And Sabrina, like everyone else, had fallen under Daisy Devlin's spell. It wasn't hard to understand why the woman was one of the most beloved actresses of her generation.

"It's kind of hard not to."

"Oh, honey, ain't that the truth?" Daisy sighed, sipping her coffee. "The only problem with those kind of men? They're tough to get over, too."

* *

Greg walked back into his suite to find Daisy and Sabrina at the breakfast bar, apparently bonding over coffee.

He knew he shouldn't be surprised. Daisy and Sabrina were a lot alike. They had the temperament to put up with difficult men.

The women turned to look at him as he closed the door.

"How is he?"

Daisy's question was almost timid, as if she was afraid to hear the answer.

Greg raised an eyebrow, asking a silent question. He had no problem discussing anything in front of Sabrina, but this was Daisy's private life they'd be talking about.

Daisy smiled and nodded. "Ever gallant, aren't you? It's okay. I like your Sabrina. She seems like good people."

Which for Daisy, Greg knew, was the highest praise.

"Did you know his mother's dying?"

"What?" From the screech in her voice, Greg took that as a no. "I didn't even know she was still in touch with him. Jesus, why the hell didn't he tell me?"

Walking to the counter, he saw Sabrina turn and grab a mug, fill it, and set it in front of him. It was such a simple gesture and it made him want to get on his knees and profess his undying devotion.

But would she accept it?

"Maybe because he didn't want anyone to know," Greg continued. "She's a pretty hardcore addict. Has been for most of his life. The drugs are finally taking their toll and she's not expected to make it more than a couple of weeks."

Daisy's eyes had started to fill with tears and now they dripped down her face. And when Sabrina reached for her hand, Daisy gripped it like it was a lifeline.

"I'm so sorry, Greg."

Greg frowned. "What? Why?"

"About Neal. I should have figured out what was wrong. I should've warned you. I knew he wasn't up for filming—"

"Daisy, none of this is your fault." Greg shook his head. "And Neal's been holding it together for the most part. The footage we've got so far is amazing. Seriously. He's waiting for you. He wants to talk. Just let him, okay? Then take tomorrow off. I'll rearrange the filming schedule. I wanted to get a few more takes with Amanda anyway."

Nodding, Daisy set her mug on the counter, gave Sabrina a smile, then walked over to him for a hug. Minutes later, Daisy was dressed and headed back to her own room.

As the door shut behind her, Greg couldn't stand the silence any longer.

"Seems like you and Daisy hit it off."

Sabrina's smile was sweet. "She reminds me of my mom a little. Crazy in love with a guy who isn't all that good for her."

Not "good enough." Neal just wasn't "good" for Daisy. Sabrina had nailed that on the head.

"So," he said. "Brunch."

"Are you really sure you can take the time? We can—"

"Yeah. I'm sure." What he really wanted to do was take her to bed, get her naked, and stay inside her for the rest of the day.

But he also wanted to get out of the city and away from everything making his life hell at the moment. He wanted to spend some time alone with Sabrina doing something as normal as sharing a meal.

He'd given some thought to surprising his parents with a visit but knew it'd probably freak out Sabrina. You didn't just throw a woman into a meeting with your parents. She'd want to take a knife to his balls.

"Let me leave a note for Sebastian, then we'll take this show on the road."

* *

They left the hotel in his car, a sleek, black Dodge Challenger that Sabrina loved on sight.

"Do you mind if we drive for a while?" he asked. "I feel like I've been cooped up in either the hotel or the farmhouse. I need a change of scenery."

"Sure. I've got the day off." And there was nowhere else she'd rather be.

"First, I'll feed you. Wouldn't want you to expire from starvation."

She laughed, like he'd wanted her to. "Which just means you're hungry."

"And here I thought you didn't know me that well."

They drove for a while, but Sabrina turned to him when it became obvious that they were headed out of the city.

"So where are we going?"

"Up to Chester County, to one of my favorite diners."

"Didn't you grow up outside of West Chester?"

"Yeah. My parents still live in the area and so do my sister and her family."

"Have you seen your family recently?"

"They came down to the set a few days ago."

He hadn't asked her to come to the set. The thought made her chest tighten. She couldn't help but think he didn't want her there. Then again, she wasn't sure she wanted to be exposed as the woman sleeping with the director.

And yet, here she was in a car with him.

Make up your mind.

"So this place," she said instead of asking more intimate questions, "what's so special about it?"

"Well, it's still owned by the couple who opened it thirty years ago. Their children run the place now. Haven't changed a thing. It still looks like a dive and no one would ever consider changing it."

"You know the owners?"

"Yep. Went to school with their daughter and son-in-law. Pam runs the dining room. Her husband, Tim, and I go way back. He's a year older but we graduated together because he lost a year fighting leukemia."

"Oh, wow. That must have sucked."

Greg's mouth tightened. "It was fucking awful. But Tim . . . he never complained. Just put his head down and barreled through. He was supposed to go to Hollywood with me but he knocked up Pam our senior year and I left without him."

"Are they still together?"

"Uh-huh. Pam's great. You'll meet her in a few minutes. She's also completely crazy." Greg's quiet laugh held wry amusement. "Guess she had to be to put up with Tim. Love the guy like a brother, but he's one of those mad geniuses. Know what I mean?"

She thought she might but she liked hearing him talk so she shook her head.

"Smart as hell but he can't remember what he had for breakfast and he always has to be doing something. That's why he's great in the kitchen."

"So he cooks at the restaurant?"

He nodded. "Make sure you get the chicken and waffles. Best damn food you'll ever eat."

"Did you warn them you were coming?"

"No." He frowned at her. "Why should I? They own a restaurant. It's not like I'm dropping by to eat at their house. Besides, they know I'm in the area and I always make a point to stop by. Every time I do, I swear my goddaughter gets more beautiful."

The smile on his face made her heart trip. "What's her name?"

"Alexis. I remember holding her for the first time when I came back for her baptism. She was so small and I'd never held a baby before. Hell, I'd practically never seen one before. But now my best friend is a dad and he's expecting me to be responsible for this little human if anything happened to him and Pam. I almost said no."

"But you didn't." And she knew he wouldn't have. Greg never turned his back on his friends.

He paused for a minute. "I sometimes wonder if he ever knew how pissed off I was at him when he wouldn't go with me to California. That had been the plan. We were both going to go. But he screwed up the works." Another pause. "Then again, I guess some things turn out the way they're supposed to."

She didn't have the chance to get him to tell her why he thought that because he turned into a parking lot.

Shifting in her seat, she almost thought maybe he'd had to make another stop before they got to the restaurant because this didn't look anything like she'd been expecting.

This looked like a fifties-era gas station, one of those really cool-looking ones that were either bulldozed or later renovated. This one had managed to remain standing but it seemed to be in pretty bad shape.

But it was surrounded by cars and Greg had to go around the back of the building to find a spot.

"I know it doesn't look like much," Greg said when she turned to him with a puzzled expression. "But keep an open mind."

With a hand low on her back, he steered her toward the front door and into the lobby, outfitted to look like the garage office it'd been fifty years ago.

The L-shaped glass case that served as the check-in counter was filled with antique motor parts. Racks full of old-fashioned candies sat on the top next to a register that looked original to the period.

"Hey, you rat fink," said the woman behind the counter as she nearly jumped over it. "Where the hell have you been? It's about damn time you showed up."

She grabbed Greg and squeezed, an embrace he returned just as enthusiastically.

"Hey, Pam. I've been a little busy, you know? But I'm here now."

After Greg introduced her to Pam by name and nothing else, Pam hustled them into the former garage bay, which now housed the dining room. There couldn't have been more than twenty tables, but they were all full.

But Pam didn't stop in the dining room. She took them straight through to the kitchen, where the tall, gangly man who was working the grill looked up when Pam yelled, "Look what I found skulking around our front door."

During the next few minutes, Sabrina was introduced to too many people to remember, most of them Pam and Tim's family, including Pam's parents, Pat and Harry, who helped on the line, and their three kids, all of whom called Greg "Uncle."

Every one of them smiled at her but she knew what they were thinking.

Who exactly are you?

Good question.

Several minutes later, Pam took them back into the dining room, where she seated them at a red vinyl booth near the back and served them the best chicken and waffles Sabrina had ever had.

No one bothered them while they ate, but after their dishes were cleared, two people came over to shake his hand. One had been a high school teacher of Greg's. The other, his parents' neighbor. No one else approached, though a lot of heads had turned their way.

"Did your friends put up some 'Don't approach the famous Hollywood guy' sign that I haven't seen?"

Greg leaned back against the booth, stuffed and more relaxed than he'd felt in days.

All of it due to the woman sitting across from him. They'd talked for the past two hours, about anything that came to mind. Mostly, he kept her talking. He knew if he started in about filming, that's all they'd discuss. And he didn't want to be that guy who only ever talked about himself.

"Most people who pass Steven Spielberg on a street outside of Hollywood don't know him. Same goes for Harvey Weinstein and George Lucas and Ron Howard. The people here who *do* know me know I deserve to have a private life."

"I guess that's pretty hard in L.A."

He thought about sugarcoating his response, telling her it wasn't that bad, but he refused to lie to her. "Yeah, it is. That's why I've been giving some thought to moving back."

Her eyes opened wide and her mouth dropped open for a

few seconds before she quickly covered her reaction. "Seriously? Wouldn't that make it hard for you to do what you do?"

He didn't answer right away, tried to get all his thoughts together. He hadn't talked to anyone but Tyler about his idea, and then only in hypothetical terms.

But the trouble he'd been having with his business partner had made him think even more about it.

"The business isn't as tied to Hollywood as much as it used to be. It's actually part of the reason I've been having trouble with my production partner. He's afraid if I move, I won't be as committed to the business and we'll fail."

What his partner didn't know was that, if Greg didn't do something, he was going to flame out and that might be a disaster of epic proportions.

Since he'd been here, he'd felt more grounded. And part of that was due to Sabrina.

Tell her. Tell her you want more.

But more what?

More sex? More talk?

Just more of her. All of her.

Sabrina looked stunned, but he couldn't tell if that was good or bad.

And he didn't get the opportunity to follow it up because Alexis stopped at their table.

"Hey, Uncle Greg. Mom said lunch is on the house and not to try to pay or Dad'll shave his head and force you to abide by your bargain."

His goddaughter's amused expression held no trace of artifice or sarcasm, so different from the kids her age he saw at casting calls.

No, eighteen-year-old Alexis was headed to college in the fall. She wanted to be a math teacher. She'd apparently gotten her mom's brains because Tim had absolutely no head for figures.

"And what was the bargain?" Sabrina asked.

Greg shook his head, a smile curving his lips. "When Greg was going through chemo, he lost most of his hair and shaved what he didn't. So I told him, whenever he shaved his head, I would, too." He turned back to Alex. "Your dad doesn't have enough hair left to lose, so tell him thanks for me. Wait a minute, kid."

Greg looked around Alex to make sure her parents weren't watching. They always made too much of a big deal about his gifts to the kids.

He reached into his pocket and pulled out the cash he'd stuffed in there. "A hundred of this is for you. The rest split between your brother and sister."

The girl's eyes got huge and she started to shake her head. "Uncle Greg . . ."

"Early Christmas present." Even though he already knew he'd be getting Alex and her siblings a few more things. "And the check is for your college fund. Just deposit it, sweetheart."

Now her eyes widened even farther and she looked ready to hyperventilate when she saw the five followed by four zeroes. "Oh, my God, Uncle Greg, I can't take—"

"Yes, you can and you will. Think of it as an investment in your future. After college, I'm holding you to that unpaid internship at the company."

Her smile spread from ear to ear as she leaned over to kiss him on the cheek. "Love you, Uncle Greg."

"Love you, too, kid."

Alexis bounded away, blond ponytail swaying.

"She seems like a smart girl." That half smile of Sabrina's was back, making his blood begin to heat. How the hell did she do that with just a look?

"Kid's a genius with numbers. She wants to be a math teacher, which is great. But if she ever decides to make a shit-ton of money, she's going to have a hell of a career as a stockbroker and I want her working for me."

Rising, he reached for Sabrina to help her out of the booth. When she laced her fingers with his, she didn't let go.

Desire raced through his veins, and his cock ached. Good thing he'd left his shirt untucked.

If he didn't get her out of here soon, he was going to kiss the hell out of her. And he wasn't sure she'd appreciate him taking their relationship even more public than he had today.

Saying good-bye to everyone took longer than he expected because he had to go back in the kitchen to say good-bye to Tim, then he stopped at a few tables to say hello. He saw two people he'd gone to high school with and a couple of his parents' friends. He introduced Sabrina by name only and no one pushed for more.

In the lobby, he got a tight hug from Pam, who smiled at him with tears in her eyes. "You're a regular son of a bitch, you know that, right? You're spoiling her."

"No clue what you're talking about."

Shaking her head, Pam turned to smile at Sabrina. "Watch this one. He's sneaky. So nice to meet you, Sabrina."

Back in the car, Greg finally felt his shoulders unkink as they headed back to the city. Darkness had fallen completely by that time.

"You look much more relaxed than you did when we left."

Sabrina's quiet voice filled the car, causing his muscles to tighten, although in this case, that wasn't a bad thing. Those muscles were lower and connected to other things that hardened and flexed.

"Helps to get away sometimes. Guess I needed the break."

"How's filming going?"

He started to tell her what he'd been telling everyone else. It's going fine, thanks for asking. Never better. Love my job. Yada, yada.

Sabrina wasn't everyone else.

"It's been tougher than I expected."

"How so?"

He paused and she turned in her seat so she could watch him.

"Because I'm second-guessing every move." Jesus, it felt like a weight had lifted off his shoulders as he started to talk. "It's been nearly a decade since I directed a movie and I feel like I've forgotten things I used to know."

"I don't think you've forgotten a damn thing. It's okay to be nervous, you know. It makes you human. I look at you and see . . ."

He frowned. "What?"

Out of the corner of his eye, he saw her shake her head. "I . . . I'm not . . . You're . . ." She sighed. "Oh, never mind."

She started to turn but he reached for her chin, holding her still for a second. "No way. Don't worry about upsetting me or pissing me off. Just spit it out."

She huffed. "I think sometimes you're just so much larger than life. There's nothing you can't do, and it's a little intimidating. I kind of like knowing you're . . . human."

"Well, wait 'til we get back to the hotel. I'll show you how human I am."

She shook her head. "Now *you're* avoiding."

Yeah, he was. He realized it was a reflex, using sex to diffuse a situation he didn't know how to handle. Which wasn't something that happened a lot.

"Possibly. Doesn't mean I don't want to get you into a bed as soon as possible, though."

He barely caught her smile, it was there and gone in seconds. "Then I guess it's a good thing I don't work tonight."

Did he hear an edge in her voice that hadn't been there before?

He didn't like the feeling he was missing something. He'd had so many balls in the air for so long that maybe he'd gotten a little arrogant about being able to keep everything going.

Okay, maybe "a little" was underplaying it. And when the hell did he underplay anything?

Silence fell as he mentally chewed over things. Sabrina had settled back into her seat and stared out the front window. Turning up the radio, he let himself fall into Sebastian's music. He'd given Greg a CD of original music, what he'd been playing for him and Sabrina.

Greg had pretty much made up his mind that he wanted Sebastian to score the film. He didn't think convincing the guy to do it would be all that difficult. Baseline Sins was on hiatus and the other band members were working on solo projects. Greg had seen the pain in Sebastian's eyes when he'd revealed that fact, although he'd tried not to let anything show. The guy blamed himself for the band's imminent implosion, and yeah, maybe it was his fault to a large degree. That didn't mean he had to continue to beat himself up about it.

So Greg was going to plead, cajole, browbeat, and basically force Sebastian to do his film. And the guy would nail it. Greg had no doubt.

Why couldn't he be as confident about where his relationship with Sabrina was going?

Maybe because he hadn't been thinking in terms of a relationship until recently. And now that he was, that's what he wanted. He had to bite his tongue so he didn't start badgering her about taking this to the next level.

And when he said next level, he meant having her tied to him through more than just sex. Sure, there'd be hurdles. But he'd become a damn good hurdler in the past fifteen years.

And if he moved his business . . .

He was still thinking about that when they arrived at the hotel. It was almost eight at night and he'd already planned to have a snack sent up so they could eat in bed.

He didn't care if George Lucas called and wanted him to collaborate on the next Star Wars film. He wasn't answering the damn phone, wasn't opening his damn door.

He didn't bother to ask her to come to his room. He just steered her toward the guest elevator in the garage and swiped his card for the fourth floor.

She didn't complain so he figured she was on board with his plans, which definitely included them naked and rolling around on his bed as soon as possible.

Dinner could wait. Hell, everything could wait.

Ten

God, she was being so stupid. She should've pleaded insanity and headed straight to her own room.

Instead, Sabrina followed Greg into his apartment, trying not to have a panic attack. It'd started about an hour earlier, after they'd gotten in the car to drive home.

He'd started to open up to her. And then he'd shut her down. With sex.

Not even actual sex. Just talk about sex.

He was never going to let her get close. Never going to let her in.

And what did you expect?

She'd broken her own damn rule. She'd gotten attached. She'd let herself fall for him.

And now he was going to break her heart.

Hadn't that been the plan all along?

Yes. But . . .

But what? Had she really expected things to change?

He'd be gone by mid-January. And she'd be here.

She couldn't breathe. She should leave now. Thank him for dinner, tell him she'd had a great time, but say good-bye.

Yes. That's exactly what she should do.

She turned—

And nearly slammed into his chest, he was that close behind her.

Gasping, she put her hands out to stop her forward motion and they landed on his chest, just below his pecs. God, the man threw off heat like a furnace.

Before she knew what she was doing, she'd leaned in and rubbed her nose against the soft cotton of his T-shirt. She breathed him in, his scent an aphrodisiac. It set all her nerve endings on alert. Her nipples tightened, her clit tingled, and her thighs clenched.

Damn, she didn't think she'd ever get used to the way he made her feel.

And that in itself should've been a huge yellow warning light telling her to step back.

But did she?

Of course not.

Instead, she flattened her hands against his chest and dragged them down his torso.

She heard Greg suck in a deep breath and mutter something, then he put his hands on her ass and dragged her hips against his.

He held her there with one hand while his other wove through her hair, tugging her head back so he could kiss her.

More like stake a claim. His lips moved over hers with a sense of possession she swore she could taste.

Urgency made her hands shake as she grabbed the waistband of his jeans. Her fingers fumbled with the button but Greg didn't seem to mind. Or maybe he just didn't notice because his hand slipped between her thighs and cupped her sex, fingers pressing the seam of her jeans into her clit, sending splinters of need through her lower body.

Moaning, her urgency became frantic, clawing need, an ache deep inside that could only be eased by him.

Ripping open the button, she shoved one hand into his jeans, wrapping her fingers around his cock and tightening them until she felt his pulse beating against her palm.

With a rough curse, he tore his mouth from hers and moved to her neck, where he pressed biting kisses against her skin.

Shuddering in his hold, her body writhed as he worked her clit. He didn't even have to put his hands on her skin for him to drive her crazy. He did it just by breathing. But apparently he wasn't satisfied with the arrangement.

Grabbing her, he lifted her off her feet and carried her to the dining area in front of the windows. The second her ass hit the top of the solid wood table, Greg had his mouth over hers again and his hands on her jeans. She had no idea when he'd released the button but suddenly her zipper was going down and then so were her jeans.

In seconds, her boots had disappeared and her jeans fell off her ankles.

She heard him practically growl *"Pretty"* before he reached for her shirt. He shoved that up around her breasts, his gaze locking onto the bare skin he'd uncovered.

"I fucking love the way your tits look in Kate's bras. I swear I'm going to force Tyler to let me invest in her."

Shivers of pure passion raced through her but she wanted more.

"Greg, less talk, more action."

His gaze flipped to hers and she saw his lips curve into a smart-ass grin. She groaned at the calculation she saw there.

"Oh, honey, you should know by now I don't take direction well."

Lifting her body onto her elbows, she glared at him as he grabbed one of the chairs he'd pushed out of the way and set it directly in front of her.

"That's because you're a control freak."

She swallowed hard as she realized all he had to do was lean in, just a little, and he'd have his mouth on her pussy. Every muscle in her body clenched in anticipation.

God, yes. I want that.

"You're absolutely right about that. And right now, your body is under my control. Take off the shirt, babe. Leave the bra."

She wanted to obey immediately but she still had some self-control remaining.

"Maybe I don't want—"

She gasped when he put this thumb directly over her clit, pressing and twisting until her back bowed from the pleasure.

"Take off the shirt."

There was a tone in his voice she'd never heard before. It made her want to give him anything he wanted.

Quicksand. Run the other way.

No, she didn't want to run unless it was straight at him.

Laying back, she worked the shirt over her head, loving the look on his face that made it clear he liked the view.

"So fucking pretty. Now just lay there, honey. This won't hurt a bit." Hooking one finger in the side of her underwear, he pulled it to the side, baring her pussy. "You're already soaking wet. You know that just makes me want to lick you, right?"

Please. "Then do it."

He smiled, so sexy her breath caught in her throat. "No need to rush. We've got all night."

"Well, I certainly hope it doesn't take you all night to— *Oh, my God.*"

He put his mouth over her sex for an intimate kiss that made her mind go blank and her body flush with the most amazing heat.

Every muscle tightened as he used his tongue and his lips to explore her. She wanted to reach for him, to hold his head, but she couldn't seem to get her hands to do what she wanted. Right now, she had a death grip on the sides of the table, giving her the leverage to arch her hips and press her pussy closer to the wonder that was his mouth.

His lips sucked at her labia, drawing the sensitive folds of skin between them for his teeth to nibble and play. With her eyes closed, she felt every sensation more fully. Her sex tingled with erotic energy, clenching, begging to be filled.

His hands had moved to her legs, holding her thighs apart so he could have unrestricted access to her. She felt his fingertips press into her skin like tiny electric prods.

Then his tongue flicked out to touch her clit.

"Greg."

"I fucking love to hear you say my name when I'm eating you out."

Her eyes snapped open and she stared blindly at the ceiling as he sucked and nipped at her clit. Alternating his sensual torture, he refused to back down or slow down at all.

And she could barely breathe through the heat building in her body.

He ate at her with a hunger that grew the more he tasted her until she wasn't sure she could stay conscious. She saw sparks flash behind her eyelids when he worked his tongue between her labia and fucked her with it.

Her body tightening to the point of breaking, she panted, trying to hold back, to let it build.

She fought against Greg's domination, although she knew she couldn't hold out for long. Because it made Greg push that much harder.

And when she finally gave over to her orgasm, letting it take her under, she heard him growl in triumph.

A second later, something hit the floor with a muffled thump and her eyes popped open.

Greg had kicked the chair away from the table and now stood at the end of the table, looking down at her. His smile was gone but the look in his eyes burned. She couldn't catch her breath, her lungs tight and heavy. Her breasts ached, and even though she'd just come, her pussy clenched, begging to be filled.

He lifted his hands and her gaze followed them as he reached for his jeans. She'd already undone the button. He gripped the zipper tab and pulled it down.

No teasing now. He looked so hungry, so *male*. She could smell the scent of her arousal in the air, knew she'd taste herself on his lips if he bent and kissed her. But kissing her wasn't what he wanted right now.

His erection had pushed out through the vee of his open zipper, and the only thing keeping him from her view was his black boxer briefs.

Then he pushed down his jeans and briefs, freeing his cock. Hard and thick, it bobbed toward her before he took himself in one hand and rubbed the tip against the wetness coating her labia. The heat of his cock felt like a brand against her delicate skin. He didn't attempt to penetrate her but he made sure when he rubbed his cock against her, he hit her clit. The little bundle of nerves was already so sensitive from her last orgasm that she practically flinched away from him.

But she couldn't seem to get enough.

Behind her, she thought she heard something that almost sounded like a door opening, but she was too far gone to care.

Only when Greg's gaze flicked away did she realize they weren't alone.

Greg must have anticipated her automatic response to cover herself because he put one hand on her stomach to hold her in place.

Her entire body flushed with heat as Sebastian froze in the doorway to the second bedroom.

"Oh, *fuck*."

It might've been mortifying if she hadn't been so turned on.

With her breath caught in her chest, she waited for Greg to tell him to turn around, to get the hell out.

In the next second, she realized he wasn't going to.

And the heat that had started to cool with embarrassment began to burn a little hotter again.

Sucking in a short, unsteady breath, she turned back to Greg, now watching her.

"Have you ever been taken in front of someone else before? Had someone watch?" Greg's steady tone made her shiver and she shook her head when he waited for her to answer. "It makes everything much more erotic. It's kind of like when I took your picture after our first time. That sensation of someone capturing you at such an intimate moment. It's so fucking hot."

Surprisingly, she understood. Already her body was reacting to Sebastian's presence with a rush of lust so hot, it made her feel feverish.

Still, she'd never done anything like this and—

And what?

Well, for starters, how the hell would she be able to face Sebastian after this? When he'd seen her like this?

Like what? asked the part of her brain that wanted Greg to continue right now.

In the midst of so much pleasure it hurt.

Hell, she wasn't even totally naked.

But Greg was about to make love to her and Sebastian was going to watch.

Turning her head again, she saw Sebastian leaning against the doorjamb, his eyes heavy-lidded, his expression unreadable. But the hint of red on his cheeks and the way his chest rose and fell in such a rapid motion belied his arousal.

God, did she actually *want* him to watch?

Would Greg expect him to do anything else?

She'd never been in a threesome. Had never considered it other than to read and enjoy the fantasy in books.

"He's not allowed to touch you," Greg continued, answering her unspoken question as if he'd read her mind. "You're mine. Only mine. He can watch because I allow it but that's all."

She bit back a moan at the absolute possession in Greg's tone. No matter that it should have grated. It didn't. It made her feel treasured.

"But Bree, you have to say it." She turned back to look at him, his expression dead serious. "You have to say yes because there's no way in hell I'd ever force you to do something like this."

Her heart melted along with her inhibitions.

She took a deep breath. "Then I say yes."

Greg's smile made her pussy clench. "Right answer."

He thrust forward without any further delay, filling her, stretching her, making her moan his name and grab the sides of the table until she swore she'd leave fingernail marks in the hard wood.

With his hands on her hips, Greg held her as he worked himself deep inside. She wanted him to go faster but he wasn't about to be rushed.

Instead, he pulled out a centimeter at a time, each tiny movement a burst of sensation that fired her arousal. When his cock slid free, she lifted her hips to try to entice him back.

Instead, he wrapped one hand around the base and tapped her clit with the tip, making her heart trip and her lungs struggle for air.

Knowing Sebastian was watching made her want to instinctively close her eyes but she forced them to stay open, to stay on Greg. His every movement riveted her attention, her gaze connected with his.

When his cock breached her again, lodging just inside her channel, he settled both hands on her hips. "Lock your legs around my waist, sweetheart."

Even though her legs felt like they had lead weights attached to her ankles, she did what he wanted.

And knowing Sebastian was watching her every move, she shimmied her hips, rocking Greg's cock the tiniest bit farther inside her.

She felt sexy. And so aroused her muscles ached with it.

Fingers tightening on her hips, Greg held her still, though she could tell his control was starting to crack. His mouth had flattened into a straight line and the muscles in his arms bunched and flexed.

"You want to play dirty?" His voice had dropped to a low growl. "I can do that."

He shoved inside her in one thrust, until she felt his balls brush against her ass.

Yes.

Now he'd pound into her like she wanted. Now—

Damn the man. He held steady, grinding his hips against her in slow, mind-splintering circles that tormented her clit.

"Greg."

She'd never experienced anything like this in her life. Having sex with Greg didn't feel like having sex. It was something else entirely. It filled not only her body but that place inside that had been empty before him.

And with Sebastian as a witness . . .

"What do you want, sweetheart?"

This time when Greg pulled out, he didn't leave her completely. She felt the head of his cock remain lodged inside the delicate opening, spreading her.

"For you to fuck me."

When he slammed back home again, she moaned and let herself sink into the table. Let him have her however he wanted her.

Greg sensed her surrender. His mouth pulled into a hard-ass grin and he started a rhythm that felt like punishment.

And she didn't mean that in a bad way. It was the most sensual form of punishment she'd ever endured. He wound her up like he was winding a clock, fucking her slow and steady. He never looked away, didn't acknowledge Sebastian's presence at all.

His entire attention was focused on her, on bringing her the most intense pleasure he could manage.

And he did, so much so she thought she might actually black out. Even though she knew her lungs were working, she felt like she couldn't get enough air. Every inward thrust forced her to exhale but each time he pulled out, she didn't have enough energy to inhale. Because every muscle in her body was waiting for that release.

That he was in no hurry to give her. He kept that steady pace going until she simply couldn't take it anymore.

She released the table and let her hand slide down her body until it rested on her mound.

Off to her side, she was pretty sure she heard Sebastian mutter something that sounded like, "Fuck yes." She almost turned to make sure he was watching but she couldn't look away from Greg.

He didn't say anything but his lips curved back into that smile that made her shiver with delight.

With one finger, she touched her clit, flicking it in time to his thrusts. Greg's gaze fell to watch her play with herself as she watched his cock disappear inside her.

She was so close, she knew if she pressed just the tiniest bit harder, she'd come. Instead, she let her finger slip off her clit so her nail grazed his cock as he pulled out.

He groaned and his next thrust was harder than the last, pushing her finger back against that tiny bundle of nerves.

"Go ahead, honey. Make yourself come. Show us how fucking sexy you are. Then I'll let go."

With her gaze locked to his, she rubbed her clit, playing with herself, knowing how much Greg, and apparently Sebastian, enjoyed watching her.

Greg's rhythm increased, giving her the internal friction she needed. The pleasure intensified and finally her eyes closed as she gasped, her body convulsing around his, pulling him deeper.

His fingers tightened on her hips until she felt his nails bite into her and then she could feel nothing but the sensation of his cock pumping deep inside her.

Her eyes opened as she felt him move, only to see him bending over her. He kissed her with a rough tenderness that threatened to crack open her heart. Wrapping her arms around his shoulders, she kissed him back with unreserved emotion.

His mouth became more demanding, his tongue tangling around hers as his arms slid beneath her back to take her with him as he straightened.

When he had her seated on the edge of the table, her head pressed against his chest, she felt him nod.

Sebastian.

For a second, doubt rushed in as she heard a door close behind her.

She'd just had sex with her lover in front of her friend.

And holy hell, it'd been amazing.

She wanted to tell Greg how she felt, wanted to know what he was thinking, but she didn't get to say anything before he wove his fingers through her hair to cup her head and tilt it back so he could kiss her again. And again. Until every thought left her head and she felt nothing but his desire for her.

When he pulled away, he stared down at her. She realized he was looking for something, some indication that she was okay.

Reaching for his head, she pulled him down again, then let her hands pet his shoulders, his chest.

Relaxing against her, he pressed a kiss to her cheek then straightened.

"Come on, babe. Off to the shower. Then we'll order up some food. You want to invite Sebastian to stay?"

She blinked up at him. "Uh . . . sure. If you want."

He stared straight into her eyes. "Better to just yank the bandage off."

She understood what he was saying, though it was going to require a hell of a lot of bravado on her part to walk back out into this room, sit down at that table, and have a meal with the man who'd watched her and Greg have sex on it.

Then again, she liked Sebastian. He'd become a good friend over the past few weeks and she didn't want to lose him. And the stuff he'd told her he'd done . . . He was lucky he wasn't dead from the amount of alcohol he'd consumed, the shitty things he'd done to his body, and the crappy way he treated it. Not to mention the women . . .

And there she went again, sounding like his mother.

She really needed to stop that.

You will. They'll both be leaving soon enough.

The thought hit her like a two-by-four and she dipped her head for a second.

"Hey, we don't have to—"

Forcing a quick smile, she shook her head. "No, it's not that. I want him to stay. I just . . . I need a shower and a few minutes to breathe. You can be a steamroller."

She pressed one finger to his lips as he opened his mouth, probably to tell her he was going to kick out Sebastian.

"That's not always a bad thing. Let me take a shower." She gave a pointed look at the table. "And maybe we want to get pizza so we can sit on the couch and eat."

Laughing, Greg picked her up and carried her to his room. "Pizza it is. Whatever you want, hon."

* *

Greg deposited Sabrina in the bathroom, kissed her hard, then left before he pushed her up against the shower wall and had her again.

He'd probably pushed her to her limit and a few miles past it in the last half hour. But she didn't want to leave and she appeared to be handling the fact that she'd just had sex in front of another man fairly well.

You're corrupting her.

The thought gave him pause.

The sexual games he played with women had evolved over the years. He hadn't started out liking three-ways and performing in front of others. Hell, he'd had a pretty damn pedestrian sex life until he'd gotten to Hollywood. And at first, even there it'd been vanilla.

Until Daisy. She'd introduced him to threesomes. And he'd liked them. A lot. Then he'd met Tyler and been invited into the Salon, where he'd discovered his inner hedonist. And embraced the shit out of it.

But he'd never forced it on anyone else.

And I didn't force Sabrina.

He'd given her a choice. She'd made her own decision.

Hadn't she?

Hell, he needed to be having this conversation with her and not by himself. And that wasn't going to happen right now.

Heading for the phone he'd left on the breakfast bar, he made the call for pizza to be delivered then knocked on the door to the second bedroom.

Sebastian yanked the door open. "Thank fuck you're dressed. Christ almighty, man, warn a guy before you decide to make him hornier than a bull in mating season and leave him hanging."

"Don't tell me you didn't just get yourself off in the bathroom?"

Sebastian's grin made Greg laugh.

"Took like three strokes for me to blow." His grin faded. "Wanna tell me why the fuck I got to watch? Not that I didn't find it hot as hell but you don't seem like the kinda guy who likes to share."

With a jerk of his head, Greg motioned for Sebastian to follow him to the seating area. "I'm not sharing her, so don't get any ideas. But yeah, I get off on other people watching. And I gambled on Sabrina enjoying it."

Sebastian dropped into the chair across from the sofa and sprawled. "Looks like your gamble paid off."

He nodded as he sat on the couch. "What about you? You like to gamble?"

Sebastian gave him a wry look. "What? It isn't obvious?"

Now was as good a time as any. "Score my movie."

Sebastian's mouth dropped open and for the first since he'd met him, the guy looked much younger than his twenty-eight years.

"Seriously?"

"Do you really think I'm the kind of guy who would fuck around with something like this?"

Sebastian sat forward, elbows on his knees, staring straight at Greg. "Why me?"

"Because I love the work you're doing. It's hard but it's not inaccessible. It's melodic but it's got bite. It's exactly the tone I want for the film."

Sebastian continued to stare at him but Greg saw the excitement in Sebastian's eyes.

"I don't have the first clue about scoring films."

"I'll help you through it. Just say yes. I wouldn't ask if I didn't think you could do it. I'm not a philanthropist."

Sebastian huffed. "No, you're a fucking crazy man."

Greg smiled, knowing he'd just gotten Sebastian to agree. "It's not crazy to know what you want and do whatever it takes to get it."

Pausing, Sebastian's gaze slid to the door to Greg's bedroom. "That include women, too?"

He didn't hesitate. "Yeah. It does."

"And what happens when you leave?"

"Who says I'm leaving?"

Sebastian's eye widened. "Does she know that?"

"No one knows. Hell, even I don't. I haven't made a final decision yet."

"But you're thinking about leaving Hollywood. Because of her?"

Greg shook his head. "It's been in the back of my mind for a while but after the last year, I've been thinking about it a lot more."

Sebastian paused and Greg swore he saw the guy's brain churning. "You going to leave the business altogether?"

"No. I'm going to bring the business with me."

"Can you make that work?"

"I'd sure as hell like to try."

His phone vibrated and he grabbed it out of his pocket. The text from Trudeau covered the length of the screen and kept going.

"Fuck. Fuck. Fuck. I've gotta order a hell of a lot more pizza. We're about to have company."

* *

Greg had warned her, but Sabrina hadn't realized just what he'd meant by "working dinner."

He'd told her his assistant, Trudeau, would be there and a few crew members.

Fifteen minutes later, Greg and six other people sat around the dining room table, shoving pieces of paper around like pawns on a chess board.

Greg had introduced her and Sebastian by name only to the three men and three women who'd shown up. She'd gotten a couple of double takes from the men. The women had smiled and shaken her hand. One had actually smacked one of the men on the back of the head when he'd stared at her a little too long.

Then Trudeau, who until now she'd only seen but hadn't spoken to, had started to rattle off action items like she was running a meeting of the joint chiefs of staff.

Greg's assistant was only a few years older than her, but had the poise and confidence of a woman twice her age. Apparently, a couple of the actors and a few crew members had come down with a violent case of food poisoning and couldn't film for at least two days, which meant they had to redo the shooting schedule.

While Greg's entire attention was focused on work, she and Sebastian had grabbed one of the pizzas and retreated to the second bedroom. Sebastian turned on the TV while she laid out paper plates, napkins, and drinks on the small table near the window.

"So, you want to talk about it or are we just going to ignore it?" he finally said.

Sabrina carefully chewed the piece of pizza she'd just bitten off and forced herself to look at Sebastian. He looked curious but she saw no hint of a leer. He just looked like Sebastian. As if nothing had changed between them.

Thank God.

"Did you get off watching?"

He nearly choked on his beer. "Well, shit. Do you really want to know?"

"I wouldn't have asked if I didn't."

He narrowed his gaze at her, his attention honed to a fine point. "First tell me something. Did *you* like being watched?"

Holding his gaze, she nodded. "More than I ever imagined I would." She paused. "Do you think I'm weird?"

He wrinkled his nose, which made him look like a teenager. "Nah. Everybody's got kinks, even the people who say they don't. And those are the ones you have to watch out for."

"I never wanted to do anything like that before . . ."

"Before Greg?"

"Yeah."

"And . . . ?"

"And . . ." She looked out the door, just able to see Greg sitting at the table. "I'm worried that I'm doing it not because I like it, but because I like *him*."

Sebastian's expression turned amused. "Seriously? That's what you're worried about? Alright, first off, you liked it, so there's nothing to be worried about. If you didn't like it but were going to do it again because he wanted you to, then I'd say you had a problem. And second, why would that be such a bad thing? I mean, it was your first time, right? How would you even know if you didn't like it if you never tried it? Don't we all do things only because we love the person we do them with?"

Love the person.

Love Greg.

Did she love Greg?

No. No, no, no.

Good sex did not equal love. And even if she did, it wouldn't matter, would it? He'd be leaving, just as soon as he'd finished filming. He'd go back to Hollywood and she'd get over him.

She'd have to. Greg wasn't the kind of guy who stuck around or did meaningful relationships.

Hell, he'd been engaged for nearly five years to a woman he still claimed to love and, even though they'd broken up, he'd cast her as the lead in his film.

And he'd just let Sebastian watch them have sex. The man wasn't possessive.

She figured a man who loved a woman wouldn't want to share her in any way with anyone else.

"Hey, Bree. What'd I say that made you go off into lala land?"

She blinked as Sebastian used the nickname only Greg had ever called her. It sounded wrong coming out of Sebastian's mouth.

And that was . . . disturbing.

What the hell have you gotten yourself into?

Way more than she'd bargained for.

"Sabrina?"

She should leave. She *needed* to leave. Her brain was telling her she needed to go now, before . . .

Her stomach churned at the thought that she'd never see him again. Never be able to touch him, kiss him, hold him. Never make love with him again.

"Hey." Sebastian sounded worried now. "You look a little green around the gills."

"Yeah, sorry. I just . . . All of a sudden I've got a splitting headache. It just crept up on me. I think I just need to go back to my room and lie down."

"Shit, what the hell did I say?"

"Nothing. Really, Baz, it's not you. It's just . . . it's just a headache."

She stood and so did he.

"Want me to walk you to your room?"

"No." She didn't have to force a smile. "But thanks. Seriously, I'm fine. Just . . . maybe it's a little stress catching up. Greg's going to be working all night. I could use a night to catch up on my sleep."

Going onto her tiptoes, she pressed a quick kiss to Sebastian's cheek. The guy looked so startled when she drew back, she had to smile.

"Night, Baz."

She thought she might be able to sneak out without disrupting Greg, but his head popped up the second she walked out of the room.

"Hang tight a minute," he said to his crew. "I'll be right back."

They didn't outright stare as he walked to the door to intercept her but a few of them did glance at her with puzzled looks on their faces. As if they had no clue what he was doing with her.

Which was something she kept asking herself. What did Greg see when he looked at her? A woman he was having fun with for now?

"Hey, I'm really sorry about this. I didn't plan—"

She smiled. "I know. I realize you're busy, Greg. I've just got this headache that won't quit and I'm going to sleep it off."

He leaned closer and, for a second, she thought he was going to kiss her.

She stiffened . . . and watched his eyes narrow as he stuffed his hands in his pockets. He didn't come any closer.

"Everything okay?"

She couldn't help herself. She reached for his forearm, brushing her fingers against his skin. His gaze dropped to where she touched him then rose again to capture hers.

"Everything's fine. Call me tomorrow."

He grimaced. "Totally fucked-up day tomorrow. When do you work?"

"Three to eleven. And I've got the seven-to-three shift Tuesday."

"We've got a night shoot Tuesday. Wednesday? No, wait. I've got a meeting in New York Wednesday, might not be back 'til

Thursday." He'd said nothing to her about a meeting in New York. "What about Friday?"

"Overnight, eleven to seven."

He grimaced. "I'm about ready to tell Tyler to just give you the rest of the month off."

Blinking up at him, her mouth dropped open. "Greg—"

"Fuck." He shoved his hand through his hair. "Sonuvabitch. Just forget I said that, alright? Put it down to frustration."

Join the crowd.

She really wanted to wrap her arms around his shoulders and kiss him until the tension left his body. Wanted to take him back to bed and make love to him until he only thought about her and left the stress behind.

Unfortunately, she knew that was never going to happen. This was his life. He wasn't going to change overnight. There would always be other demands on his time. More important demands on his time.

And no matter how much he might care for her, his company would come first. His films, his actors, his crew. They all held demands on his time that she never would.

Wow, feel sorry for yourself much? Grow up.

Yeah, maybe it was time to grow up. And cut her losses.

"Give me a call Saturday." She tried out her smile again but his gaze narrowed even more. "We'll see what we can work out."

"Hey, before you leave, I've been meaning to ask if you're planning to go to the New Year's Eve party."

She nodded. "Annabelle and Kate practically made it mandatory. I work until eleven that night. I'll go after."

She'd had the fleeting thought that maybe he'd ask her to go with him but as the date grew closer and he hadn't said anything, she'd thought maybe he planned to be gone by New Year's Eve.

And then she'd pushed that thought out of her mind because she didn't want to think about it.

"Good. I'll see you there. We'll be finished with filming and I've invited the cast and crew. But . . . I'm hoping to spend some time with you that night."

One last hurrah before he left?

Her smile might've turned a little sharp. "Well, I'll be there. I'm sure we'll see each other."

He stared at her, his eyes narrowing as he contemplated . . . what? "Yeah. I'm sure we will."

Opening the door, she slipped through but, when she turned to say good-bye, he walked out after her. Shutting the door behind him, he caught her before she could make a clean getaway.

"What's going on?"

She shook her head. "Nothing."

His arms crossed over his chest. "Bullshit. Just spill it, sweetheart."

Oh, there was no way she was having this conversation in the hall. Or at this minute. "I'm tired, Greg. That's all. I just . . . need a decent night's sleep."

He paused. "Okay. Then go back to your room, pack a bag, and spend the night with me. As a matter of fact, tomorrow, just move everything down here."

Her brain stuttered to a stop as she stared up at him. Was he serious? And if he was, why was he doing this to her now? Because he'd somehow seen she was getting ready to shut him down? When he was going to leave in only a few weeks.

"And when you leave? What then?"

He didn't blink. "Come with me."

Her lips parted but she quickly closed them because she had to think about a response. She didn't have to think that long. "What about my job?"

"Quit."

"Are you serious?"

"As a heart attack."

And he was. She saw blazing sincerity in his eyes. He wanted her to throw away everything she'd worked for and be his fuck buddy.

Anger boiled in her gut with lightning-fast intensity. What kind of a bastard—

"Shit. *Shit.*" He shoved a hand through his hair. "I fucked that up completely, didn't I? I can see it on your face. Damn it, Bree—"

She held up one hand. "Greg, slow down. Just give me a minute to process."

"I don't want you to have to process. I want you to say yes." He took a deep breath. "I also realize I blindsided you and that wasn't my intent. Especially not now."

She had no idea what to say, her emotions shifted like waves on a stormy sea. She couldn't honestly say she didn't want to do it. Which sucked. Absolutely sucked.

But what about her job? Her friends and all her family were here. He wanted her to leave everything and everyone and blindly follow him for an affair that would eventually end? And who got to say when it ended?

And who the hell are you and what happened to the person who knew exactly what she wanted in life and was making it happen? And what happens when he decides he's done with you? Where does that leave you?

Back where she'd started, only older and more pathetic.

"Why not now?" she finally managed to ask, almost afraid of the answer.

"Because there's so much going on right now that even I'm not sure which way's up." After a few seconds, his expression cleared and he took a deep breath. "Look, take the night, think about what I said. And know that you're only the second woman I've ever asked to share my space. I know you have a lot more questions that we can't even get into right now. Take the night. Think about it. Hell, take the week because I may not get to see you until Friday. And think about this, too."

He put his hands on the wall on either side of her head, caging her in. His mouth opened over hers and she suddenly couldn't breathe, couldn't think. Could only be right here with him. Her arms wrapped around his waist as her head tilted to give him more access. He kissed her like he wanted to inhale her. To conquer her.

She responded with a rush of heat so strong, she couldn't help but moan. A second later, Greg had her plastered up against the wall, every ounce of his will in his kiss. His desire brushed against her skin like a physical caress. His mouth moved over hers without letting her up for air.

Spreading her hands across his back, she pressed him closer. He did what she wanted but only, she knew, because he wanted it, too.

His hips locked onto her lower body and he bent at the knees until his erection pressed against her mound. Moaning, she tilted up into him, pressing against him, an almost frantic sense of desire threatening her sanity.

God, what would she do when she couldn't kiss him like this? When she couldn't feel his body pressed against hers, the heat and hardness of his erection making her pussy clench in agony for it?

Rubbing against him, she thrilled to hear him groan, to feel one of his hands twine in her hair and hold her head at the angle he wanted it. His other hand locked onto her hip, his grip hard, almost too tight.

His.

Why did the thought make her shiver when she should be running the other way?

And what happens when he doesn't consider you his anymore? Because you know it'll happen. You know he's not always going to want you.

Still, his kiss almost tasted like he wanted her forever.

Fool.

Did she care?

She should. She knew she should, but when he kissed her, she lost herself.

Did he feel the same?

Lifting her hands, she sank her fingers into his hair. She loved the way his curls felt against her skin. Loved that he let her pull his head back, breaking the kiss so she could stare into his face.

A heavy flush rode his cheeks but his gaze was sharp.

"Tomorrow. Move in down here."

She shouldn't want that so badly. "For how long?"

He shook his head. "For however long you want to stay."

And what if she wanted to stay forever? What happened when he went back to Hollywood?

"I can't make that decision at the spur of the moment."

"Yeah, you can. You just have to decide if you want to badly enough." And on the heels of that, he sighed and grimaced. "I'm pushing. Again. That's really *not* how I intended to handle this. And I wasn't planning to *handle* this. Shit."

He took a step back while she remained against the wall, trying to get her bearings. "Just tell me you'll think about it."

She nodded.

He continued to stare, as if he could get her to comply by simply looking at her.

And man, did she want to.

Get a backbone, girl. Do you want to be like your mom, never happy unless she had a man in her life?

"I'll talk to you tomorrow."

"Alright. Sleep tight, Bree." That smile of his nearly ripped all her careful plans to shreds. "Dream about me."

Turning on his heel, he went back into his suite. The door closed behind him with a click she barely heard.

Her mind raced, thoughts ping-ponging between wanting to walk back in there and telling him yes and running back to her room and texting him to say she never wanted to see him again.

Behind her, she heard the door open again. Taking a deep breath, she steeled herself against another onslaught.

But when she turned, she saw Trudeau, tablet computer in hand. Sabrina thought maybe it'd been surgically attached to her hand.

The other girl smiled at her but Sabrina saw the strain behind the smile.

"Hi. Sabrina, right?" Trudeau stepped forward, hand out. Sabrina took it automatically. "I don't know if you remember me. I'm Trudeau, Greg's assistant."

"Of course. Can I help you with something?"

"Actually, Greg wants to know if you'll need help with anything. Which is his code for 'Get this done.' So can I help you with anything?"

Confused, Sabrina frowned. "Anything meaning . . ."

"Well, I assume he means helping you move your belongings into his suite."

She blinked. "Did he tell you that?"

"No. But the reason we work well together is that I anticipate what he wants. And he wants you to move in with him."

She felt every hair on her body stand on end. "And does he typically get everything he wants?"

Trudeau raised delicate eyebrows over sky-blue eyes. "You know Greg. What do you think?"

Well that answered that question, didn't it?

"No, I don't need your help, Trudeau. Thank you."

Greg's assistant nodded but didn't leave, and Sabrina knew the girl wanted to say something else.

Sabrina wasn't sure she wanted to hear it, but waited anyway.

Finally, Trudeau sighed. "Please forgive me if I'm overstepping, but Greg's got a lot on his plate right now. More than he may have told you. Things I'm not at liberty to discuss."

Her patience started to buck at the reins. "Then maybe you should keep your mouth shut. He's busy. I get it. I'm not going to interfere in his business. Trust me, you won't have to worry about me causing problems for much longer."

Trudeau's expression didn't change at all. Cool didn't come close to describing her. Sabrina wished she had a little of that cool right now.

"Sabrina, please don't misunderstand me. It's not my intention to interfere in his personal life. I'm sorry if you think that's what this is. My job is to smooth as many bumps in his professional career as I can. Right now, there's a lot of bumpy road ahead and I'm trying to make sure he doesn't get thrown off course. If he needs me to help you then that's what I'll do."

"I'm not part of his business life, so you can just take me off your to-do list. There is such a thing as a private life. But maybe you don't know that."

"I get that." Trudeau flipped the cover on her tablet. "I just don't have much of one. And neither did Greg." She smiled, surprisingly sweet. "Until you. If you decide you do need me, please let me know."

Turning, Trudeau headed back into Greg's suite.

Head spinning, Sabrina turned to head for the elevator then stopped in the middle of the hall.

She didn't want to go back to her room. Not alone. Didn't want to sit and wonder and worry. She wanted to do . . . something. Anything.

She wanted to not think about anything for just a little while.

And she knew just the woman to help her.

Eleven

"He told you *what*?"

"Basically, he told me to quit my job and become his fuck buddy full time."

Kate's mouth dropped open and the look of shock on her face made Sabrina snort out a dry laugh. That's probably what she'd looked like when he'd told her.

Good. She hoped he realized just how much of a shock she'd had.

"Holy shit. Seriously?" Kate's shock quickly morphed into a gleeful smile. "Well damn. The man is smarter than I gave him credit for."

Grabbing Sabrina's arms, Kate pulled her into Tyler's apartment. "Don't worry. Ty's not home. He's meeting with someone about something. I totally wasn't listening when he told me. He should know better than to talk to me when I'm sewing. But I'm done now, so spill. Oh, wait. I can see we're going to need alcohol. What are we drinking tonight?"

Sabrina flopped onto the couch as Kate headed straight for the fridge.

"Whatever you're having. I don't care. And how can you think this is a good thing? The man wants me to drop my entire life and do nothing but be available to screw him when he has the time."

Kate pulled a face at her while she poured wine in the kitchen. "You know that's not what he wants. He's just a guy and guys aren't great about saying what they really mean."

After Kate handed over a glass of white wine, Sabrina took a healthy swallow then sighed.

"And that's bullshit because the man can write dialogue so real you think you're watching two people have a conversation and not watching a movie."

"Totally different." Kate dismissed her argument with a head toss. "And if you were thinking straight you'd know that. Now tell me exactly what Greg said and what you were doing when he said it."

Sabrina knew it actually had more to do with what they'd been doing before he'd asked. Something had changed between them when she'd agreed to let Sebastian watch. She almost felt like she'd passed some test.

"Why are you turning a really interesting shade of red?" Kate asked when Sabrina didn't answer right away.

"If I tell you something, will you promise to keep an open mind?"

Kate rolled her eyes. "Please. My mind no longer has any doors left to blown off. Seriously, whatever you say will not—"

"Greg and I had sex while someone else watched."

Kate blinked as her mouth snapped closed. "Only watched? This other person was male?"

Sabrina nodded, a little thrown by Kate's response. It was almost like she'd expected this.

And maybe she had. Greg and Tyler were good friends. Of course, Kate would know things about Greg . . .

"What do you mean, only watched?"

Now Kate looked uncomfortable. "I mean, this other person didn't . . . participate?"

"No, he didn't. Greg told him he couldn't."

Kate's eyebrows lifted in surprise. "Wow. Okay." She paused. "So . . . did you enjoy it?"

"First tell me why you aren't shocked."

Kate hesitated, biting her lip. A sure sign she had something to say but didn't want to say it.

"Kate, please, just spit it out, whatever it is. I know something happened between you and Greg. And I know it happened before he and I became involved. Just spit it—"

Oh, wow.

All the pieces clicked together and Sabrina couldn't decide whether she wanted to laugh or cry.

"Sabrina."

Kate reached for her but Sabrina drew back instinctively. She felt like she'd gotten kicked in the stomach. The visceral reaction nearly made her double over as she tried to breathe.

"Shit," Kate muttered under her breath. "Just . . . *shit.* Sabrina, please, *please* don't freak out. I wanted to tell you. I really did. But how do you tell someone that you had a threesome with the guy you love and his best friend who *your* friend was lusting after?"

She should leave. Get up and walk out the door. But she couldn't move.

Breathe. Just breathe.

The words got through the static in her brain, as did Kate's reasoning. The only problem was, she couldn't get past the fact that her friend had had sex with Greg.

Which is total bullshit. You weren't even seeing him then.

No, he'd been treating her like a kid, patting her on the head, while she'd been totally in lust.

She grabbed her wine and took another swallow. She was lucky she didn't choke on it.

"I'm sorry," Kate continued. "I'm *so* sorry I didn't tell you before. I know it feels like a huge betrayal of trust but—"

"Wait. Just . . . wait. Let me catch my breath."

Kate bounced up from her chair and started to pace, which did nothing for Sabrina's ability to process. She couldn't decide whether it was the fact that Kate had had sex with Greg or that Kate hadn't told her.

And she had no right to be upset that Greg had shared Kate with Tyler. Kate loved Tyler. Tyler loved Kate. And apparently Tyler trusted Greg enough to share his lover with him.

Maybe Greg had feelings for Kate that went deeper than friendship? Maybe Sabrina was the rebound.

Wow, that hurt. Pretty freaking bad. Her heart threatened to pound out of her chest.

What if Greg only wanted her because he couldn't have Kate?

"Sabrina?"

What if he was still sharing Kate with Tyler?

"Are you still—"

"NO!" Kate practically shouted, waving her hands in front of her. "Oh, my God, no. It was just that one time. Honestly. Sabrina, I love Greg. But not like I love Tyler. Greg's a great guy but . . ."

"But?"

Kate's lips smashed into a straight line "But he's not mine. Not like Tyler. Do you understand?"

Yes, she did.

And the more she thought about why she was hurting, the more she realized it was because Kate hadn't told her. Hadn't confided in her.

She didn't feel this way around Daisy, and she and Greg had had a relationship that lasted years.

"Sabrina?"

She held up one hand. "Still processing."

"Could you do it a little faster?" Kate sighed. "I don't know what else to say. I certainly never meant to hurt you. You know that, right?

"I know. I do. It's just . . . I think I love him."

"Oh! Oh, man. That's not a bad thing. Why do you look like you want to cry? Or hit me? Don't do either, please. If you cry, I'm going to have to, too. If you hit me, well, maybe just not in the face. How about the arm?"

Sabrina started to laugh, which was exactly what Kate had wanted, if her relieved smile was any indication.

"I'm not going to hit you. I'm just so . . ." She released a short, frustrated groan that made Kate grimace in sympathy. "I don't know what I am."

"You're hurt. I get that and I'm sorry. But, I gotta say, the fact that he didn't want to share you should tell you a hell of a lot."

Sabrina snorted, shaking her head. "If it does, I'm not seeing it."

"Then try harder. Seriously, if the man didn't consider you his, he would've had another guy join in."

Okay, that made a little bit of sense. Then again . . . "What if he just doesn't care enough to want to share me?"

"Please." Kate rolled her eyes again, which made about a hundred times just in the past few minutes. "The man cares. Anyone can see that any time he looks at you."

"What if it's not enough?"

Frowning, Kate finally stopped pacing. "What do you mean?"

"What if love isn't enough? He's married to his job. To his company. I'm just the girl he bangs when he's not busy. And what about my job? Am I just supposed to give that up and follow him wherever?"

"No." Kate drew that one word out into three syllables. "But sometimes you have to decide what's more important. And I really hate to use this old cliché but you know that saying, 'When one door closes, another one opens?' It's kind of true."

"Yeah, I never noticed all that many open doors in my life. Usually they're hitting me on the ass as they close."

Kate made a sympathetic face. "For so long, the only thing I wanted to do was be a costume designer for a New York theater. And then I met Tyler and my entire world upended. I was offered my dream job and I could've taken it. But the boutique . . . how could I turn that opportunity down? And honestly, I didn't want to leave Tyler. But if I'd decided to take that New York job, we would've made it work. I totally believe that. So I guess you have to ask yourself if you believe in Greg enough to give his . . . arrangement a chance."

"You make it sound so logical."

Kate snorted. "And when have you ever known me to be logical?"

Sabrina pulled a face at Kate, prompting Kate to stick out her tongue, which made them both laugh.

"Wow, I totally feel like I lost the boulder sitting on my shoulder." Kate's smile returned but so did Sabrina's uncertainty. Not to mention the well of hurt she continued to hide deep inside.

"I'm glad you finally told me. But . . . this doesn't exactly help me with my dilemma. What do I do?"

"What do you *want* to do? Not what should you do or what do you think other people think you should do. What do you want, Sabrina?"

"I want it all." She shrugged. "But I know that's impossible."

"No, you don't want it all because, honestly, you wouldn't be able to handle it all. Who can?"

"Now you're just depressing me."

"I don't mean to. But seriously. Do you love Greg enough to give up something you've worked for your whole life? That's the question you have to ask."

Her mom had given up most of her life to raise her children. She'd given up dreams of college and a decent job to raise Sabrina. She'd given her heart to a man who'd broken it with his death. Then she'd given it to another who'd broken it when he'd walked out on her and his children for another woman. And she still hadn't forgiven herself for falling for a man who might have molested her daughter.

But she never gave herself credit for keeping their family together, for putting food on the table and clothes on their backs by working two and sometimes three jobs. And her mother hadn't stopped looking for a decent man to love.

"Greg didn't say he loves me. Only that he wants me to move in with him so we can have sex whenever he has a few minutes free."

Kate's eyes went wide. "You sound like he's treating you like a fling."

"And how do I know that's not all this is?"

"Have you asked him?"

She pulled a face.

"Of course you haven't," Kate continued. "So ask him."

"Just come out and say, 'Hey, is this just sex or do you have actual feelings for me?' And when exactly am I supposed to do this? When there are ten crew members, two assistants, and five actors in his room and he's trying to finish the movie he's been working on for years? Or should I wait until he's finished filming and ready to hop on a plane back to Hollywood? Right before he pats me on the head and says, 'Hey, thanks for the fun. Catch you the next time I'm in town.'"

Kate had started to shake her head near the end of her monologue. "Greg's not like that and you know it."

Taking a deep breath, Sabrina rubbed her temples, feeling the throbbing headache lurking there. "Yeah, I do know it. I know he likes me. I know he cares about me. I also know he collects strays. Like me. And Sebastian."

Kate shook her head until her hair swung around her face. "No way. I've seen how he looks at you. He doesn't consider you a stray. When he looks at you, I see hunger. And I don't just mean sex."

"Then what the hell am I supposed to do?"

"You need to get him alone."

She snorted. "Yeah, that's not going to happen any time soon. He's too damn busy. And I don't want to be the bitch who tells him to make a choice between his work and his girlfriend. And I'm not even *at* the girlfriend stage yet."

Kate heaved out a sigh. "Alright, I see your point there. I just . . . Don't make a decision you can't take back now. Wait until he's finished filming. New Year's Eve. He's planning to be at the party and so are you. I have your dress finished, by the way. The man will not know what hit him."

"If he even goes."

"He will. Even if I have to make Tyler threaten him with bodily harm, he'll be there. And . . ." Kate got a look in her eye that Sabrina had grown to be wary of. That look meant she was plotting something. "What are you doing the night after Christmas?"

"I work three to eleven and then I'm off the next day. Why?"

"Because I have an idea. Give me a minute." When Kate got that look on her face, people usually backed away slowly. Sabrina watched her with rounded eyes as she grabbed her phone and made a call.

"Hey, Jared. I want to show Sabrina the Salon and I know she needs to sign a waiver. Yes, I know that. No. No. Yes." Kate rolled her eyes. "Seriously? Now, you're just being a dick."

Sabrina heard Jared's laughter come through the phone though she couldn't hear his side of the conversation.

"Fine. Yeah, I know where you keep them. I'll leave it on your desk. Thanks. Love you. Give Annabelle a hug for me. What?" She laughed. "No, you're a perv. Gotta go. Bye."

Kate jumped up off the couch, grabbed Sabrina's hand, and tugged her toward the door. "Come on. I've got something to show you."

* *

"Hey, Uncle Greg, why do you look like you're gonna eat somebody?"

Greg cracked an eye and found his four-year-old nephew, Adam, standing beside the sofa where he'd sprawled just minutes ago.

Dressed in *Toy Story* pajamas that Santa had brought him just this morning, Adam looked so much like his brother-in-law, it was hard to believe there was any Hicks in the kid at all. Until you noticed the hair his sister hadn't cut in weeks. More waves than the Pacific.

The kid was gonna be a heartbreaker in a few years. His mom, Greg's sister Sam, had already told Greg he had to wait until Adam knew exactly what he was getting into before she allowed him to be in one of Greg's movies.

"Maybe because your mom's cooking just makes me hungry for real food."

Sam was vegan. Enough said there. Luckily, their mom took pity on Greg and had brought one of her amazing prime ribs to Christmas dinner.

Adam's little face screwed up in a frown and then he leaned in close. "Even the dogs don't like it."

Greg burst out laughing, grabbing his nephew and pulling him in for a hug and a tickle until his brother-in-law came to take him away to bed.

"I have no idea what you two are conspiring about," Art said, "but it's time for bed, little man. Kiss your Uncle Greg good-night."

Greg gave the little ball of energy to his dad with reluctance. He felt like every time he saw the kids, he'd missed years. Which wasn't true, but still . . .

His sister walked in, having just said good-bye to their parents. The three of them had been exchanging "the look" all night. And he could see from his sister's expression that they'd all come to the same conclusion: Greg needed to talk. And since it was true and, since Sam was the one person he trusted absolutely, he guessed that was why Art hadn't come back downstairs.

"So." Sam sat next to him on the couch. "Spill it. What's got you looking like you want to crack some heads?"

"Besides the fact that even the dogs won't eat your cooking?"

Her eyebrows barely even lifted at his dig. "I'll have you know they love my cooking. Adam feeds them enough of it. Come on, Greg. What's up?"

Leaning his head back against the cushion, he stared at the Christmas tree in the corner, all colorful lights and mismatched ornaments. Just like his parents' tree at their house. He couldn't remember the last time he'd put up a tree in his house in L.A.

He wondered if Sabrina would want to put up a tree.

"So I met this girl."

Sam's eyes widened until he thought she might hurt herself. With a little grin, she stared at him. "Wow. Seriously. This is about a girl? Who is she?"

He saw no trace of snark on his sister's beautiful face. She was two years older than him, but looked ten years younger. They shared the same nose, though Sam's was much more delicate, the same eyes, the same chin, and if he let his hair get any longer, they'd have the same hair. He made a mental note to get a trim.

"She works at Haven. We've been seeing each other for a couple months and she's thirteen years younger."

Sam's mouth opened. Closed. Frowned and opened again. "You've been seeing her for a couple months? While you've been filming? Damn, that's, like . . . well, damn. Must be true love."

"You're seriously not going to say anything about her age?"

His sister held up a hand and waved it in his face. "Oh, just wait, we'll get to that. First things first. How'd you meet?"

Settling more comfortably into the couch, he told his sister everything, from the first moment he'd seen her and thought she was the most beautiful woman he'd ever met, to the last time he'd seen her at Haven. The only parts he left out were the sex. There were limits to what he discussed with his sister, after all.

When he finally stopped, so did Sam. Which was not what he'd expected.

"Now you go silent? When I'm counting on you not to be?"

Sam held up one index finger in front of his face. "I'm lining this all up. Give me a sec." Of course, she didn't need one. "First of all, you haven't mentioned a problem so I'm a little lost as to what that might be. Second, so she's thirteen years younger. She's legal, right? Yeah, you're a little older but, Greg honey, no one will accuse you of being too mature."

He burst out laughing, knowing that's exactly why she'd said it. "Thanks. You always manage to put me in my place."

Sam nodded. "Good. Haven't lost my touch. Keeps me on my toes for the kids. Now, explain to me why this relationship is causing you such problems."

"Maybe because I have the feeling she's not so sure she wants to take me on."

"What? A catch like you? What's her problem?"

He heard not only the implied jab at his ego but also her indignation on his part. And loved his sister just a little bit more.

"Her problem *is* me."

"No." Sam waved that index finger at him again and he felt as old as Adam. "Her problem is you haven't told her you love her. And you probably haven't spent enough time together to know for sure, have you?"

"No, I'm pretty sure I love her." Actually, he was damn sure.

Sam's eyes narrowed. "But you haven't told her."

"Not sure she's ready to hear it."

"And you know this how?"

"Hell, the girl doesn't even want to move her stuff into my suite to spend time with me. I tell her I love her and she'll run the other way."

"Guys." Sam rolled her eyes. "Jesus, for such a smart one, you're extremely dense."

"So clue me in to the error of my ways, oh great one."

"Lay your heart out, you idiot." Sam reached out and smacked him on the back of the head to punctuate her statement. "Tell her how you feel, not just what you want. And then back it up with action. Show her you mean what you say. And don't screw it up. Voila! Happy ending. Fade to black."

"Hey, who's the filmmaker in this family?"

"That would be you. But sometimes you can't see beyond the end of your lens, Greg."

"And what if this is a tragedy and not a romantic comedy?"

"With you directing? Please, I'm sure there'll be some explosions but there's always a happy ending."

Twelve

Greg walked into Haven the day after Christmas with a plan.

He liked having a plan. He could make things happen with a plan.

And he had his target in his sights.

Sabrina was alone at the desk, her head bent over a terminal, but as soon as he cleared the front door, her head popped up.

He couldn't tell if she was happy to see him or wished like hell he'd never shown up again. That was a real kick in the ass. Didn't change his objective but it did make him that much more determined to get what he wanted.

He headed straight for the desk, holding her gaze as he navigated the lobby. No one milled around. The doorman was helping an elderly couple into a taxi for their trip to the airport.

"Mr. Hicks. Can I help you?"

"Yes, you can. Come out with me tonight."

Her eyes widened and she glanced toward the door that led to the reception office. "I was actually hoping to see you today. I thought maybe we could meet for dinner. We need to talk."

Sounds like maybe Sabrina had a plan, too. Too bad he couldn't tell if her plan ended with them in the same bed, like his plan. Usually when a woman wanted to talk, a man didn't necessarily want to hear what she had to say.

But since he couldn't say what he wanted here and now, he'd just have to make sure he got in the last word tonight.

"Sounds good. Where do you want to go?"

Her gaze dipped for a second. "We won't be leaving the hotel. I'll meet you at your room around eight. Is that okay?"

Greg started to get a sinking feeling in his stomach. She looked nervous. He couldn't remember ever seeing Sabrina nervous.

"Sure. How was your holiday?"

She nodded, her smile a little less brighter than normal. "Nice. And yours?"

Fuck. This conversation just continued to suck. He wanted to walk behind the counter, kiss the hell out of her, and coax a smile from those beautiful lips.

"Good. How's your family?"

And there was the bright smile he'd wanted. "Christmas is always a madhouse but it's fun. The younger kids still believe in Santa so that makes it special."

"Yeah. My nephew and nieces are only eight, six, and four. You kind of forget the magic when there's no one around who still believes."

They fell silent then, an awkward silence that made him want to tease her, make her blush. Make her smile for him.

"So," he said. "Tonight."

"Tonight."

"I'll see you then."

He forced himself to push away from the counter and head for the elevators. Just as he stepped off on the fourth floor, his phone rang.

"Greg, we have a problem."

He sighed at Trudeau's voice. "When don't we have a problem?"

"This is bad."

He paused. "How bad?"

"Bad like I've already booked you on a flight that leaves in ninety minutes. You need to leave for the airport in five. I'll have a taxi waiting."

"What the fuck. Trudeau, I can't—"

"You need to talk to Amanda. Mark just called. He said she's been AWOL since five days before Christmas. The AD covered for her until someone called Mark. Mark tracked down Amanda but she'll only talk to you and only in person. Mark tried to downplay it but Fred said he got calls from *EW* and *Variety* and now he's threatening to shut her down."

"Fuck."

He was going to fucking kill Fred Jamieson the minute he had his hands around the guy's thick neck. His business partner might just have found a way to get him to sell the company. It's what Greg had been waiting for him to do for months. Apparently the guy had finally gotten the balls to do it.

Nearly breaking the door handle in his rush to get into his suite, he headed straight for his bedroom to pack.

He heard Trudeau take a deep breath. "I think Fred is—"

"Yeah. You're not wrong. Fred wants to sell. The Japanese must have upped their offer. He's gonna try to force my hand."

"Do you want me to find out?"

"Yeah. Whatever you can. But Trudeau . . ."

"Yes?"

"I might not be able to fix this."

She didn't say anything for a few seconds. "I understand." Another pause. "Do you want me to start looking for office space? I'm sure the Greater Philadelphia Film Office will be thrilled to welcome you to the area."

Greg snorted as he grabbed his overnight bag and stuffed a few things in it. Yeah, he'd been thinking about moving but he'd wanted it to be on his terms. That Fred was forcing his hand made him want to dig in his heels and fight with everything he had.

"You're kinda scary, Truly. Remind me not to get on your bad side."

"You should know that already by now. And if you call me Truly again, I'll make sure your flight is so turbulent you will puke all the way to Iowa."

Now he laughed though it was kind of lame. "I have no doubt you can do it. Alright, I've got a bag packed. I'm on my way down."

"I'll meet you in the lobby with your ticket."

Already on his way back to the elevator, he realized he was about to disappoint Sabrina again. And that sucked.

Shit.

He stepped off the elevator and headed straight for the desk. Trudeau stood at the front door and he saw her start to move toward him. But she stopped when she realized where he was headed.

Sabrina watched him come closer with that pleasant employee smile firmly pasted on her face.

"Are you leaving us, Mr. Hicks?"

"Not for long. And if you don't give up the Mr. Hicks bit, I'm going to spank you when I get back. And you're going to like it."

Her eyes went round, her mouth dropped open, and he had the satisfaction of seeing that fake expression erased by a flush of color. And he didn't think it was embarrassment.

Then she turned to look over her shoulder for a second before turning back to him. "I take it your schedule has changed."

"Yeah. I'm not happy about it, and I'm gonna be even less happy if I have to fight for control of my own damn company and pull another director's ass out of the fire. But when I get all of this shit taken care of, you and I are going to settle this."

Surprise quickly followed by sympathy flashed through her eyes, and he could tell she wanted to say something but all that came out was, "There's nothing to settle."

"Yeah, there is, but we're not doing this now. I'm literally catching a plane in an hour. I'm flying to Iowa for a few hours before I catch another flight to L.A. Then I'm gonna do battle with my business partner who wants to break up our company and sell it to the highest bidder. Once I take care of that, I'm catching the first flight back here. Then we'll talk this through. Or we won't talk at all and we'll still figure it out. Understood?"

She got that stubborn look on her face, the one he always wanted to kiss off her lips. When his gaze fell to those lips, he heard her suck in a breath.

Yes. She understood.

Smiling, he nodded, then turned on his heel and walked away.

* * *

"So no word from Greg?"

Sabrina sat next to Sebastian on the piano bench, watching the man's hands work the keys. "Well, technically, yes. I got texts the past two nights. 'How are you' and 'sleep tight' qualify as words."

"But he hasn't called?"

Sebastian sounded pissed off and she rested her head on his shoulder for a few seconds, drawing comfort from his righteous anger on her behalf. "No. Is this for the film?"

"Yes. Don't change the subject. You want me to—"

"So, this is where you've been hiding. Nice digs, Valenti. Daddy wanted his little boy to have a nice quiet place to recuperate. Did Daddy also tell you to quit? When the fuck were going to tell your fucking band?"

Sabrina nearly got whiplash as she turned toward the door to the music room, where Sebastian had asked her to keep him company. Since she'd been feeling pretty lonely, she'd agreed.

Now, she almost wished she'd gotten Sebastian to take her out. Because the man who'd walked through the door was nothing but trouble.

His spiky black hair glinted blue in the light, handsome face punctuated by multiple piercings in his brows and lips, and his thickly muscled body covered in black leather and denim.

She'd known exactly who he was the second he'd opened his mouth. She'd listened to enough Baseline Sins music by this time to know they'd just been graced with the presence of lead singer, Nikky Gerhart.

"Nik. What the hell are you doing here?"

Sebastian's voice sounded almost strangled as he rose from the piano bench, stepping in front of Sabrina. She had the instant thought that he was shielding her, but a quick shift to the side and she had a front row seat to what was about to be a shitstorm.

Nik had a mean look on his face, and Sebastian's expression quickly mirrored it.

"I'm here to find out if you're going to fuck us over after you nearly destroyed us."

"I'm not planning to fuck anyone over."

After a glance at Sabrina, Nik's sneer made her feel like an outsider at a private party. "She doesn't look like one of your regulars, Baz. She actually looks like she could string a sentence together."

"Sabrina, you better leave." Sebastian didn't take his eyes off Nik, as if the guy was dangerous. And yeah, he looked dangerous. But there was no way she was going to leave Baz alone with him.

"What?" Nik sneered. "Afraid I'll hurt her? You suck, asshole."

"You know that's not what I meant. Why are you always trying to fuck with my head?"

"I'm not fucking with your head. I'm here to find out if we're still a fucking band or if I gotta go out and look for a new fucking guitarist."

"Did I say I was leaving?"

"No, you haven't said one fucking word since you left. Four *fucking* months ago, Baz." Nik punctuated each word with an index finger pointed in Sebastian's direction. "No one knew where you were."

"Like you fucking cared." Sebastian's voice sounded strangled. "You never tried to track me down."

"And why should I? You left."

"I had a mental fucking breakdown. I couldn't hack it. The touring, the drinking, the drama. Hell, I'm lucky to still be alive. Do you get that?"

"And that was my fault?"

"Part of it, yeah. I told you I needed a break. But did you fucking listen? You never fucking listen, Nik. You never have."

"And you never fucking *talk*." Nik's voice had risen and Sabrina heard total frustration in every word. "Not really. I had no clue you were so close to dying. I had to hear that from your dad."

Dying? Sebastian had nearly died. He'd never told her that.

"Yeah, well, I didn't."

"And that's supposed to make me feel better? You son of a bitch."

Sabrina let out a little yelp as Sebastian launched himself at Nik and the two men went to the ground in a churning mass of arms and legs.

By the time she made it around the piano, they'd already landed more than a few punches. The piano bench skidded across the floor as one of them kicked it as they rolled. Sebastian had had the upper hand until then but now the bigger, stronger Nik was on top, and Sabrina was afraid Sebastian would be seriously injured.

As Nik drew back to throw a punch, she caught his arm before its downward swing.

She startled Nik into turning, but he did it with enough force that he knocked her off her feet and sent her sprawling.

She was still shaking her hair out of her face when the door opened again and Greg walked in.

"What the *fuck*."

Greg covered the ground between them in seconds, pulling her to her feet and running his hands down her arms.

While the other two men continued to pummel each other again, he asked, "Are you okay?"

She nodded, thinking he looked like he hadn't slept in days. Or weeks.

She wanted to wind her arms around his waist and hang on but she cringed when she heard Sebastian grunt.

"He's going to get hurt. Please do something."

Nodding, Greg turned and grabbed the first man he could reach, which turned out to be Sebastian. Ripping Sebastian away in one direction, Greg shoved Nik in the other.

"Back the fuck off. Both of you. Right now."

Sebastian immediately turned to Sabrina, checking her out from head to toe.

"Are you okay? Goddamn it, Nik, if you fucking hurt her . . ."

"She got knocked on her ass. She's fine. Right, babe? You're fine. I'm fucking bleeding."

"You fucking deserve it."

Sabrina released the breath she'd been holding when she no longer heard the bitterness that'd been in both men's voices before their fight.

Turning, Sebastian put an arm around Sabrina's shoulders. She felt Sebastian sway and wrapped her arm around his waist to steady him. Out of the corner of her eye, she saw Greg's gaze narrow and had the childish urge to stick her tongue out at him.

She knew she should be mature about this but she wanted Greg to know she wasn't just going to wait around for him to have time for her. It hurt too damn much to know he couldn't spend two minutes to pick up the phone and call her.

Sebastian had been here.

Of course, she didn't want to wrap herself around Sebastian and lick the hollow of his throat.

Damn it. Why couldn't she move on?

Because he wouldn't let her. Whenever she thought maybe today was the day he told her he wasn't coming back. And yet here he was again.

The mixed signals should be making her head spin.

"So you wanna tell me why you're really here, Nik?"

Nik's expression went serious. "Because it's time for you to come back. We need to write. I got all this shit in my head and you know I can't get it out on paper without you to write the music."

Sebastian stiffened beside her and it almost felt like he was struggling to get air into his lungs. Almost like he was having a panic attack.

"I'm not ready to come back. I told you I'd call when I had my head on straight."

"Or maybe you just found something else you want to do more and you don't want to say anything."

"That's not it."

"Then what is it, Baz?" Nik looked confused, and Sabrina felt almost sorry for the guy. He really had no idea what was up with Sebastian. "Are you really gonna throw away a twenty-year friendship over a girl?"

Sabrina's shock must have shown on her face because Nik sneered at her. "Oh, sorry. Didn't he tell you? His breakdown involved a piece of ass who fucked us both over."

Sebastian practically vibrated beside her but she couldn't tell if it was rage or hurt. She wanted to do something, say something to make this better but she didn't have a clue. She could only hold him closer.

"I think it's time for you to go." Greg stepped in front of Nik, cutting off his view of Sebastian.

"Yeah, I guess it is." Although the men seemed evenly matched, the fight must have gone out of Nik. "He knows how to reach me."

Nik left without a backward glance, while Sebastian continued to breathe so heavily she could hear his every exhale.

When the door closed behind Nik, Sebastian released her, only to lean forward and grab the piano. He bent to rest his head on the lid and, for a second, she was afraid he was going to start banging his forehead against it.

"Baz."

"Yeah."

"You wanna talk?"

"No, I really fucking don't."

Sabrina watched Sebastian, taking in the swollen lip and the eye that was definitely going to be black and blue. She was about to tell him he needed to get some ice when he turned and kissed her.

She had no time to react and, this time, he didn't hold back. He kissed the hell out of her and she let him. Mostly because she knew he was hurting and she cared about him. And yeah, a little because Greg was watching.

When he released her, she sucked in a deep breath, biting her lip as he stalked out of the room.

After a second, she turned to face Greg, knowing he'd watched. He didn't look angry. He looked . . . resigned. And tired. But he didn't say anything. Or move closer.

Finally, she couldn't stand the silence. "When did you get back?"

"Twenty minutes ago."

"And how did things go?"

"Things went." His tone held a distinct note of finality.

"Oh. Okay."

She'd never seen him like this. Like he'd been beaten. Maybe a little lost. Too quiet. A silent Greg wasn't the man she knew.

"So I'm sure you're tired."

He nodded. "I am but I've got two more days of filming."

"And then you're going back to L.A."

Amazingly, her voice didn't break when she said that.

His gaze narrowed. "Yeah. I have things I need to take care of."

"Your company?"

He looked like he was grinding his teeth. "That's one."

She waited for him to say more, to confide in her, but he only continued to stare. "Do you want to talk about it?"

His terse "No" made her gut clench.

She swore she could feel his walls snapping shut, keeping her out.

And when have you ever really been inside those walls? Sure, the sex has been great but when has he ever indicated that it's been more than sex?

Swallowing down the hurt, she said, "So what do you want?"

"You."

Yes, she could see that in the intensity of his gaze and the tightness of his jaw. If she looked lower, she'd probably be able to see the proof through his jeans, as well.

"You look like you could use some sleep," she said truthfully.

"Sleep can wait."

Her body wanted to give in on the spot, let him bend her over the piano and take her. She could practically feel his hands on her hips as he held her steady for his cock.

Her heart ached because she wanted him to talk to her, to let her in. Lately, it'd seemed all they'd had time for was sex.

And maybe you should've seen the writing on the wall.

She took a deep breath. "I'm not sure I'm willing to wait anymore."

His eyes narrowed. "And maybe you haven't."

It took her a second to get his implication. Then her body flushed with heat, even as her heart felt flash-frozen.

"I'm going to leave before—"

"Damn it." His expression twisted with frustration. "God*damn* it. Bree, I didn't mean—"

"Yes, you did. That's exactly what you meant. We never made rules about this . . . relationship, Greg. You've never made me any promises and I respect that. And it's been fun but I think it's time to walk away."

She was proud of the fact that her voice sounded steady, even if it hurt her inside to say the words.

"And if I don't want to walk away?"

"Then you're just prolonging the inevitable."

His jaw clenched even tighter and his voice sounded strangled. "You've been waiting for this, haven't you? For me to say thanks for the good sex and leave. All this time. You've never let me in, have you?"

If he only knew . . . "And isn't that exactly what's going to happen? We both knew one of these days you were going to walk out that door and I'd never see you again. I understood that from the first night we slept together."

His gaze narrowed. "And is that what you want?"

"It's what *will* happen."

"And *if* that happens, what then? That's it? You cut me off like this never happened?"

"We both knew this affair had an expiration date. My life is here. Yours isn't. I understand that."

"Maybe you don't understand things as well as you think you do."

Maybe not. She only knew that she had to get out of here before she broke down in tears.

With all the strength she could muster, she walked to him and kissed him on the cheek. "And maybe I don't want to play this game anymore."

She walked out, managing to hold back her tears until she got to her room.

Then the floodgates opened.

* *

Greg sat in a dark corner of the hotel bar, nursing a 7&7 and barely listening to the music. Tyler had stopped by earlier but Greg growled something at him and he'd wandered off.

"So, you look like you could use a good swift kick in the ass. I thought you took care of everything."

Without asking, Trudeau slid into the booth across from him, her trusty tablet clutched in one hand.

She looked as adorable as ever, her hair in a ponytail, the blue of her sweater bringing out the blue of her eyes. The only thing out of place was her jeans. She typically wore a skirt and flat boots or shoes that she could switch out for pumps if she needed to handle press or money men on short notice.

"I didn't know you owned a pair of jeans."

She raised one eyebrow in classic Spock fashion. "And I didn't realize you were that drunk. What do you need me to do?"

Her straightforward statement made him blink. "What do you mean?"

"Tell me what you need me to do."

"Are you worried you won't have a job tomorrow?"

She gave him a steady look. "No. There are aspects of your business you have no idea how to handle. Now that you and Fred have divided the company, you're going to need me more than ever."

Damn, this girl was smart. If he were half as smart, he'd be upstairs working his way back into Sabrina's bed and spilling his guts about the major changes happening in his life.

Instead, he was sucking down whiskey and about to get life advice from his assistant.

His very bright, very loyal assistant.

"You're absolutely right. As always. That's why I'm promoting you. You're now the managing director of ManDown Films."

The unflappable Trudeau's mouth fell open as her eyes rounded and he thought he saw actual tears in the corners of her eyes until she blinked and they were gone.

Then the grin that lit up her face made him smile despite the pain deep in his gut. The one Sabrina had put there by walking away.

And she'd been right. What right did he have to expect her to give up everything for him when he couldn't do it for her?

Yeah, he'd just made the first step toward moving his business to the East Coast, but he'd also just dug himself into a very deep hole financially and career-wise. Hell, his time was about to get even more tight.

Or . . . he'd find the balance he hadn't been able to get in L.A. And that balance had to include Sabrina.

"Oh, my God!" Trudeau squealed like a little girl and practically fell out of the booth as she moved over to his side and wrapped her arms around his neck. She nearly cut off his air supply before she pulled away and jumped back to her feet.

"Oh, my God, I have to call my parents. And my grandparents. And I cannot *wait* to tell my sister. When I left for L.A., she told me I'd be home in a year. I can't wait to rub this in her face. She's such a bitch. Oh, my God, Greg, seriously?"

He laughed. "Well, I couldn't exactly take it back, now, could I? Not when half of Philadelphia just heard you. And to think I was a little worried you wouldn't want it. Seriously, I wouldn't know what to do without you, Tru. But we're not going back to L.A. You know that, right?"

Trudeau rolled her eyes. "I knew that as soon as you said you were filming out here. Hell, with video conferencing, it doesn't matter where we set up shop. And over here, maybe you can do more directing."

"Yeah, I think I'd like that."

"And maybe have a private life, too?"

He winced. "Not so sure I'm cut out for one of those."

Trudeau blinked. "I thought— Shit, never mind. I'm sorry, but I thought . . . you and Sabrina . . ."

"I'm not sure she thinks I'm the right fit for her anymore."

Trudeau cocked one hip and gave him a look he couldn't mistake for anything other than disbelief.

"Are you kidding me? Have you *seen* the way she looks at you? Or are you blind? She loves you. Don't you love her back? What did you do to her?"

"Why is this automatically my fault? Maybe we just aren't a good fit." Although he knew that wasn't the problem. *He* was the problem. "Or maybe I'm a prick who thinks everyone should do what I say."

Trudeau rolled her eyes at him. "Bull. That's not you and you know it. Now, since I don't plan to spend the next six months with you moping around while we're trying to put this business back together, how are you planning to get her back?"

* *

The picture showed up the day before New Year's Eve.

It had been shoved under the door and she almost didn't open the manila envelope because it looked suspicious. Until she saw the note on the front and recognized the handwriting.

I promised you the SD cards. I made no copies except for this one. I want you to see what I do.

Sighing, she set the envelope on the tiny dining table near the kitchen nook in her room.

Yesterday, she'd scoured the paper for apartments, but still hadn't managed to find one a) she could afford and b) that was close enough to work so she could walk.

But she couldn't stay here much longer. It'd become increasingly obvious that she needed her own space. Being here every minute of every day would be unbearable. She saw reminders of Greg everywhere, even if she hadn't seen him.

He had finally listened to her and stayed away.

Which totally sucked.

And if that wasn't enough, Sebastian seemed to have deserted her as well. Which was unfair of her. He'd thrown himself into scoring Greg's film and had little time for her.

Annabelle and Kate had busy lives and men who took up most of their spare time.

And aren't you just feeling sorry for yourself.

She glanced at the envelope.

Just open the damn thing.

With a huff, she grabbed it, ripped it open, and dumped the contents into her hand. She'd expected the SD card. She hadn't expected the snapshot.

The four-by-six photo fell into her hand and her breath caught when she saw it.

She looked . . . amazing. Sexy, sweet, playful, rumpled. And smiling at the cameraman like she adored him.

Blinking back tears, she tossed the photo on the table and, as it fluttered down, she saw writing on the back.

This is how I see you.

Damn that man. Damn him, damn him, damn—

Someone knocked on her door and she grabbed the photo and stuffed it back into the envelope then stuffed that under a pile of magazines before she opened the door.

"Hey. I was just thinking about you." Before she'd gotten sidetracked by Greg.

Kate hustled in, a dress bag in her arms. "I hope it was good thoughts, considering I come bearing gifts. Namely, your dress for the party."

It was on the tip of her tongue to say she'd changed her mind about going, but she knew Kate would argue her into the ground.

"Thanks. I appreciate it."

Kate gave her a wry look as she lay the dress bag over the nearest chair. "Yeah, it totally sounds that way. Spill it. What's the problem?"

"Nothing. Well, apartment hunting is a drag, but that's a given."

Kate waited, her eyebrows lifting higher. "And . . ."

Sabrina turned away to pick up the dress. "And nothing. Leave it, Kate. Please."

Kate huffed. "Fine. You don't want to talk, we don't talk. But before I leave, I want you to try on the dress."

"I'm sure it's fine."

A couple of heartbeats passed.

"You know if you don't show up tomorrow night, I'm going to be really pissed," Kate said.

Sabrina's cheeks flushed and she turned toward the armoire along the wall to hide her expression. "I'll be there."

"You better be. And I'm sure Greg and you—"

"There is no more Greg and me."

Kate's mouth dropped open but nothing came out. Wow, she'd finally managed to render Kate speechless.

"What the hell happened? And why am I just now hearing about this?"

"I don't want to talk about it. Not now." *Maybe not ever.*

"But . . . Sabrina, what—"

"No. Just don't. Please, Kate."

Something in her tone must have gotten through because Kate went silent again and her eyes narrowed.

"Well, shit. I'm going to kill him."

"No, you're not. You're not going to say anything. It's over. I need to focus on my career now. And that's all."

"That's exactly what you don't need." Kate's arms crossed over her chest. "You need balance in your life. All work and no play makes people suicidal."

"Gee, you're just a big ball of wisdom this morning."

Kate sighed. "No, I'm just a friend who doesn't like to see you looking like your favorite cat just died."

"I don't have a cat. Too much trouble. Just like men."

Kate's expression softened. "Not all of them. I thought . . ."

Shrugging, Sabrina tried to smile. "We tried. It didn't work. I've got to let it go."

"Sometimes a guy needs a second chance."

"And sometimes it just doesn't work."

"And sometimes things are worth fighting for."

"And sometimes they just run their course."

Kate threw her hands in the air. "Argh! You are the most stubborn person I know besides Tyler."

"Then I guess I'm in good company."

"But he got the girl in the end. Don't forget that." Kate huffed. "Make sure you try that dress on before New Year's Eve. You look like you've lost some weight."

Kate left Sabrina with a hug and a stubborn vow that she would drag her to the party if she didn't show up. She had no doubt Kate would do it, too.

God, she was miserable without him.

And even though she knew that eventually the feeling would pass, or at least fade, she wasn't sure she wanted it to.

And maybe . . . neither did he.

She picked up the picture again.

No. She didn't want to read something into what could be his way of saying good-bye. He'd given her the pictures. Maybe he was writing her off.

Later that night, she'd nearly talked herself into calling him, but the cast and crew arrived for their wrap party.

She'd known they were coming. It'd shown up on the hotel schedule a couple days ago. Obviously, they'd finished filming.

And Greg looked happy. He was laughing as he walked into the hotel, his arm around Amanda Patton.

For several seconds, she felt like she'd been stabbed in the gut as she stared at them. At the huge smile on Greg's face and the way Amanda stared up at him like he was a god.

Oh, God.

Like a coward, she dipped her head and made herself real interested in whatever was on the monitor screen.

"Hey, you're off at eleven, right? Come to this party with me. I'm not going to know anybody but Greg twisted my arm."

Sucking in a deep breath, she dug out a smile for Sebastian. "I'm sure you don't need me there to hold your hand. You're a big boy. Besides, I'm tired, Baz. I just want to get some sleep."

"Would it help if I told you Greg told me to ask you to come?"

Her smile died a quick death. "What? So I could see how he's moved on? No, I don't think I need any help in that area."

Sebastian frowned. "What the hell are you talking about?"

She shook her head. "Nothing. Forget it."

"No way. I won't bug you now while you're working, but later we're gonna talk. Tonight I just want you to come with me."

And that was a whole other issue, wasn't it?

"Come as my friend. I miss you, Bree. And so does he."

She so wished she could believe that. "It's better this way, Baz. I just need to get through the next few days and then he'll be gone."

With a sigh, Sebastian crossed his arms over his chest. "Alright, Sabrina, since you're so obviously going to be difficult tonight, I'll leave you alone. But I'm warning you, you better be at that party tomorrow night. You're dancing with me if I have to drag you out on that floor."

"Wow, such a gentleman."

He grimaced. "And you know that's exactly what I'm not."

He turned and headed for Greg's group. Most had already gone into the atrium, where they were holding the party in an event room.

Greg must have already gone through because she no longer saw him.

And now she was going to spend the rest of her shift wondering what he was doing. And with whom.

*   *

Greg wondered if Sebastian was having any luck coaxing Sabrina into coming to the party. He hadn't heard from her after sending her the SD card and the photo. Maybe the note had been too subtle.

And maybe she just doesn't want to see you again.

Which is why he'd sent Sebastian to invite her. He'd thought if he could get her in the same room, he'd be able to get her to talk to him in a setting where she didn't feel trapped.

He chewed on that for most of the party. They'd wrapped earlier today and, for the first time during the entire filming, he felt like he finally had a grasp on everything. The film, his business . . .

Except the woman he wanted by his side.

When Sebastian walked in and shook his head, Greg knew what he had to do.

I want to use the Salon tonight.

He filled the time waiting for Tyler to text him back talking with his cast and crew, making sure he shook every hand and spent a few minutes talking to everyone. Word hadn't yet filtered out about his new venture, so he spent some time dodging questions about his next plans. A few of the crew picked up on what he wasn't saying but no one pushed for more. Tonight wasn't for that.

He spent more than a few minutes with Daisy and Neal, who were still having problems that he couldn't help them with. Greg could only tell them how thrilled he was with their work and hope like hell they understood that he'd be there for them in any way he could.

"So will Sabrina be here after she finishes her shift? I like her, you know. She's sweet. Not at all your normal type, though."

Daisy's quiet question made Greg pause before answering.

"I'm not sure she'll show. I think I may have scared her away. This life isn't for everyone."

Beside Daisy, Neal snorted. "Hell, sometimes it isn't for us, either."

"Have you ever thought about getting out?" Greg asked Neal. "Living like a normal person?"

Neal looked at him like he was nuts. "Who the hell wants to be normal? You just gotta find the people who love you despite your freak tendencies, man." Neal's glance at Daisy was so full of tortured wanting, it almost made Greg uncomfortable to see. But when Daisy smiled up at Neal, that intensity eased just a little. "Then it doesn't matter what anyone else thinks."

An hour later, Greg was still thinking about Neal's comment when Tyler texted him back.

Just you and a guest?

Greg frowned before he realized what Tyler was asking.

Yeah. Leave a contract. I'll have her sign it.

Tyler didn't answer right away and when he did, he was pretty sure Tyler hadn't typed out the message.

If you're asking who I think you're asking, she already signed a contract. If you're not, you & I are going to have a talk.

His brain froze for several seconds but his thumbs were already flying.

WHEN THE HELL WAS SABRINA IN THE SALON?

When neither Kate nor Tyler answered him right away, he had to force himself not to stalk out to the lobby and demand Sabrina talk to him.

Luckily, he didn't make that mistake. He forced himself to continue making the rounds, waiting for an answer.

And when he got it, his grin made Trudeau, who looked like she'd been gritting her teeth as she talked to Sebastian, frown at him.

Checking the clock, he realized it was just after eleven p.m. and his time was running out. Greg jerked his head toward the door and Trudeau met him there.

"I'm slipping out. Say I got called away. Frankly, I don't care if you say I'm leaving to grovel at a certain female's feet. Just don't tell them who."

Her nose screwed up in an offended grimace. "I hope you know I can come up with a much better excuse than that."

"And that's why I hired you, Truly. I'll see you tomorrow night at the party. I expect you to save me at least one dance."

Her expression finally lightened, and he made a note to ask what the problem was. Tomorrow.

Tonight he had to fix his own problems.

"Good luck, Boss. Personally, I think she's a fool if she doesn't take you back."

He pressed a kiss to her temple, sealing a deal they'd made official only this morning. "Have fun, Tru. January second will be here soon enough."

New year. New business.

New start.

*   *

"Just a minute. I'm coming."

Whoever was knocking on her door at quarter after eleven could have at least had the decency to do it quietly, Sabrina thought as she hurried for the door.

She'd thrown on her robe, because she'd already been undressed and ready to get into the shower.

When she opened the door, no one was there.

"What the—?"

The envelope sitting outside her door was white and stood out against the blue-and-black-patterned carpet in the hall.

Greg's handwriting made her heart pound, and she quickly looked both ways down the hall but she saw no one.

Open now.

Bending to pick up the envelope, she frowned at the weight.

Curiosity got the better of her as she straightened and closed the door.

When she ripped open the envelope, a red keycard slid out with a sticky note attached.

Just in case.

He thought she might have given up her card for the fourth floor. She'd meant to. Had planned to. Sooner or later. As it was, it still sat on her bedside table.

There was something else in the envelope as well.

Tipping it again, an eggshell-blue, drawstring bag with the words Tiffany & Co. on it fell into her hand.

Her mouth dropped open and she could barely draw in enough air to breathe.

With shaking fingers, she opened the bag and turned it over her palm. A chain fell out. It was silver, probably platinum, as was the skeleton-key pendant encrusted with sparkly bits that sure as hell looked like real diamonds.

This time the note was stuffed in the little blue bag.

Meet me in the Salon at midnight.

Her gaze automatically went to the clock on the microwave. She had just enough time for a shower.

If she was going.

She stared at that necklace for a full minute before making up her mind.

* *

Greg sat in the Salon, fingers tapping an impatient rhythm on the arm of his chair.

He'd been staring at the door into the Salon for the past half hour, willing it to open.

The fact that it wasn't midnight yet didn't make him any less anxious.

He wanted her now. He'd wanted her to pick up the envelope,

read the note, and want him so badly she couldn't wait until midnight to get here.

Obviously, that hadn't happened.

The ornate clock on the fireplace mantel in one corner of the octagon-shaped room ticked over. One minute to midnight.

He'd set the fire and turned off the lights, the glow of the flames setting exactly the right tone for the seduction he'd planned.

The fire couldn't illuminate the entire room but it did give enough light to show the silk wallpaper, the plush carpets, and the lush fabrics that covered the chaise lounges, chairs, and ottomans.

Jared's vision for this room had been inspired by Victorian salons, and Greg knew if he ever did a period piece, he was hiring Jared to consult on set design. The guy had one hell of an eye.

A crystal chandelier in the center of the ceiling hung directly over a mahogany game table. Tyler's baby grand piano held court in the corner across from the fireplace, while several seating areas were set up around the room.

If you didn't look too closely at what Jared had on display in the floor-to-ceiling glass-front display cabinet on another wall, or notice the few pieces of furniture equipped with sturdy rings for attaching handcuffs or ropes . . . well, then, you kind of missed the point of the room.

Maybe he should've told her to meet at his suite. But he'd wanted to meet somewhere they wouldn't be disturbed. Hell, he'd even left his phone in his room.

Kate had told him Sabrina had made plans to use the Salon with him before he'd left the last time. Maybe she'd taken one look and decided to stay far, far away. Maybe she thought—

The door opened and his heart tripped over itself to keep beating.

The low light from the hall backlit her so he couldn't see her face. And since he sat out of reach of the glow from the fire, she might not be able to see him.

He held his breath as she hesitated in the door for several seconds, only releasing it when she walked through and closed it behind her.

"Greg?"

"I'm here, Bree."

She turned toward the sound of his voice, taking another step into the room before stopping. The fireplace was at the other end of the room from where he sat, and far enough away that she probably couldn't see him clearly.

"Where exactly is here?"

Rising from his chair, he walked toward her until they could see each other clearly.

She'd taken the time he'd sat here worrying to change, and he barely contained his growl of approval. Or the urge to rip the dress off her.

Made of some silky material he couldn't wait to get his hands on, the simple black dress molded to each and every curve the way his hands wanted to. If he was right, he'd only have to tug on the bow at her hip to get it open. The neckline plunged far enough that he could see the black lace of her bra beneath.

"You got my messages."

Her eyebrows arched and he'd already started to smile when she said, "I'm here, aren't I?"

"And I'm grateful for that."

Tipping her head to the side, she waited for him to continue.

He sighed. "Not gonna give me any leeway, are you?"

"Should I?"

"Probably not. So . . . Kate told me you signed the waiver days ago. Wanna tell me why?"

"Do you think it's any of your business?"

"I'm hoping it is, yeah."

Instead of answering, she motioned toward the fireplace. "Can we sit for this conversation?"

"Only if you sit next to me and, when we're done, I get to pull on that bow and unwrap you like a present."

She started to smile then bit her lips like she was trying to hide it. "Greg . . ."

"No debate."

He scooped her up in his arms and held her against his chest as he walked to the loveseat near the marble fireplace.

Her eyes widened but she slid her arms around his neck and held on. When he sat, he kept her on his lap.

He already had an erection, and it throbbed even harder at the press of her ass against his thighs. He barely controlled the urge to kiss her and forget the talking, at least for now.

"Now, talk."

She wrinkled her nose at his command. Fucking adorable. "Fine. I planned to meet you here one night but you left."

"And that's why you told me we were through? Because you realize life with me would be a series of interruptions?"

She shook her head. "No, I realized I loved you, but I knew that when you left after the movie was finished I might not see you again, and I couldn't handle it."

His mouth curved in a hard grin. "And what if I told you I don't want to leave you."

Her answering smile was bittersweet as her hands sank into his hair, winding through it and tugging, which made his cock tighten even more. "I might be willing to give up everything to make it happen. But I'm not sure I want to be that person, the woman whose life is defined by the guy she's seeing."

"What guy in his right mind would want a woman like that? Not me, babe."

"Then what do you want?"

"You. Do you trust me?"

"If I didn't, I never would've let you take those pictures of me."

He smiled, hope making his heart pound. "Then trust me when I say I don't want to wake up in a bed without you ever again. And yes, I know that's gonna be impossible but here's my propo—"

She kissed him, short-circuiting his brain and anything he might have added to the rest of that sentence.

It didn't matter now. She'd given him her answer whether she'd said the words or not. And he was going to hold her to them. And hold her against him for as long as he could. Preferably forever.

Of course, he still hadn't told her about the move. That could wait. Because she was kissing him like she was afraid she'd never see him again.

Her hands cupped his jaw as her lips moved over his, demanding a response he was only too willing to give. His hands tightened on her hips, lifting her so she could straddle his lap. And he really fucking liked this dress because it split apart to let her.

Now on her knees, she was slightly taller than him, and he had the unfamiliar sensation of looking up at her when she pulled back.

Her hair fell around his face, brushing against his shoulders until he wanted to take off his shirt so he could feel it against his chest.

Actually, he wanted her to remove his shirt. And maybe he was just a little bit telepathic because she drew back then, reached for the hem, and began to lift it over his head.

"I'm guessing this won't be the first time people have had sex in this room. Although I'm thinking it might be the first time there were only two people in here having sex." She got rid of his shirt then rested her hands in the middle of his chest. The warmth of her skin seeped into his, made him breathe like he'd just run a flight of stairs. "Kate told me about you and her and Tyler."

Now he couldn't breathe at all. "And?"

"And it's in the past. Yes?"

"I haven't been with another woman since the night I met you."

Her eyes rounded. "Seriously?"

"As a heart attack."

Instead of making her happy, that seemed to throw her off. "I don't know what to say to you sometimes."

"Then just say yes. Or, 'Please, Greg, take me now.'"

Her smile returned, sexier than ever. Bending closer, she made sure her lips were only a hair's breadth away from his when she said, "Please, Greg, take me now."

He threaded his fingers through her hair, rubbing the silky strands against his skin. "As long as you realize that when I do, I'm not giving you up."

"Then you better know the same goes for me."

"Wouldn't have it any other way. Now . . ."

He let his free hand fall to that bow and give it a tug, watching as the dress fell apart at the front, revealing the black lace and gold satin bra molding her breasts. And the silver chain with the diamond-encrusted key hanging between her breasts.

"Jesus, Bree." His words sounded strangled but he hoped she heard the sincere, loving sentiment behind them. "You're absolutely gorgeous and I fucking love you."

"And you have the dirtiest mouth I've ever heard on a man." Her hands had fallen to his pants, where they were busy working to open the button and the zipper. "Good thing I love you, too. Otherwise, I might have to punish you for it."

He grinned so wide, his face hurt. "Promises, promises."

He didn't ask about her panties. He just tore them off her hips and dropped them on the floor.

She either didn't notice or didn't care. And frankly, neither did he, because she wrapped one hand around his cock and stroked him, hard and fast, until he thought maybe she planned to make him come outside her.

No fucking way.

He grabbed her hips and brought her down until his cock split her wide.

"Mine."

On a gasping breath, she agreed. "Yours."

* *

"Go ahead, Sabrina. Just leave already. These last fifteen minutes aren't going to matter. Get changed. Have a good time."

Teresa had been trying to get her to leave for the past hour, but Sabrina had resisted. They'd been busy earlier and she didn't want to leave Teresa with all of the work.

But now that they were caught up . . .

"Are you sure you don't mind?"

Teresa rolled eyes. "Please. I was young. Once. If I was going to the party, you would've bet I'd have left you to fend for yourself an hour ago. Go. Have fun. Dance with a hot guy. Maybe do a little more than dance."

Sabrina gave Teresa a quick hug then took her coworker up on her offer.

The New Year's Eve party had been in full swing for about an hour. She knew Greg was already there with Jared, Annabelle,

Kate, and Tyler, along with the members of his cast and crew who hadn't left for home already.

She hadn't seen Greg but he'd texted her to let her know she should look for him when she got there.

As if she wouldn't.

Sebastian had stopped by the desk on his way to the party and she'd nearly laughed herself into the hiccups. Instead of a costume like Julius Caesar or the Blues Brothers, all of whom she'd seen walk by, he'd been dressed as himself. His stage self, complete with spiked hair, combat boots, ripped jeans, and a Black Sabbath T-shirt with the sleeves torn off that showed his spectacular arms in all their tatted glory.

Sabrina knew Teresa thought that's who she was meeting. Which was fine with her. Greg hadn't said anything about taking their relationship public and she figured that was okay. For now.

They hadn't really talked about how they were going to work their relationship other than they didn't want to give up on it. She figured she'd better get used to making the most of their alone time because who knew when he'd be back.

Or how long their exclusive arrangement would last.

She tried not to think about that as she took a quick shower, styled her hair, did her makeup, and dressed in the slinky red, sleeveless gown she'd found at a secondhand store. Kate had altered it to fit her like a glove and when she turned sideways, she could almost see the resemblance to Jessica Rabbit, which is who the dress had reminded her of when she'd bought it.

Now, she wondered if it wasn't a little too revealing.

Too late.

Grabbing her black lace mask, she hurried back down to the ballroom with only fifteen minutes to spare until the new year.

Jared was at the check-in podium when she walked up and he took one look at her and whistled.

"Please don't sue me for harassment but, Sabrina, you clean up well."

She laughed, as she knew he'd meant it, and she loved Jared for making her feel beautiful.

"You don't look bad yourself, boss."

He shook his head. "Not your boss tonight, sweetheart. Just a friend. Make sure you save a dance for me. Then again, your dance card might be filled." His smile made her blush. "Annabelle and Kate have been texting me relentlessly for the past half hour. Please go tell them you're here so they can stop asking."

With a smile and a wave over her shoulder, she made her way into the ballroom.

The amazing color of the costumes should have made her want to stop and stare, but she wanted to see Greg. Even if they weren't going to take their relationship public, they could at least have one dance tonight. And later . . .

She smiled and that's when she saw him. He'd already noticed her and was making his way across the ballroom toward her.

Her breath caught at the sight of Greg in a tux. Oh, my God. The man cleaned up well. Her heart began to race and she forgot she was on her way to sit with Annabelle and Kate until Greg was close enough to touch.

She thought he'd smile and continue on but he stopped in front of her.

"Hello, Greg."

"Jesus, Bree. Let's blow off the rest of the party and leave right now. You look beautiful, sweetheart."

She blushed, grateful for the mask that covered most of her face. "You look pretty gorgeous yourself."

Then she glanced around to make sure no one was close enough to hear. "Sorry."

He frowned. "For what?"

"I just thought . . ."

"Whatever you're thinking, unless it's how much I want you, it's wrong. Take the mask off, Sabrina. No more closed doors. No more hiding how much I want you by my side or in my bed."

She didn't hesitate as she reached behind her head to release the mask then held it out to him. He took it and stuffed it in his jacket pocket then took her hand.

"Come and celebrate with me."

"What are we celebrating?"

"The start of a beautiful relationship."

Her mouth curved into a smile, her heart kicking into a bass line similar to one of Sebastian's songs. "I think I've heard that line before. But I think I like it."

His answering smile held more than a little victory. "Guess it's a good thing I'm moving my entire base of operations to Philadelphia then." He bent to steal the look of shock off her face with a kiss.

When he pulled back, she blinked up at him. "Seriously?"

"I've been thinking about it for months." He lifted one hand to run a finger down her cheek. "But when I met you, I realized I'd do just about anything to make sure I could keep you with me. I want to be with you. I can work from anywhere. You can't right now. Yeah, it's gonna take some adjustments, but what relationship doesn't?"

Only one word kept popping into her head. "Seriously?"

He laughed but his expression quickly turned intense. "Absolutely." Bending down, he kissed her, lingering over her until she couldn't breathe. And didn't care that she couldn't.

When he finally pulled back, he kept his gaze locked on hers. "Mine."

Her smile widened until she couldn't help herself, and she started to laugh as she threw her arms around his shoulders. "No. All mine."

headline
ETERNAL

FIND YOUR HEART'S DESIRE...